The Version You Hide

eve blakely

To those who've stood still for far too long.
It's time to live again.

GRACE

No one else on the pier today would know that she's been crying. Not unless they're giving her their undivided attention. The stoic expression she wears is enough to hide the emotional pain that lingers beneath the surface.

But I *am* paying attention.

Even from where I stand, a short distance from the grassy hill she sits upon, her back leant up against an old gumtree, I can sense the air of vulnerability surrounding her.

The way she dips her chin as she tucks an unruly curl behind her ear, the ever so subtle swipe of a lone tear from her cheek. These little signs are invisible to the preoccupied bystanders as they go on about their day, but then again, they don't have anything in common with this young, brave woman. And I am no doubt tuned into her body language because it's so like my own.

She isn't exactly how I pictured her to be. She's stunning, sure. More beautiful than I ever thought possible, but it's the trauma behind her light blue eyes that captures my attention the most. They bear witness to how this cruel world she's had to survive has shaped her.

My mind journeys back to that night. Her face plastered across the television screen, the mention of her name on every channel. The coloured assortment of vegetables scattered over my tiled kitchen floor between broken fragments of cornflower blue porcelain. I hadn't even heard the plate fall to the ground, my ears only registering the sound of her name as the news reporter vaguely detailed her alleged kidnapping.

I'd crumpled to my knees, an ache twisting through every sinew of muscle, bleeding through every vein. An ache that still exists even now. One I fear will never leave me.

This girl has been betrayed. Suffered at the hands of a violent man. One that she most likely had trusted at some point.

One that should have protected her.

Loved her.

And I had failed her too.

I'd prayed that she had someone in her corner.

Anyone.

Someone to help her through all the times that life had let her down. I'd wished with every fibre of my being that I could have made things different for her. That I could have waved a magic wand and made all the bad stuff go away. Knowing she was out there somewhere, possibly all alone, had terrified me.

But now I've found her. I've finally found her.

A young brunette approaches her, pausing to click on the

brakes of the pram she pushes before sitting down at her side.

Her posture straightens instantly as she sits a little taller, a smile melting the chaos in those stormy grey irises. She laughs at something the brunette says, her strength evident as her uncertain frown disintegrates. My girl here's a fighter. It's in her blood after all.

A firecracker, just like her mother.

She pulls what looks like a sketchbook from her faded black backpack, turning the cover over in her lap. With the flick of her wrist, she releases the hair tie that holds her messy bun, and her curls fall around her shoulders in the same way that mine do. Her friend points at the page, admiration in her eyes.

A deep yearning tugs at me from within as the realisation sets in.

I *need* to know her.

I'm no longer content watching her from afar, but I've missed so many years of her life. I can't help but wonder whether too much time has passed, whether our lives are too different to merge.

That we're just a pair of strangers on opposing sides of a coin.

Two people bound by blood yet disconnected in life.

She doesn't owe me anything. I know that. I know there's a possibility she may not care to get to know me at all. But I need her to know that I'm here now.

I'm here now.

Please forgive me.

My dear, sweet Mackenzie.

Chapter 1

MACKENZIE

I'm falling. And not in the way that makes your heart flutter in your chest or clumsy butterflies roil in your stomach. It's definitely not the kind of falling associated with that overwhelming euphoric sensation of dopamine flooding your brain cells.

Not that I would know what that feels like.

Nope. This is just plain old falling. Arms flailing. That sinking drop in the pit of your stomach as you attempt to fight the Earth's undeniable gravitational pull. I'm caught in that moment when you know you're about to meet your doom, aka faceplant. When everything plays out in slow motion for just that little bit, before catapulting back into real-time.

Somewhere, between all of it, I manage to cry out. "Holy shit!"

An arm reaches out across my waist, suspending me in mid-air, my long blonde hair draping mere inches above the bonfire

I've almost tripped into. The sudden jolt causes the margarita in my hand to slosh forward into the open flames. I rare back as it flares up, the heat of it stifling, the flames licking dangerously close to my left eyebrow.

"Easy there," I hear him say as I'm dragged backwards, his solid arms clamped around my midsection. He pulls me further, drawing me a safe distance away from the fire. Firm palms steady my shoulders, before his hands awkwardly drop to his sides. "You okay?"

"Yeah," I say, huffing out a breath, and smoothing out the uncomfortable cocktail dress that suffocates my frame. I'm not one for playing dress-up and this frock is definitely not me. It's too sophisticated, too frilly. Give me a t-shirt and shorts any day of the week.

"You sure?" His head tilts to the side, concern painting his features.

And there it is. The indisputable glare of pity that I'm so often subjected to in this town.

"I'm fine," I say in an unreasonably annoyed tone. "Relax. You don't have to act like I'm some sort of damsel in distress."

I hate that I sound like a bitch, but if one more person treats me like I'm a fragile porcelain doll, I might actually break.

I look up in time to see Dylan's sideward smirk, his eyebrows shooting upward. "Sure," he casually waves off my statement, then adds, "I mean, you almost dove headfirst into an inferno, but I'm sure you had it under control."

A slight frown builds on my brow, but I can't help the way the corners of my lips turn upward. I actually appreciate his sarcasm. Maybe he doesn't think I'm so fragile after all.

"Whatever." I roll my eyes and offer a sigh as I flop down

onto the makeshift log seat nearby, sticking my now half-empty margarita glass into the sand beside me.

I let out a groan of relief as I begin peeling off the strappy high heels that adorn my pained and blistered feet — the culprits of my almost-fall into the flames mere moments ago.

These shoes have been killing me, but Kristen insisted I borrow them for Liv and EJ's wedding. The only shoes I had brought with me to Cliff Haven were the ones I'd been wearing when Henley helped me escape from my abusive ex-boyfriend's house in the middle of the night.

A pair of casual sandals, of which the soles were wearing thin, would simply just not cut it for such an elegant event, but these death traps Kristen has me wearing tonight are not exactly ideal for the uneven ground behind the tavern or the sandy shore where I now sit. Especially when I'm a little more than mildly tipsy, and I'll admit, not accustomed to prancing around in such high-fashion footwear.

"Why aren't you up there enjoying the party?" Dylan nods toward the outdoor dance floor where Kristen, Liv, Henley, and EJ sway merrily, and albeit a little drunkenly to an upbeat, punk-pop cover of a Taylor Swift song played by the live band.

I could tell him the truth. That being up there with my newfound half-sister and her friends had felt both heartening and unbearable. That even though I love my sister and her fiancé, the man that saved my life, being around them reminds me that we are worlds apart.

Instead, I choose to deflect his question. "Why aren't you?"

"It's more chill down here." He shrugs, shoving his hands into the pockets of his navy-blue suit pants. "I'm not much for crowds, I guess."

"Same," I agree.

Dylan and I are not all that well-acquainted, but as his eyes dart to the wedding party behind the tavern and then back down to me, I get a strange sense that we're kindred spirits. That maybe in some way, through our mutual introversion, we understand each other.

Though I know he couldn't possibly comprehend. That nobody really knows what goes on inside my head. I make damn sure of it. Letting people in is dangerous and not something I'm interested in doing any time soon. If ever.

Of course, Dylan knows of things that have happened in my life. Everybody in this town does. It's kind of hard to escape prying eyes when your face has been plastered all over the evening news.

But none of them really know me. They couldn't possibly.

"How are you?" he asks.

He moves toward me and takes a seat to my right, carefully positioning himself on the smoothest part of the log.

I pick up the glass near my feet and drain it in about three gulps. "Fine," I answer stiffly, turning my gaze on him. "How are *you*?"

"Nice deflection." He nods once but his chestnut eyes don't leave mine. There's a warmth and sincerity in them I'm not entirely used to. He tilts his head to the side, then tries his question again. "I mean, really. How *are* you?"

I inhale a breath, hoping I appear calmer than I feel. "Kinda sick of people asking me how I am actually."

I know my words come off rude, which is why the subtle smirk that pulls his lips up at the corners surprises me.

He nods again, his eyes glimmering under the glow of the festoon lights. "Fair enough."

"How are *you* though? I mean. Really." This time my tone

is serious, and his chest rises subtly with a sharp intake of breath as he contemplates his answer.

Dylan had been the one to find Henley after the attack, something I'm sure will stay with him forever.

"I see what you did there. Yet another deflection," he replies with a mischievous wink, his pointer finger tipped in my direction. I know he doesn't owe me an answer when I didn't give him one for the same question, but he gives me one anyway. "I'm okay most of the time. When I'm not seeing images of stab wounds and blood. I guess it all could have been a lot worse."

I think he says something else, but I'm not listening anymore. His words have taken me somewhere far away to a place I don't want to be. I've been trying so hard to leave the past behind, but all it takes is a phrase, the mention of a name or place, and I'm right back there.

I can vividly recall the pain inflicted by my ex-boyfriend, Ethan. The dull thud as his fist struck my cheekbone before he savagely pulled me from the foreshore on my early morning run. The way his hands clawed at my face to smother my screams, the air inside his van thick with the scent of marijuana.

"Shit." Somehow a muttered curse word pulls me back into the moment. "I'm sorry."

Dylan's eyebrows are pinched in a frown as he brings a hand to his forehead, guiltily raking his fingers through his chestnut brown hair. I can tell he's berating himself for the way his words have affected me.

"It's fine." I shake my head, as if doing so will rid my mind of the thoughts my screwed-up brain has just concocted. "Seriously."

He looks uncertain. Like he isn't sure if I really am as fine as I say I am. I worry he's going to keep talking, to make a big deal of this. The last thing I need is to rehash the tragic events of the past, so I'm relieved when he says something completely unrelated.

"So, listen," he begins, rubbing a hand over the back of his neck. "I wanted to talk to you about something."

"Me? Why?" I can't help my defensive tone. It's how I'm wired, though I'm still thankful for the subject change.

"I heard you were interested in a job at the tavern."

"Really? And where would you have heard that?" His assumption has piqued my curiosity, but mostly my distrust.

He isn't wrong. I'd asked Henley months ago if he could put in a good word for me at Steve's Tavern, the local pub where he works, but he hadn't wanted to complicate things with Kristen at the time. I've been struggling to find work in Cliff Haven since my arrival almost five months ago now.

Kristen's mum, Pamela had offered me a few shifts helping out at her veterinary clinic. Honestly, I'd probably get more enjoyment working with animals than I would people, but she was unable to offer me a position with regular hours so I'm yet to find something solid.

"Henley may have mentioned it to me," Dylan answers. "And if the rumours I've been hearing circulating this wedding tonight are true, I'm going to need to find a replacement for him when he gets his business off the ground. The job's yours if you want it."

"You're offering me a job? Just like that? No questions asked?"

And after I've been less than polite to him, though I'm not going to voice that argument. I squint at him in suspicion wondering what the catch is. There's that distrust rearing its ugly head again.

"Well, yeah." He shifts uncomfortably on the log seat, and I almost feel bad for my accusatory tone. "Come on. It's not like you're a complete stranger."

"Right."

Except that's exactly what I am to him. If he thinks he's learned anything about me from some silly little news article, he's sorely mistaken. My life has been way more complicated than most people care to imagine.

"So, what do you think?" He splays his hands out, elbows resting on his knees as he awaits my response.

What do I think? I think hell yeah. I need that job more than anything right now. I could hug this guy and dance a jig right here on the spot I'm that ecstatic, but I'm not the type of girl to let my emotions show.

"I'll think about it."

"Okay," he replies. "Let me know then."

"Mackenzie!" I look up as my name is called, echoing across the expanse. My sister, Kristen stands on the edge of the lawn, smiling and waving her arms wildly at me, her hot pink gown shimmering beneath the soft glow of the lights strung above. "Hurry!"

My chest deflates with a heavy sigh, my eyes rolling involuntarily knowing that my reprieve from the party is now over.

Dylan lets out a soft chuckle beside me. "Looks like you're being summoned."

"I guess so."

There's a moderate tugging sensation as I stand, followed by the sound of fabric tearing. I cringe as a draft of warm air wraps itself around my knees. Knees that should be covered by the long dress I'm wearing.

My eyes snap to Dylan's in time to catch one dubious eyebrow shoot toward his hairline. His lips have curled into a thin line, fighting to keep a grin contained.

"Please tell me that was just a rip in the time-space continuum." I squeeze my eyes shut as I anticipate his response, knowing it won't be the one I want to hear.

"Yeah. Sure. That," he says, obediently playing along. "Or… the bottom of your dress got caught on that log and tore clean off."

"Dammit!" I cry as I inspect the once-floor-length frock that now resembles a mini dress.

"Bad luck really seems to be following you around tonight, huh?" Dylan laughs, but the grin is wiped clean from his face when he sees the hurt in my expression. "I'm sorry. I didn't mean that how it sounded. I just meant… how you tripped and then…" He gestures to the gaping flap of material at my feet.

I'm sure he probably didn't mean it how it sounded, and I don't know why his remark even upset me. This notion that my life is somehow cursed isn't new to me.

I huff out a breath, ignoring his apology. "Kristen is going to kill me."

Because of course, I'd borrowed this from her closet too.

"No, she won't. You know Kristen. She'll understand." His tone is sympathetic, his eyes kind.

I haven't known Dylan all that long, but despite my natural tendency to suspect the worst in people, I have to admit he seems dependable.

When Henley had been in trouble, he'd been there. When Kristen needed a friendly face, he'd been the one to console her. But right now, his words of comfort irritate me.

They shouldn't. But they do.

Because I've just realised what irks me about my future boss right here.

He's nice. He's too nice.

And I can't trust nice.

"Mackenzie!" Kristen calls again from behind the tavern, waving me to the makeshift dancefloor. "Let's go!"

I look up to see all the female guests of the wedding grouping on the dancefloor behind Liv, our blushing bouquet-toting bride.

"Ugh," I groan. "You have to be kidding me."

Despite it all, Dylan lets out another chuckle.

"You better hurry. Looks like you're up for the bouquet toss."

I scoff. "As if! Like I want to catch that stupid thing."

Dylan is subjected to one of my filthiest scowls as I sling the pair of heels over my shoulder and hike up the torn pieces of my dress.

"Finding a man is literally the furthest thing from my mind," I mutter, as I stomp up the slight incline in the direction of the crowd, the tattered material trailing behind me.

A crease forms between Kristen's brows as I approach. No doubt she's assessed the discomfort on my face, but she might just be inebriated enough to bypass the current state of the dress she loaned me.

"Are you okay?" she asks.

"Yeah. Fine," I sigh. Though, to be honest, I wish I was at home watching Netflix in my pyjamas.

"What was that all about?" she waves an arm between me and Dylan, still standing near the bonfire down on the beach.

I open my mouth to tell her it's nothing, that everything is fine. But the words are knocked straight out of my mouth as Liv's bridal bouquet sails through the air in my direction, colliding so forcefully with my teeth, I fear an inevitable trip to the dentist. I splutter, puffing away the tiny petals that have embedded themselves in the shiny lip gloss that Kristen also insisted I wear.

Once I've recovered from the initial shock, I spare a glance down at my hands where my fingers clumsily grip the flowers, my black nail polish a stark contrast to the pale pink.

"Eww!" I screech. "I don't want it!"

I drop the bouquet in an instant and several women dive down at my bare feet, clawing at each other in a desperate attempt to claim the prize I've rejected.

Pamela Riley rises a moment later, lifting the bouquet to the sky in victory. "I got it!" she squeals.

Still gaping, I turn around slowly to find Kristen giggling beside me.

Henley is doubled over in laughter too. And behind him in the distance, his skin aglow in the firelight, Dylan watches the scene play out.

In his defence, he does try to disguise the smirk that's intent on making its way across his features. Too bad I can see the glint in his eyes from here as they crease at the corners.

My stare locks on his for a fleeting moment before Kristen's shriek pierces the night. "Hey! What the hell happened to my dress?!"

Chapter 2

MACKENZIE

"Hey, what happened to that pallet out back?" Dylan looks uncharacteristically perturbed, a veil of annoyance falling over his face.

"What pallet?" I ask, seemingly uninterested as I shuffle dirty glasses into a drink tray.

"The one that was supposed to be delivered this morning," he replies, an impatient breath leaving him. His hand comes up to swipe at his forehead as he begins to second guess himself. "I'm sure Corey said it was coming today."

This is possibly the most agitated I've ever seen him, and I can't deny that it amuses me. I know which pallet he's referring to, of course. I just like watching him sweat it.

It's my third week working here at the tavern and I'm liking it so far. There's always something to be done and I'm not one to shy away from hard work. After what feels like months of standing still, not knowing what the hell I'm doing with my life, keeping busy is good for me.

Not that I'm any closer to knowing what the hell I'm doing with my life. I have a feeling the jury will be out on that one for a while to come.

Tormenting Dylan has become the highlight of my day. He strolls into every shift beaming with positive energy and a sunshiny-ness that is honestly nauseating. So, I've taken it upon myself to knock him down a few pegs when the opportunity arises. I don't even have to try. Pessimism is second nature to me.

"Oh, that pallet!" I say, my tone one of mock aloofness. I watch as his eyebrows shoot up in panic and let out a laugh. "Relax. I've unpacked it already."

"You unpacked it," he deadpans. "An entire pallet of alcoholic beverages. Yourself. Before lunch."

"Yeah. It's my job, isn't it? The fridges were empty. I stocked them. The rest is in the cool room." Balancing the tray of glasses, I push past him to get to the sink.

He glances at the fridge behind the bar, then turns, following my movements. "Wow, that's impressive. Corey's gonna have to pick up his game. Great job, Kenz!"

He holds up a hand for a high five.

"It's Mackenzie." I correct him as I roll my eyes and slap my palm to his.

And holy Jesus. How the hell are his hands so soft?

"You should probably go for your lunch break while it's quiet," he suggests, sparing a quick glance at the Garmin sports watch wrapped around his left wrist.

"Sure," I reply as I watch him return to the office at the back.

"You get off on torturing that poor guy, don't you?" A voice draws my attention away from the hallway Dylan has disappeared into and I look up to see Jade, one of our regulars, perched upon a bar stool to my right. She grins as she readjusts her aviator sunglasses atop her dark waves.

I don't know a lot about Jade. Only that she comes into the tavern almost daily, sometimes arriving with Dylan, sometimes leaving with him when his shift ends. If I had to guess, I'd say she was a few years older than him, somewhere in her late twenties.

I huff out a laugh and shrug. "Gotta pass the time here somehow."

"You're evil," she snickers. "I like it."

"So how do you know Dylan so well?" I ask her.

"Oh, we go way back." She doesn't look up from the cocktail menu she flips back and forth in her hand.

Her answer is vague, and I don't know why it doesn't satisfy me, but I feel the need to pry further. "Are you his girlfriend or something?"

"Ha! No. Nothing like that. He's not exactly my type."

I don't like the sense of relief that washes over me at hearing this, but it's quickly replaced by confusion. A chiselled jawline, chestnut eyes, and golden skin stretched over sculpted muscle? I fail to see how Dylan couldn't be anyone's type.

Not that he's *my* type.

I don't have a type.

"Don't get me wrong. He's cute and all," she says, as if she's read my mind. "But I have a girlfriend."

"I see." That explains it, I guess. "Cool. Well, can I get you anything before I head out to lunch?"

"No, thanks. I was just hoping to catch up with Dylan."

"Sure." I nod, realising she never really answered my question about their connection. "You want me to go get him for you? He's in the office."

The 'office' is a glorified storage room out the back with barely enough room to house a desk cluttered with invoices and receipts.

Jade's mouth opens in answer, but her words are rudely cut off by a deep, agitated voice travelling from the other end of the bar. "Hey! Hello?! What do I have to do to get some service around here?"

I turn around slowly, adrenaline beginning to course through my veins as I come face to face with an intimidatingly angry, muscular man in his thirties dressed in a fluorescent tradesman's uniform.

He glares at me with mean, dark eyes, but I don't react. I won't allow him to see how much his presence bothers me.

Instead, I reply calmly and confidently. "Excuse me?"

"Oh no, excuse me!" he mocks. It takes everything in my power not to flinch as he slams his hands down on the bar, his jaw jutting out in aggressive annoyance. "I'd hate to interrupt your little gossip sesh down there."

I sense Dylan behind me before I see him in my peripheral, taking long strides down the hall to meet me behind the bar. He comes to a stop next to me, his hands finding their way to his hips as his nostrils flare warily.

"Is there a problem, mate?" He directs his question at the guy, his tone firm but professional.

He has patience. Something I'm lacking.

"I've been waiting here five minutes for your bar wench to quit gasbagging with her friend down there." The man's brow pulls together in frustration, the vein is his neck now clearly visible as it protrudes out from underneath the stubble on his chin. "What does it take to get a fucking drink around here?"

I should be bothered more by his use of explicit language, but it's the term 'bar wench' that has weirdly aroused a whole new level of anger from within me. Who does this guy think he is?

Dylan tenses beside me, a sign that he's clearly feeling threatened, but I won't allow this guy to walk over me. I raise an eyebrow, a bitter smirk twisting my lips.

"Oh no. A whole five minutes?" I say in mock surprise. "I don't think so, buddy. You literally just walked in."

"No. *I* don't think so," he replies. His eyes narrow to dark slits as he leans in across the bar. "Bitch."

Dylan steps in front of me protectively. He holds both hands up in defence, but his professionalism remains. "Excuse me, sir. We don't tolerate abusive language here. I'm going to have to ask you to leave."

"Or what?" the guy retaliates, a spray of saliva raining down on both of us.

I don't have time for arrogant pricks today. And this one is getting on my last nerve.

If there's one thing I can't tolerate, it's a man who thinks he can use his physical size and the sheer fact that he's male to belittle and overpower. I've seen my fair share of egotistical jerks, been abused into submission by one in particular for far too long. If this one thinks he can get the better of me, he's sorely mistaken.

Not today, asshole.

I reach in front of Dylan and grip the water dispenser, pulling it out and aiming it at the man's head. I squeeze the tap and the valve releases, shooting a steady stream of good old H2O into his face.

"Mackenzie!" Dylan shouts in surprise, his eyes wide as he fumbles with the tap in my hand.

"What did you do that for?" the man shouts. His hands fly up to his face, attempting to redirect the flow of water.

"Oh, I'm sorry sir," I say politely, calmly returning the dispenser to its hook. "Your face was going a little red there. Thought you could use some cooling off."

"Mackenzie," Dylan says again, this time through gritted teeth.

"What? He deserved it," I mutter under my breath.

Dylan's stern expression tells me I'm going to be reprimanded for my little stunt. His jaw is clenched, his lips clamped together in a thin line. Despite not regretting my actions, I begin to worry that I've crossed a line. I really need this job and I hope I haven't jeopardised it.

I wait for him to scold me, but then his expression slackens, and he gives a small shrug. He turns back to the burly man in front of us. "She ain't wrong."

The guy staggers back, swiping at droplets of water that cling to his short beard. "You just lost a customer," he grumbles.

As he walks away, I swear I hear the words "stupid, crazy bitch" on his breath.

Jade's laughter pulls my attention to the other end of the

bar. "Oh, I like this one!" she says to Dylan, a finger pointed in my direction.

Dylan palms his face, shaking his head. "Mackenzie, there are rules and protocol we have to follow in situations like this. Remember your training?"

"Whatever." I shrug, shaking off the seriousness in his tone. "That guy was a dick and he deserved worse."

Dylan nods but he doesn't share the same amusement as us. "You're right. He was a dick. But that situation could have gone a whole lot differently had he been dangerous. What if he'd had a weapon?"

My face drops, my eyes softening with guilt. I'd never considered the fact that Dylan has had firsthand experience with criminals with weapons in this very bar. That, like me, maybe he harbors some post traumatic anxiety after what he'd experienced the day Henley was attacked. He knows what it's like to witness the wrath of a 'dangerous' man.

But so do I.

It's the last thing I need advice on. I've been there. I've already lived through that nightmare, and he knows it.

"I just don't want to see anything happen to you," he says quietly with such sincerity that it makes me uncomfortable.

That's another thing about me. I tend to shy away from serious conversation and open displays of emotion, covering my unease with bad jokes and sarcasm. Which is exactly what I'm about to do now.

"Right," I say confidently. "Okay. Next time I'll just let you handle it."

"Thank you," he says, seemingly satisfied, resting his hands on his hips again.

"Because, you know," I continue in a matter-of-fact tone. "Dangerous guys respond really well to just simply being asked to leave. Maybe you could offer to walk them home and tuck them into their beds too."

Dylan rolls his eyes and sighs as Jade snorts out another chuckle.

"Sorry," she blurts out, then quickly cups her hands around her mouth. She's trying to hide her laughter but the way her eyes crinkle at the corners gives her away.

"Don't you encourage her, Jade." Dylan points a finger at Jade, the beginnings of a grin threatening to ruin his composure.

"Oh, come on!" she cries, throwing her hands up in the air. "The guy was a total wanker and she got him to leave. The girl is badass. I like her."

"Thank you, Jade," I say self-assuredly. "Now if you'll both excuse me, this badass is overdue a lunch break."

"Yeah," Jade agrees. "She needs a lunch break. And I need a Jack and coke. What does a girl have to do to get a fucking drink around here?" She slams a heavy hand down on the bar attempting to imitate our disgruntled former customer.

A laugh bursts from me as Dylan turns to Jade. "Oh, come on! That's not funny. I'm going to make you wait now. In fact, I'm cutting you off!" He waves a dismissive hand as he turns his back to her.

"I just got here!" Jade cries, her eyes widening as her jaw drops in surprise.

"Well, you should have thought about that before you opened your smart mouth," he retaliates before moving down the corridor back to the office.

"Looks like I'm not the only one around here that enjoys torturing him then," I say with a conspiratorial smirk, pouring a shot of Jack Daniels into a scotch glass.

"Yeah, you're right." Jade brushes her dark hair over her shoulder. "It's a pretty fun way to pass the time."

"Told you." I wink, topping her glass with Coke and sliding it across the bar. "I'll catch up with you later, I guess."

She offers me a nod before taking a sip of her beverage while I head to the storage room to grab my backpack.

I wander down the esplanade, relishing the afternoon sun on my face and the way the ocean breeze gently whips my hair. After the events of recent years, it's the little things that make my heart happy. The unmistakable sensation of white sand slipping through my toes. The sound of a seagull cawing, the crashing of the waves.

Things that can't turn on me, abandon me, crush my heart to dust.

These are the things I can let in.

The pier has become my usual lunch time stomping ground. Or more precisely, the patch of grass in front of the large gum tree. I let my backpack fall to the ground, then sit, setting my back against its smooth bark. I pull my sketch book out and rest it on my knees while I dig around for the set of pencils at the bottom of the bag. Then I survey my surroundings, searching for my muse.

What to draw today, I wonder. The sailboat on the horizon, the surfer girl that waxes her board on the shore. Or maybe the pelican that digs for leftovers in the trash can a few metres to my left. None of these subjects really capture my attention. At least not long enough to spend the required effort needed to put them on paper.

But then I see her. A woman on a park bench, her gaze lost on the ocean in the distance, her wiry long waves curling behind her in the soft breeze. There's an emptiness within her eyes, yet they portray more emotion than I've ever seen. She looks lost. Or lonely. Or both, and my chest aches with sympathy for her.

I drag my pencil along the paper, sketching the lines of her face, unsure if I really have the capability to capture the aching in her expression. To truly do justice to this woman's portrait. I continue anyway, mindlessly detailing the curve of her jaw, the fullness of her lips and the turmoil in her light blue irises.

It's not quiet on the pier today, and I'm glad for that. I don't do well with the quiet. The calm.

It's when things are quiet that the doubts creep in. When I begin to wonder whether this path I've taken is the right one for me.

You'd think it would be easy for me to pack up and start a new life. Especially when the one I've left behind was less than ideal. I mean, as if having a mentally preoccupied father and a physically absent mother wasn't enough, the abusive, drug-dealing boyfriend that constantly pulled me into his web of deceit took the cake.

But of course, leaving behind the girl I used to be comes with a new set of challenges. I've only ever been Mackenzie Riley.

The girl with the alcoholic father.

The girl with no friends.

Ethan Davis's punching bag.

Two questions keep me awake at night, when anxiety creeps

in like an oxygen thief, emptying my lungs of air. The first one is, who the hell am I if I'm no longer the girl I've been my whole life? The second, do I really belong here?

I'm desperate to break free from the girl I used to be, but I still feel her there. She exists below the surface. Unsure, fragile, and absolutely terrified she's going to blow this second chance she's been given.

And I know that Cliff Haven isn't the worst place I could have landed. I mean, its small. Like, tiny. There's only one supermarket in town and the nearest shopping mall is a half hour drive away. Things are so backward here I'm surprised they aren't still using dial up internet.

And because it's so incredibly tiny, everyone knows everyone else's business. Which would be fine if *my* business wasn't the business that the town was preoccupied with.

Sometimes I pray for a natural disaster, a flood, or some giant event to rock Cliff Haven. Nothing that would threaten anyone's lives. Just something big enough to override the magnitude of a lost girl from out of town being kidnapped by her boyfriend and bringing with her the evil that resulted in one of their own being hospitalised for life-threatening stab wounds.

But it isn't all bad. I have my half-sister. This one person that connects me to my new beginning. And I love Kristen. I really do. I'm grateful that fate brought us together.

I glance back up to the woman on the park bench. I've got her main features pencilled in on the page and I've begun to shade in the definition of her eyes, nose, and jaw when she stands, folding her arms around herself and walks away.

I watch her leave, wondering where she could be going and

who would be waiting for her when she got there. And how the hell I'm going to finish the finer details of this drawing now that she's gone.

"Hey, girl." I'm pulled from my thoughts in an instant as Harper clicks on the brakes of the pram beside me and drops down onto the grass in a crossed-leg position. "Wow, that's amazing," she adds, pointing to the A4 sized sketch book in my lap.

"Oh, it's nothing," I say modestly, covering the graphite drawing of the woman I've just been sketching.

"Seriously!" She reaches forward and snatches the book from my lap and begins flipping through it.

"Hey!" I fling out an arm in an attempt to retrieve it, but she has a firm grip on it, and I'd rather let her have it than rip its pages. Instead, I run a hand through my long hair and try not to seem uncomfortable as she surveys my work.

"These are so good," she says, her eyes lighting up as she studies each page. "You could sell them, you know?"

"I don't want to." I shake my head at her suggestion. "I draw for my own enjoyment, not others."

Sketching gets me out of my head. It's always been the one thing that helps me relax. Putting prices and deadlines on doing the things you love only turns them into chores.

"Suit yourself," she resigns, placing the book back in my lap.

Harper and I became fast friends in my first week of working at the tavern, although I'd seen her around many times before that. She'd served me at the Haven café almost daily, which is situated across the road from Steve's Tavern.

For three consecutive days, we walked out of our workplaces for lunch at the same time, which somehow lead to us bonding over our hatred of men.

Since then, we've shared our lunchbreaks almost every day with Harper even joining me sometimes on her days off, and vice versa, though I wasn't expecting to see her today. She'd told me she was so tired she wouldn't leave the house unless absolutely necessary.

"What brings you to the pier today? Is baby Noah having a bad day?" I ask, tucking my sketch book and pencils into my backpack.

"Baby Noah is having a fantastic day," Harper says with an exhausted sigh that lets me know that her day is less awesome than Noah's. "In fact. Baby Noah has been calling all the shots. I've tried absolutely everything to calm him down but this whole teething thing is a bitch."

I wince. "I can imagine."

Except I can't. I've really never given two thoughts as to what it must be like to be a mother. Especially not a single mother like Harper here. But for all the struggle she tells me she experiences I have to give the woman credit. She hasn't up and left her child yet and that's a whole lot more than I can say for my own mother.

I peer into the pram. Noah is peacefully sleeping, his cherubic face and long eyelashes so angelic they make a liar out of his mother. "He looks pretty freaking cute to me."

Harper stares me down with her 'I'm not impressed' face. "Of course, he does *now!*" She blows out a long and dramatic breath. "I'm just thankful he's finally asleep. All I need is five minutes of quiet."

"Have you heard from Ryan?" I dare ask.

She sighs again, disappointment brewing in her eyes. "No.

And frankly, I'm not holding my breath."

"He's an asshole," I tell her.

I only met Ryan once, when he came into the Haven café a few months ago, but I instantly disliked him. I guess I've got "asshole radar" because a week later he was gone, leaving Harper in the lurch and six-month-old Noah without a father.

Hence, our bonding over our hatred of men.

"Yeah," she mutters. "I guess the lesson here is not to get knocked up at nineteen."

I shake my head. "You're doing an amazing job, Harps. Noah is awesome, and that's because of you."

"Yeah," she agrees, a slow smile warming her expression. "Awesome and completely devious."

This makes me laugh, but I truly meant what I said. I have so much respect for Harper.

When she'd become pregnant, she worried that bringing a child into the world might not be the best idea for someone in her circumstance. Although she and Ryan had been in a committed relationship for years, she was concerned about the toll having a baby at a young age might take on them, not to mention the financial difficulties they may face.

It was Ryan who convinced her that keeping the baby was the right choice. That they could do anything in this world if they did it together.

And it was Ryan who left her when the pressure became too much.

I see the way that Harper loves Noah, like he's the best thing in her world. I admire her courage to raise him on her own.

"Seriously though, I could really use a night off," she says, mindlessly picking at a blade of grass in front of her.

"Yeah. I know how you feel," I reply automatically.

"No, you don't," she laughs, throwing the tiny pieces of grass at me.

"No, I don't." I agree. "I just mean, Henley and Kristen. I feel like I'm crowding their space. They're getting married and they're so in love. You should see them after dinner. They sit on the couch so loved up and all cutesy and then there's me on the other side of the room in the single armchair, scrolling through my phone pretending I can't hear their kissy sounds."

"Oh, wow. Okay, you win. Sounds like you need a man of your own," she says, nudging me in the ribs with her elbow.

"Hell, no. You know that's the last thing I need."

Hear hear, sister," she raises her hand as if holding an imaginary wine glass and I mirror the action as we mime a cheers.

I'm not looking for a man. Been there, done that.

It only ends in heartache. Or in my case, a few broken ribs, and a trip to court to have my beloved contained to a prison cell.

Chapter 3

DYLAN

Things have been running like clockwork at the tavern today, and I know I owe a lot of that to Mackenzie. She's efficient, to say the least, always taking the initiative whenever a new task arises. We breezed through the onslaught of lunch time customers, without any complaints this time, and now we're in that in-between lull.

The calm before the happy hour storm.

Not that I need to be concerned with that today. I clock off in exactly thirteen minutes. One of the things I love about this job is that I don't have to take it home with me. There are no urgent emails to tend to during dinner time, no after-hour phone calls.

I slide a couple of clean glasses into the cabinet behind the bar, looking up in time to see Jesse stroll in through the tavern's bulky doors, raking his shoulder length hair back from his face.

I'd been sharing the managerial tasks with Corey since I started here, but Jesse was hired as a third bar manager when I'd expressed to Steve that I wanted to step back a little from my role to focus on other commitments. I'd been afraid to raise the subject, but Steve had been nothing but supportive and had hired Jesse within a week.

I doubt he could have found a better co-manager to run this place. Jesse is never late to a shift, and he knows his shit. He's a hell of a lot easier to work with than Henley had been, but knowing what I know now about Henley, I can't say I blame him for his tardiness and unlikeable attitude. The guy had a plane load of baggage. I realise now that he was just trying to survive, to get through his days without drowning.

In hindsight, I regret how I treated him. He didn't deserve the way I'd blatantly dismissed his behaviour, simply labelling him an asshole. Normally, I'd apply more effort in getting to know a person, to find out what was going on inside their head.

But I wasn't myself. I was preoccupied with my own drama at the time. I had a lot riding on this gig at the tavern. I still do. I can't take any chances with anyone messing it up for me.

"Hey, Dylan." Jesse greets me from the other side of the bar, a backpack slung over his shoulder, his nose ring glinting under the overhead lights. "Did we get that order this morning?"

"Sure did," I answer. "Mackenzie has already unloaded it and updated the inventory."

Mackenzie's head snaps up at the mention of her name.

"Could hardly leave it to you two slackers. The job would never get done," she chides as she slides another drink across the bar to Jade.

I know I can always count on Mackenzie's sarcasm to amuse me in some way. I get the impression she likes to keep me on my toes. Though the stunt she pulled this morning with that aggressive customer had been unethical, I have to give her props. The girl has guts.

"You are a force of nature," I tell her, an unexpected grin playing on my mouth.

"Yeah. I've heard that before," she says smugly and then turns to Jade. "Seriously. You have no idea how painful it can be to work with this one." She throws her thumb over her shoulder in my direction as Jade's eyes find mine.

My smirk spreads wider when Jade's left eyebrow arches in question. I give a subtle shake of my head, signalling her to stay silent. What Mackenzie doesn't know is that Jade knows exactly what it's like to have me as a co-worker, but I'm not ready to reveal that side of me just yet.

I turn back to Jesse to fill him in on the details of today's shift, something we do at every handover. "So, as I said, that order has been received and sorted. Bad news is the seafood delivery we were supposed to get is delayed so we'll have to cut the salmon from tonight's menu. Shouldn't be too much of an upset though. And I had to hire an electrician to fix that light that kept flickering." I turn to the back of the tavern to where said electrician stands, a tall ladder leaning up against the side wall. "But he shouldn't be too much longer and …. Oh my god."

I'm only mildly embarrassed by the gasp that escapes me

and the way it demands the room's attention.

Jade's eyebrows furrow, Mackenzie's rise and Jesse offers a "You okay, bro?"

"Yeah, sure," I say with a wave of my hand. "No big deal. Mackenzie just walked underneath a freaking ladder is all."

Mackenzie glides toward me, a tray of empty glasses in hand. "And?"

"And? Are you kidding me?" I exclaim. "Well apart from the fact that that is a serious workplace health and safety issue, it's also extremely bad luck, Mackenzie!"

I'm met with the blank stares of all three of them, and probably countless others in earshot. I only notice Mackenzie's though, her grey irises rimmed with navy blue as they bore into mine. There's a cynicism in them that no one should bear. I'm instantly transported back to the bonfire at Liv and EJ's wedding when I'd made the mistake of telling her that bad luck followed her around.

"I mean…" I begin.

"You mean I'm a walking, talking jinx," she says matter-of-factly, her expression void of emotion as she shoves the tray of empty glasses upon the bar.

Shit. How the hell am I going to get myself out of this one?

"Come on," I say. "That's not what I… I just don't want you to get hurt is all."

"Whatever," she says, the iciness in her tone defrosting somewhat. "It's fine. I'm fine. But some of us don't have the privilege of believing in luck."

I drop my gaze to the ground, knowing I've really put my foot in it this time. I can understand why she might not believe in luck. I know things about her. About her past. I know she hasn't had what one might call a typically fortunate life.

And those that know me might assume that I've been blessed with all the luck that life could possibly offer. But appearances are deceiving. Sometimes we think we know someone when we've barely even scratched the surface.

"Just be careful, okay?"

When I bring my gaze back to hers, I expect to find annoyance, but she stares back at me with amusement. "Sure, boss. Time for you to get out of here, isn't it?" She flicks her pointer finger at the clock behind us.

"Yeah." Relief washes over me. I'd never take joy in hurting anyone's feelings but for some reason the idea of offending Mackenzie kills me. Maybe it's the fact that she's been through enough. Or maybe she's starting to get under my skin. "I'll see you guys tomorrow afternoon."

"And I'll see you tomorrow morning," Jade pipes up.

"Right," I say. My eyes involuntarily find Mackenzie's again. I see the slight confusion in them, but she doesn't ask questions. I turn again then remember today is a big day for my friend. "Hey, aren't you meeting up with Jaclyn tonight?"

"Yeah. I'm meeting her parents." Jade winces.

"I thought that was tonight," I say. "You've got nothing to worry about. Her parents will love you."

"I hope you're right. I'm nervous as hell." She lifts her third Jack and Coke up to her lips just as Mackenzie's grip tightens around the glass pulling it back down to the bar.

"Maybe that's enough of these then," she says. "I'm cutting you off. For real this time."

Jade pouts and crosses her arms over her chest. "I take back what I said before, Dylan. I'm not sure I like this one anymore."

I huff out a laugh as Mackenzie shrugs her shoulders. "You'll thank me tomorrow."

"She's right," I agree, glancing back at Mackenzie one last time.

She may have only been here for three short weeks, but in that time, she's infused herself into this place, filled it with her sarcastic, yet spirited energy.

A small smile tugs at the corners of her mouth as our eyes lock, before I turn and exit through the heavy tavern doors and out onto the street.

I round the corner, moving down the alley that leads to the carpark, clutching the keys to the old white 1998 Toyota RAV4 in my palm. I throw myself into the driver's seat, slamming my head back against the worn cloth headrest.

A silent prayer forms within my already overwhelmed mind that it will start this time. It should after all the money I had to put into repairing it last month. I flip the key in the ignition and feel the satisfying spread of relief through my chest as the engine rumbles to life.

"Yes!" I give an audible cheer, throwing a fist into the air and slamming it victoriously down on the steering wheel.

This piece-of-shit, hunk of metal may not be the best thing money can buy. But it's *mine*, and for that reason alone, I love it.

I cruise down the main boulevard, or more accurately, putt along, towards the winding road that leads across town to Cliff Haven beach. It takes less than five minutes before I'm parked out the front of the tiny, wooden shack I call home.

I take the stairs two at a time, the wood splintering under my weight as I bound up to the faded blue front door. I turn the key in the lock and jiggle the handle, something I've learned has to be done in just the right way to gain entry, then swing the front door wide open. I'm about to step inside when I'm almost knocked off my feet from behind by a solid mass of black and tan fur.

The friendly, yet clumsy brute that's made himself a home with me barges past, galloping his way over to the sofa where he proceeds to jump on it, making himself comfortable. His tongue protrudes as he pants heavily, his eyes wide with pride as a string of drool descends to the sofa cushion.

"Nice to see you too, Chance," I say with a shake of my head. "You crazy mutt."

I found Chance on my second day in Cliff Haven. Or maybe he found me. He'd turned up on my front doorstep after a storm one morning, his coat matted in mud and sand. Pamela, our local vet assumed him to be a kelpie border collie mix. She helped me search high and low for his owner, but to no avail.

I'd thought he looked like he needed a friend, but in hindsight, maybe I did. Which is why I decided to take him in and share my home with him. A choice I sometimes regret when I find him sprawled over the couch or huddled up under my duvet when I return home from work. There are no fences around the beach house. He's free to come and go as he pleases, yet he always finds his way back here.

Besides the stench of seaweed that's obviously coming from Chance, there's another pungent odour that fills the tiny beach cottage that wasn't here this morning. A musty sort of dampness. I round the kitchen bench, the worn-out floors creaking under my toes, and discover the problem. A large puddle of water has pooled in the kitchen. Droplets trickle out one by one from the cabinet below the sink.

I groan, glancing down at my watch. Even if I report this to the landlord, there's no way they'll be able to get a plumber out until tomorrow morning. I'd learnt that lesson a month ago when the bathroom sink sprung a leak.

It won't be the first DIY job I've done since moving in six months ago. Home repairs had never been my forte, but when your budget is low and professional help is scarce, you'd be surprised how well you can cope with a few dollars' worth of hardware supplies and about eight different YouTube video tutorials.

I throw open the cabinet doors and crawl underneath to inspect the damage and as I do, a flood of water sprays me directly in the face as the pipe gives way completely. I guess this one is going to take a lot more skill and patience to repair.

I let out a frustrated growl and then a sloppy tongue glides up my cheek, a wet nose nuzzling my ear. "Chance!" I shout. "What are you doing, boy? Stop!"

I turn and try to direct him away from me but the water still shooting out from the broken pipe makes it almost impossible. Surrendering, I scratch the spot behind his ears as he flops onto the floor, flipping onto his back into the puddle, tail wagging madly.

Despite the kitchen filling with water and knowing I'm likely going to be spending all night googling how to solve this problem, a laugh erupts from my chest. No one could wipe my smile away if they tried. Because this place is mine.

This mess is mine.
This is the life I chose.
And I wouldn't change it for the world.

Chapter 4

MACKENZIE

"Oh my gosh! Remember that little dance routine you did back in third grade?" Pamela gushes as she lifts a bright pink tasselled skirt from the dusty box she's just manoeuvred from the corner of the loft. "Check it out!"

"Oh mum," Kristen whines. "I hated that stupid performance. And that stupid skirt. It constantly gave me a wedgie."

A quiet snort escapes me. I'm still getting used to this quirky side of my half-sister. When we'd first met, she'd come across as moody and serious and far too into her career.

Not that being driven is a bad thing, but I could sense that she was hiding behind it all. I understand now that she was going through so much. Her efforts to keep herself busy had purely been to keep her mind off the things she didn't want to face.

She pouts at my reaction, swatting me playfully on the wrist which causes the handful of photographs I'm grasping to slide from my grip. She offers an apology as they fall to the floor, but I barely hear it.

I'm too focused on the shiny, smiley faces that stare back at me from the glossy polaroids below. I try to mask my sorrow but it's too late. Kristen sees through me. She always does. She drops to the ground in a flash, hastily scooping up the pictures with both hands.

But I've already seen.

An image of a happy father cradling his newborn daughter, another of a doting dad holding his baby girl upon his shoulders. Reminders that although we share a biological father, we've both grown up having very different experiences in life.

I was bitter when I first learned of Kristen's existence, believing that she had been raised on the proverbial 'right' side of the tracks and I on the 'wrong' one. I realise now that Kristen was fighting battles of her own and I've let go of my resentment, but I can't deny the piercing sting in my chest at seeing those photographs.

I don't blame Kristen. At one point I did, but I had been blinded by my own insecurities. I'd thought that she'd had the perfect life, but it turned out I was wrong about that too.

I might have been the one that grew up with the alcoholic version of our father, but for the first eight years of her life, Kristen had been raised by a financially stable family man. The same man that turned out to be a total douche that abandoned her and her mother for another life. That other life included me, so if anything, she should be the one resenting me. But

Kristen has only ever made me feel welcome in this town, and in her home. Even when I didn't deserve it.

"Are you okay?" she asks sliding the rest of the polaroids from my grip, a frown of concern etched in her brow.

"Fine." I tuck a strand of hair behind my ear. A tell-tale sign of my vulnerability. Then in an effort to change the subject, I gesture to the countless boxes that crowd the other side of the loft. "Do we really have to go through every single one of these boxes? It could take years."

Pamela scoffs. "That's a slight over-exaggeration, Mackenzie. There's not that many. I just need to clear a decent space."

"Why are we cleaning out the loft again, Mum?" Kristen asks. "Which one of your crazy hobbies is going to be performed up here this time?"

"It's not crazy," Pamela retaliates. "It's yoga. I want to create a lovely calming space where I can realign my chakras."

Now it's Kristen's turn to snort and when her eyes find mine, I can't help the smirk that forms on my lips.

I love Pamela so much. She's like the mother I never had. Since my arrival in Cliff Haven, I've loved spending time with her, and I'd enjoyed volunteering at her veterinary clinic on occasion.

Kristen had warned me about her crazy hobbies and ventures, but I never realised just how many extra-curriculars this woman went through. I have to give her credit though. No one could ever say she didn't try anything new. She knows how to get the most out of life. Maybe we should all aspire to be like her.

"Oh! Look, Mum. I found a box of all your discarded

hobbies," Kristen says sarcastically. She lists each item as she pulls them out. "A scrapbooking kit, a bunch of knitting needles and yarn. Oh, and a tennis racket."

"I only quit when I got tennis elbow!" Pamela interjects.

"You got tennis elbow? After playing for what… like… five minutes?"

"Don't tease me, Kristen. I was in pain for a month. And I still plan on learning how to make that Christmas sweater for Ben," she adds as she reefs the knitting needles from my grip and places them aside.

"Well, that's bound to be uncomfortable," I remark.

"Why?" She takes on a bold stance, her hands resting defiantly on her hips. "You don't think I'm capable of making it the right size, Mackenzie?"

"Actually, I was referring to the fact that it barely gets below twenty-eight degrees Celsius in this town over the Christmas period. Are you planning on going to the snow?"

Pamela tilts her head, dropping her hands to her sides. "Hmmm…You make a good point," she admits. She reaches forward and tosses them into the box we've set aside to donate.

"Hey, Mum," Kristen says, holding up a set of paint brushes and oil paints. "Remember when you were going to be the next Picasso?"

"Oh, you stop it right now, Kristen Riley!" Pamela holds up a finger at her daughter. "You know damn well I only took that painting class for your benefit."

Kristen's face softens as she gently places her arms around her mother's shoulders. "I know. I'm only teasing. You know I love you, Mum. And thank you. It really did get my mind off Henley for about all of five minutes."

I smile, realising now that they must be referring to the art class that Pamela took Kristen to after Henley left town in a desperate attempt to help her daughter move on with her life after his abandonment.

"How is Henley going, anyway," Pamela asks.

A smile lights up Kristen's face. "Really great, actually. Things are better than they've ever been. His business is doing well. He's booked out for the next few months but I'm still driving him crazy with wedding plans."

"I'm happy for you, kid. I really am." Pamela gazes upon her daughter lovingly, tossing her arms around her shoulders and giving her arm a gentle squeeze.

The sinking weight of envy wraps itself around my ribs. I'm suddenly conscious of the gaping void inside of me. What must it feel like to have that one person that knows you inside and out, who will love you unconditionally? For the first time in a long time, I feel completely robbed.

"It makes everything we went through worth it, you know?" Kristen looks up at Pamela and then to me, radiating happiness.

I nod. Even though I don't know. I can't imagine ever having the kind of life that would make all the shit I've been through worth it.

"I'm glad everything worked out between you two," Pamela adds, then turning back to the task at hand she points to the box Kristen has just opened. "I don't need the art supplies. They've served their purpose. Would you like them, Mackenzie? I've seen those sketches you do in that little art book of yours. You're probably the only one in the family with any talent."

My heart aches hearing the word.

Family.

I've never really known family until now. At least not the kind that counts.

I grew up with an alcoholic father that was generally absent, whether it be emotionally or physically. My mother ran off when I was three for reasons unknown to me. I guess I've always blamed myself for that. For not being the kind of kid she could love enough to stick around.

Henley coming to give our father a piece of his mind had been the best and worst thing that had ever happened to me. The best because it led me to Kristen, Pamela and her stepdad, Ben. The worst because it upset my crazy, criminal boyfriend enough to hunt me down and kidnap me.

God, why does my life have to be so complicated?

Even now, after finding Kristen and Henley, Pamela and Ben, I still feel out of place. Like I haven't quite found a home.

"Hey, look. Here's another set of brushes and a blank canvas. Everything you need to make a masterpiece." Pamela holds the art supplies out to me. "There's even an easel. It's still in the box."

"Thanks, but I'll pass," I say, with a shake of my head as I pick up a box to relocate it to the other side of the room. I am grateful for the offer but I'm feeling less than inspired right now.

"Oh well," Kristen sighs, tossing it onto the pile. "Hopefully someone else can make use of it."

I feel Pamela's eyes on me, and I know she's sensed my mood change. "How are things going at the tavern, Mackenzie," she asks.

"Yeah, good," I reply, not caring to elaborate.

"And how's Dylan?" Kristen says in a tone I can't decipher.

"He's a pain in the ass," I reply, my face void of expression, remembering the weird comment he'd made after I walked under the ladder by mistake yesterday. "Next question."

"He's a hot pain in the ass though." Kristen slaps me on the forearm, her left eyebrow wiggling up and down. I stare at her with dead eyes. When I don't give her the reaction she's hoping for, she points a finger at me and adds, "You can't deny it."

"He's my boss, Kristen," I state flatly.

She eyes me sceptically, a devious smile stretching across her face. "But you're not denying it."

I shrug. "I don't see him that way. I don't see anyone that way." I turn my back to the two of them as I move to the other side of the room, my arms laden with yet another box.

"Oh, come on now, honey!" Pamela exclaims. "I'm almost forty-ni-. One. Almost forty-one. And even I can see that boy is damn fine!"

"Mum!" Kristen gasps. "Dylan is half your age! Your real age. Not the age you tell everybody."

"Well, he is," Pamela shrugs as she dives into yet another storage box. "That golden brown hair and those deep chocolate eyes. Don't even get me started on that body and those…"

"Okay, Mum!" Kristen shouts, cramming her hands over her ears. "That's enough!"

I reach into the box in front of me and try to focus on its contents, pretending I can't feel Kristen's gaze boring a hole into my soul.

"You can't shut everyone out forever, you know." There's

just enough sympathy in her tone to shatter my composure.

I pause, leaning on the edge of the box, swallowing my emotions down. "I can try."

I don't look up as I reach inside and scour through the contents, but I know Kristen and Pam are sharing a look. And I know what they're thinking. That I've closed myself off from the world. That I'll never be happy until I open myself up to possibility.

But I know they're wrong. I let someone in once. Someone I thought was one of the good guys. Someone I never imagined would hurt me in a million years.

I can't trust anybody. Not ever.

I know the mental health professional in Kristen is just dying to pick apart my psyche, but she lets it go, not saying another word.

We work for another hour, slowly shifting things around the loft until we've created a decent space for Pamela to set up her yoga space. There's even a good amount of natural light pouring into the loft now through a window that had been previously covered up by two large stacks of storage tubs.

"Thanks so much for your help girls. All we need to do now is cart this stuff downstairs." Pamela wipes the dust from her palms onto her thighs while Kristen and I glare at the pile exhaustedly.

I lean into Kristen and jokingly mutter the words, "Your mother is a slave driver."

She lets out a giggle before Pamela screeches, "Hey! I heard that, Mackenzie!"

My muscles are already fatigued from unpacking that pallet at work yesterday, but I hoist a box up over my right shoulder and begin shifting it down the stairs. Kristen and Pamela follow suit and after four loads each we've successfully emptied the loft of unwanted things.

"Okay, I'm beat." Kristen huffs out a breath, then turns to me. "You ready to go home?"

"Please," I almost plead. "I'm missing out on serious Netflix time."

"Thanks again, girls," Pamela says as she throws an arm around each of us. "I really appreciate it."

"Of course, Mum," Kristen replies, giving her mother a peck on the cheek.

"Have fun doing yoga," I add awkwardly, offering a stiff wave.

I turn on my heel, caught off guard as Pamela's arms reach around my shoulders, drawing me into her warmth. I've never been much of a hugger, but the scent of her floral perfume infiltrates my senses and I relax into her fleetingly.

"Don't be a stranger," she whispers. "You're always welcome here."

"Thanks." I offer a small smile as I pull away and turn to follow Kristen down the front porch steps to her brand-new VW Golf.

When I say brand-new, I mean literally brand spanking new. As in, it still has plastic film over the dash. She only picked it up last week.

After her car had pretty much died a few months back, she'd been sharing Henley's ute. But now that she has a fully-fledged job in a psychologist clinic, she was able to take out a loan.

Ben had of course gone along with her to the car yard to

ensure she got a good deal and a safe car. He'd told me that when the time comes for me to get a new car, he'd offer me the same gesture. I've started saving, but at this rate I'll be fifty-five by the time I can afford one. Lucky for me, this town is so small that all the places I need to go are in walking distance from each other. Maybe I could settle for a bike.

I know I told Kristen I wanted to get home to watch Netflix. The latest season of Outer Banks has just dropped, and I can't wait to watch it, but after the week I've had, I suddenly feel that I need a different kind of release. I can almost hear my sketchbook calling out to me from here.

I climb into the passenger seat and fasten my seatbelt, staring out the windscreen ahead. I wait for Kristen to do the same, noticing the items Pamela discarded sitting on the front porch in my line of sight. The canvas and boxed easel stick up from the top of the pile and a thought crosses my mind.

I've only ever sketched with pencils and graphite, but maybe it's time to broaden my horizons and experiment with paint. I unclick the seatbelt and open the door.

"What are you doing?" Kristen asks in surprise. "Where are you going?"

"I'll just be a second," I tell her. "Pop the boot."

She squints in confusion but does what I say.

I march over to the stack and pull the canvas and easel out. I have to dig a little to find the paints and paintbrushes, but I get there in the end.

Maybe I'll take these after all.

Chapter 5

DYLAN

"Hello, father." I cradle my phone between my cheek and shoulder as I use one hand to open the skip bin and the other to throw in the bag of empty glass bottles. I glance around the tavern's unoccupied courtyard, ensuring I'm alone.

This was the fourth time my dad had tried calling me this morning, and talking to him is really the last thing I want to be doing, but I know if I continue to ignore him, he'll continue to call. I figured at some point I'd have to listen to his criticism. May as well just get it over with now.

"Dylan." My father's voice echoes sternly across the line. "How are things?"

I scoff under my breath and shake my head, knowing my father could care less about what I'm up to these days. "Things are great, Dad. How are things for you?"

"Why don't we just cut through all the pleasantries," he suggests curtly.

"Of course," I say. "I'm sure you don't want this conversation to take any longer than necessary. You are a busy man after all."

I hear his exasperated sigh and I picture a hand coming up to his forehead, his fingers smoothing out the frown lines that have accumulated there from… well, too much frowning. "When are you going to come home?"

"I told you already, Dad. I am home."

I've lost count now of how many times we've had this conversation. This push and pull routine is getting old.

He clears his throat loudly, a sign he's becoming agitated. "We both know this is just another one of your little projects. It's a phase. I don't want you making decisions you're just going to regret later."

"This isn't a project. This is my life." His condescending tone is exhausting. I lean my weight into the tavern's external brick wall behind me and slide down till I'm sitting on the ground with my knees bent upward. "You make it sound like I'm a child. I told you a long time ago that this is what I want, Dad. I have a plan."

"Oh, I see. A plan, huh?" he retaliates arrogantly. "You mean the plan that entails you slogging it out in a bar and squatting in some poorly maintained beach shack?"

Despite his words, a laugh burst from me. "You just don't get it."

"No, son. I don't think *you* get it. I've worked hard to give you a good life and now you're squandering any chance you have at being successful, all because you're too damn proud to admit that you've screwed up. If you'd just come home, we can move past all of this. We can support you if you make the right decision."

My jaw clenches as the weight of his words sink in. "So, what you're saying is you'll support me on your own terms, but you won't support me following my dreams?"

I'm about done with this discussion. I knew he would refuse to see things my way. The same way he always has.

Another audible sigh fills my ears. "Don't be stubborn, son. It's okay to admit when you're in over your head."

"Over my head? It's like you're not even hearing me," I mutter as disappointment floods through me. I've had enough. "This conversation is over, Dad."

With that, I hang up on the call, tossing my phone across the courtyard in frustration. I shake my head, raking a hand through my hair, pulling my knees in closer to my chest. I'm sick to death of having this same damn fight with my parents. I realise to them that it does look like I gave up everything to work in a bar. That I'm unthankful for the life they provided me.

That isn't the case though. My parents have given me everything and I'm more than grateful. I've been given opportunities that most people can only dream of. I'm guaranteed success in life because of them, but it comes with one condition.

That I follow in their footsteps.

I try to believe that my parent's defiance comes from a place of love. That maybe they're afraid to see me fail because it will break their hearts to watch their only son struggle. But more than likely, they're worried I'll embarrass them.

To be honest, I think I probably already have.

I've tried to keep my activities here on the downlow but it's important to me that I forge my own path. And yeah, there's a chance I'm going to fall on my ass doing it, but failure is a risk I'm willing to take.

I want a life of adventure.

Of passion.

And I know I won't have that back home. They see me working at the tavern as the biggest mistake of my life. I see it as my ticket to bigger, better things.

They're incapable of envisioning the bigger picture.

Or they don't want to see it.

"Geez. Looks like your day just turned to shit." A voice echoes off the tavern's brickwork, startling me out of my pity party for one.

"Jesus!" I grasp at my chest in shock, pivoting to my left in time to see Mackenzie creeping out from the corner of the building. "Where did you come from? Have you been standing there this whole time?"

"Guilty," she says, placing her hands up in the air as though in surrender. "Came out for my break and then I heard you talking. It sounded serious so I didn't want to spring out from nowhere. You know, until after it was over."

I snort out a laugh. "Your honesty is refreshing."

"Sorry," she offers, suddenly having the sense to look a little sheepish.

"It's okay."

"What's with the temper tantrum?" She nods her head at the ground where my phone lies, probably with a cracked screen.

"Parental problems," I admit. "My father is really overbearing."

"Oh." I'm a little surprised when she wanders over to where I'm sitting and slides down onto the ground next to me. "Can't say I know what that's like."

"Shit," I murmur. "I'm sorry."

I'm always putting my foot in my mouth around this girl.

She waves my apology away with a hand. "It's fine. It seems we both have issues. Just on different ends of the spectrum. Not having parents at all comes with a whole set of different ones." Despite her obvious sadness, she smiles and if anything, it shows her strength.

"What happened to them?" I dare to ask.

I feel her stiffen beside me and for a second, I think she isn't going to answer. That maybe she'll throw some sarcastic comment into the air and be on her way, but she stays silent, her eyes locked on the vines that wrap their way around the trellis attached to the far wall. I'm usually great at reading people, but she has me completely baffled. Mackenzie isn't like everyone else, and it doesn't take a genius to see that.

"You don't have to answer that. I shouldn't have asked. I'll mind my own business."

She looks down at her hands where they fall into her crossed-legged lap. "It's okay. I'm sure you heard my dad is an alcoholic. Mine and Kristen's dad, I mean. He's on his third stint of rehab."

"Yeah. I'm sorry."

I had overheard pieces of conversation between Kristen and Liv about their father's situation. From what I'd heard, he'd come to Cliff Haven on his way to rehab the first time.

"Who knows? Maybe third times a charm." Her nostrils flare as she chews on her bottom lip. She's trying to act cool about it but it's obvious it bothers her. "My mother left when I was young. I don't really have any memories of her."

"Do you have any idea where she went?"

She shakes her head slowly. "No. I have no idea where she is or why she chose to leave."

"I'm sorry," I say again, feeling stupid that at this point, these are the only words I can think of to say.

Her shoulders lift in a shrug. "It's fine. I guess you can't really miss what you don't remember."

Her words make my heart ache, my problems seem that much smaller. Mackenzie and I have come from extremely different worlds but right now, the one thing I can empathise with is her loneliness.

It seems you can have nothing and be lonely. Or you can have everything, and still be lonely.

"Have you ever tried to find her?" I ask.

She shakes her head. "No. I don't have any interest in looking for someone who clearly doesn't want to be found."

She's giving off those tough girl vibes again but something about the way she speaks has me thinking she might not actually mean what she says.

"Fair enough."

"I know how people see me," she continues. "After what happened with Ethan. It's hard having everyone in town thinking that they know me because they saw my face plastered all over the evening news, or they read what some stupid newspaper printed about me. Like that's my whole story right there on that tiny piece of paper. The damsel in distress from the wrong side of the tracks." She uses her fingers to air quote that last part as she lets out a weak laugh. "I didn't make that up, by the way. That was an actual headline."

"Really? I hope whoever wrote it got fired because that's cheesy as fuck."

She chuckles at my lame attempt at a joke, but I can't help thinking that this is the most I've ever heard her say. At least about something so personal. I'm suddenly hyperaware of what a privilege it is to have been given an insight into the mind of Mackenzie Riley.

I can't imagine what she has been through in her life. It's one thing to have absent parents. It's a whole other thing to be wrapped up in an abusive relationship with a criminal. I only know what the news has reported and random things I've heard from Henley and Kristen, but I have the good sense to recognise that that's not even close to her whole story.

I know from my own experience, albeit a very different one, how easily the media can twist the narrative to their favour.

Mackenzie is right. Those that judge her based on a bunch of news reports are shallow. It's becoming more apparent to me with each conversation I have with this girl that she has so much more depth, so much more personality and strength than she's probably ever been given credit for.

And there's something else I know about Mackenzie. Something I've known since I met her. She doesn't want my pity. Or anyone's for that matter. She doesn't need it. And though she might possibly be one of the strongest people I've ever met, she carries with her the sense that she doesn't really belong.

Another feeling I'm more than familiar with.

I watch as she tucks a blonde ringlet behind her ear, the silver stud in her helix glinting in the sunlight that pours in from the open alfresco.

"For what it's worth, that's not how I see you." I lay a palm on her knee, my fingertips unintentionally grazing the patch of skin that peaks through the shredded threads of her distressed, baggy, light blue denim jeans.

She looks up and her grey eyes meet mine, uncertainty swirling in their midst. "But you don't really know me."

"Maybe not. But I know you're not that. You know," I lift my hands to air quote the phrase she had used earlier. "A damsel in distress."

She nods and then we sit in silence as the moments pass by. Finally, she playfully digs an elbow into my ribs. "Are you planning on slacking off out here all day, boss?"

"I'm thinking about it." I snicker as I nudge her back with my shoulder.

"I mean, it really says a lot that no one has seemed to notice that you're gone." Her tone drips with sarcasm but there's a slight grin twisting the corners of her mouth upward. "You're obviously invaluable around here."

A laugh surges from me as I rise to my feet. I'm getting used to these sassy one-liners. "You know I could fire you for being such a smartass."

"Then who would unpack your deliveries and give you hell," she says. "Face it. Life would be boring around here without me."

I know that she's joking. That she doesn't really regard herself that highly.

But as we return to the bar to serve customers, wash dishes and clean tabletops, all I can think about are those grey-blue eyes and the way her smooth, tanned skin felt underneath my fingertips.

Chapter 6

MACKENZIE

I may not always do well with the quiet, but somehow, I find the most peace at the river. When I need to free my mind of unwelcome thoughts, this is where I come. To the small jetty at the back of Henley and Kristen's house.

Well, it's my house too, they tell me. But that feels weird to say. And honestly, that's another reason I come here. To give them privacy.

I know I'm welcome in the house. They've never done anything to make me feel otherwise, though it's hard to imagine them not wishing they had more time to themselves. I know my time staying here with them is limited.

I'll have to get my act together and find my own place one day. I can hardly stay here when they're newlyweds or even worse, and I know I might be getting ahead of myself here but, new parents.

I balance my art book in my lap, a half-drawn sketch of the old oak tree across the bank filling its current page. This one has taken me a while because I've been trying so hard to get every detail perfect. To capture the way the light hits its leaves making them glisten like tinsel and the depth of each groove in the bark of its trunk.

My concentration is strained today. I can't seem to get the conversation I had with Dylan yesterday out of my mind. It isn't like me to be so open, to share my thoughts so easily and disclose information about my past. In fact, I usually do everything in my power to keep it all inside.

I've been silently reprimanding myself ever since, but there was a vulnerability in the way he spoke to his father on the phone that intrigued me. Dylan gives the impression that he just cruises through life, but obviously things aren't all sunshine and rainbows within his family. Still, I should have known better than to trust him so quickly. God knows I've made that mistake before.

"What are your plans for today?" Henley's voice disturbs the silence of the creek, and my pencil falls from my grip onto the jetty.

Startled, I turn to find him standing behind me, sipping from an extra-large mug, barefoot and shirtless wearing nothing but a pair of green and blue boardshorts.

"Shit, Henley," I curse. I knock the pencil forward trying to grasp it and it slips through the crack between the planks of wood. "Don't fucking creep up on me when I'm in the zone. That was my favourite 6B pencil!"

"Sorry." He lets out a chuckle. "Kristen just left to get groceries. I'm about to go for a surf if you wanna join me."

On any other day, I would have taken him up on his offer. If someone had told me a year ago that one day I'd be living in a small coastal town where I'd learn how to surf, I never would have believed them. Surfing has never been something I've aspired to do, but it didn't take Henley long to show me the ropes. I sucked at first, of course, but I like to think I'm getting the hang of it.

"Thanks for the invite but I've got lunch plans at Steve's Tavern with Harper." I slide another pencil out of the pencil box beside me and turn my attention back to my sketchbook.

"You're having lunch at your workplace?" he questions. "On your day off?"

"I know. It's weird," I agree, looking back up to the tree I'm detailing. "But the chicken parmigiana is the best in town."

I see Henley shrug in my peripheral. "That's fair. You know I perfected the sauce when I was working there?"

I tilt my gaze to his, my expression unbelieving. "No, you didn't."

"No," he says shortly, his lips curling into a straight line before he tips a finger in my direction and adds, "But it was my idea to add thyme to the schnitzel crumbs."

"Sure it was." I deadpan.

"I swear," he replies boldly, his eyes wide. He glances down at my pyjama pants and bare feet. "Anyway, shouldn't you be getting ready for lunch if you're meeting Harper?"

"Why? How late is it?" I ask, picking up my phone to check the time. "Oh, shit! It's eleven thirty already?"

That was the other thing about the river. It was a time-warp. I so often became immersed in its tranquillity, my sketchbook transporting me to a better place, and I'd lose myself to it all.

I hastily shut the sketchbook and slide the pencil box containing my graphite pencils into my pyjama pants pocket, before running back up the jetty and into the house, leaving Henley to make his own way back.

I shower quickly, then slip on a cropped tee and a pair of cargo pants. Swiping on a light CC cream and a hint of lip gloss, I allow my blonde waves to cascade down my shoulders. I always kept a hair tie around my wrist for when my hair's unruliness got to me, and I know it will be swept up into a messy bun before the day is done.

Henley has already left to go for his surf by the time I start making the short walk to the boulevard that runs the length of town.

When I step into the bustling tavern, a quick scan of the open plan bar and bistro lets me know that Harper is yet to arrive. This doesn't really surprise me, given the sleepless nights little Noah has been imposing on her lately.

I take a seat over by the window, looking up just in time to see Dylan arriving for his shift, once again with Jade in tow. He heads straight behind the bar, seemingly unaware of my presence, but Jade gives me a friendly wave before settling on her usual barstool.

I pick up the menu and peruse the lunchtime specials, despite already knowing what I'm going to order. I hear Harper coming before I see her. Or rather, I hear Noah.

I glance up to find her barrelling toward me, flustered as all hell, a screaming baby perched on her left hip. She tries her hardest to manoeuvre his pram through the sea of tables, her right shoulder weighted by the largest nappy bag I've ever seen.

I stand up, ready to go to her aid, when Dylan swoops in to save the day.

Of course, he does. Because he's that quintessential nice guy.

"Harper, are you okay?" he asks, holding his arms out to baby Noah.

Harper practically throws her son at Dylan, ready to take all the help she can get. "I'm so sorry for the noise, Dylan. He's teething and it's a complete nightmare. I'm at my wits end."

"I have no idea what that means," Dylan admits. "But obviously no judgment here. It must be tough."

"Sorry I'm late, Mackenzie," she says breathlessly. "I'm running on pure adrenaline at this point."

"Are you kidding? Please don't apologise," I say, waving off her apology. "Seriously, though. Are you okay?"

The giant nappy bag falls to the floor with a thud as she flops down into the chair across from me. "I'm wrecked."

I nod in sympathy and it's then that I see her. Like, really see her. The dark circles that underline her eyes, the unkempt strands of auburn hair that haven't quite made it into her ponytail. Her expression is one of pure exhaustion and frustration. Motherhood must be a real bitch.

"You look…" I begin searching for a compliment. Her eyebrows lift in hopeful anticipation, but I decide to be honest instead. "Wrecked."

Harper squeezes her eyes shut, her face scrunching as if she's about to cry, but then suddenly her attention is shifted back to Noah. Her jaw drops, her eyes widening in awe. When I follow her line of sight, it's not hard to understand why.

Baby Noah is soundless as he bounces up and down in Dylan's arms, apparently fixated on the beaded bracelet he wears around his left wrist. He reaches for it, a cherubic smile forming as he stares up at him in wonder.

"Hey, little man," Dylan says gently as he removes the bracelet, rattling it in front of him. Noah's big, blue eyes track the beads as Dylan swings them from side to side. He's completely mesmerised.

"Oh my god," Harper practically sobs. "Miracles happen."

"Shhh," I hiss cautiously, warning Harper not to break the spell. "Don't speak too soon."

"You like these, little dude?" Dylan allows baby Noah to safely grip the beads in his chubby little fingers, which seems to work in settling him down completely.

We watch as he slowly places Noah in the pram, the beads still curled up in his tiny fist as he rests back against the quilted lining, completely content.

"What the hell are you? A fucking baby whisperer?" I ask.

"Mackenzie!" Harper whisper-yells. "Don't disturb the peace. Look. He's asleep!" She lays her palms over her heart in relief.

We all gaze down at baby Noah, snuggled up in his pram, silent and finally sleeping.

Dylan folds his arms smugly across his chest. "My work here is done," he says, turning on his heel toward the kitchen. He only takes a few steps before he turns back to us. "Obviously, don't let him choke on those. I don't need that on my conscience."

"Obviously," we both reply in unison.

When Dylan has returned to his position behind the bar,

Harper turns to me, fanning her face with her hand. "Oh my god. Is it weird that that did something to me?"

"What?" I ask her. "Who? You mean Dylan?"

"Yes! Of course, I mean Dylan!" she whisper-shouts at me again as she leans across the table.

"God. Not you too." I groan, remembering the way Pamela had described Dylan in her loft that night and the way Kristen had shamelessly admitted that she thought he was hot too.

"Huh?" Harper throws a confused look my way.

"Nothing," I say with a shake of my head. That was not a conversation I wanted to get into right now. Or ever.

"Seriously though. He is so hot. I can't believe you get to work with him almost every day. You're so lucky."

"Who? Dylan?" I ask again just to annoy her. The deadpan stare she aims at me tells me I've succeeded. I let out a chuckle and then put on my best serious face and wave an open palm at her. "Please, he's lucky he gets to work with *me*."

This earns me a laugh from her, before she snatches the menu from my hands, her gaze skimming back and forth from the lunch specials to Noah.

When I first arrived at the tavern I was starving, but I'm suddenly not thinking about food anymore. Much to my own apprehension, Harper's comments have me thinking about Dylan. And I don't want to be thinking about Dylan. Or any guy, for that matter.

But I get it. I get the appeal. What he did to calm that screaming child may have also made *me* melt just a little inside. And not because I want kids of my own. I mean, I'm having trouble most days just taking care of myself.

I can lie to Harper. And Pamela and Kristen. But I'm not

sure how much longer I can lie to myself.

Harper is right. What Dylan did just now with Noah was hot.

My boss *is* hot.

And for someone who is intent on keeping men at a safe distance, I sure am having a hard time trying not to think about the way his touch felt on my knee in the courtyard yesterday.

I might be in trouble here.

"Hello. Earth to Mackenzie." I hear Harper's voice, distant with a hint of impatience.

"What?" I ask, realising that as my thoughts had wandered to a place they should never go, I'd missed whatever Harper had said to me.

She follows my gaze to the bar where Dylan serves up a beer to a local tradie. She squints at me in suspicion, a smirk twitching the corners of her mouth. "How's work going?"

"It's fine," I reply with a nonchalant shrug, knowing I've been busted.

"I'll bet," she responds, one eyebrow arching upward.

I shake my head at her and toss a coaster in her direction. "Let's order. I'm starving."

"I'll bet," she says again brazenly, throwing a look over her shoulder at Dylan.

"Stop! You're seeing things that aren't there."

"If you say so," she resigns, stiffening as baby Noah stirs in his sleep. It's only when he settles back into position that she releases a long breath. "Oh, thank God. I need for this kid to give me just a little more than five minutes peace. I love him, you know. Like I honestly love him so much it hurts, but sometimes I wish I could have just one night off."

"You deserve a night off," I agree.

"Maybe I should take my mum up on her offer," she muses.

"What offer?" I ask.

"She's always saying that she would have Noah for the night if I wanted to get out of the house. I just never have because the thought of leaving him makes me feel so bad. Mum guilt is the absolute worst."

"Well, I think you should take her up on it. A night off might be just what you need to reset."

"Would you come with me?" she perks up at my suggestion.

"Sure," I say. "Why not? But where would we go?"

"We could go to a night club. Or we could just come here. I honestly don't care if we spend the night walking circles around this town if it means I don't have to hear a baby cry," she says with a laugh.

"Hey, guys." Harper and I look up just in time to see Jade swiftly drag a chair over from a nearby table and seat herself beside us. "I'm sorry, I didn't mean to eavesdrop, but I couldn't help overhearing what you guys were talking about."

Harper and I look back and forth from each other and back to Jade.

"Which part?" I ask.

"The part about poor Harps here needing a break. I thought I could offer a suggestion."

"Oh," Harper replies happily, her posture straightening. "What is it?"

"Well, I'm not sure if it's your thing, but there is this amazing snorkel and scuba tour that leaves twice daily from the marina on the other side of town. I know it's not the same as some seedy nightclub but maybe a fun day in the sun could be just what you need."

Harper seems to mull this over in her mind and before too long she breaks out in a huge grin. "You know what? I think that would be amazing."

"You do?" I ask dubiously.

"Yeah!"

"The morning session is the best in my opinion," Jade adds. "The dolphins and turtles are always out to play."

"So, you've done this before?" I question Jade.

"Yeah," she replies, her shoulders jumping in a small shrug. "I've done it a few times."

"What do you say Mackenzie? Are you free tomorrow morning?" Harper's voice is laced with anticipation.

I'm not due to start my shift at the tavern tomorrow until three and I'll be working into the night but in all honesty, I'm not sure if snorkelling is really my thing. I could probably think of a million other things I'd rather be doing, but Harper's expectant expression lets me know that I'm probably not going to be let off the hook that easily.

I throw my hands up in the air. "What the hell. I guess I am."

"Great! I'm texting Mum right now to see if she's free," Harper says as she taps frantically at her phone.

"Cool." Jade stands up, flinging the chair back under the table next to ours. She holds up two fingers and adds, "Oh, it's called Two Tanked, by the way."

"Two Tanked?" I ask. My uncertainty is surely written all over my face, but Harper only smiles with glee.

"Yeah," Jade replies, looking to the bar where Dylan has just emerged from out the back. "The tour is Two Tanked. I'll catch you guys later."

"Yes!" Harper cheers as her phone chimes, signalling an incoming text. "Mum said she's free all day. This is going to be so epic."

I'm not sure what could possibly be so epic about diving from a boat named Two Tanked, but Harper's joy is adamant. And I know my friend needs this.

I wait while she types out another message and pulls up the details for the tour on her phone. She continues to scroll and tap for another moment as I throw a glance toward Jade who grins back at me from the bar. Is it me, or is it more of a conspiratorial smirk than your average friendly smile?

"I just booked us in for tomorrow," Harper says excitedly.

She slams her phone down on the table loud enough to wake Noah. He lets out a shrill scream that could wake the dead. I cringe as Harper groans, thrusting her head into her hands.

"Damn it," she curses. "Bring on tomorrow."

Chapter 7

DYLAN

The beach is calmer today, which doesn't make for great surfing, but sitting on my board out past the breakers as the sun begins to rise is still the best way to spend the morning.

I start most of my days out here in the ocean, something I feel has become more of a necessity than a want. A way to clear my head before I get on with my day.

Tilting my head to the side, I release the kink that's been there since the other day. I could put it down to the crooked way I slept, trying to accommodate for the giant canine that insisted on sharing my bed. But it most likely stems from the anxiety that has plagued me since that phone call with my father.

It isn't like me to worry about the things I can't change. I've always had a laid-back nature. Maybe that's why I always found it so hard to fit in at home.

I usually don't have to try so hard not to let things get to me, but ever since this situation with my parents escalated, my stress levels have been sent through the roof.

Finally, I sense what I think will be a decent wave and position myself on the board, anticipating the water's movement. I begin to paddle as the wave builds, synchronizing myself with its energy. I speed up, popping up swiftly when I feel its sheer force lifting my board, guiding me into the shore.

I don't think I'll ever not be in awe of the ocean's power, of the push and pull of the tides, the way it can be both tumultuous and serene.

Chance barks at me from the sand, bounding up to me like the ever-loyal companion as I wade through the shallows.

"Hey, boy," I say as I reach down to scratch his head.

He responds with another bark, shaking wet sand and seawater all over me. I drag my board across the shore, then hoist it up under my left arm, heading for the beach house. The greatest appeal to living here is having the ocean in my backyard.

Though this modest little beach shack definitely has its issues. It's always filled with sand, no matter how much I sweep or vacuum, and there are mysterious sounds in the night that I don't think I'll ever get used to. The house needs constant maintenance, which I know should be the sole responsibility of my landlord, but I've learnt that if I wait for him to get his act together, I'm waiting all day and night.

My impatience with that sort of stuff generally gets the better of me and I end up taking matters into my own hands. Nobody could ever accuse me of not being proactive. Although it did take me two trips to Bill's hardware and four hours to fix that leaky pipe the other night. Maybe next time I will leave it up to the landlord.

Pausing halfway to the house, I pick up a twisted lump of driftwood and throw it for Chance to fetch. He gallops off after it, collecting it as he goes. His bark resonates through the side passage between our house and the one next door. This isn't unusual behaviour for him but the way his yelping intensifies tells me something has caught his attention.

When I round the corner to the outdoor shower, I realise why. My blood pressure rises a little higher, undoing the work of the salty waves.

My sister, Claire leans up against the side of the house, one hand on her hip, the other scrolling something on her phone. Her red locks fall loosely down around her shoulders. In her black stiletto pumps and business formal dress and blazer, she looks wildly out of place against the backdrop of beach grass that divides my house with the next.

"Finally, Dyl," she says as she slides her phone into her bright red Gucci handbag. "I've been waiting here forever."

"Nice to see you, sis," I offer, and I do mean that. I'll always hold a special place in my heart for my big sister, even if she has just been sent here to do my parent's dirty work. "So… Something serious must be going down for you to have driven down from the city this early."

"Actually, I was in Little Beach. I stayed with a friend last night." She folds her arms across her chest, a sign she doesn't want to be pressed with questions.

Too bad she's in the presence of her annoying little brother.

"A friend, huh?" I query with a single raised eyebrow. "Anyone I know?"

"Nope." She doesn't offer any further information.

"But you *have* come here with ulterior motives, right?" I bend down and pull the stick from an impatient Chance's mouth and toss it into the distance.

"Can't a sister check up on her baby brother every once in a while?"

I aim a cynical glance her way as her phone begins to ring. She retrieves it from her bag, swiping the answer key.

"Hi, yes," she says to the caller. "No, they need to be round… White ones, yes…With the floral centrepieces. They go much better with the lighting…Okay… Thank you. Bye."

"What was that all about?" I flip on the outdoor shower tap and begin rinsing the salt from my skin, goosebumps forming at the sudden drop in temperature.

"Just finalising plans for the party next weekend," she informs me, absently tapping away at her phone screen. "Which brings me to why I'm here."

"Oh." I turn the tap off and reach for the towel hanging over the deck railing.

Claire's head snaps up in my direction. "Oh? What do you mean 'oh'? Please don't tell me you've forgotten. You have to be there."

I hadn't forgotten. My parents had been planning their 30th wedding anniversary party since last year, but with everything that has gone down since then I worry that if I go, I'll just be giving them another chance to corner me. "I'm not sure yet, Claire. I might have to work."

Chance returns with the driftwood stick. He proudly drops it at my feet and then moves over to my sister, nuzzling the bottom of her skirt, leaving a slimy string of drool. She huffs out a frustrated breath at the sight of it but doesn't deny Chance a pat on the head.

"Work?" Her tone is incredulous. "Dylan, do you know how ridiculous that sounds? Dad has offered you a job. They want you to run the family business. I still can't believe what you're giving up."

"I like my life," I tell her. "I love it. And it's not that I'm ungrateful for the offer. I really appreciate it, but I know if I took them up on it, I'd be miserable. I wasn't built for pushing papers around an office desk."

"I get it," she says, unfolding her arms and blowing out a breath. "But I'd take that position in a heartbeat."

I nod sympathetically. "I know you would. And I wish they'd just offer it to you instead."

I might have an MBA, but Claire's qualifications are astoundingly more impressive than my own. At twenty-eight, with an MBA and several other business admin qualifications, plus a doctorate degree under her belt, Claire is more than capable of running the company. Way more so than I am.

"Yeah, well," she says with a frown. "I guess neither of us can help the fact that Dad is a misogynist that doesn't believe in successful women in business."

"I'm sorry, Claire Bear."

Chance impatiently jumps for the driftwood stick as I pick it up, trying to secure it between his teeth. I chuckle as I move it from side to side teasingly, watching as his eyes follow it.

"Get it, boy!" I shout as I toss it as far as I can down the beach.

From my peripheral, I can see Claire watching me. "You really are happy here, aren't you?"

She gestures to the house, then her gaze moves to the waves crashing on the shore and the crazy stray dog galloping back toward us.

"Yeah. I really am." I grin. "I know it's not the life that was planned for me, but it's what I want. I love what I do. And speaking of what I do, I need to get ready for my second job."

I grab the stair railing, ready to take the rickety back steps up to the house when the urgency in Claire's voice stills me. "Dylan."

I spin back around. Her eyebrows are knit in a frown as she lets out a sigh. I get the sense she's about to say something I don't want to hear.

"Look, I didn't come down here to pester you. I came to warn you." Her voice is stern, her facial expression serious to match it. "You need to be at this party. Mum has said in no uncertain terms that they aren't above coming down here to convince you to come home."

"Look, Claire, I'm sorry they're giving you such a hard time because of me," I begin. "I just think going to the party could do more harm than good. Dad and I just can't seem to see eye to eye. Things are tense."

"Yeah?" she retaliates, folding her arms across her chest again. "Well, you know how many high-profile guests will be in attendance. Just how tense do you think things are going to get if the press gets wind of the fact you didn't show up to the party of the year?"

Pinching the bridge of my nose, I blow out a defeated sigh. "I know."

My sister has made an excellent point. And it's not one that I hadn't considered. If word got out that I didn't attend my own parents' anniversary party, the media will have a fucking field day.

And word always gets out.

"Please, just be there." Claire has always been the peacekeeper in our family, the buffer during family arguments, but it's not often I witness her pleading. This is either really important to her or she knows something I don't.

"Okay," I nod. "I'll see what I can do." I bound up the stairs onto the balcony, then call back out to her before she slips around the side of the house. "Hey, Claire?"

She turns her gaze upward to find me. "Yeah?"

"You don't think they'd actually come here, do you?" I ask. "To Cliff Haven?"

"I wouldn't put it past them. Just be ready.

Chapter 8

MACKENZIE

"Dad called yesterday."

Kristen's words stop me in my tracks, my hand pausing in place on the refrigerator handle. I spin around slowly, unsure how to react. I hadn't been in contact with our father since his first failed stint in rehab. I didn't realise Kristen had been.

"What?"

Her lips curl inward, mashing together as she looks down at the bowl of cereal in front of her on the wooden kitchen table, her shoulders hunching inward at the hostility in my tone. "He's earned phone privileges," she says, a little more softly this time.

"Shit," I mutter. "What did he say? Actually, no. I don't want to know." My hands go up defensively in front of me.

"I'm sorry. I didn't mean to drop a bomb on you like that." She at least has the sense to look a little uncomfortable.

"Yeah. Well, you did anyway." My jaw clenches in irritation and I'm suddenly not in the mood for my coffee. "How did he even get your number?"

"I called him first," she admits. "A couple of weeks ago."

"So… what? You and Dad are like besties now?"

I can't hide my agitation. Our father hasn't been there for either one of us. He'd left Kristen and Pamela for my mother when Kristen was barely eight years old. I don't remember a time when he'd ever been there for me. Not really. The fact that she's seemingly having casual conversations with him now cuts deep, resurrecting the feelings of resentment I'd once held for my sister.

I was jealous that she had known family, parental love, and a father that doted on her. Even if only for the first eight years of her life. Now I envy her for a different reason.

When I'd first come to stay with Kristen in her apartment, I'd found a bunch of letters in a drawer addressed to our father. I never read them, but I did march them down to the local post office, bought a stamp each for all sixteen of them and slipped them in the bright red post-box out the front. I later learned that she'd written one for each of her birthdays that she'd spent without him, never intending for him to read them.

Maybe that had been a shitty thing to do, but I didn't send those letters to hurt Kristen. I sent them to hurt him, hoping that something in them might tip him over the edge.

I got my wish.

A week later, he showed up here in Cliff Haven on his way to the city for rehab, making a pitstop at Kristen's apartment to let her know that her words had been a godsend. That they made him realise just how pathetic he was.

I'd never admit this out loud, but a part of me resents the fact that it was Kristen's letters that finally pushed him to see his mistakes and check himself into rehab. Not me blatantly telling him over the years that he needed help. Nor any of the times he'd neglected basic parental duties like cooking meals and cleaning up after himself, let alone me. I'd lived under his roof all along, completely invisible to him, my pleas falling on deaf ears.

Kristen stands, shuffling over to the sink with her bowl. "I wouldn't exactly say that. He has a long way to go to earn my forgiveness, but these programs don't usually work without the support of family and friends. And we're all he's got."

"Nope," I say. "*You* are all he's got."

"Look, Mackenzie." She sighs, flipping on the kitchen tap to rinse her bowl and coffee cup. "I'm not going to make you do anything you don't want to do. And like I said, I haven't forgiven him either. I just wanted you to know that we're in contact. If you want to speak with him I could–"

"No thanks," I interrupt abruptly.

Kristen knows better than to follow me as I storm down the hallway to my room, but I feel her eyes burning holes in my back all the same.

When I'd first woken up, I'd contemplated not going for my morning jog. I'd even pondered the possibility of a sleep in, but like clockwork, my body had got me out of bed at six-thirty anyway. This conversation with my sister has me so worked up now, I need somewhere to direct this pent-up aggression.

I pull open my second drawer, reaching in for my workout

gear and slam it shut with a little too much force. I slip the black and purple Lycra crop-top over my head, pull on my leggings and running shoes and sneak out the front door before Kristen gets out of the shower.

I head for the trail near the river, jogging through the undergrowth until I reach the fork. The left side will take me out to the beach, the right to the lagoon behind the tavern. Today I decide to be brave and take the right side of the fork. I veer down the path, winding my way through it until the salt of the ocean hits my senses.

I pause to catch my breath. I love this time of the day in Cliff Haven. When everyone but the surfers and joggers are yet to wake. Nothing destresses me quite like the seashore, but as the tension from this morning's conversation with Kristen evaporates, a new sense of dread arises.

Not many people can say they've been kidnapped by their ex while out for their morning run but that's exactly what happened to me.

My forehead crumples as I try to shake away the memories that unfortunately live rent free in my head of events that happened right here, in this very spot. The taste of blood and sweat as Ethan's palm clamped over my mouth, my heels digging into the ground in an attempt to gain traction as he dragged me backward.

Sometimes I swear I can still feel the icy cool blade he held to my throat, already tainted with blood. Hear the gravel in his voice as he spat out cruel words, describing in detail what he'd just done to Henley behind the bar at Steve's tavern before opening hours. I hadn't wanted to believe him, but I'd been involved with Ethan Davis for long enough to know what he was capable of. Thank God Henley survived. I never would have been able to forgive myself.

I suck in another breath, willing it all away. I focus on my gratitude. That I'm able to be standing here, free, no longer bound by the chains of an abusive boyfriend.

It had taken a while for me to work up the courage to jog alone after what happened with Ethan. To really let it sink in that he was behind bars and could no longer touch me. And even on the day that I'd finally dared to jog my usual morning route, I'd panicked, hearing heavy breathing behind me, only to turn and realise it was Henley.

He joined me for the first couple of weeks, despite being told by the doctors that he wasn't in any condition to run. He never said anything about the trauma we both experienced. Instead, he cracked some joke about not wanting to lose his Thor-like physique, but I knew he was looking out for me. Just like he had ever since the day we left Coledale together. It's ironic. My sister's fiancé is the only man in this entire world to ever earn my trust.

Kristen has tried to get me to talk about what happened, though her questions have never been specific. She never asked me why I stayed with Ethan as long as I did, probably because she knew I wouldn't have told her anyway.

Whenever she shot a question my way, I clammed up, unable to speak. At some point she stopped asking. Nobody else has ever asked. Maybe they're scared I'll react and dive off the deep end. Maybe they don't want to know. Or worse, they think they already know everything there is to know.

A quick glance at my watch tells me it's just after seven. Harper and I had agreed to meet at the Haven at 8am and walk to the dive boat tour from there, knowing it would take around twenty minutes to walk across town to the marina. I turn, readying myself to head back through the trail the way I came when something catches my attention further down the banks of the lagoon.

A woman stands motionless, her eyes trained in my direction. I recognise her from the pier during my lunch break that day. Gone is the look of anguish she'd worn in her expression, replaced by one of pure shock. I glance around behind me, searching for something or someone that may have caught her eye.

But there's no one else here. She's staring at me.

And she looks as though she's seen a ghost.

Suddenly, my phone rings, disturbing the serenity, and I hastily reach into my pocket and slide it out. Harper's name lights up the screen.

"Hey," I answer, still slightly out of breath.

"Hey, Mackenzie." Disappointment fills her tone, echoes of a crying Noah in the background.

"Uh oh. What's wrong?" I can already sense without her saying anything that things are not going to go as planned today. "Is Noah okay?"

"Not exactly," she replies, sadness dripping from her voice. "He'll be okay but he's running a really high fever. I'm not going to be able to come today."

"Oh shit," I say. "Poor Noah."

"Yeah," she says regretfully. "Look, I'm so sorry. I just can't leave him when he's like this. He needs me and…"

"Of course," I tell her. "You absolutely need to be with him. It's fine. We can reschedule the snorkelling trip for another day. It's no problem at all."

"Well." She drags the word out and I picture her wincing. "There might be a slight problem."

"What do you mean?"

"The tickets I got were non-refundable and non-transferrable. It was like a last-minute kind of deal. I couldn't pass on the discounted price."

"Oh."

"I think you should still use them," she blurts. "I'll email them to you. Maybe you could see if Kristen wants to go." She seems to perk up at this suggestion, but it only brings to mind my altercation with my sister this morning.

"I don't know. I'm happy to forfeit the tickets and wait till you can go." It's not like the dive boat tour was my idea. In fact, I'd much rather stay on dry land than commit my day to a boat named Two Tanked.

"Please go, Mackenzie," she begs. "I might be a single mother, but you never take the time to do anything fun for yourself either. You deserve a nice morning out in the sun. Besides, I'm kind of living vicariously through you at this point."

"Oh really?" Her comment makes me laugh. "Well, if you're depending on me to fill your quota of excitement and adventure, you're in for a world of disappointment."

"Come on, Mackenzie!" she pleads. "Do this for me then. Please go. Slip into a gorgeous bikini, get onboard that boat and send me some insta-worthy pics. Bonus points if you can get a selfie with a hot dive instructor."

"That is not happening," I tell her.

"I hope you just mean the last part because I really want

you to get on that boat. I mean it, Mackenzie. You deserve to have some fun too."

I contemplate Harper's suggestion. I guess it could be fun to try something different. "If it means that much to you…"

"It does," she interrupts.

I suppose I could see if Kristen wanted to join me. It is her day off. And I hate fighting with her. Maybe this would give us a chance to have some sisterly bonding time or whatever. "Sure. Okay. Email the tickets."

"Yes!" she squeals. "Okay, I've gotta check on Noah and then I'll send them through."

"Okay," I say. "Take care of him. Give him a hug from me."

"I will," she replies. "Oh, and Mackenzie."

"Yeah?"

"Don't forget to get a pic with a hot instructor."

My eyes roll as I shake my head, but I'd be lying if I said my lips didn't twitch with the hint of a grin as I hang up on her call.

I slide my phone back into my pocket and glance back down the lagoon to where the strange woman had been standing. She's no longer there, but as I jog home, I can't seem to erase the image of her or the expression on her face from my mind.

Chapter 9

DYLAN

The weather stats blink brightly from the iPad screen I'm holding. All blue skies and sunshine icons for today and tomorrow, with a high of thirty-two degrees Celsius. However, a quick glance at the rest of this week and next shows predicted storms. I hope that won't affect business too much.

I was running late today. Claire's unexpected visit this morning had thrown me out of routine. Then, after my shower, Chance had given me sad puppy dog eyes which lead to an extended game of beach fetch, which is why I'm surprised I beat everyone to the boat.

I close down the weather app and pull up the guest register. Two Tanked can only take out a maximum number of twelve passengers and a minimum of eight. Looks like we're at full capacity again today.

I hear Jade coming, her footsteps falling heavy on the dock.

"Hey, what's up amigo," she says as she climbs aboard the thirty-foot catamaran.

"Morning," I say, my eyes still on the iPad. "Just checking the register for today. We have another full tour."

"Third day in a row. Cool," she responds casually. "Cameron will be happy."

"Yeah," I agree. "Especially considering the storms predicted for later this week."

"Cameron will be happy about what?" Our boss is next to board, his usual tattered blue backpack hitched high over one shoulder.

"Full tour today," Jade informs him.

"Nice," Cameron replies, slapping her palm with a high five.

Cameron is our trip director and part owner of this boat. He only started up these dive tours about six months ago. Business hadn't boomed right away, but now Two Tanked is vying for the top spot in diving tours in Cliff Haven. I only joined the dive crew about four months ago, but it's been the best thing I've ever done.

For the most part, the weather has been on our side, having only needed to postpone a few tours here and there. Having these full capacity days helps make up for the loss of business on days when it's too risky to go out. And looking at the forecast, we may have a couple of cancelled trips later on this week.

My eyes are still trailing over the names on the guest register when one in particular stands out from all the rest. "Huh," I mumble, my gaze hovering at the bottom of the list. "What's this?"

Jade's head snaps up. There's a hint of mischief in her eyes as they slice to mine. "What's what?"

"Harper Conway and Mackenzie Riley?" I question her, my gaze narrowing in suspicion. "Did you tell them we work here?"

"Nope," she says slyly.

"Jade." I drag her name out cautiously. "Why do I sense a but coming on?"

"They don't know we work here." She shrugs before making her confession. "But I may have told them this snorkel tour was the best in town and that it would be a great way for them to blow off steam."

"Jade!" My eyes go wide with accusation as I follow her to the small storage area where the supplies are kept. "Are you serious?"

"What's the problem?" she asks as she digs through the refreshments. "I don't know why you're being so secretive about your second job."

"I'm not secretive," I retaliate. "I just like to keep all aspects of my life segregated."

"Right." Jade scoffs. "You work with Mackenzie nearly every day. She's bound to find out eventually. I don't get why this is such a big deal. Unless..." she pauses, her finger on her chin, her eyes wide in astonishment.

"Unless what?" I ask with my hands splayed out awaiting her response.

"You're harbouring an even bigger secret."

My posture stiffens as I contemplate the possibility that Jade knows more about me than she's let on. We haven't known each other long, but if she wanted to find information on me, it wouldn't be hard to find it.

"There's no secret," I say quickly.

"Oh my god!" she exclaims, her bright green eyes narrowing as they pierce mine. I hold my breath, awaiting her next words. "That's it. You have superpowers. Are you Clarke Kent? Wait…no. Aquaman!"

My shoulders slump, releasing the tension as I let out an irritated sigh. I stare back at her with dead eyes. "You are the literal worst."

She chuckles as she shoves a case of bottled water into my chest. "Come on. Help me load up the fridge." She leads the way, moving in front of me, but turns back when she senses my persistent apprehension. "You're not mad at me for this, are you?"

I relax my glare. "Of course not."

I realise I seem like the world's biggest overreactor right now. Jade and I have grown close since we started working together and she's way too sweet for me to ever be mad at. It's not like it really matters if Harper and Mackenzie know the reason I cut my shifts at the tavern.

It's the rest of the world I worry about.

And none of that is Jade's fault. In hindsight it wasn't fair of me to ask her not to tell the staff at the tavern that I also work on the dive boat. She has no idea the extent of the impact it could have if the wrong people discovered my whereabouts, the media storm it would unleash on my family. I know it's only a matter of time before I have to deal with it all though, because this is the life I chose.

"I guess I've just liked having this extra side job as mine. I have goals to accomplish, and I don't want anything getting in the way of that." It's technically not a lie.

"Well," Jade says, looking towards the pier. "You've got about ten seconds to jump overboard if you don't want them to know."

I roll my eyes at Jade and then follow her line of sight to where Mackenzie strolls casually down the dock, flipping her long, blonde curls behind her. A beach bag with rope handles is slung over her shoulder, the cropped, white, crochet top she wears revealing her midriff. I search the line of awaiting passengers for Harper, but there's no sign of her.

Cameron greets the first few passengers as they file onto the boat. "Morning guys," he says, his tone chipper as he rakes a hand through his sun-bleached hair. "You've picked a great day to come out. Weather's going to be crazy towards the end of the week."

He begins escorting them down the aisles, directing them to where they can sit. When Mackenzie steps aboard, the first thing she notices is Jade. She blinks in surprise as she recognises my co-worker. "Jade? Are you doing the tour too?"

"Sort of," Jade says, her hands finding their way to her hips. "I work here."

"Oh, wow. You should have said," Mackenzie replies, tucking an unruly blonde wave behind her ear. "That's really cool."

Jade shrugs and steps aside, unblocking her view of me. I'm still hovering near the fridge behind the bar area, the case of water suddenly heavy in my arms. I release it and it drops loudly on the countertop.

I'd be lying if I said I wasn't affected by those grey-blue irises and the way that crochet crop top she wears fits so perfectly around each curve. The tavern is mutual territory for us and it's weird to see her outside of it. Here, she isn't my employee. She's… different. Her eyebrows furrow in confusion as she takes another step toward me.

"Hey," I offer with an awkward wave of my hand.

"Um, h-hi," she stutters. Her gaze drops to the bottled water in front of me that I slowly start to unpack. "Is this your boat or something?"

"Ha! He wishes!" Cameron half shouts as he appears from nowhere, slapping a hand on my back. "It's my boat. Well, mine and my brother's, but he's off diving in the Galapagos."

"Uh, Cameron," I say, nervously scratching the back of my neck. "This is Mackenzie. We work together at the tavern."

"Oh, I see. So you know all about how much of a pain in the neck this one can be," he says slyly, throwing a thumb in my direction.

I try to hide my discomfort behind an awkward laugh, half expecting Mackenzie to come back with a smart-ass comment in agreeance with my boss here. But she just watches our interaction with curious eyes.

"I'm just kidding," Cameron continues. "This guy is one of the hardest workers I know. Nice to meet you, Mackenzie. Welcome aboard Two Tanked. If you need anything at all, I'm sure Dylan will be able to help you out."

Mackenzie nods, a small smile tugging at the edges of her mouth before her bottom lip disappears between her teeth. I'd be lying if I said I wasn't affected by that too. "So, this is what you get up to when you're not busting my ass at the tavern."

"Uh, yeah." I move out from behind the bar, realising too late that the space is too small. Despite the closeness of our bodies, she doesn't take a step back. "I think you have that the wrong way around, though. Aren't you the one busting my ass most of the time?"

That earns me another sly smile, her eyes glinting as they roam the length of my body. Any thoughts I have of whether that was her attempt at checking me out are cut short as Jade appears, slamming my wetsuit against my chest.

"Come on. Time to suit up," she declares, the seriousness in her demeanour dissolving with a wink as she adds, "Aquaman."

If looks could kill, the one I'm giving her right now would annihilate her right where she stands. Her wicked grin is wider than that of a cheshire cat, one hand perched on her hip, the other carrying a bunch of snorkel masks.

"Yeah. Okay. I should go… change," I stammer, aiming a thumb behind me to the back of the boat.

Mackenzie nods, but her eyes don't leave mine. I can still feel them on me, burning into the skin of my back as I turn.

And I'm not complaining.

"Come over and I'll get you some equipment," I hear Jade say as I'm walking away, then to the rest of the group forming behind Mackenzie she calls loudly. "If everyone would like to head over this way, I can hand out the snorkels and fins. If you will be scuba diving today, please see Dylan at the back there and he can get you fitted up with wetsuits and your dive equipment."

A young woman and two middle aged men trail me to the back of the boat. The snorkellers usually outnumber the scuba divers and today is no different.

"Hey guys," I say to the three people that have joined me. "I'll just get you to come over this way and we'll sort out what you need. Are any of you first timers today?"

All three of them shake their heads, the men letting me know they're PADI certified divers. The young woman explains that one of them is her uncle and the other her dad, and that she has done a couple of dives before. The fact that the two men are certified makes my job a whole lot easier, which I'm thankful for, because as I steal a glance at Mackenzie down the other end of the boat, I realise I'm going to be struggling to keep my main focus on the job today. I watch as she walks to the back, taking a seat on the bench outside.

There's a sudden jerk as the boat glides away from the dock and we begin the journey out to the reef. I busy myself helping the divers find what they need. Then I give them a full debriefing, explaining how the tour will run and answering any of their questions along the way.

After I've pulled my own wetsuit on, I take the opportunity to find Mackenzie, knowing we still have ten minutes before we reach the dive location. She's still sitting on the bench at the back of the boat, her tanned legs stretching out in front of her. She looks up as I approach.

"Hey," she says.

"Hey." I take a seat beside her. "No Harper today? I saw her name on the register."

"No, unfortunately," she replies with a quick shake of her head. "It was her idea to come out on the tour, but she cancelled last minute. Noah got sick."

"Oh." My forehead pulls in a frown. "I hope he's okay."

"Yeah. Me too. She didn't seem to think it was anything too serious, but he had a fever," she explains. "I asked Kristen if she wanted to come instead but she had a thing."

"Well, I'm glad you still came."

She glances up at me, squinting in the sunlight, her hair glistening like strands of white gold. She looks away and then back down at her feet. "So do you have any other sneaky jobs I don't know about?"

"Ha. No. Just this one."

"How many tours do you do a week?" she asks.

"I work the morning dives for five days of the week, but every now and then I take on an afternoon one."

She nods. "So that's why you cut your hours at the tavern and had Steve hire Jesse?"

"Yeah." I rake a hand through my hair, then smooth my hands along my wetsuit covered thighs. "It was kind of always the plan. I still like working at the tavern though. Steve has been really good to me."

"Does he know about your side job? Why so secretive about it?"

"He doesn't know. He didn't ask." I suck in a deep breath as I contemplate the best way to answer the second part of her question. "My parents aren't exactly thrilled about my life choices. I guess that's kind of stopped me from shouting it from the roof tops."

"Ah. Hence the heated phone call at the tavern the other day," she assumes.

"Yeah. Sort of." There's a lot more to it than that, but I don't want to go into that right now. "Plus, it's nice to have something that's just mine, you know?"

She tucks her hands under her thighs and her shoulders jump up in a shrug. "Not really."

"No? You don't have a hobby? Or something that you do just for you? Something that you're so passionate about that you need it like you need air?"

She gives me a sideward glance. "Okay. Settle down there." She seems to ponder my question for a moment and then finally she says, "I don't know. I guess I have my art. I like to draw, but it's nothing special."

"Something tells me you're probably not giving yourself enough credit," I tell her. "Maybe you could show me sometime."

She gives me a sceptical look, like she can't understand why I would possibly want to see her work. But I do want to see it. There's something about Mackenzie that I'm drawn to. I just haven't figured out what it is yet.

"Yeah, maybe," she responds, then in true Mackenzie style, she deflects the attention back onto me. "So, why diving?"

My answer is automatic. "I love it. I love the ocean and everything in it."

"Everything?"

"Yeah. Everything. You'll see."

For a second I think she's going to make some smart-ass comment like she usually does, but instead the corners of her mouth twitch subtly with the smallest hint of a grin.

And I make it my mission, right here and now, to make this girl smile a real smile one day.

Chapter 10

MACKENZIE

I'm totally out of my comfort zone here, bobbing around in the middle of the ocean participating in a water sport that I've never tried before, without the friend that actually booked it.

But I'm still glad I came.

The reef is beautiful, brimming with fish of all the colours of the rainbow and corals so articulate in their design. I make a mental note to thank Harper for pushing me to come out here. It has been exactly what I needed.

When we'd arrived at the reef, Jade had given us a thirty-minute guided tour, pointing out different species of fish and rattling off facts about turtles. She'd also shown us some interesting reef formations and explained how corals are actually animals and not plants, which was something I'd been unaware of until this point. After the tour, we'd been told we could explore freely until it was time to get back on the boat.

I dive down deeper and come face to face with another sea turtle. Behind it, two others float in the depths. I'm mesmerised by their grace and the way the rays of sunlight penetrate the water in silver streaks, highlighting the colours in their shells. I find myself thinking about the canvas and art supplies I retrieved from Pamela's loft. Maybe I've just found my next subject.

Further down, I can make out Dylan and the other scuba divers. I'm not sure I have any intentions of learning how to dive, but I am impressed by it. It must feel super-human to be able to walk along the ocean floor. Although I'm not sure I'd be prepared to face the many creatures that lurk out in all that deep blue.

I glide upwards, taking a deep breath as I break through the surface.

"It's beautiful, isn't it?" Jade treads water next to me, her snorkel mask perched upon her forehead.

"Yeah," I agree, sliding my mask up onto my forehead in the same way. "It really is."

"Told you you'd like it," she says with a smile. "It's a shame Harper couldn't make it."

"Yeah," I say. I feel a pinch of guilt at being out here knowing it was my friend who really needed this escape. "It's too bad. She would have really liked it."

"Another time," she says.

"For sure. I'm definitely bringing her back out here once Noah feels better."

A moment later, four dark figures resurface near the boat, their excitable voices carrying across the water as they whoop and holler.

"Did you see that?" The young woman says to the rest of the group. "It was so cool!"

The man to her left responds by high fiving her. Whatever happened down there below the surface has no doubt gotten the adrenaline pumping through their veins. Dylan slides his mask up onto his forehead, his eyes finding mine across the turquoise ocean.

"Well, Dylan's back," Jade announces. "That's our cue. Morning teatime."

"Okay." I paddle to the boat while Jade collects the rest of the snorkellers.

By the time I've reached the boat ladder, all of the scuba divers have already climbed back aboard. Except Dylan. He hovers at the side of the boat. "How'd you go today, Jade?"

"Yeah, good. Heaps of turtles out to play," she answers as she hoists herself up the ladder.

"Awesome," he replies. Then he turns to me, his eyes warm like coffee flecked with gold. "What about you? Did you have fun?"

"Yeah, I did," I tell him.

I reach for the ladder, but his hand comes up to stop me. I pause, glancing down to where his golden skin meets my own.

"Wait," he says. He smiles, exposing a brilliant flash of bright white teeth. "Come with me. I want to show you something." He slides the oxygen tank off his back and thrusts it up into the boat where Cameron collects it, then he begins to move toward the bow. "Over here."

I paddle over as quickly as I can. "What is it?"

"Something really special. Just come with me. You'll see," he says, sliding his mask back down over his eyes with the biggest grin I've ever seen. "Put your mask on. We're gonna dive down a few metres. Hold your breath, okay?"

I pull the mask back down over my eyes as instructed, then his palm is in mine, firm and reassuring. We glide downwards, tiny blue and yellow fish flying past, the underwater world breathtaking in its beauty. I feel freer than I ever have before, so grateful to be alongside Dylan for this adventure.

Then my heart slams against my ribs when I see a large grey mass a few metres below us. I panic at the sight of a dorsal fin, several rows of jagged teeth and the beady eyes that watch me from their peripheral.

I pull my hand frantically from Dylan's. He turns. Seeing the fear in my eyes, he realises I'm freaking out. Then grasping my hips with strong hands, he propels us both to the surface. He doesn't let go of me until I'm gripping the boat's ladder.

"Kenz, are you okay?"

His question maddens me. I clench my jaw, my body still trembling with fear.

"Am I okay?" I shout. "What the hell, Dylan? I need on this boat now!"

I try to hoist myself up, but the fins I'm still wearing keep getting caught in the rungs of the ladder, making me slip and slide all over the place. I cry out in frustration, slamming my fist into the side of the boat in anger. "These fucking things!"

Dylan watches me patiently from the water with an amused glint in his eye. After a moment, he sighs. "Can I help?"

I turn myself around stubbornly, managing to seat myself on the bottom rung of the ladder, awkwardly holding my feet above the surface. With the patience of a saint, he gently slips my fins off one at a time. I give him a defiant look, my nostrils flaring, chin jutting out, before I turn and climb aboard. He follows closely behind me with way more grace than I'd been capable of.

"I'm sorry, Mackenzie," he offers. "I thought you'd like it."

"Like what?" I cry. "Being lured to the depths of hell straight into the jaws of... Jaws!"

He raises an eyebrow, rolling his lips together. I can tell this is him attempting not to laugh, which only infuriates me more. "It was just a grey nurse shark, Kenz. They're actually really peaceful. And they're endangered."

"Endangered? *I* was just endangered!" I shout, not caring that we now have the attention of the rest of the boat.

"No, you weren't. I'd never put you in harm's way." Another sigh escapes him as he swipes a hand through his wet hair. "I'm sorry. I didn't peg you as someone who'd be scared of..."

"You didn't think I'd be afraid of a shark?" I cut him off. "Most people on this planet are afraid of sharks, Dylan!"

"Sharks are actually really misunderstood creatures," he says calmly and matter-of-factly.

"*I* was just a misunderstood creature! As in, *you* misunderstood that *I* would want to be fed to a shark."

At this point I realise I may be overdoing it with the dramatics, but adrenaline is coursing through my veins after our close encounter with The Meg and I'm not in the mood.

He clamps his lips together, his eyes crinkling at the corners as the laugh he tries to contain bursts free in the form of a snort.

"I would never feed you to a shark, Kenz."

"It's Mackenzie," I tell him, for the four hundredth time as I thump a fist into his chest.

And damn it, his pecs are firm.

"Okay. I'm gonna let you calm down a little while I go get these lovely people some refreshments. I'll bring you something in a minute, okay?"

"Whatever," I mutter as I make my way across the boat to my bag.

I grab my towel and begin drying off, then I throw on the shorts and crop top I'd worn here back over my bikini. The boat is set in motion as I take a seat on the same bench I sat on for the journey out to the reef.

A short while later, Dylan is standing in front of me, his wetsuit pulled down to the waist so low it reveals his eight pack and a scripted tattoo across his right rib cage.

Great. Now he's decided to use his hot body to distract me from being angry at him.

"How's it going, Kenz?" he asks as he holds out a selection of sandwiches on a small plate to me.

I swear he's just going along with this annoying nickname to piss me of now.

"As good as it can be after a near death experience." I answer stiffly, plucking a cheese and ham portion. He doesn't say anything. Just stands there grinning at me, one hand on his hips, the other balancing the plate of sandwiches. It's irritating. "Stop smiling at me!"

God, I wish he'd put a shirt on. I also wish he'd never put a shirt on. I don't know what it means that I can't stop gawking at him, but I really hope it isn't obvious.

"Okay, okay," he says, raising his hands up in the air. "I'm sorry I scared you. You hate sharks. Duly noted. Friends?" He holds out his hand in a peace offering.

I'm not usually the type to overreact and I'm starting to realise that's exactly what I've done. Although I don't know Dylan well enough to trust him – I don't think I'll ever know anyone well enough to trust them – I know he'd never put me in immediate danger.

He's a dive instructor who is clearly passionate about his work. The grin that he's worn this entire boat tour is a testament to that. He just wanted to show me something that he thought was special to him and I freaked out about it.

I huff out a breath. "Fine. I'm sorry too. For overreacting." I accept his handshake and then he sits down beside me, placing the plate of sandwiches on the bench in between us. "But I am gonna get my revenge on you for that stunt you pulled."

"I'll sleep with one eye open." He chuckles. "Any word from Harper?"

I reach into my bag with my free hand and pull out my phone, casually scrolling through the notifications. "Not yet. I'll send her a text."

I type out a quick message asking Harper how Noah is doing.

"I meant what I said before, you know." He shifts his body towards mine on the bench seat.

"Which part? That sharks are misunderstood and endangered?"

"No." He shakes his head, laughing quietly.

"Oh, so you made that part up?" I quirk an eyebrow as I take a small bite of my sandwich.

"I didn't. Those things are true," he replies earnestly.

"Oh. What then?"

His eyes soften and he lifts his right shoulder subtly in a small shrug. "I'm glad you came out today."

"Yeah. Me too," I admit.

Despite the last five minutes of the snorkelling trip sending me into a panic, I have really enjoyed today. And whether I care to admit it or not, Dylan's company hasn't been all that bad either. My phone chimes with an incoming text from Harper, and I break my gaze away from his to steal a glance at the screen.

> Noah's fever has broken.
> I think he's on the mend.

"Noah's starting to feel better," I relay to Dylan.

"That's good," he replies, taking a bite of one of the sandwiches. "He's such a cute kid."

"Yeah." I can't help my mind shifting back to yesterday, to the way he'd calmed Noah down so effortlessly, which in turn reminds me of Harper's comments. My phone chimes with another text.

> So tell me... On a scale of 1 to 10...
> How hot are the instructors? 😏

> Can't believe you still haven't sent me a pic

I almost laugh out loud. Her timing is impeccable. If only she knew. Before I've even had a chance to slide my phone into my pocket, it chimes again. Twice.

"Must be important," Dylan says gesturing to the phone in my back pocket.

"Hardly," I scoff.

He arches an eyebrow in question.

"It's just Harper being… Harper," I say, rolling my eyes and retrieving the phone again.

Remember I'm living vicariously through you.

Selfie!!

Mama needs her eye candy!

"Is everything okay? Is it Noah? What's she saying?"

"Nothing. He's fine," I tell him, barely stifling a soft laugh.

Harper's texts, as outrageous as they may be, seem to be lifting me from my sullen mood and I don't think I'm doing a very good job of masking the smirk that seems intent on blowing my cover here.

"Then what is it?" He leans into me, analysing my face. "Wait. Are you smiling?"

"No," I lie. "It's nothing."

And then he's swiping the phone from my grip. I try to reclaim it, my fingers grasping at his muscular forearms to no avail. I surrender, squeezing my eyes shut in embarrassment as he skims over Harper's words. When I open them, he's still reading, the corners of his mouth downturned, his eyebrows arched in surprise.

"Hmm," he murmurs, his expression unreadable. "Well, we better give the woman what she wants."

My jaw drops. This is the last thing I expected him to say. "What? No."

"You heard her. Mama needs her eye candy." Dylan grins deviously as I shake my head in mortification. At this point, I'm wishing that a strong wind would force me overboard, but he's already opened the camera app, positioning the phone to capture a selfie of the two of us. "Smile."

I grimace, then lean into the shot and put on a cheesy grin for Harper's benefit. He sends the pic and hands me back my phone.

"She's gonna freak out," I tell him.

I glance down at it. It's actually a pretty decent pic of Dylan, his perfect white teeth a stark contrast to his suntanned skin, his right hand forming a peace sign. My eyes catch on the ink adorning his rib cage and I can't help myself seeking it out in real life.

"What's this?" I ask, my hand trailing the script as I read the words aloud. "Fortune favours the brave."

When my gaze drifts upward I find his eyes locked on mine and its then I notice the goosebumps that have formed beneath my fingertips. "It's just an old saying. You've heard of it, right?"

"Yeah," I say. "But I mean, what does it mean to you?"

He pauses, still looking at me, seemingly contemplating his answer. He opens his mouth to say something, but Cameron's voice echoes across the boat.

"Dylan!" he calls impatiently. "You wanna come help me out here or what?"

His eyes snap to Cameron somewhere behind me and I draw my hand back, suddenly aware of the heat traveling through my core.

"Duty calls," he says in a low voice, then with a wink he adds, "You're gonna get me into trouble, Kenz."

"Oh, you don't even know what trouble is yet," I hit back.

"I take it I still need to sleep with one eye open then?"
I lean back in my seat, crossing my arms over my chest. "I'm plotting my revenge as we speak."

There's a gleam in his eye when he replies. "I'll bet you are. I can't wait."

As he strides away from me, my phone chimes again.

ARE YOU FUCKING KIDDING ME!!! 

Chapter 11

DYLAN

"Well, if it isn't Cliff Haven's own resident dive master." Harper teases me from behind the counter at the Haven café. She wears a smile despite the bags underlining her eyes.

A sheepish smirk creeps across my face as I remember the selfie I'd sent to her from Mackenzie's phone yesterday. I choke out a half laugh. "I guess the cat's out of the bag then."

I'd delighted in stirring Mackenzie up yesterday when I'd sent that message, but I realise now that I probably should have thought through the consequences before I did.

"Guess so." She shrugs, pulling a muffin from the cabinet with a set of tongs and bagging it for the elderly woman to my left. "There you go, Mrs. Mayfield. Enjoy!"

How this woman can sound so peppy when she's clearly exhausted as hell is beyond me. "How's Noah?" I ask. "Mackenzie said he wasn't well."

"He's still not great, but he's a lot better than yesterday." Her forehead crumples and the corners of her mouth turn down in a frown. "Mum's taking care of him today so I can work."

"That's no good. Hopefully he's back to normal soon."

"Yeah, thanks. I hope so too," she says. "What can I get you?"

I blow out a breath, remembering the text I'd received from Claire barely half an hour ago relaying the news that our parents were on the way to Cliff Haven to discuss 'things' with me and that they were 'on the warpath.'

"I think I need a coffee," I blurt.

"A coffee?" Harper stares at me like I've lost my mind. "You've literally never ordered a coffee from me ever."

"Yeah. I don't drink coffee." Another wave of anxiety ripples through me at the thought of my parents impending visit. I smooth out the linen button-down shirt I'd chosen this morning, my palms slick with sweat. "My parents are visiting. I need something to calm my nerves. What do you recommend?"

She raises an eyebrow but doesn't ask questions about the information I've just revealed. "Not coffee, dude. That's literally the last thing you need."

"Okay. Have you got any suggestions?"

"Chamomile tea?"

I blow out another breath. "Yeah okay. That will do."

She rings up my order and I swipe my card. She turns to the back wall, busying herself with preparing my tea.

Suddenly, I'm thrown off kilter by the girl that barges in front of the line. Her forearm nudges mine as fingertips adorned with chipped blue nail polish meet the countertop, champagne waves spilling down around her shoulders.

"Harper!" she calls. "Have you got some cream we could borrow?"

"Uh, I guess?" Harper answers as she turns around, confusion marring her features.

"Sorry. There's this posh woman at the bar demanding some cocktail that's not even on the menu and Corey just put the last of the cream into his precious potato bake recipe." She pushes her hair back off her face, revealing that flawless golden skin I've become so familiar with of late.

"Everything okay, Kenz?" I ask.

"Not exactly. This woman is fucking awful," she replies.

At that moment a text chimes through my phone and I pull it from my top pocket. It's my dad.

> We're waiting for you. You're late.

I let out a groan. They're already here. And I'd put money on who this awful woman making Mackenzie's life hell might be.

Harper hands me the tea, which at this point I don't even think I can stomach. I set off across the road, leaving Mackenzie there to source the cream.

When I enter the tavern, the first thing I see is my father, seated at a table smack bang in the middle of the room. He sticks out like a sore thumb in his black Hugo Boss suit and matching shiny shoes, no doubt made from the finest Italian leather.

The second thing I see, or hear rather, is Faith Abbott. Dressed elegantly in a burgundy designer cocktail dress, she screeches at Corey from the opposite side of the bar. "Where has that wretched girl gone with my drink?"

Corey mutters an apology to my mother as I place an arm around her shoulder. I begin steering her in the direction of the table. As if on cue, Mackenzie comes barrelling through the doors of the tavern, a small tub of cream in hand.

"I'm sure your drink won't be too much longer, mother," I say loud enough for Mackenzie to hear.

Her head snaps up as she catches my words, a knowing look passing over her face. Mackenzie doesn't know the inner workings of my relationship with my parents, but she knows that things are strained between us. I'm counting on her to help me make this experience as pain free as possible but when her eyes meet mine, they're full of mischief, crinkling at the corners as she aims a devious one-sided smirk my way.

My mouth forms a grim line in response. I shake my head at her as if to say, "Now is not the time to give me any shit," but she only lets out a low chuckle.

My lips part, another quiet sigh passing through them as I take a seat between both of my parents. I'm about to ask them how they both are, to entertain the usual small talk, but my mother speaks before I get a chance.

"Seriously, Dylan. This place is lacking." She picks up the laminate card in front of her between her forefinger and thumb, eyeing it as though it's a plague-infected rat. "The menu is bare. There's hardly any choice."

I resist the urge to roll my eyes and take a sip of my tea. It's too hot and it makes me splutter. "How are you, Mum?" I ask, ignoring her remarks. "What have you been up to?"

"I'm splendid," she answers, folding her hands into her lap, the precious gemstones gracing her fingers and wrist shimmering under the light. "I trust that Claire told you all about the party arrangements for Saturday? It starts at 6pm sharp."

"Yes.' I nod as enthusiastically as I can manage. "She mentioned it."

"Here you go, mam." Mackenzie's voice is the epitome of fake politeness as she smiles down on my mother. "Your Ramos Gin Fizz."

She places a tall glass filled with white liquid that barely resembles the cocktail my mother has asked for. I don't blame her though. My mother has clearly requested one of the most difficult-to-make cocktails there is and I can honestly say I wouldn't have been able to do any better.

Mum glares at her, but Mackenzie's smile doesn't falter. I admire this about her, I realise. Mackenzie doesn't give a fuck what anyone thinks of her and nor should she. Despite all she's been through, she knows who she is, and she doesn't bow down to the demands of others. She's unapologetically herself.

My father clears his throat loudly, leaning back in his chair. "Let's just cut to the chase, shall we?" His tone is condescending as usual. "When are you coming back home?"

I hear Mackenzie shuffle from side to side behind me as she busies herself at a nearby table. The sound of the salt and pepper shakers clinking together repeatedly could not make it any more obvious that she's eavesdropping.

I sigh again, my head falling into my hands. "I've told you time and time again. I am staying here in Cliff Haven. I don't want to run the business."

"But don't you want more for yourself, darling?" Now it's

my mother's turn to weigh in. "You should be thinking about your future. Don't you want a steady career? To find a nice girl and settle down?"

Mackenzie giggles softly somewhere behind me and I drag my hands over my face, frustrated to be having this same conversation over and over. "Yes, Mum. I do want more for myself. That's why I'm here. But I don't need a girlfriend."

"And why not?"

I'm fighting a losing battle here. I shake my head before taking another long draw of my tea.

"Because he already has one." Mackenzie's voice fills my ears, more chipper than I've ever heard it as she slips into the empty chair beside me. She slings a toned arm around my neck.

I'm so shocked by her words, I choke on my tea, the hot liquid spluttering from my lips as I try to suppress my shock. I have no idea what this girl is doing, but she sure knows how to put on a show.

I swipe the moisture from my chin and dare a glance at my my mother. Mum's expression is as expected; one of absolute horror. She looks from Mackenzie and then back to me.

"Dylan," she says, her voice stern. "You neglected to tell us that you were in a relationship. Do you care to elaborate here?"

My eyes go to Mackenzie's, a twinkle of trouble playing in them, a smirk turning up the corners of her mouth. My eyes plead with hers, silently asking where the hell she's going with this. Her gaze softens and I think for a second, she might dial it back, but instead she winks.

She. Fucking. Winks.

My jaw goes slack as I realise her diabolical plan. This is her revenge. For the 'incident' with the shark yesterday. She raises her eyebrows expectantly, daring me to go along with this insanity.

"I didn't," I admit to my mother. This is my chance to shut this down. To tell my parents she's only kidding. That I'm as single as I've ever been and I'm not looking to be tied down. But instead, I find my face mirroring hers, my gaze lingering on her bottom lip. "But that's just because it's so new."

"Super new," Mackenzie agrees with an exaggerated nod, her arm still draped around my shoulder.

"This is Mackenzie," I tell them.

"How did you two meet?" my father asks.

"Funny story," Mackenzie says. "Dylan saved me from being eaten by a shark. I knew right away that he was the one for me."

I stifle a laugh. "Ha. That might be a slight exaggeration."

"Which part?" My mother mumbles.

"I don't think so," she says sweetly, tapping me comically on the nose. She turns to my parents, her grin growing wider. "He's being modest."

"Well, you weren't actually in any real danger."

"It had huge teeth," she interrupts. "And it was massive." She stretches her arms out wide as if demonstrating the size of said shark.

"Really?" My father seems unconvinced.

"Yeah, it was really scary. It was staring me down with its beady little black eyes." Mackenzie squints her eyes comically in an over-the-top impersonation.

My hand goes up to my forehead, then I drag it back down

over my mouth to stifle a groan.

"I thought I was going to die," Mackenzie continues melodramatically, slapping a hand over her heart. "But this amazing man right here, your son, he swooped in and pulled me to safety. He's my hero and …"

"Yep," I cut in, desperate to stop her from saying anything else. "And she's been my girl ever since."

"Your very best girl." Mackenzie tilts her head to the side and pretends to gaze at me lovingly.

My father clears his throat. "And just how serious is this thing between the two of you?"

"Well…" I begin to explain as the tavern door swings open.

Jade and her girlfriend, Jaclyn stroll past, Jaclyn laughing at something Jade has said before Jade's eyes find us. She does a double take, noticing our entwined embrace.

"Really serious," Mackenzie interrupts.

"So, then I guess we'll be seeing you on Saturday night then, Madison?" My mother's tone is friendly enough, but her stiff posture and pursed lips say otherwise.

"It's Mackenzie, Mum," I correct her.

Mackenzie looks at me, uncertainty in her features. "Saturday night?"

"That's right. You remember, don't you, Kenzie? My parent's big anniversary party?" I say with a teasing smile, curling my arm around her back and squeezing her a little too tightly.

"Of course." She grunts softly at my abrupt touch but barely skips a beat. "We'll be there."

"Right," my father clears his throat again. "Well, with that settled, I think it's time we made our journey home. Faith? Are you ready?"

"Yes. This drink is inedible anyway." Mum pushes the cocktail into the centre of the table and clutches her handbag.

My parents stand, and I follow suit, ready for this uncomfortable event to be done with. My mother places a steady hand on my forearm. "Please reconsider your options, Dylan."

"Can I have a word, son?" My father ushers me to the side as Mackenzie stands awkwardly next to my mother. "I don't think I need to warn you about gold diggers, Dylan. Be careful."

"Sure, Dad," I say, stifling another groan.

It's not until the tavern's doors have closed behind them that I finally let my shoulders slump. This encounter has completely drained me of energy.

"Well, they seem nice." Mackenzie folds her arms over her chest, a smirk once again playing on her mouth.

"What the hell was that?" I laugh, splaying my hands out in front of me.

"I could ask you the same thing," she says. "What the hell was that whole thing about some party?"

"Oh, that?" I say, spinning around to face her, a conspiratorial grin spreading across my face. "That was you volunteering yourself to be my date at my parent's anniversary party on the weekend."

"Ha!" she laughs. "As if! You do realise I'm not actually going. I was just trying to get payback for what you did yesterday."

"Mission accomplished," I say. "But you *are* coming with me. I can hardly show up without my best girl now, can I?"

Her smile falls, her eyes squinting at me warily. "You're the worst." She pauses, seemingly contemplating her options. "I suppose it would give me more opportunities to embarrass you further."

"Don't even think about it," I warn.

"I'm not going anyway," she says defiantly.

"Oh, yes you are."

"Where even is your parent's place?"

"You'll see." I tell her. "I'll pick you up at five."

"Fine." She uncrosses her arms, allowing them to fall to her sides. "But I have another question."

"What is it?"

"Does your father accuse all of your fake girlfriends of being gold diggers? Or does this outfit I'm wearing scream 'I'm here panning for riches'?"

"I'm sorry you had to hear that." I sigh. "And yes, he does."

She quirks an eyebrow in curiosity, clearly having no idea why my father would assume something like this about her. Her stare has me in a chokehold, until something captures my attention behind her.

"Hey, don't look now. But there's a woman outside watching us through the window. I think she's staring at you."

Ignoring my instruction not to look, Mackenzie swings around. The woman startles, caught off guard, the sad smile falling from her face before she rushes off down the street.

"That's weird. Do you know her?" I ask.

Mackenzie shakes her head, a troubled expression on her face. "No," she replies.

But there's something in her voice that suggests otherwise.

Chapter 12

MACKENZIE

The pier is packed on Friday afternoon. People come and go from the local businesses and cafes. Surfers flock to the waves despite the dark clouds that linger in the distance, but I am in the zone.

A quick glance at my watch lets me know I've been sitting here on this park bench for close to two hours now, completely lost in my art. I've only found the crowds of people distracting when the odd surfer or dogwalker gets in the way of my view of the horizon.

I've decided to try my hand at colour drawings. Up until now I've only ever worked in black and white, and while I'm excited to try a new skillset, I'm having a difficult time trying to work out the right hues to capture the sunset as it hits the ocean. A task made more challenging by the fact that the sun keeps moving lower with every passing minute.

I worked most of the day at the tavern, but other than Harper dropping in to say a quick hello, my shift had been uneventful. Dylan was meant to work too, but he hadn't been there. In fact, I haven't seen him since that weird encounter with his parents on Tuesday. I assume he must be taking on those extra afternoon shifts he mentioned on the dive boat.

I'm noticing more often when he isn't around and that's weird for me. It's almost like work is better when he's there. I'm not familiar with this feeling. Of depending on someone else to make my day better.

"That's beautiful."

I'm startled, suddenly aware of the presence on the bench next to me. I swivel my head in the direction of the voice, stunned to see who it has come from. It's the woman that watched me from the pier the day I went for my morning jog. The same one from the windows of the tavern yesterday. The woman from my sketch.

"The drawing. It's beautiful," she repeats.

The fact that she's suddenly sitting beside me should freak me out. Her behaviour seems stalkerish if anything, but I suppose it could be pure coincidence that I've now seen her multiple times.

I contemplate confronting her about it, asking her what her deal is and whether she's been following me, but there's something about her demeanour that stops me. Just like the first time I saw her on the pier, I sense a sadness surrounding this woman. An air of longing.

Being so distrustful of every person I meet is a quality I'm beginning to like less and less about myself. I don't want to be so quick to judge this woman. God knows I know what it feels like to be taken at face value.

So instead of throwing out some sarcastic snide comment I choose to appreciate her compliment.

"Thank you," I say. "I don't normally use colour, so I didn't know if it was going to work out."

She smiles, her light eyes twinkling in the golden glow of the sunset. "It's very good. Especially if that's your first attempt. Do you paint too?"

"Not really," I answer, but then I think of the supplies that Pamela had offered me. They're still sitting untouched in the corner of my room but after experimenting with coloured pencils, I suddenly can't wait to dip into the paints. "I'm going to give it a try though."

"You should. I bet you have a natural talent." I'm not sure where she's gathered this assumption from. She shifts closer to me on the bench and begins pointing to various parts of my drawing. "If you add some shadow to the sides of the water here, it will really emphasise the light reflecting from the sunset here in the middle."

I tilt my head on an angle, contemplating her suggestion. She's right, I realise. "Yeah, that makes sense."

"And if you deepen the hue of the storm clouds over here, the oranges and yellows in the middle will really pop."

I turn my head, watching as she examines my drawing, fascinated by her observation. This woman clearly knows what she's talking about. "Are you an artist?"

"I am," she nods, lifting her blue eyes to mine. "I run art classes from a studio a few towns over. In Seabright Cove."

"Wow, that's really cool," I say.

Her smile radiates a certain warmth, and I can't help but

think about how comfortable I am in her presence, despite the strange circumstances under which we've met.

"You should come down and check it out," she offers. "We do all kinds of things there."

"Oh, I don't know," I say, not sure whether I should entertain this idea. "I don't know if I'd be able to."

"Oh," she says. A veil of disappointment falls over her for a moment before she straightens herself, a glint of hope entering her gaze. "The first two lessons are free. It's a promotion that I'm running at the moment."

For whatever reason, she's being awfully persistent.

"Oh, okay. I guess I could think about it."

I say this only to be polite. I don't have any intention of taking up her classes, but I don't want to break what seems to be an already fragile spirit.

She nods, looking ahead to the waves. "Sure. Well, it's on Palmwood Drive if you decide you'd like to come. It's called the Abstract Palette. Here's one of our cards."

She holds out a pink and yellow business card to me and I take it, flipping it over in my palm. "Cool name."

"Thanks," she says, her voice suddenly thick with emotion. "Well, it was lovely talking to you."

Before I can say anything else, she's standing up, smoothing her dress with the palms of her hands, and readying herself to walk away.

I pluck out the indigo pencil and begin adding depth to edges of the water as she had recommended. The conversation between us replays in my mind. I keep seeing the gutted look of rejection she'd given me when I'd turned down her offer to come to her studio. I try to remember if I'd been harsh in my answer, but I can't think of any particular reason that she should be offended. I'm sure I hadn't been rude.

There are so many red flags relating to this woman's behaviour, but I chose not to confront her about them because she seems completely harmless. In fact, I welcomed her presence. She exudes a calmness that most people don't have, an ability to make those around her feel comfortable. Maybe she is just a loner.

I find myself considering her offer to partake in those free classes. I can't deny that I'm intrigued about learning new techniques. I've never had the opportunity to participate in something like that.

Hell, I've never really had the chance to take time to do anything but try to survive.

But the bus trip into Seabright Cove would be long and I'm not sure how it would fit into my work schedule at the tavern. I push the idea from my mind as I pack my art supplies into my backpack and head home for dinner.

It starts to sprinkle just as I'm stepping up onto the front porch and when I open the front door, my senses are overtaken by the scent of garlic and rosemary.

I continue down the hall, rounding the corner into the cottage-style kitchen where Kristen is hunched over a baking tray, carving a seasoned lamb roast. Two plates of baked vegetables rest on the island bench beside her.

"It smells delicious in here," I say, letting my backpack fall to the floor in the corner.

She looks up from the leg of lamb, aiming a warm smile my way. "Henley got stuck at a job so it's just dinner for two tonight. I thought I'd make us a roast."

"Oh."

When I'd seen the two plates, I'd automatically assumed that they were for Henley and herself. Not that she doesn't cook for all of us, but because I hadn't let her know that I'd be home. I nod subtly, a stab of guilt piercing my chest.

It's not like we haven't been on speaking terms or anything, but I'd never really apologised properly for the way I'd treated her the day she told me she was in contact with our father. I know she's only trying to do what's best for everyone and most of the time, that can be a real balancing act. Pleasing one person can easily upset the next, and ultimately, she needs to do what's right for herself too.

She brings her eyes to mine, worry swirling in their depths. "Are you okay?"

"Yeah. Thanks. It all looks amazing." I manage a smile, but she sees right through it.

"What's wrong?" she asks. "You look upset."

"I do?" My eyes begin to sting with the threat of tears and at first, I'm not even sure why. "It's nothing. I'm fine."

Kristen isn't buying it. "Mackenzie, you can tell me."

A tear rolls down my cheek and I quickly swipe it away. I'm not normally this emotional. It feels completely foreign to me.

"They aren't sad tears, I promise. I'm just... not used to coming home to ... this." I wave a hand at the delicious food my sister has clearly spent hours preparing.

She nods sympathetically. "I know. I'm sorry."

"You have nothing to be sorry about. I never should have snapped at you last week about wanting to talk to Dad. I'm just... I get so angry when I think about him."

"Hey, you have every right to be mad at him," she says. "I'm angry too."

"Why do you want to talk to him then?" I ask her. "How could you ever possibly forgive him?"

She shrugs. "I don't know. Selfish reasons, I guess."

"What do you mean?"

"There's a release in forgiveness. I've held a grudge for so many years now, it's like this weight that's lived inside of me for what feels like forever is finally lifting. And maybe if I can find it in myself to just let go, I could be free of it."

I nod slowly, contemplating her words. "I guess that makes sense."

I know what she means. I know that sinking weight she describes and it sure would be nice to release some of it. I just can't see it happening in the foreseeable future.

"Maybe I need to forgive him because it's the right thing to do," she continues. "He's my flesh and blood. Maybe he's paid for his sins. Maybe he's paying for them right now."

She could be right. Maybe our father being stuck in his own private hell is enough punishment, but it doesn't make any of it right. It could never make any of it right.

Kristen places the knife down gently on the countertop, then takes a few cautious steps towards me. "And because of you."

My brows pinch together in a frown. I don't understand. "Because of me?"

"Yeah. I know this is twisted." She lowers her gaze to the ground momentarily before looking back up at me, her hazelnut eyes glistening with moisture. "But if he hadn't left us to be with your mother, then we wouldn't have you in our lives at all. So, I guess I owe him a thank you."

The breath is knocked out of me. I'd never considered this way of thinking before, never entertained the possibility that Kristen could find a silver lining in this messed up situation.

Or that the silver lining was me.

"That is twisted," I agree. "But it's also the nicest fucking thing anybody has ever said to me."

A tear escapes down her cheek and I lunge forward, wrapping my arms around her.

I've never believed in fate. It's absurd to think there is some higher power in control of my circumstances. I mean, if there is, they've been doing a really shitty job with me. But moments like this with Kristen have me believing there must be a reason we came to find each other.

We stay like that, encased in each other arms for a moment before she pulls away, a smile on her lips. "I really think we should eat now before our dinner goes cold."

"I couldn't agree more," I say, unfurling myself from her warmth. "I'm starving."

She lets out a soft laugh as she moves back to the island bench. I set the table for two while she finishes plating up our meals.

Over dinner, I ask her about her day, and she asks me about mine. She tells me about a promotion she's going to go for, and I tell her about the mysterious woman I met at the pier today. I explain how she had invited me to her art classes but that I didn't intend to go.

"It might be good for you to go. Art is your thing," she says.

I'd never considered art to be 'my thing', but her words get me thinking about Dylan and what he'd said on the boat that day. About how he liked having something all of his own. I've never had something all of my own.

But maybe it would be nice to.

So, when I'm lying in bed later that night, unable to sleep, I take out my phone and google the Abstract Palette. Then I do a search for the local bus timetable.

Chapter 13

DYLAN

My phone rings from the top pocket of my dress shirt as I'm getting into the car. It takes me by surprise, and I almost hit my head on the car door frame as I fumble to retrieve it. There's only one person I can think of that would be calling me right now. Just as I suspect, the word 'Mum' lights up the screen. She's been texting me sly comments ever since her awkward and impromptu meeting with Mackenzie.

"Hi, Mum," I answer as I turn the key in the ignition.

"Dylan," she says, her tone almost as firm as my father's this time. "Where are you? Please tell me you're still coming to the party."

"Of course. I'm already on the way," I tell her.

This is a lie. I'm running fifteen minutes late and I haven't even picked up Mackenzie yet.

"Are you still bringing Maxine?"

I roll my eyes, knowing full well my mother doesn't forget names that easily.

"Mackenzie," I correct her. Again. "And yes, I'm just picking her up now and we'll be there in about forty-five minutes."

Or an hour.

"Okay," she replies. "Please be on your best behaviour tonight though, Dylan. You know how important this party is to me. I've been planning it forever."

I pull the phone away from my face so she can't hear the defeated sigh that leaves me. It does little for my self-esteem that my own mother thinks I'm capable of ruining her anniversary party. I can't deny that in the past, there had been sporadic periods where my behaviour could have been described as borderline reckless, but I've turned over a new leaf. It's a shame my parents can't see that.

"I know, Mum. It's going to be great. Stop stressing."

"I want the oyster tower over there!" She shouts and I need to pull the phone away from the side of my face again. This time to avoid having my ear blasted. "And the canapes are to come out no later than six thirty."

"What?"

"Not you, Dylan. Ugh, these caterers need to get their act together." She huffs loudly into the phone, pausing before she throws another question at me. "Are you sure this girl is a good fit for you?"

"Why wouldn't she be?" I surprise myself by how protective I am over my fake-date for the evening.

"She's not like any of the other girls you've dated."

"Maybe that's the point," I argue.

"Oh, Dylan," she almost groans. "Seriously! You need to think this through."

"Why?" I ask. "Just look at how well all those past relationships turned out."

I realise I'm defending a relationship that doesn't actually exist. But more than that. I'm defending Mackenzie. Whether I want to face it or not, I've started to care about her. To enjoy having her around. And the thought of anybody saying anything negative about her has my hackles rising.

"You know that being a member of this family comes with responsibility. We can't just bring anyone into it and expect them to be able to keep up."

"I know." I drag my hand down over my face, knowing that she isn't wrong. "She can handle it."

I believe my words to be true. There are expectations involved with being a part of the Abbott family, or by association with any of us, but something tells me Mackenzie would do just fine.

I consider that I should give her a little insight into my background, but there's no sense involving her when this is a one-time only fake date. After tonight, she won't have to deal with my parents again, and weirdly that sends a ripple of disappointment through me.

"If you say so. I'll see you soon." My mother's clipped tone echoes through my ears.

Without another word she's hung up on me and I'm left with the choking sounds coming from the engine and impending thoughts of this car breaking down before I can make the journey out to the cape.

This car is so ancient it doesn't even have electric windows and it's unbearably stuffy in here with no working air-conditioning. I quickly wind down the driver's side window before throwing the gears into drive.

A ball of dread builds in the pit of my stomach when I think about the expectations my parents will have for me tonight. No doubt they will want me to network with people I'd rather be leaving behind. To bend the truth for the sake of our family's reputation.

Somehow, knowing that I'll have Mackenzie by my side eases a little of that pressure. An unexpected smile makes its way across my face. I suddenly can't wait to see her.

I step on the accelerator, eager to make the short distance across town to her house.

Chapter 14

MACKENZIE

"What do you think of this one?" Kristen thrusts yet another page of her bridal magazine under my nose, interrupting my view of the sketch pad in front of me.

We're both sitting on the couch, me working on a drawing inspired by my underwater adventures last week, her flipping through the pages of her wedding planner as though her life depends on it. I didn't have to work today, so we've pretty much spent the day together.

"I guess?" I say unhelpfully. I'm not sure I'm qualified to give an opinion on the subject of weddings.

"Ugh!" She groans in frustration. "There has to be something good in this magazine, but seriously, it all just seems so unrealistic. I mean, look at this. This woman is supposed to be having a backyard wedding. Where the hell does she even live? In the middle of a forest? And her hair! There's no way it's actually going to stay like that all day."

I look up in mock horror. "You mean to tell me that the elaborate photo shoots in magazines that require an entire team of professionals and hours of work don't simulate the real-life wedding experience?" I finish my rant with a 360-degree eyeroll which earns me a dead-eyed stare from Kristen.

"Okay, okay. I get it, smart ass."

"Sorry," I say with a sigh, not looking up from my sketch book. "I thought Liv was coming over to talk wedding stuff with you anyway."

"She is," she replies, slapping me on the knee with her rolled up magazine. "I just thought I'd ask my sister's opinion too."

"Hey!" I cry. "You bumped me!"

"Oops." She winces, leaning over my shoulder to get a look at my work. "Hey, that's actually really good. I wish I had your talent."

I scoff. "And I wish I had your brain. Look, I'm really not the best person to be asking about wedding stuff. Liv's married. She'll be way more helpful than me."

As if on cue, the doorbell chimes. "Oh, that must be her now," Kristen says as she rises from the couch, her coffee cup in hand. "Would you mind getting the door while I toss this in the sink."

"Sure," I say, placing the sketch book aside.

I wander over to the door, rubbing the kink in my neck that's most likely been caused from staring into my lap for too long. When I pull it open it isn't Liv standing there to greet me.

Instead, I'm met with eyes the colour of freshly melted chocolate and flawless, bronze skin, and what looks like an expensive dress shirt stretching over toned biceps. "Uh, what are you doing here?"

"Picking you up," Dylan answers with a megawatt smile that could power Luna Park. His grin fades when he sees my genuine confusion. "For the party, remember?"

"The party? I didn't think you were serious about that." I fold my arms across my chest, falling back against the door frame.

It's become a habit for Dylan and I to rib each other every now and then, but for me to go to his parent's party with him? That's taking things too far. It serves no purpose having me along for the ride.

Still, he persists, like having me there is something that he actually wants. "What do you mean? You have to come."

"I'm sure you'll have a whole lot more fun without me." I straighten and then begin to close the door.

"Wait!" His palms come up, pressing against the timber to hold it open. "That's really not true. To be honest, I don't even want to go. The only thing keeping me sane the last couple of days was knowing that you were going to be there with me."

I stop in my tracks, my forehead creasing in a frown. His words are so honest, so open.

So *not* what I'm used to.

There's a pleading in his eyes, only thinly veiling the hurt behind them. For whatever reason, he's decided he wants me at this party. I'm taken aback by the way my own body responds to seeing him upset, my heart sinking with the weight of knowing it has something to do with me.

Then he smiles and warmth spreads through my chest.

"Please?"

"Fine. Whatever," I say nonchalantly, throwing my hands up in the air, an eyeroll deliberately employed to mask my growing enthusiasm. "Wait here and I'll go get changed."

His face lights up as he fist-pumps the air. "Yes! Okay, I'll wait out here."

I turn, closing the door behind me and march up the hall to my room. "Hey, where's Liv?" I hear Kristen call out.

"It was a salesman!" I call back.

"Selling what?"

"Solar panels or some shit." The last thing I need Kristen to know is that Dylan is outside waiting to take me to his parent's anniversary party. I'll never hear the end of it.

It only takes me five minutes to swipe on some lip gloss and slip into a sundress. I guess getting ready for a party takes less time when you aren't spoilt for choice.

I give myself a once over in the floor length mirror, smoothing out the skirt of the ditsy floral sundress I purchased from Target on a day out shopping with Kristen and Liv. It's the nicest one I own, so it will have to do. I throw my curls on top of my head and secure them in place in a messy updo and head back to the front door.

When I pass the living room, Kristen is back in her position on the lounge, the bridal magazine once again spread open in her lap.

"Hey, I'm going out," I call.

Thankfully, she doesn't question where I'm going, barely looking up from the magazine. "Oh, okay. See you when you get home."

I never thought I'd see the day that Kristen turned into Bridezilla, but here we are.

I throw the door wide open, almost walking straight into Dylan where he stands on the porch waiting.

"Come on, let's go." I grab his hand and drag him down the steps, eager to get away before Liv turns up and blows my secret.

"Wow," he breathes as we approach the car. "Is that what you're wearing?"

"Yeah." I shrug. "Why? Is it okay?"

"Yeah. It's perfect," he replies, his eyes wandering over the fabric down to the sandals I'd borrowed from Kristen's wardrobe. "I mean, it's fine. It's nice."

"Okay," I say, slowly drawing the word out. "You're being weird."

"Sorry." Dylan directs me to the passenger side, and I can't help giving him a curious look as he opens the door for me.

"You don't have to do that," I say. "It's not like this is a real date or anything."

"Ah, yeah. Sorry. I know." He sounds almost sheepish as his hand goes up to rake through his golden-brown hair. "It's just that… Sometimes the handle gets stuck."

"Oh, right," I say, strangely disappointed that he had another reason for appearing so chivalrous.

I climb in as he slips around the other side into the driver's seat. The car takes a while to click over, and Dylan breathes a sigh of relief when the engine finally roars to life. "Thank fuck," he sighs. "I swear this car likes to test my patience."

A small smile twitches my lips hearing him curse so brazenly. Maybe we have more in common than I realised. He throws the car into reverse and backs out of the driveway and within minutes we're merging onto the highway.

Several vehicles overtake us as the car struggles to reach full speed and it occurs to me now that I have no idea where we're going. Dylan had never answered when I'd asked.

"So, where is this party anyway?"

"Cape Charlton," he replies.

"Huh." I'm not originally from this area. I've heard of Cape Charlton, commonly known as 'the cape', but I've never ventured out that way. Hell, before Henley found me, I'd never ventured anywhere.

"We'll be there in a little less than an hour. I can't push this baby too far or she might die on me." He chuckles as he gives the dashboard a playful slap.

"An hour!" I complain, although somehow the thought of being in close proximity to Dylan for an extended period of time doesn't irk me quite the way it should. "Does this thing at least have aircon? It's so stuffy in here my skin is about to melt off."

I reach forward and begin twisting random dials on the dash when Dylan's hand shoots out to stop me. A bolt of electricity arcs up my spine when his hand connects with mine, his fingers pulling back too fast the only sign I get that he feels it too.

"It doesn't work," he says, his eyes locking briefly on mine.

"Oh." Did it just get even hotter in here? I reach downward, gripping the winder and attempt to lower the window to allow airflow. "You must have the only car left in the world with manual window winders."

The window has barely budged when I hear a crack. "Shit," I curse, pulling my hand away from the door, the winder still gripped between my fist. "Um, sorry?"

Dylan glances over at me to see what the problem is. I tense, fearing he's going to be angry when he sees me clutching a small chunk of his car in my palm, but instead he lets out a roar of laughter. "Damn. This car is such a bomb."

I relax, sinking into the seat, relieved that he can see the funny side. If this had been Ethan's car, I'd have been dragged from the passenger seat by my hair and left behind on the side of the road somewhere.

In fact, that very thing did happen once. Not because of a broken piece of plastic, but because *he* had slapped *me* over something trivial, causing my drink to spill into my lap, soaking the front seat and leaking down onto the floor. I can still hear his voice as though it happened just yesterday.

"Look what you've done, you clumsy bitch."

"Hey." I flinch at Dylan's touch as his hand brushes my elbow. My head snaps in his direction. "Where'd you go just now?" he asks.

I exhale a shaky breath, brushing the thought away. "Nowhere."

"You sure?"

"Yeah," I say as convincingly as I can.

He looks as though he wants to question me further but then thinks better of it. "Okay."

His concern fades into a smile. A smile that makes me forget all about Ethan and the horrors of my past.

At least, for a little while.

Chapter 15

MACKENZIE

I'm learning that Dylan has this uncanny ability to make me feel comfortable like no one else can. Conversation flows easily between us, filling what would otherwise be awkward silence. During our little road trip to the cape, he's mostly spoken of his experiences out in the ocean, but he mentioned his sister a couple of times and I got the feeling that the two of them are close.

When he finally merges off the highway, following signs for Cape Charlton, we find ourselves navigating quiet roads that lead to large, expensive-looking vacation rentals. We travel along a secluded road that leads out to the sea when Dylan abruptly turns, stopping outside of a tall ornate metal gate.

"What's wrong?" I ask. "Is there something wrong with the car?"

I can think of no other reasonable explanation we would be

stopping here on this secluded expanse of road.

"We're here," he says.

"Uh, where exactly?" I ask, confused.

He doesn't seem to hear me. He's already reaching out the window, tapping out a six-digit pin number into an electronic keypad situated on a sandstone wall. The gates swing open, revealing a winding driveway lined with trees and tall lamp posts strategically placed every few metres.

I'm stunned into silence as we pull up to an extravagant two storey building lit up like a beacon. Even the trees adorning the property are illuminated by fairy lights, a soft glow radiating from an elaborate fountain in the centre of a horseshoe driveway. It looks like something I've only ever seen in movies.

"Dylan, what the hell is this?" I finally ask, disbelievingly, my mouth agape.

He pulls the handbrake up noisily. "This is the party."

"Your parents live here?"

"No," he replies bluntly.

"Oh," I say, relief washing over me. "For a second I thought you were going to say that..."

"They live in the city. This is their vacation home."

"Oh," I stare at him wide-eyed, unsure of what else to say.

I guess I should have assumed when meeting Dylan's parents at the tavern that they came from a higher socioeconomic background but I'm just now starting to see why Dylan's father had questioned my intentions.

Why he'd wondered whether I had been a gold digger.

"Come on," he says, looking less than enthusiastic. "Let's get this over with."

He exits the vehicle, leaving me in the silence of the empty car. What the hell have I gotten myself into?

Snapping out of it, I fumble with the door handle. It takes two goes to get it to open but I eventually succeed. I round the front of the car and join Dylan near the fountain, the mansion looming high above us.

It's as though the energy has been drained right from him. Gone is the carefree, adventurous guy I've come to know. The sadness in his eyes as he stares at the front doors and the way his jaw is set hard are definite signs of his reluctance to enter his family vacation residence. I'd known from the phone call I overheard with his father that things were strained with his parents, but it's becoming blatantly obvious to me now just how much.

His hand reaches for me, but my instincts kick in and I brush it away. In my peripheral I see his head swivel in my direction. I slowly turn, expecting to find annoyance in his gaze. Rejection even.

Instead, I only see his concern for me. I hate that this is how I'm programmed now. To refuse all human touch. Ethan did that to me and I'll never forgive him for it.

Dylan drops his gaze to the ground, his shoulders slumping. For reasons unknown to me, he really doesn't want to be here.

I don't even want to go. The only thing keeping me sane the last couple of days was knowing that you were going to be there with me.

Suddenly, my fingers are gently grazing his, my palm looping around until our hands are flush together, his skin warm against mine.

"Come on," I tell him, nodding towards the house. "We've got this."

His mouth slowly curves in a smile, a glint of gratitude in his eyes. Knowing that I might be able to somehow make this night easier for him fills me with something I'd thought I'd lost long ago.

It fills me with purpose.

We enter through the wide, double front doors, echoes of laughter and music filling the space. I'd thought the exterior of the house was impressive, but the interior is exquisite. It's like nothing I've ever seen before.

Decorative woodwork adorns the ceiling and every wall. Fancy pendant lights and chandeliers hang from above, but what really captures my attention is the art. There are multiple original paintings in immaculate frames. I might be passionate about art, but I'm still learning. I don't know all that much about it. Still, if I had to guess, these pieces are worth thousands of dollars. Maybe even hundreds of thousands.

A less than subtle squeeze of my hand has me turning my attention to Dylan, his expression stoic as we approach his parents.

"Oh, Dylan! You made it!" his mother turns to greet us. Well, him. She greets him. She throws her arms around her son lovingly, but I hear the words she says through gritted teeth. "You're late."

I grimace inwardly knowing that I contributed to his tardiness.

"Hi, Mum," he says, his discomfort obvious as he pulls away awkwardly from her and his father takes his hand in his. "Dad. Happy anniversary to you both."

"Happy anniversary, Mr and Mrs. Abbott," I say as confidently as I can.

"Mackenzie." His mother smiles stiffly. The judgmental way her eyes survey me from head to toe isn't lost on me. "So nice to see you, dear."

Her tone tells me she'd rather not be seeing me at all.

One glance around the party is all it takes for me to realise that I'm severely under dressed for the event, but I won't allow it to phase me. I've spent most of my life feeling like I haven't been enough.

Not enough for my mother to stick around.

Not enough for my dad to stop drinking.

Never enough for Ethan.

This world is filled with all kinds of people but at the end of the day, that's all we are. People. Regardless of status, income or fashion. I am enough. And dammit, so is my store-bought Target dress.

"Dylan, why don't you show Mackenzie to the champagne tower," Dylan's father suggests. "I'm sure she could use a drink after the drive here."

"Oh, thank you but…" I begin, waving a hand in front of me. Champagne has never been my drink of choice.

"Sure." Dylan interrupts me, curling his arm around my waist as he steers me away from his parents.

He directs me to the corner of the room where a literal tower of champagne glasses has been set up. It's taller than I am. Knowing my luck, it can't be safe for me to be anywhere in its vicinity.

Much to my relief, Dylan stops us before we reach it, moving around in front of me, his arm still looped around the small of my back protectively.

"I don't drink champagne, Dylan," I say.

"I figured." He says, leaning into me. I catch the scent of his cologne, a summery blend of cedarwood with a hint of something fruity. "But they gave us an out and I took it."

"I see."

I know this display of closeness is for his parent's benefit. We're supposed to be dating after all. So why this sudden onset of arrythmia that seems to increase in severity when his hand comes up to comb a stray curl behind my ear?

"But you do need a drink," he says, his fingertips gliding along my jaw before his hands fall to his sides. "What can I get you?"

"What do you have?"

"Literally anything. There's an open bar out the back."

"There is?" I ask, peering toward the back of the house.

I see a pool illuminated by bright aqua lights, and sure enough, there's a bar set up on one side. I can just make out two bartenders mixing drinks behind it between the groups of mingling people.

"I'll just get a Coke or something," I tell him. "I'll come with you."

"Of course you will." He winks. "I'm not leaving you here with the vultures."

I know he's only joking but when we step through the doors out onto the expansive balcony with several sets of eyes pinned on us, I'm overcome with relief as his hand grips mine.

He ushers me through the crowd of people until we reach the bar. Then he orders us two Cokes and we move to take a seat at a small table.

"Dyl! I'm so glad you made it!" comes a perky voice to my right. "Now Mum and Dad can get off my case. Oh, hi! You must be Mackenzie!"

This girl's excitement level is off the Richter.

"Yeah. Hey," I say, extending my hand.

She takes my hand in hers but then bends down in her wickedly high heels to air kiss me on both cheeks. It's a gesture that I'm not familiar with in any sense. She seems friendly enough. I'm just not used to people encroaching on my personal space.

"Uh, Mackenzie," Dylan smirks, clearly amused by my discomfort. "This is my sister, Claire."

"Oh, hey. Cool. It's nice to meet you." For some reason I've been reduced to one syllable words.

"You too," she replies. "Dylan's told me so much about you."

Dylan shakes his head with a frown, making a subtle 'cut it out' gesture across his throat. "Nope. Not really."

"Anyway, I'll leave you to it. I have to make the rounds, but I'll catch up with you guys again soon." With that, she turns on her crimson, red stiletto heels in search of the next social circle.

"So…" I grin, eyeing him curiously. "You told your sister about me?"

"No. Not much. She's confused." He shakes his head adamantly before taking a sip of his beverage, then gesturing to where Claire animatedly greets a friend, he adds, "I mean, obviously she's been drinking."

"Right," I say, huffing out a laugh.

I stiffen as Dylan's dad approaches the table, his presence sucking the energy straight from the air.

"Dylan," he says sternly. "Can I borrow you for a moment?"

"Now isn't a good time, Dad," Dylan says, his jaw clenching. "I'm talking with Mackenzie."

It solidifies the respect I have for Dylan that he doesn't want to leave me alone to go and to talk to his father. He's been the perfect gentleman since the moment he picked me up, offering me a kind of protection that I've never really known. But right now, I can see his father isn't ready to let whatever he has to say to him go.

"It's important," his father presses.

A vein in Dylan's neck bulges as he takes a mouthful of Coke. "Dad, this is a party. Can we leave it?"

His dad lets out an agitated sigh.

"It's fine," I say. "Go with your dad. I'll be okay for a minute."

Dylan's nostrils flare in defiance as he stands and follows his father back inside, leaving me twirling the straw in my glass at an empty table.

I'm only mildly uncomfortable sitting in the middle of the fanciest party I've ever set foot in, but I'm not alone for long. I glance up as two women that seem to be only a few years older than me seat themselves on the opposite side of the table.

One has long platinum waves and the bluest eyes I've ever seen. Her lashes are fake. Her lips are swollen, the result of too much filler. The other, a brunette with piercing green eyes, wears the tightest, lowest cut dress I've ever seen in person. She looks like she just stepped off the red carpet.

"Uh, hi," I stammer.

"Hey," the blonde says, her voice surprisingly low and sultry. "You must be Dylan's new girl."

"Yeah," I say without hesitation. That's what I am tonight, for all intents and purposes after all. "I'm Mackenzie."

The blonde eyes me like she has a million questions to ask, the brunette like she doesn't trust a word that's coming out of my mouth. Smart girl.

When an awkward silence fills the atmosphere, I finally ask, "And you are?"

"I'm Skye, and this is Madison," the blonde says, gesturing to the brunette next to her. "Madison and Dylan dated for like… ever."

"Ah, I see." A light bulb flickers on somewhere in my brain. Dylan's ex. Noted. No wonder she doesn't trust me.

I look at Madison, but her eyes don't meet mine. She's too busy staring down at her manicured nails. She looks bored by our interaction. Another awkward silence passes before she finally makes eye contact with me.

"You know, you don't seem like his usual type." She tilts her head to the side, staring me down with her green gaze, before shrugging condescendingly. "But I get it. You're pretty in that girl-next-door kind of way. Be careful though. You know what they say. Once a player, always a player."

"Sure." I nod knowingly.

I can see what's going on here. The jealous ex is trying to spook me, but what she doesn't know is that Dylan is only my fake boyfriend. For tonight only. There's nothing she could say right now that would have any effect whatsoever on me.

"He seems quiet tonight, though. More reserved. He's usually way out of control at parties, but I guess the night is still young." Madison snickers, then turns to Skye beside her. "Oh my god, Skye. Do you remember that party he had here when his parents were overseas on business?"

"Yeah." Skye sounds only vaguely interested.

Madison turns back to me. "Someone called the cops to make a noise complaint and he was so high he threw a pound of weed on the bonfire to hide the stash." She says this with a less than impressed look upon her face, making air quotes when she says 'hide.'

She expects me to be horrified by this information, but knowing she probably made half of this story up in her head, I give her the opposite reaction. I laugh. "Wow! That's chaotic! Sounds like a real rager. I bet everybody left a little light-headed that night."

A giggle escapes Skye's Barbie-pink pout. I think I'm beginning to like this one.

"Anyway," Madison scoffs. "If you've managed to tame the party boy, then good for you. I guess the one thing we're really struggling to understand is how you got him to abandon his career."

"His career?" I shake my head at this crazy notion. "No. He's not abandoning his career."

What the hell are they talking about? Dylan works two jobs.

"Yes, he is." Madison replies, blinking at me as though I'm stupid. "He quit the hotel industry."

"Hotel industry," I echo dumbly.

"I mean, the guy's obviously already loaded but walking away from running the Abbott Group is costing him millions. Maybe even billions. How'd you get him to do it?" She rests her chin on her hand, staring me down with contempt.

"What?" I look to Skye, hoping she has something else to offer that might explain the insanity coming out of this woman's mouth, but she just sits there, casually watching our interaction play out.

"I mean, the Abbott hotel chain is booming," Madison continues. "I overheard his father say they're going to be starting up a new boutique hotel soon. I guess I just can't understand why, given the opportunity, Dylan wouldn't want to run it."

Evidently there's more family drama here than I'd banked on. "I… I don't know. I guess that's something you'd have to ask him."

I realise now that Dylan wasn't kidding when he used the term 'vultures.' These women are brutal. Madison clearly has it out for me, and I've managed to hold my own up until now, but I'd be lying if I said her words hadn't begun to blister under my skin.

Not because I care what Dylan's job prospects are or whether he has money or not, but because he's beginning to sound untrustworthy. Secretive.

The idealisation of him being this carefree, open book begins to shatter like glass, the lines of what I'd thought to be the truth beginning to blur at the edges.

According to Madison and Skye here, Dylan is loaded.

A loaded, party boy player.

And now I've found myself wondering if it was intentional when Dylan's mother had called me Madison the day we met at the tavern. Is this woman sitting in front of me the kind she has always envisioned for her son?

I may have encouraged this fake relationship that day in the tavern, but Dylan had been more than happy to bring me along to his parent's party. In fact, he had insisted on it. And I had believed him when he'd said he wanted me here. That having me here would make this night easier for him.

But the more I think about it, the more I question it. Because I am nothing like the two women sitting here in front of me. I'm obviously not Dylan's type at all.

Did he bring me here to parade me around in front of his parents in some futile attempt to piss them off? Am I here as some kind of revenge act?

I glance across the yard, noticing that there are now several sets of prying eyes trained in my direction. I stiffen, suddenly wishing I were invisible. I need to get away from these people and their potent stares.

Pressing my hands against the crisp, white tablecloth, I rise to my feet. "Well, it was great meeting you, but I need to use the restroom."

"See you later, Mackenzie," Skye says, her tone not unkind.

Madison scowls at her, then raises her piercing emerald glare to mine, a fake smile plastered over her perfectly made-up face. "Bye. Oh, and nice dress, by the way."

I look down at the floral sundress I'm wearing, and I'm taken back to the moment I stepped out onto my front porch tonight.

"Is that what you're wearing?" Dylan had asked. "It's perfect."

Was it perfect? Or was it the perfect way to embarrass his parents at their big anniversary party?

Was he hoping for me to look out of place here?

I think about the way he'd held the small of my back as he'd ushered me through the crowd tonight.

Had I mistaken possession for protection?

I don't want to believe that Dylan is here to make some kind of statement tonight, but this war against his father is obviously bigger than I'd thought, and he must be using me as leverage. It's the only thing that makes sense to me now.

I storm back inside the house and take the hallway on my right. I enter the first door that I see and slam it behind me. It's pitch-black inside. I whip my phone out and turn on the flashlight function, using it to investigate my surroundings.

Damnit. I'm in some sort of linen closet, albeit a large one. I don't bother trying to find a light switch. Instead, I pull up the internet browser on my phone and type Dylan Abbott into the search bar. My heart sinks when his photo appears on the screen above a formal caption printed below it.

Dylan Ivan Abbott, born 24th August, 1999. Australian business magnate and son of hotelier, Ivan Abbott, founder of the Abbott Group. The Abbott Group owns and operates multiple brands in many segments of hospitality including The Abbott, Gateway, and Boxborough hotel chains.

Holy shit. The guy has his own Google profile.

What the actual fuck?

I don't even know what to think. All I know is that I need to get far away from here. Now.

As I pry open the closet door, stepping out as discretely as I can, I scan the room for the nearest exit. I see Dylan standing off to the side of the large open plan living and dining area. He seems to be engaging in some sort of heated discussion with his father.

His nostrils flare as he places the glass of Coke he's still clutching onto the granite tabletop in front. I can't interpret the expression he wears, though the way his jaw hardens as he adjusts the collar of his shirt lets me know he isn't happy.

I'd thought that shirt had looked expensive, but it strikes me now that it probably cost more than my entire wardrobe and Kristen's combined.

Whatever his father is saying to him has him tense, but I don't care all that much anymore. Dylan lied to me.

He catches sight of me as I move forward, but when our eyes meet, I can only shake my head in disappointment. The tension in his stare immediately evaporates into hurt.

"Kenz!" I hear him call.

I don't turn around, instead pushing directly through the middle of a group of people until I've reached the front door. I barge through it and take the steps two at a time, my hand skimming the white, metal railing as I go. I've barely reached the bottom of the stairs when a warm hand wraps gently around my wrist. I spin around, only to find myself flush up against Dylan's chest.

"Leave me alone, Dylan," I shout angrily as I shake off his grip.

"What happened?" He looks genuinely confused. He's a great actor.

"Who are you?" I whisper, my eyes searching his for answers he probably isn't going to give me. "I mean, really? Who are you?"

He lets out a shaky breath, his guilty stare dropping to the ground. At least he has the decency to look ashamed.

"You completely blindsided me!" I continue. "You brought me here under false pretences."

"No. That's not what…"

I ignore his attempts to defend himself, cutting him off before he has a chance to spin me another story. "You neglected to tell me major details about yourself and your family. I don't even know you."

"Mackenzie, I can explain."

"Is that why you said this dress was perfect?" I hate that my eyes are stinging with tears.

I am not this girl. I'm not.

He drops his hands to his sides. "What?"

"Because you knew your parents would look down on me in it? Because it's not the kind of dress that Madison would wear?"

His eyebrows draw up in surprise at my question. "Madison?"

"Yeah." I nod. "I had a lovely chat with your ex."

"You don't understand." He shakes his head, his hand coming up to pinch the bridge of his nose.

"No. You don't understand. I am not ashamed of this dress or the person wearing it, but I won't stand here and let you use me in some ploy to piss your parents off." I point an accusatory finger in his direction. "You're the one that should be ashamed."

I turn away from him and begin marching down the ridiculously long driveway.

His voice follows me. "You can't leave like this, Kenz. Come on. I'll take you home."

"I can find my own way home." Even as I say this, I know

it's next to impossible.

I could call Kristen or Henley, but the thought of being such a burden to them when they've already done so much for me has me rethinking my options. I wonder how long it would take for me to get a bus out of here.

I'm probably not even halfway down the driveway before grasping the fact that I seriously underestimated its length, but it's not until I make it to the tall metal gates another ten minutes later that I realise my mistake.

The fence around the property is ten foot high and appears to be fitted with some sort of security system I'm not familiar with. There's no way out of here without being able to open that gate and I don't know the code. I should have paid more attention when Dylan was keying it in instead of gaping at him like some naïve loser.

I wrap my arms around myself and trudge down a small, pebbled path that leads to a gazebo. If I wasn't so pissed off, I might be able to appreciate the gorgeous floral vines that wind their way around each post or the fairy lights that give it a warm, whimsical glow. Releasing a long breath, I slump onto the swinging seat in the centre of it.

A moment later a set of headlights are making their way toward me, the familiar chug of a struggling engine drawing nearer.

Chapter 16

DYLAN

I step out of the car, closing the door as softly as I can. Mackenzie sits on the swing in the gazebo, wearing her sadness like a second skin. I hate that I'm the one that's made her feel this way. I feel awful.

She doesn't look up as I approach, and I can't say I blame her. It appears to her that I've mislead her, and I guess to an extent, that's exactly what I've done.

I haven't lied to her. Not once. But I have omitted things from conversations with her. Things that I haven't told any of my friends in Cliff Haven yet. The truth is, if I could trust anyone with the sordid details of my life, that person is probably Mackenzie.

I move closer to the gazebo, hands shoved deep into the pockets of my suit pants. Stopping at the entrance, I lean up against the post.

"What exactly happened, Kenz?" I dare to ask. "What did Madison tell you?"

Knowing Madison, it can't have been anything good.

"Oh, not much," she answers spitefully, the hurt in her light blue eyes sending shockwaves to my heart. "She just accused me of being the reason you're abandoning the hotel industry. Oh, and she may have mentioned you're a major player with party boy tendencies. Not that any of that should matter to me, seeing how our relationship is fake and all."

"Fake?"

We may have been putting on a show for the benefit of my parents tonight, but nothing about any of this feels fake anymore. I'd wanted her to come to the party, fake-date or friend, and if I've hurt her, I hate myself.

"Yeah, well it's not like we're really together." She pushes off the ground with her foot, setting the swing in motion.

"Why are you so upset then?"

Just as quickly, she slams her foot down and the swing comes to an abrupt halt. The pain in her stare has me wishing the ground would open up and swallow me.

"I'm upset because you've been hiding shit from me, Dylan," she cries. I wince at the disgust in her tone. "You aren't the person that I thought you were. You actually led me to believe that we had something in common."

"We do," I say, my eyes pleading with hers.

A bitter laugh escapes her. "Dylan, you used me tonight. You brought me here to shock your parents and your ex-girlfriends. I'm not like these people and you took advantage of that."

I shake my head defiantly. "No. I didn't even know that

Madison was going to be here."

She raises her eyebrows in disbelief.

"That's not the point though," I continue. "I brought you with me because I like spending time with you. I wasn't lying when I said that having you here with me made this whole party more bearable."

At least it had until my father dragged me away from her.

"Yeah, well it feels like you literally just fed me to the sharks. For the second time since I met you, by the way." She folds her arms across her chest, leaning back into the swing.

I exhale an unsteady breath as I step up into the gazebo and fill the empty space on the swing beside her. My chest physically aches knowing I've been careless with Mackenzie. She's right. She deserves more than what I've given her. I'd been stupid not to have been upfront with her.

"I'm sorry, Kenz. I should have given you a little more background information. About me, and about this whole situation. I wanted to. It's just… complicated."

"I googled you, Dylan," she admits. She thrusts her hand in the air, her phone held tightly within her grip before dropping it back into her lap. Settling her gaze on the stars in the darkened sky ahead, she lets out a groan of frustration. "God, you're fucking googleable."

I sigh, stealing a glance at the phone in her hand. Cringing, I squeeze my eyes shut before I ask her, "How much did you read?"

"Enough, I guess."

I slowly reach for the phone, my breath catching in my throat as my fingers brush hers. She opens her palm, allowing me to take it. I bring up the internet browser, still open on the google search page. Sure enough, my face fills the screen, a bunch of words below it that only describe me in vague detail.

I press on the news tab and a bunch of articles follow. I hold the phone back out to her, and she reads the top headline aloud.

"Future of Abbott group in jeopardy as Dylan Abbott, son of Ivan Abbott exits company."

My lips form a thin line as I look down toward the ground. "My dad wants me to stay on and work for him so that I can take over the company when he retires."

"But you don't want that," she correctly assumes.

"No." Leaning forward, I rest my elbows on my knees. "I tried it. I worked for him for a few years while studying for my MBA but honestly, I hated it. I'm not cut out for that type of work. But you're right. I should have told you that I…"

"That you what?" she retaliates. "That you're the heir to a billion-dollar fortune?"

"Was."

"Was?" she questions, a crease forming between her brows.

"When I left the company, my parents cut me off. I think they figure that without my trust fund and credit cards I'll eventually come crawling back," I say with a subtle snicker. "Joke's on them, I guess. Living in Cliff Haven makes me happy. The tavern, the diving. Even that stupid bomb of a car."

Mackenzie is silent for a moment as she allows my words to sink in. Then she finally says, "I was wondering why you drove that hunk of metal if you were a billionaire."

My lips lift slightly in a subtle grin, my shoulders jumping up as I let out a short laugh.

"My Ferrari is in the garage round back," I admit.

"You're joking."

"I'm not."

Her eyes lock with mine, scepticism in their midst, the growing smile on her lips mirroring mine. She doesn't know whether to take me seriously and I don't blame her.

How can I when I've been keeping this huge secret?

A moment later, her smile fades. "Money doesn't impress me, Dylan."

"That makes two of us," I tell her.

"None of this makes sense. Why Cliff Haven? I mean, you could go anywhere."

"What's wrong with Cliff Haven?"

"I don't know," she replies, looking down at the ground. "Sometimes I think about leaving. Just buying a bus ticket to anywhere and starting again."

There's an honesty in her words that I don't deserve. A vulnerability that I don't feel worthy enough to witness. Not after I've hidden these parts of myself from her.

Mackenzie doesn't show her heart often, but I can see it now. She isn't as tough as she lets on. The things that have happened in her life have affected her beyond repair. She's become an expert at hiding away parts of herself too. Maybe even more so than I.

"How do you think Kristen would feel if you left town?" I ask.

"I don't know." She shrugs. "She's got her own stuff going on."

"I think she'd miss you," I say.

She gives a little shrug, pushing the ground with her feet

again to move the swing back and forth.

Stopping it suddenly with my own feet, I lock my gaze on hers. "I know I would."

Her eyes stay on mine for a moment, then she shakes her head. "As if."

"I would," I argue earnestly.

"Whatever." She dips her head, pushing off the ground again, setting us in motion.

"I mean it. Besides, those beers at the tavern aren't gonna be pouring themselves."

This earns a chuckle from her and I'm so happy to have made her laugh, I don't even care that she almost shoves me off the swing. "You're the worst."

"Come on. Let's go home."

"I'm not going with you, remember? I've already googled the nearest bus stop. I just need you to put in your magic code and let me out of here," she says, nodding toward the gate.

"If you think I'm going to leave you on the side of the road an hour away from home at this time of night, you're seriously deluded."

"I'm perfectly capable of getting myself home, you know. I don't need saving," she whips around to face me, and not for the first time, I see the fire inside of her.

She may be vulnerable, but she's also the strongest woman I've ever met. A fighter.

"Well, thank God," I joke. "Because I'm no knight in shining armour and that right there is hardly a white stallion." I turn and point at my beat-up car.

"Well, no," Mackenzie agrees. "But it is white. If you don't count all the paint chips."

My head falls back as I bark out a laugh, then I turn and plead with her. "Please Kenz. Just get in the car."

"I'm okay here," she argues, crossing her arms over her chest again.

"What are you gonna do? Wait till I drive up to the gate and sneak out behind me?"

"If I have to."

"Fine. You're stubborn as hell, so I guess there's no point in arguing with you." I stand and ready myself to get in the car. I'm only calling her bluff. I still have no intention of leaving her behind. "But just so you know, I really am sorry. For dragging you into this mess. I shouldn't have kept all this stuff from you. I should have trusted you with it."

She looks up at me, not moving from her spot on the swing.

"I never lied to you though. I do like spending time with you. I did want you here with me tonight." I swallow down the lump in my throat, remembering the hurt that I'd caused her, hating that I wasn't able to protect her from Madison's wrath.

She looks over toward the gates, like she's planning her escape from me. "Have you finished?"

"No." I shake my head. "There's one more thing."

Her eyebrows jump up as she looks at me expectantly. "Well?"

"When I said that your dress was perfect, I meant that you look perfect in it. That's all."

I turn away from her, stepping down from the gazebo. I've only made it halfway to the car when I hear her footsteps crunching on the pebble path.

"You better figure out a way to fix that window winder." Her voice cuts through the night somewhere behind me. "Your rich ego is bound to take up all the oxygen in the car and I'm going to need some air."

A smile stretches across my face as I open the driver's door. I wait for Mackenzie to round the car to the passenger side, then I hear her wrestling with the handle.

"Do you need help?" I call.

"No," she cries out, yanking it so hard, I think it might break.

A few seconds later, the door opens, and she climbs inside while I try to deny that those long, toned legs have any effect on me.

We drive toward the security gate, and she watches as I wind down the window to press the large black button on the side panel.

"Are you kidding me?" she asks, completely livid. "You mean all I had to do was press that button and I would have been free?"

I couldn't contain my laughter if I tried.

Chapter 17

MACKENZIE

I've been awake for an hour, but I can't seem to find the motivation to shift myself from my bed.

What I have done though, is google Dylan about twenty-five times. I've read article upon article about his exit from the company, scrolled through countless images of him at important events. There are even photographs of him as a child, his sister alongside him with his parents, Faith and Ivan Abbott. A cute little wide-eyed boy beaming at the cameras.

I've also read his google bio, which is full of pointless facts that I have to admit don't even nearly capture the essence of the person I've come to know these past few months. What his life must have been like, growing up in the limelight, his every move described by reporters.

And what it still must be like.

I understand now why he felt the need to keep his job at

Two Tanked a secret. What he meant when he said he wanted to have something that was all his own.

I'm not rostered on to work at the tavern today, and I feel relieved about that. Maybe by the time tomorrow's shift rolls around, I'll be in a better headspace to handle this situation with Dylan, but for now I think space from him is what I need.

It's not that I don't want to see him. Despite everything that had happened last night, we were able to fall back into easy conversation during the trip home. When he'd dropped me off, I was still reeling from the things I'd learnt about him, but something was telling me to trust the person that I'd come to know, and not the things his bitter ex had said about him. We all have a past after all.

I toss my phone on the bedside table where my art books lay, the brightly coloured business card that peaks out from the pages grabbing my attention. I pinch it between my fingers and pluck it from the book, then I flip it over in my palm, tracing the bold font with my forefinger.

The Abstract Palette.

Maybe it's time for me to have something that's all my own too.

If I take the next bus into Seabright Cove, I could be there not long after opening. I mull it over in my mind for the next few moments, weighing up the pros and cons.

What if I go and hate it? But then what the hell am I going to do around here all day? If I stay here a second longer, I might end up googling Dylan's name a hundred more times, and after that there's always Facebook and Instagram profiles to stalk.

Screw that. Suddenly the decision isn't such a hard one to

make after all. I'm going.

I take a quick shower, then pull on a pair of shorts and a black t-shirt. Then I toss my art book and a random handful of pencils into my backpack, dumping it on the kitchen table while I turn on the coffee machine.

The house is otherwise quiet with Kristen and Henley having already left for work. Once my coffee has dispensed into my keep cup, I grab my backpack and head out the door in the direction of the bus stop.

According to the trip planner app, it will take forty-five minutes to reach Seabright Cove by bus. I spend the journey lost in my sketch book, adding details to the drawing of the tree across the creek out the back of our house. I feel like I've been working on this one forever, but I'm a perfectionist when it comes to my art, and I really want to get this one right.

As the bus approaches my destination, I pack up and race down the aisle, thanking the driver as I skip down the stairs.

Once out on the street, I scan the area. The bus has stopped right near a marina, not unlike the one in Cliff Haven. It's not until the bus pulls away from the curb that I see it.

Situated directly across the road from the bus stop is The Abstract Palette. A quaint and charming little shopfront on a street lined with planter pots overflowing with colourful petals. The art studio is on the ground floor, forming only a small part of a large Victorian style three-storey building. It has an old school vibe that, for a moment, has me feeling as though I've been transported somewhere else in time.

Crossing the street with my bag slung over my shoulder, a woman becomes visible in the window as I approach. She stands bent over a table, engaged in casual conversation with a group of elderly women. She straightens, laughing, before turning her attention to the street outside. Her smile falters ever so slightly when she catches a glimpse of me. Only for a moment though. Then her hand comes up to wave at me as I push through the door. A bell chimes above my head, signalling my entry.

"Hi," she says as she steps forward to greet me. "You made it."

"Yeah," I say, eyeing the various paintings that hang from the walls. There are large shelves lining the far wall, scattered with several sculptures and pottery pieces. "I thought I'd take you up on your offer after all."

"I'm so glad," she replies, wiping her hands on her apron, her blue eyes beginning to glisten with moisture. "I'm Grace, by the way."

She extends her hand and I accept, grasping it gently in a weak handshake. "Mackenzie."

"Mackenzie," she echoes, her hand still clutching mine. "It's a pleasure to have you here."

I gently slide my hand from hers, stepping further into the room. "These are so beautiful." I point at a group of charcoal drawings hanging along the nearest wall. "Are they yours?"

"A few of them, but most are from students that have attended my workshops over the years. Come." She ushers me over to a table where the group of older women sit, bent over canvases speckled with brightly coloured splotches of paint. "I run a small senior's class on Sundays. We call it Canvas Connoisseurs."

The women look up from their work when I approach the table. "Sorry, I don't mean to interrupt."

"Nonsense," says an older lady with short, bright white hair. "Pull up a seat, girly!"

"Uh, thanks," I say awkwardly, pulling out a chair.

"This is Betty," Grace informs me. "And this is May, Ava and Liz. Ladies, this is Mackenzie."

They all regard me, nodding their hellos, except for Liz who stares at her canvas intently, clearly lost in the zone.

"What brings you here today, Mackenzie?" May asks me.

"Uh, well, I met Grace on the beach, and she took an interest in my drawing," I explain, retrieving my art book from my backpack.

"Well then. Let's see it!" Betty says excitedly, rubbing her hands together.

"Uh, okay," I say with a soft laugh. I'm taken aback by her enthusiasm. I flick through the pages until I find the sketch of the beach with the sun on its horizon.

"That's pretty good," May says to my right. She helps herself to my book, pulling it from Betty's grip and thumbing through its pages. She makes soft sounds of agreement. Or maybe it's disagreement. I can't tell. "Hmm. You're talented, that's for sure. But there's something missing from these drawings."

"There is?" I ask.

My left eyebrow quirks involuntarily as I spare a glance over at Grace. I hadn't realised that coming to this art studio would result in my work being critiqued by a bunch of old biddies.

"Hmm. This one is interesting though," Betty muses. "What inspired it?"

I look down at the drawing she refers to. It's one I'd started the day after the snorkel tour but since abandoned. So far, I'd outlined the turtles and some fish, pencilled in the rays of sunshine, leaving an expanse of blue in the centre. "Oh, that. I went on this snorkel tour, and I guess I was moved by the colours, the ocean, you know? But it's not very good and I haven't finished it."

"Oh, that sounds lovely. Who did you go with?" she asks, her eyes twinkling with wonder.

"No one," I reply flatly. "I was meant to go with a friend, but her son got sick, and she had to cancel."

"So, there were no other people there?" the old woman's eyes crinkle as she squints at me suspiciously.

"Well, not exactly," I answer. "There were other people in the group, but I didn't know them."

"You didn't know any of them?" May asks dubiously.

A smile makes its way across my face. "What is this? An interrogation?"

"Just answer the question, girly," May demands.

"Okay. Okay." I resign with my palms raised, then dropping them back into my lap I say, "Well, I knew this one guy, I guess."

"Ah ha! There it is!" Betty shouts, a finger pointed in the air. "That's what these drawings are lacking."

"What do you mean?" I laugh. "They're lacking a guy?"

"No dear. They're lacking a real subject. Passion!" she slams a hand down on the table, letting those of us in the room know that this is something she herself is clearly passionate about.

"Oh." I'm not really sure how else to respond. I'd be lying if I said I wasn't slightly weirded out by her blatant display.

"This man you speak of. Maybe he belongs in your drawing," she suggests.

"Pfft. No." I shake my head at her out-of-left-field notion. "It's not really like that. He's no one. He was just one of the instructors."

Just one of the instructors that I fake-dated last night who turned out to be an ex-billionaire and who is also my boss.

I attempt to pull the book away from May's grasp, but she tightens her fists around it. She's got a solid grip on her for an old lady.

"He's important enough that you mentioned him," Betty argues.

I scoff at her statement. "I only mentioned him because you asked me who was there with me!" I reef the book away from her, smoothing out its pages. "Let's all critique your work then, shall we, Betty?"

"Go right on ahead. I have nothing to hide," Betty retaliates.

"Whatever," I sigh.

Getting into an argument with an eighty-year-old woman had not been my intention today.

I turn to Grace, who has been quietly watching my interaction with the group from the corner of the room. She wanders over to the table now, her arms laden with art supplies.

"Now, now, ladies. Mackenzie has inspired me to show you a different activity today," she says, placing a set of watercolour pencils in the centre of the table.

After laying down an A3 sheet of watercolour paper in front of each of us, she takes a seat beside me. "Let's see you work your magic with these, Mackenzie. They're great for drawing seascapes."

"Yes, Mackenzie," Betty agrees. Then she picks up a cyan pencil and lays it across the top of my page. "Perhaps you could draw the boy from the ocean for us."

I squint at the old woman, wondering why she won't let this go. My reply comes out through gritted teeth. "Why, thank you for the suggestion, Betty. Maybe I will."

Grace stifles a soft laugh beside me, a small smile lighting up her face. It has the corners of my mouth tugging upwards too. Of all the ways this day could have gone, this is definitely not how I'd pictured it, but I have to admit that despite these feisty women, I am enjoying myself.

I pick up the cyan blue. Then, hoping to translate the picture forming in my mind to paper, I drag it across the middle of the page. An image of the sea turtles floating so gracefully in the ocean's depths. Only this time, Dylan is there, gliding seamlessly below, his black wetsuit and dive gear a stark contrast to the white, sandy ocean floor.

An hour passes by easily, all of us lost in our projects. I listen as the five women make small talk of the weather, their families and random chit chat. They seem to have given up on their interrogation, only throwing the occasional question my way, to which I give them brief answers. When the class is over Betty, May, Ava, and Liz carry their work over to a table along the window. I follow their lead and do the same.

"Not bad," Betty says as she gestures to my work.

It's unfinished, but most of the details are there.

"I'm glad it meets your expectations, Betty."

The narrowing of her eyes is the only sign I get that she's

picked up on my sarcasm. Still, we both wear slight grins as we wander over to the sink to wash our hands in silence.

After thanking Grace for her time, the four older women exit the studio, dispersing into different directions out on the street.

I linger at the table, packing the watercolour pencils back into their tin. When I look up, Grace is watching me from the window. "Thank you, Mackenzie. You didn't have to do that."

"I don't mind. Thank you for having me along today. I had fun."

"Of course," she says. "I'm glad we ran into each other."

The way her hopeful gaze lingers on mine implies that her words hold deeper meaning for her. I'm not sure why. It should make me feel uncomfortable, but somehow it doesn't. Maybe she's just a people person.

"Where do you keep these?" I hold up the set of pencils.

"Just in the top drawer over here." She points to a set of drawers next to her, then slides the top one open as I approach.

I place the pencils neatly inside and as I turn around, a large canvas on the wall above captures my attention. It's incredible. Haunting, yet beautiful.

"Wow," I breathe.

Grace watches as my feet carry me towards it, mesmerised by its colours and the painstaking detail within. I'm completely and utterly intrigued, moved by the emotions it conjures.

The canvas itself is massive in size. Probably about five feet long, the painting created from an underwater perspective. In the centre, a young woman floats, her white dress billowing around her slender body, her back to the ocean floor. Her arms are outstretched, her long, wavy hair wafting around her. Its melancholy in a sense, or peaceful, depending on your perspective. The woman could simply be letting go, or she could be drowning.

"This is incredible," I say in awe. "Is it one of yours?"

"No," Grace says, clearing her throat. "Not that one. But it was done by someone very dear to me."

"It's amazing. The texture, the use of fine lines to capture the light rippling through the water. The artist obviously had a steady hand and…" I end my rant when I see that Grace has turned her back to me, hunching her shoulders as she rests her hands on the sink. I hear her sniffle and begin to worry that she's started to cry. "I'm sorry. Did I say something wrong?"

She hesitates a little longer, before wiping her eyes and turning back around. "No. Of course not." Her cheerful voice is forced. Her smile too. "Why don't you tell me something about yourself, Mackenzie?"

It's obvious she wants a subject change. For whatever reason, she isn't interested in talking about that painting.

I shove my hands into the pockets of my shorts. "There isn't much to tell."

"Oh, I doubt that," she says. "Have you always lived in Cliff Haven?"

"Me? No." I shake my head. "I'm actually from Coledale."

"Oh. So, you were raised in Coledale and moved recently?"

"Raised?" I can't help scoffing at the word before letting out a short laugh. "Yeah, sure. If you want to call it that."

Her brow furrows as she watches my reaction inquisitively. "What do you mean?"

"Sorry," I say, waving off her concern. "It's nothing."

"Doesn't sound like nothing," she says. "You can tell me."

I hadn't planned on opening up to this woman about my life story, but it seems like a safe enough space. "It's just that I pretty much had to raise myself. My dad was an alcoholic. Is. He *is* an alcoholic. He's in rehab."

I'm only just now realising how often I refer to my father in the past tense, as though I've already erased him from my life.

She frowns, turning her sights out the window. When her eyes return to mine, there's an unmistakeable sadness swirling in their midst. Her throat bobs as she swallows, seemingly thinking over her next question. After a long pause, she finally asks, "And your mother?"

"No idea where she is," I answer, a bitterness in my tone. I wander toward a set of paintbrushes resting in a jar, plucking one out and absent-mindedly brushing it over my fingers. "I honestly wouldn't know her if I passed her on the street."

Her frown deepens. This time when she sniffles, there's no mistaking it. She's holding back tears. "Oh, Mackenzie. I'm sorry."

I force a smile. "It's not your fault. You have nothing to be sorry about."

"No, of course." She shakes her head, swiping at her eyes. "I just mean, I'm sorry you had to go through all of that."

"It's fine. And I'm fine. I mean, I'm here, right?" I shrug, placing the paintbrush I've been fidgeting with back in the jar.

"Yes." She nods. "You are. And I'm so glad." She wipes her hands on her apron and moves to a cork board on the other side of the room. She unpins an A5 flyer, returning it to me with shaky hands. "I wanted to show you this."

"What is it?" I ask, taking the paper.

"Every year, we run an exhibition night here at the studio. It's a chance for us to showcase the great work we've been doing here to the public. Students can offer their art for sale. I've seen the kind of work you do, Mackenzie. I think you should join us."

"This is next month," I say. "I don't have anything to show."

"Come back to the studio," she says, resting a warm hand on my shoulder. "You can work on something here."

"I don't know. I've never considered putting my art on display like this. Or selling it." A nervous laugh leaves me at the thought. "I'm not sure anyone would buy it."

"Well, you never know until you try." Grace shrugs. "But your talent is too good to be wasted."

I nod, taking another look at the flyer. "I guess I could think about it."

"Take your time. Well not too much time," she laughs.

"Okay." I glance down at my watch. "I better start making my way back home. The next bus is in five minutes."

"Good timing," she says. "Will I see you again soon, Mackenzie?"

There's something in her tone that I can't quite decipher, though it borders on desperation. My interactions with this woman have no doubt been strange. She seems like a highly emotional person which would normally send me running for the hills.

Yet, I do want to see her again. I don't mind being in her company. I appreciate the sense of peace and calm that being in her presence brings and I like the atmosphere in this studio.

I've had fun today. My soul has been nourished.

I understand now what Dylan had been talking about when he'd asked me if I had something I loved to do. Something that I needed like I need air.

"Yeah," I nod. "You'll see me again."

I turn and leave the studio, heading for the bus stop across the road. Only once I've reached the bus shelter do I turn around to realise she's still standing at the window beaming at me. I look down at the exhibition flyer, still clutched within my right hand, then when I look back up, she's gone.

The bus approaches and I find a seat at the back. As we wind our way down the coastline, I get lost in the view of the waves crashing against the rocky cliffs below. I smile when I think about Betty and May. Those women had been savage today, yet somehow, I'm sure that they're just the kind of women anyone would be lucky to have in their corner.

Then I think about what Grace said about my talent being too good to waste and for the first time in a long time, I'm instilled with a sense of hope. As though I could handle anything that life throws my way. As though I'm ready for my future.

Something catches my eye in the distance. I squint, holding my hand up to shade the sun from my face. For a second, I think that maybe I've imagined it, but then I spot movement in the water. Three dolphins rise from the waves, looping up and then diving back under the surface. Another two spring upward and a wide grin stretches across my face. I can't wait to tell Dylan about this.

Dylan.

The thought stops me in my tracks. Of all the people in my life I could sit and talk about my day with, Dylan was the one that came to mind first.

It should terrify me. Especially after what happened last night. And I know I could sit here and question that choice. Try to talk myself out of it. But it would be pointless.

Because I want to talk to him.

Instead of taking the bus all the way to the end of the boulevard, I decide to hop off outside the Haven and cross the road to see if Dylan is still working. When I push through the tavern's heavy doors, I find Jade, perched in her usual position at the bar. She lifts her hand in a wave when she sees me.

"Hey."

"Hey, Jade. Is Dylan still here?" I ask.

"Sure is," she smiles. "But he just stepped out the back."

"Thanks."

I round the bar and skip down the narrow hallway to the back of the tavern, figuring he must be out emptying the trash into the skip bins. At first, I can't see him. I turn, thinking he may have already gone back out around the side, but stop short when I hear voices.

I peer around the corner, down the alley between the tavern and the next building. Dylan stands face to face with an older man dressed in a torn flannelette shirt. The man's appearance is scruffy and unkempt, a lit cigarette pursed between his lips as he reaches around to the back pocket of his jeans.

"Did you get the good stuff this time?" I hear Dylan ask.

"Top grade, just what you need," the man says to him with a laugh as he retrieves something I can't quite see, placing it in Dylan's palm. "Best on the market, I'm told."

"Thanks, man," Dylan replies, digging deep into his own pockets. He pulls out a few rolled up notes and something else

I can't quite distinguish. "I appreciate it. This is for you. But keep it on the down low though, okay?"

"Yes, boss," the man replies, accepting Dylan's offering in a tightly closed fist. He immediately shoves it into his back pocket, nodding once.

What the hell am I witnessing right now? A shady deal in the middle of an alley in broad daylight?

I flatten my back against the tavern wall, exhaling a long breath, a string of questions swirling through my mind. My heart sinks, disappointment flooding me at the realisation of the one thing that I am finally sure of.

I need to keep my distance from Dylan.

He's proved once again that he isn't the guy that I thought he was. Things between us need to remain strictly professional.

No more fake dating for his family's benefit.

No more thinking of him as the one person I want to share my day with.

He is my boss. And nothing more.

Chapter 18

DYLAN

"Hey, Dylan," Harper calls to me from the other side of the bar. "Have you seen Mackenzie? I feel like I haven't spoken to her in days. Is she working today?"

"She's supposed to be," I answer, frowning at the antique grandfather clock on the wall. "Her shift started ten minutes ago."

Mackenzie has never been late to a shift, so I find her tardiness to be somewhat concerning. I hadn't heard from her since dropping her home after our eventful night at my parent's party. I'd walked her to the door, fumbled through another apology for my bad behaviour and she'd laughed it off, throwing a sarcastic comment my way.

It had seemed as though she'd begun to let go of any resentment she'd been harbouring towards me, but that hadn't done anything to resolve me of the guilt I still feel.

I know I should have done better.

I need to *be* better.

I slide my phone from the top pocket of my shirt, but as I'm finding her name in the contacts, the tavern's doors swing open and Mackenzie barges through them looking mildly dishevelled.

"Oh, here she is now," Harper says, stating the obvious. She lifts a hand up to wave at her friend, an expectant smile on her face. "Hey!"

"Hey," Mackenzie says abruptly as she rounds the bar. She doesn't return the smile.

I spare a glance at Harper. Her frown tells me I'm not the only one that's noticed the aura of defensiveness surrounding Mackenzie. Something is wrong and I need to find out what it is.

I follow her into the storeroom where she dumps her backpack aggressively in one of the lockers.

"What happened?" I dare to ask. "Are you okay?"

"Fine," she says, slamming the locker door.

"Are you sure?"

She ignores me, looking away as she piles her long hair on top of her head, securing it with an elastic.

"You've never been late to a shift before," I add, awkwardly rubbing the base of my neck. "It kind of had me worried for a second."

"I said I'm fine," she scowls, pushing past me to get back out to the bar.

I guess she still isn't over what happened on Saturday night. I'm going to have to try much harder to win back her affections.

And I *want* to win back her affections. That's something I'm sure of now.

"Hey, what's up?" she asks Harper, offering her a weak smile. "How's Noah doing?"

"He's finally over this virus. Thank God!" Harper cries, her hands held together as though in prayer. "It's been a long week."

"I'll bet," Mackenzie says, busying herself with wiping down the bar. "I'm glad he's okay though."

"Yeah, me too. He's with my mum right now actually. Grandmothers are the best babysitters, I swear," she says, resting her chin on her hands. "Speaking of, I'm ready to take that raincheck. You ready to go back out on the snorkel tour again?"

Mackenzie glances in my direction, her nostrils flaring, but she doesn't make eye contact. "Uh, I don't know. Maybe we could do something else instead?" she suggests. "We could go shopping or do dinner?"

"Oh, come on!" Harper complains. "I want to do something different. You said it was really good and I want to see for myself."

I can't help but grin hearing this, but my smile fades when I hear Mackenzie's reply. "I said it was okay, but I'm sure we can find something better to do."

I feel a crease form between my brows. "Ouch," I mutter under my breath.

What is Mackenzie's deal today? I guess I had seriously misread her. I know things had become complicated between us over the weekend, but I thought we'd overcome that. She had been fine on the drive home from the party. Hadn't she?

"But I really want to go," Harper persists. "I've got total FOMO over the pics you sent me. Don't make me go without you." She gives her best attempt at puppy-dog eyes, forming a pout, but not even this can crack a smile on her friend's face.

"The pics *I* sent you, you mean," I snicker, wiping a wine glass dry and hanging it on the overhead rack.

Harper lets out a laugh. "I was referring to a really great pic Mackenzie sent of the water, but yes, Dylan. Your pic was great too."

Mackenzie doesn't react to my comment or to Harper's reply. I feel the crease between my brow deepen. This is not just Mackenzie being her usual grumpy self. She's completely pissed. And it's obvious it has something to do with me.

I bend down, bringing my mouth so close to her ear that I can smell her coconut shampoo. "Hey," I say in a low voice. "Can we talk for a minute?"

She rolls her eyes at me, then turns her attention to Harper. "I'll be back in a second."

She barges past me in the direction of the courtyard. I follow closely behind, not speaking until we've cleared the crowded tavern and the doors of the courtyard are closed behind us. There are two women sitting in the corner, but the area is otherwise unoccupied.

"What's going on Kenz?" I ask in a softer tone. "I thought we were cool."

"Yeah," she scoffs, then mutters almost inaudibly. "That was before."

She begins to move past me, but I catch her arm. She stares intently at the place where my fingers wrap gently around her bicep, her nostrils flared in defiance, and I realise I've made a mistake touching her so unexpectedly. I draw my hand away swiftly, as though her arm is on fire, disappointed in myself for encroaching on her personal space like that.

I take a step backward. "Sorry. I didn't mean to grab you. What do you mean 'before'? Before what?"

"Before I saw you out back making deals with the devil," she accuses, fury in her icy eyes.

"When?" I'm dumbfounded by her cryptic statement.

"Does it matter?" she retaliates.

"Kenz, I have no idea what you're talking about. Please. Tell me what you mean," I plead.

She leans back up against the courtyard wall, exhaling as she crosses her arms over her chest. "I came looking for you yesterday. I saw you."

"You came looking for me?" Despite the situation, I feel a warmth spread through my chest.

"You're missing the point."

"Okay?" I draw the word out, wondering where this is leading to.

"Look, I'm just here to do my job, okay? We don't have to be friends. You're my boss. Let's just keep it that way. I've had my fair share of dirty money in dark alleyways. I can't be a part of that life anymore."

I let out a breath as understanding dawns on me. She came looking for me yesterday. She saw me in the alley. She saw an exchange of money, heard words that out of context, may have sounded dodgy.

"It's not what you think," I begin, shaking my head profusely.

"Yeah. It never is," she says sarcastically. "Look, whatever you're up to is your business. I don't want any part of it."

"I mean it, Mackenzie. You have to know I would never do that."

The next words out of her mouth cut through me like a knife. "I think we established over the weekend that we really don't know each other at all."

Despite how upset I am, I manage a laugh. "You know, it kind of hurts my feelings how little you think of me."

I mean it as a joke, but honestly, if it was Madison or any other girl I've dated standing in front of me making these accusations, I'd be walking away right now, not bothering to look back.

But this is Mackenzie and I need to remember what she's been through. God only knows what that asshole of an ex-boyfriend has put her through.

"Putting on the guilt trip," she says, pushing off the brick wall. "Nice. The first sign of a narcissist."

I sigh. "Please meet me tonight. I'll explain everything."

"No, thanks," she says, her palms raised defensively as she backs toward the doors.

"Please Kenz," I plead. "Look. I know I haven't given you a whole lot of reasons to trust me, but I'm not out to hurt you."

"I don't care."

"I'll pick you up tonight." I'm determined to prove to her that I'm not the monster she thinks I am.

"No, you won't." With that, she turns and pushes through the doors into the bustling tavern.

Like hell I won't.

Chapter 19

MACKENZIE

After dinner, I retreat to my room. Like an idiot, I still can't seem to let what happened with Dylan go and I have no idea why. It shouldn't mean anything to me. *He* shouldn't mean anything to me. But the disappointment of it all has fallen heavy, like a weight in my bones. Even after last weekend, I'd thought Dylan was different.

But he's just like the rest of them.

Wishing I had something else to occupy my thoughts, I decide to set up the easel I'd retrieved from Pamela's unwanted hobby pile. Then I pull the canvas out from the corner of the room and perch it on its rail, hoping it will provide me with a much-needed distraction.

I sit back on my bed examining it and try to envision something, anything, that I could paint on it. Thanks to Betty and May's commentary yesterday, the only subject that comes to mind right now is the very person I'm trying to avoid.

It doesn't matter anyway. I'm feeling less than inspired right now. I had begun to seriously consider Grace's invitation to the exhibition night, but if I can't find my muse, I'll be attending as a visitor and not an exhibitor.

Frustrated, I throw myself back onto the bed, staring at the ceiling.

"Mackenzie!" I hear Kristen call from down the hall. "Someone's at the door! Can you get it? I'm naked!"

"Ugh. Where's Henley?" I grumble, then thinking better of it I add, "Don't answer that."

I stomp down the hallway to the front door and swing it wide open.

"Hi," Dylan says cheerfully from the other side of it, his eyes the colour of burnt caramel.

"What are you doing here?" My glare narrows in suspicion.

"Picking you up, remember?"

I shake my head in annoyance, huffing out a sigh. "I told you I'm not going with you."

"Yes, you are," he says cheekily, his eyes travelling down to the Scooby-doo pyjama pants I'm wearing. "I'll wait here while you get ready. Or you could just wear those if you like. I don't mind."

"You can wait out here all night for all I care. I'm not going anywhere." I prepare to shut the door in his face, but what he says next catches me off guard.

"I thought you might say that. That's why I brought a book along with me."

"You're kidding," I say, calling his bluff.

"I'm really not."

I roll my eyes as he reaches into his jacket and pulls out a thick, heavy book, his grin spreading wider. He wasn't kidding.

I read the title aloud. "'Shark Biology and Conservation: Essentials for Educators, Students and Enthusiasts.' Well, have fun with that."

The hinges creak as I begin to close the door, but his hand comes up to hold it open. "I'll wait as long as it takes, but I'm not leaving until my reputation is intact."

"Whatever." This time I do slam the door with way too much force and the sound reverberates throughout the small cottage.

I storm back to my room, passing Kristen in the hallway as I go. She frowns at my sullen expression. "What's up with you?"

"Nothing," I mutter as I enter my room and fall back onto my bed, resting my head up against the bedhead.

Stupid Dylan and his stupid, persistent attitude.

No more than a minute later, Kristen is back, arms folded as she leans against the doorframe. "Um, Mackenzie? Why is Dylan sitting on our front porch reading a textbook?"

"He likes reading?" I offer.

"Mac, come on. What's going on?" She moves into the room, taking a seat at the end of my bed.

I sigh, knowing she isn't going to leave until I give her an answer. "He wants me to go somewhere with him."

"Why?"

My answer rushes out of me in one breath. "Because I may have accused him of participating in illegal dealings and he wants to clear his name."

Kristen narrows her eyes at me, a sceptical smile spreading across her face. "Dylan? He's like… the nicest person."

"Sure." I shrug. "They all seem nice until you find out they're not."

Her grin fades. "I know your past experiences make it hard for you to trust, but I really do think he's a good guy," she says earnestly. "And something tells me he likes you."

"Oh yeah?" I question cynically. "What could possibly make you think that?"

"The fact that he's sitting on our front porch reading a book when he could literally be anywhere else," she deadpans.

My eyes roll back until they're focused on the ceiling. "Fair point."

"You owe him the chance to at least explain whatever it is you're accusing him of."

She's right. As much as I hate to admit it. If Dylan says he can explain the interaction I saw in the alley yesterday, then I owe it to him to at least listen.

"Fine," I grumble, springing upright. "But if my body turns up dead in a ditch somewhere, don't say I didn't warn you."

"Your dramatics are truly something to be admired." Kristen stands up, then a moment later I hear her feet padding gently down the hallway.

"Kristen!" Henley calls out from their bedroom. "Hurry up and get your ass back in here!"

Ugh. Getting out of the house for a while suddenly sounds more appealing than ever. I change into my denim cut-off shorts and pull on a pair of ankle boots before marching back down the hall. I throw the front door open with a little too much gusto. It clangs against the wall with a thud before swinging shut. Dylan looks up from his book, his eyebrows raised in question.

"Let's get this over with," I say as I strut over to his car.

I can hear the smirk in his voice as he casually follows behind me. "Always such a ray of sunshine."

"Don't push your luck, Abbott."

I'm at war with the passenger side door handle when I feel his breath on my neck. "Need some help?"

Frustrated, I step aside, my posture stiffening as I cross my arms over my chest. Dylan gives the handle a jiggle and the door swings open. It only aggravates me further when he stands there waiting for me to climb into the car so he can close the door behind me.

He energetically throws himself into the driver's seat and pulls on his seatbelt. I almost smile at the way his eyes squeeze shut in silent prayer as he turns the key in the ignition, only opening them once the engine has roared to life. When I see him like this, it's hard to envision the version of him that drove a Ferrari through the city streets.

"Please tell me you're not taking me on another hour-long journey to the cape," I complain, combing a hand through my hair as I shift my sights out the window.

"Nope," he replies.

"Where are we going then?"

"Not far."

He is true to his word. Within minutes we're parked out the front of a warehouse just down from the marina. It's not a well-lit area and there are barely any other people around. I had only been kidding when I made that comment to Kristen about my body ending up in a ditch, but seeing how derelict this end of town is has me on high alert.

"What is this?" I ask.

"Come on," he says, opening his door. "I'll show you."

Hesitantly, I step out of the car and follow him to the padlocked doors of the large building in front of us, the ocean behind it black in the night. The lone streetlight above us flickers on and off, emanating an eery glow.

Dylan shuffles around the side of the building, climbing up on a stack of tyres to peer in through the high windows. His actions don't exactly scream legit.

"So let me get this straight," I begin. "In order for you to explain the shifty conversation I heard you having in an alleyway, you've brought me to the shadiest looking place in town to perform a break and enter."

His laugh echoes across the bay as he jumps down from the stack of tyres. Then he pulls out a single key from his jacket pocket. "I have a key, Kenz."

"Then what the hell are you doing spying in the windows of a building you already have a key to?"

"I just wanted to make sure…" he stops short, taking a breath before he goes on. "Okay. This is going to sound weird no matter how I say it, so hear me out. Promise you'll let me finish."

"That depends," I say.

He scratches his forehead, seemingly contemplating the best way to explain himself. "I was checking the windows to make sure that Roy wasn't inside."

"And who exactly is Roy?" I ask.

"The guy you saw me with in the alley."

I nod once, then taking a step backward, I turn on my heel.

"I'm out of here."

"Kenz, please," he pleads, rushing around in front of me, his hands held up in defence. "It isn't what it looks like. I lease this warehouse and sometimes I let Roy stay here."

"Why?" I ask, throwing my arms up in the air in frustration. Nothing he's saying is making any sense.

"He's homeless."

My feet pause in their place as my eyes snap to his. "Okay. You have my attention."

"He isn't a bad guy, but he has nowhere to go. I met him at the back of the tavern one day looking for food in the dumpster. I've kind of gotten to know him over the past few months and I allowed him to use this space for shelter."

"Okay," I say. "Then why the exchange of money in the alley the other day? What was that all about?"

"He offered to help me out with some odd jobs. To pay me back for letting him stay here. I gave him some money to buy some supplies. He brought them here to the warehouse and then delivered the change to me at the back of the tavern."

Showing generosity towards a homeless person is definitely not a crime. It's admirable even, but still, something doesn't sit right with this situation. I have more questions. Questions I really hope he can answer. "But I saw you give him something too."

"Yeah. The spare key to the warehouse," he explains. "Plus, I gave the change back to him and told him to buy a meal at the tavern on me."

"You told him to keep it on the downlow."

He lifts his arm, scratching the back of his neck. "Yeah. I did. Otherwise, I could end up with a whole bunch of people trying to take shelter in this warehouse."

That makes sense to an extent, I guess. "What kind of supplies did he buy you?"

"Paint."

"Top grade paint?" I squint at him sceptically.

"Marine grade," he fires back.

I stare at him in awe, the silence of the night falling over us for a moment before I find the words I want to say next. "You trusted a homeless guy with your own cash, then let him stay in a warehouse that your name is assigned to. He could be anyone. How can you do that?"

His shoulders jump up in a small shrug as he tucks his hands into the pockets of his jacket. "I guess I just choose to see the good in people."

There's an ache in my chest hearing those words. Not only have I chosen to jump to the worst possible conclusion about Dylan, but I'm also constantly looking for the worst in everyone. I squeeze my eyes shut, then look away. "And I'm a complete asshole."

"No, Kenz. You aren't," he sighs, reaching forward to comb my hair behind my ear. I flinch as his fingers graze my jawline. His touch is slight, but it sets my skin on fire. "I get why your mind went to a dark place. And you don't owe me anything. Not your trust. Not anything. Look, I'm not perfect. In fact, I'm far from it, but I swear to you, I would never do anything to hurt you."

He steps toward me, closing the space between us. My heart beats out of sync when I feel his hand in mine. "I can promise you that."

A hurricane of thoughts whir through my mind.

I'm hearing him, but all I can see is flashing lights and neon signs of warning. My heart longs to let him in, but my mind looks for reasons to push him away. I'm not ready to open up to him.

Not yet.

I swallow down the lump in my throat, sliding my hand out from his. "Why do you have a warehouse anyway? Why do you need marine grade paint?"

"Will you let me show you?" It sounds like such a simple question, but it carries with it a cathartic undertone. He trusts me with whatever he has in that warehouse.

"Okay."

He turns, moving toward the building where he slips the key inside the padlock. The doors squeak loudly as they slide along their tracks, revealing a vast black space. He beckons me to come forward, holding out his hand despite the pitch-black darkness inside.

Hesitantly, I step forward and slip my palm into his again, ignoring the wave of electricity that shoots through my core. He pulls me into the shadows, drawing me into his warmth as his other hand searches the wall for the light switch.

A few seconds later, a fluorescent light flickers above before bathing the whole space in bright light. The warehouse is huge, taking up twice the amount of space as Kristen and Henley's house would. A pitched roof hangs high above us and there are random pieces of hardware scattered on its outskirts. Tools, paint cans, buckets full of various cleaning products, and there in the centre of it all, a work in progress.

A passion project.

A boat propped up on stands.

"Wow," I whisper, my mouth gaping open as I take it all in. I wander toward the huge vessel, trailing my fingers along its paint-chipped hull. I don't know much about boats, but I can tell this one needs a lot of work. "Is it yours?"

"Sure is."

He motions for me to follow him around to the stern, where a ladder rests up against it. He swiftly climbs it, jumping into the back, then he leans forward to take my hand as I follow him up.

I clamber aboard, looking around in amazement. There are several seats at the back and a few at the front, a cabin in the centre where a steering wheel sits on a dash that looks a little worse for wear.

"You bought a boat? How?" The second I ask the question I realise how silly it sounds. "Oh, of course. You're rich."

He lets out a laugh. "*Was* rich."

"Sure. Okay. So you bought this back when you were rich?" I smirk.

"If I'd have been loaded when I bought it, I would have bought one that didn't need so much work."

I contemplate this. "Fair point."

"Actually, that's probably not true." He tilts his head to the side in thought, a hint of aversion in his tone as he continues. "My whole life I've had people there to do everything for me. Clean my house, cook my food, dry-clean my clothes. I mean, I've grown up with a mother who pays people to organise her closet and a father that has someone drive him to his meetings. It's kind of sickening when I really think about it."

I quirk an eyebrow, absorbing his words. It's moments like this that make me realise how vastly different our lives have been. "Does this little diatribe of yours have a point?"

He aims a smile my way, then he turns and runs his hand along the edges of the boat. "I know. I know. I sound like an ungrateful asshole. It's just that, in all honesty, I grew tired of paying people to do things I'm capable of doing on my own. That's why I chose this boat. I wanted to take something that needed some love and make it my own. Rebuild it from the ground up. Does that make sense?"

"Yeah. It does."

"When I first told my father that working for the company wasn't working out for me, I had my suspicions that he might try something extreme," he explains. "And I was right. I was supposed to receive my trust fund when I turned twenty-one, but he pulled some strings and had the funds withheld until I turn thirty."

"He can do that?"

"Sure. It pays to have friends in high places, I guess." He huffs out a sour laugh. "I knew from that moment that this was the way he was going to control me. With money. And that was the same moment I decided I didn't care. I just wanted to do something worthwhile. Something that made me happy. So, I worked for him for a bit longer. Then I took what I had left in my account, paid upfront for a couple of years to lease this warehouse and I bought this boat."

"You did all of this before you even moved to Cliff Haven?"

He nods. "This is it. This is my dream."

"To have your own boat?"

"To have my own charter boat," he corrects. "I want to start my own company. To specialise in taking people out to see endangered species and educating them on conservation."

"Endangered species, huh?" I say, quirking an eyebrow. "Like the one you tried to show me?"

His chuckle reverberates off the warehouse walls. "You're never going to let that go, are you?"

"Probably not." I fight to keep a grin contained.

He walks to the front of the cabin, wrapping his hands around the steering wheel. "I can see it now. This baby all fixed up, the open sea ahead." He playfully waves an arm in front as though imagining the ocean before us.

"So, this is it?" I ask, moving in beside him. "This is why you gave up all of your money."

"This is the dream."

"Does she float?"

"Probably not," he laughs. "But she will. Hey, you should have seen her when I first got her. She was in even worse shape than this."

"Even worse than this?" I mock, jabbing him in the ribs. It has me remembering the tattoo I'd seen the day of the tour. The script that made its way across his torso. "Fortune favours the brave, huh?"

He lets out a breath, dipping his chin to his chest before his eyes find mine again. "You think I'm insane, don't you."

"No," I say, daring to lean in closer. "Right now, I think you're the coolest person I've ever met."

"Really?" he whispers, lowering his head to mine. His breath is warm on my cheek as I inhale the scent of cologne and fresh linen.

"Yeah," I whisper back, touching my forehead to his. "But don't get too excited. That could change tomorrow."

He smiles, his eyes lingering on my mouth before his lips gently graze mine. Then I close the gap between us. I seemed to have somehow quietened the negative thoughts, given my heart free rein.

Heat shoots up my spine as his tongue caresses mine, slowly but with purpose. His arms curl around my waist, pulling me in against him. When my hands find their way into his hair, I surrender myself to the moment. I lose my breath, the butterflies bouncing off the walls of my chest as his fingers glide upward from my hips, his thumbs dragging along the skin there.

And that's when everything falls apart.

I haven't experienced this feeling in what seems like a lifetime, but the memory is there, raw and real. There's only been one other time I've ever felt remotely like this.

And it didn't end well.

And just like that, the spell is broken.

It's too much. Too soon.

My palms push against Dylan's chest as I gasp for air, hating myself, but hating him more.

Ethan.

The one who broke my spirit. Who left me a mere shell.

Dylan lets me go immediately, but I don't miss the hurt in his expression.

"I'm sorry," I say, backing away, my body trembling.

"Don't be," he rasps, his gravelly voice low but unexpectedly comforting. "It's okay."

I shake my head. "It's not. I'm sorry," I repeat as I stare at the floor of the boat between us.

"Kenz." I close my eyes as he utters the nickname he's given me, his voice a mere whisper as he slowly steps forward. He reaches out, tilting my face up to meet his. The sincerity in his gaze crushes me. "It's okay. Come on. I'll take you home."

I nod, allowing him to lead me down the ladder and back to the car.

Chapter 20

DYLAN

The surf is warm this morning, but my usual energy doesn't follow me into the water. I find myself mostly just sitting on my board, allowing the waves to pass underneath me. I've even lost my concentration and been pummelled by a bomb or two.

Mackenzie has had an effect on me. One I don't know what to do with.

I'm drawn to her in a way that I've never been to anybody else. It's not a secret that I've dated a lot of women, but I've never had serious feelings. Not like this. I'd wanted her last night. That kiss had been everything, but with Mackenzie, I know I need to have patience.

Chance is waiting for me when I arrive back at the beach house. He bounds off the back porch, tailing wagging, tongue hanging out as he picks up a piece of driftwood between his teeth. He nudges my thigh, begging me to initiate a game of fetch. I drop down onto the top front step, staring out at the ocean in the distance.

"Not now, boy. I'm not in the mood."

He lets out a whine then flops down on the deck beside me.

"I don't know what the hell I'm doing anymore, Chance. I feel like I'm losing my mind," I say out loud. "I mean, obviously I am. I'm talking to my dog." I blow out a long breath. "I just really like her though, you know?"

I glance over at the furry canine beside me like he has the ability to answer, then shake my head at how absurd I'm being.

I've never really cared too much about what other people think, but when Mackenzie had doubted my character, it had cut deep. I want her to like me. I just didn't realise how much. Now my every thought seems to revolve around her, but I know I need to take things slow. The last thing I want is to scare her away.

Chance lifts his head, then his tongue swipes my hand. I give his head a rough scratch. "I've got you though, right? We're a team."

A soft whiny whimper leaves him as he sits up, suddenly at attention, his eyes scanning the beach ahead. Out of nowhere a white dog about the same size as Chance comes bounding from the right. He lets out a bark and then takes off down the steps, running toward his newfound companion.

"Oh, come on!" I throw my hands up in the air, then mutter under my breath. "Traitor."

My ringtone blasts from the jacket I'd left hanging over the railing this morning before my surf.

I throw my head back, a low groan rumbling through my chest. "What now?"

I haul myself up, rifling through the pockets until I retrieve my phone. The word 'Mum' flashes across the screen and I slump my shoulders, defeated. Well, this is going to be fun.

I swipe the answer key. "Hey, Mum."

"Don't you 'Hey, Mum' me." My mother's patronising voice comes sternly through the line. "You better have a good explanation for why you disappeared from the party the other night."

I shift uncomfortably, lifting the beach towel from the railing and dabbing at my chest. I'd known these questions were coming. Had I not been so wrapped up in proving myself to Mackenzie I would have better prepared for this conversation.

"I had some stuff I had to deal with." I attempt a weak explanation, knowing it won't even nearly be satisfactory. "I'm sorry I left."

Despite our current family drama, I do feel remorseful for leaving the party early. It wasn't my parent's fault that Madison and Skye had dredged up the past with Mackenzie, or that I hadn't been open with her about the lion's den she was walking into. That one's on me.

"What kind of stuff?" she persists.

"Mackenzie needed to get home is all," I reply, realising as I say it that it was not the best choice of words. It only gives my mother fuel to further dislike her.

"Of course," she says, reading into my words.

I decide to steer the conversation in a different direction. "Did you have a good time at the party? I know you put a lot of effort into planning it."

Or Claire and the party planner did. Nonetheless, flattery

will get you everywhere with my mother and it's a sure way to change the subject.

"It was fine." Her tone is clipped. "The caterers made some errors and there was an issue with the oyster tower, but the rest of the evening went off without a hitch."

"That's great, Mum. I'm really glad to hear it," I say. I mean it. My parents work hard, and they deserved to enjoy their celebration. "Listen, I just got out of the water and I need to take a shower so..."

"Ah yes," she says, as though she's just had a lightbulb moment. "That reminds me."

"Me needing to take a shower has jogged your memory?"

"Don't be a smartass, Dylan," she chides. "No. You gallivanting around that miserable beach town has. I don't know why you insist on staying there when you have responsibilities here."

"Not anymore, Mum. I quit. It's time you both accepted that."

She lets out an audible frustrated sigh and continues as though she hasn't even heard me. "The reason I was calling was to ask you to please reconsider your decision not to come home."

"Of course it was," I mutter.

The demanding tone she uses with me is unappealing. "You know how happy it would make your father if you just came back to the Abbott Group."

I have no doubt it would make my father ecstatic, but at what cost? I'd be trading my own happiness for his.

"Mum," I sigh. "I'm trying to forge my own path in life and all I keep hearing about is how much I've disappointed you all.

I'm sorry I'm not the son Dad envisioned I'd be, but I'm happy here."

"You could be happier," she retaliates. "And you know what your father is like. I'm worried if things don't go his way, he might resort to something drastic."

"I doubt it."

He's already disowned me from the family. What else could he possibly do?

"I'm not so sure," she says. "You know what he's like when he gets upset, Dylan."

"But he shouldn't be upset." I'm losing my patience now. "I'm a grown adult capable of making my own decisions."

I hear her scoff from the other end of the line. "You sure have a funny way of showing it. You've bruised his ego. His pride is damaged."

His pride? What about mine? "What are you talking about?"

"He'll be retiring in a few years from now. How do you think it looks to the world that his only son doesn't want to take over the family business. Surely, you've seen the things that are circulating in the press. The things they're saying about you."

"I've never paid attention to gossip, Mum." I groan, hanging the towel around my neck. The wooden floorboards creak below my feet as I move down the hall to the shower. "And I'm not about to start now."

"You're impossible."

"I love you too, Mum. I'll talk to you soon."

With that I end the call, placing the phone down on the basin. I flick on the faucet, awaiting the water to heat. I almost wish I had to work today. That I had something to distract me from what my mother had just said, but my shift at the tavern doesn't start until tonight.

Would my dad really do something radical? I shake away the irrational thought. This was just my mother's way of manipulating me to come back.

I step under the hot water, hoping it will wash away the tension.

It doesn't.

But when my thoughts become too much, I think of Mackenzie.

Chapter 21

MACKENZIE

The bus ride into Seabright Cove takes forever. Or maybe it just feels that way because I can't stop thinking about Dylan and the kiss we shared last night.

I don't even know what came over me. It was completely out of character for me to make such a bold move, but I'm not that far deep in denial to know that there are some serious feelings at play. At least, there is on my part.

Those feelings go hand in hand with overwhelming insecurities. I can't stop wondering what they mean and whether my trust is something I can just offer up on a silver platter to somebody who has inadvertently deceived me on more than one occasion.

Dylan is a good guy though. Kristen knows it. Harper knows it. On some deeper level, even I know it, and yet, that is the very quality that made me so wary of him in the first place.

Go figure.

My head is not a safe space for me to be today, full of second-guessing and denial. I'd decided a trip to the one place that managed to get me out of it was in order, which is why I'm currently skipping down the steps of the bus onto the street across from the Abstract Palette.

There's an almost whimsical glow surrounding the studio as I enter, the sunlight penetrating the bay windows at just the right angle. Grace looks up from what looks to be a small lump of terracotta clay that she's delicately moulding between her fingers. It isn't just her attention the tiny bell resonating above the door has captured though. Betty and May are also watching me, lifting their palms in greeting.

"Well, look who the cat dragged in." Betty is all sass, a smile letting me know that she means her words light-heartedly.

"Mackenzie!" Grace beams. She rises from the table, moving swiftly in my direction. "What a lovely surprise."

"Hi," I say, fidgeting with the strap on my bag. "I hope it's okay that I came by."

"You're always welcome," she replies warmly, resting a hand on my upper arm. Her gentle touch takes the edge away, that sense of serenity I've come to know in her presence washing over me.

"Thank you."

"Come and sit with us, Mackenzie," May shouts across the room, her slender hand raised high in the air as she waves us over.

Grace lets out a soft laugh. "Looks like you've made fast friends with those two."

I can't help but smile as I head over to the table where the two older women sit, both of them working on some type of handmade pottery projects.

"Here," May says, tossing a chunk of modelling clay in front of me. "Make something."

"Uh, okay." I take the clay and begin kneading it. It's tough at first as I compress it between my palms, but it gradually softens as I continue.

"So, you decided to come back, hey?" Betty says, giving me side-eye. "I'm glad we didn't scare you off."

I turn to her, my lips pulling in a one-sided grin. There's something endearing about this old, white-haired woman and the attitude she exudes. In many ways, it's like looking into a mirror. One in the distant future anyway.

"Oh, you'll have to do a lot worse than that to scare me off."

"Did you get a chance to think about what we talked about the other day, Mackenzie?" Grace asks, dropping down into a chair beside me.

"The art exhibition night?" I ask. "Yeah. I thought about it. I'd really love to, but I can't figure out what to paint on my canvas."

"I'm sure you'll figure something out," Grace says, picking up the piece of clay she'd been moulding when I arrived.

"It can't be that hard to think of something. Maybe your sexy diver friend could be your muse," Betty states.

I'm so stunned at her remark I nearly drop the handful of terracotta, my mouth gaping open in shock. "What!? I never said he was sexy!" I retaliate.

She hums in response, a small shrug lifting her petite shoulders. "In my mind he is."

"Of course, he is," May responds gruffly. "Because you're a horn dog, Betty."

I glance over at Grace and see her lips pressed into a tight line. Like me, she's suppressing a fit of chuckles. A few seconds later, we fail to control ourselves and bursts of laughter explode around the table. Even Betty herself can't help but giggle.

May slumps her shoulders, leaning into me. "Is he though?" she whispers loudly.

"Oh, sure, May," Betty chides. "Now who's the horn dog?"

"Ladies. I think we've established that you're both clearly horn dogs." I dump the clay on the table in front of me. I expect the two women to carry on with their art but instead their eyes remain eagerly trained on me, awaiting my response. "Fine. Okay, yes. He is."

"I knew it!" Betty says excitedly, slamming her bony hands down on the table.

As hard as I try, I can't stop the smirk that spreads across my face.

"Wait a minute." From the corner of my eye, I can see May watching me intently. "Something happened with this boy, didn't it? You're different today."

"I am not," I argue.

I avoid eye contact with the three women, choosing to retrieve the clay and focus my attention on it, but with every passing second, I can feel my face warming with the blush that creeps up from my neck.

"Yes, you are," Betty joins in.

"Now now, ladies. Let's give her some breathing room," Grace says. "If Mackenzie wanted you to know her business, she'd tell you."

"I kissed him," I blurt.

The women are silent as I let out a long breath. It had felt good to offer that information up to these virtual strangers. I mean, sure, I could have confided in Harper, but she's biased and would tell me straight up to go for Dylan when that could be the worst idea ever.

I look up to find three pairs of eyes fixated on me before Betty's shriek carries across the table. "Slay!"

The rest of us can't help but laugh at her response. "Slay?" I repeat.

"Yeah. Isn't that what all the kids are saying these days?" she asks, waving a hand at the rest of us.

"Oh, stop trying to stay relevant, you old biddy," May grumbles.

"It's a thing, May!" Betty argues. "I heard it on the TikTok!"

I shake my head, restraining another giggle as I absent-mindedly manipulate the terracotta.

"You really like this boy." Grace muses.

My eyes snap upward meeting her cool, icy irises. "Yeah," I sigh. "Unfortunately, I think I do."

Normally it would take a lot for me to admit something like this. I couldn't even admit it to Harper, but here in this circle of women I barely know, I feel as though my secret is safe.

"Unfortunately?" Grace's forehead crumples as her gaze softens.

"I don't exactly have the best track record." I let out an anxious laugh. I may have felt comfortable to share with them my feelings for Dylan, but I'm not sure unpacking the baggage I've accumulated over my lifespan would be a fantastic idea today. "It's complicated."

"Life's complicated, girly," May says, a finger pointed at me.

"You're telling me," I begin. "I don't -"

"I wasn't finished," she cuts me off. Her lips are pursed together in a thin line. It's honestly kind of scary.

"Sorry, May," I apologise begrudgingly. "What were you saying?"

"I was saying, life is complicated." She pauses deep in thought and for a moment I begin to think she might have forgotten what she was actually going to say. "But it ain't worth living without love in it."

My eyebrows shoot upward as I absorb the old woman's words. "You make it sound so simple."

"Hey, what's that you've got there?" Betty asks gesturing to the clay in my hands.

I hold it up for her to see. Without even thinking about it, I've moulded it into a miniature shark, much like the one that Dylan had led me to on the snorkel tour.

"Oh, she's good," May says to Grace, nodding toward the clay shark in my palm.

"She sure is," Grace agrees. "I knew this one had artistic talent the second I saw her."

I smile back at Grace. Her words are kind, but I remember the first time Grace saw me.

It wasn't the day she'd spoken to me on the park bench, my art book resting in my lap as I'd shaded in the colours of the sunset. It had been the day she watched me from the pier as I went for my morning run. Then again, when her stare had found mine through the tavern's windows. I still haven't been able to erase the image of her, the expression of anguish I'd witnessed on her face. I still wondered where that sadness came from.

"Well, I'd love to stay and chat some more, ladies, but I have lawn bowls in twenty minutes, and I need time to warm up these old muscles." May rises from her seat and ambles over to the table on the far side of the room where she lays her project gently.

"I need to get moving too," Betty adds. "I'm going to the matinee session of Chicago at the Seabright theatre. Found myself a gentleman friend that loves musicals as much as I do." She gives us a wink as she too, stands with her art piece – a tiny planter pot.

"Horn dog," May mutters as Betty shuffles past her.

Grace shakes her head, chuckling under her breath. "These two. I swear, you never know how things are going to play out when they're in the same room together. Great artists though."

I laugh, moving to the table to place the small shark I've just made down. Betty and May wander to the sink to wash their hands.

"Don't worry about cleaning up, ladies. I've got it under control," Grace says.

"Are you sure?" They both say in unison as they hold their soapy hands under the running water.

"Oh, yes. It's fine." Grace waves a dismissive hand their way. "I'd hate for you to be late to your activities."

"We'll be back for tomorrow's oil painting class, Grace," Betty hollers. "And Mackenzie?"

I swivel around at the sound of my name. "Yes, Betty."

"Grace is right. You are very talented." She pats her hands dry with a piece of paper towel, then tosses it into the waste basket. "That blank canvas of yours. Something tells me it could be the best work in the exhibition if you just paint something that moves you. Something that makes you feel alive."

I give her a subtle nod, forcing a smile. If only it were that easy.

A moment later, the two of them disappear out the door and I turn my attention back to Grace.

"I can help you clean up," I offer.

"There really isn't a whole lot to be done. I just need to wipe down the tables and get set up for the next class. I have about fifteen people joining me for some charcoal drawing. You're quite welcome to stay."

"That sounds fun." I contemplate her offer. I'd have to catch a later bus home, but I could make it work. "I'll start wiping down the tables."

Grace smiles warmly back at me as I turn for the sink and grab a sponge. "Thank you for your help, Mackenzie."

"It's the least I can do. I haven't even paid for a lesson yet." I swipe the clay from the tabletop, scrubbing at the parts that have dried on the surface. "Which reminds me. My two free sessions are up. How much are your weekly classes? I'm pretty busy with work but I'd love to come down once a week and try out some new techniques."

Plus, I could really use the escape from reality.

I feel Grace's eyes on me as I wander back to the sink to rinse out the sponge. I squeeze it under the running water, watching as the terracotta-coloured swirls circle the drain.

"You'd really like to keep coming back?" she asks.

"Yeah, of course. I like your studio. I think it's really cool."

Grace's smile grows wider as she moves toward me, though her expression is contradictory. Her eyes don't mirror the happiness in her smile. Instead, they're haunted with sadness.

"Um… are you okay?" I ask.

She clears her throat, turning to gather some art paper from a drawer underneath the bench. Her voice is clipped when she replies. "Yes. I'd love for you to come back. For as many classes as you'd like. Free of charge."

"I don't understand."

Why would she offer me these classes for free? It doesn't make sense.

There's a faraway look in her vacant teary-eyed stare that sends a sense of unease through me. The speed at which her mood has changed from pleasant to tortured is unsettling. I watch as she picks up the little shark I'd moulded mere minutes ago.

"You seem to have a natural talent," she says, delicately turning it over in her palm. "Your mother was the same."

Her words hit me like an ice-cold rush to the head, an almost physical jolt wracking my body. I'm frozen, unable to respond, my breath caught in my throat.

I must have heard her wrong. I must have.

It feels like forever before I finally manage to choke out a reply. "What did you say?"

Her gaze snaps to mine, her clear blue-grey stare wide with shock as the realisation of her admission begins to sink in.

"Oh, I'm sorry, Mackenzie," she gasps. "I shouldn't have just blurted that out. I wanted to say something to you sooner." A single tear rolls down her cheek as a wrinkled hand comes up to her mouth. "I just didn't know how."

"To tell me what?"

Her eyes close as she inhales a shaky breath, but still, she says nothing.

My heart thrashes against the walls of my chest. "What are you saying, Grace? Do you know my mother?"

"Yes," she croaks. "Very well."

"How well, exactly?" I whisper.

She shakes her head, her clear, blue stare focused purely on mine as her brow pulls down in sadness. She doesn't answer me though.

She doesn't have to.

Because when I look at her, really look at her, the answer is staring me in the face.

I see myself in the reflection of her storm-blue eyes. Her wavy hair, ash blonde streaked with grey, is wild and untamed. So much like the girl's golden strands in the painting hanging above us.

So much like mine.

It doesn't make any sense that she's standing here before me. A woman I never knew to exist. And yet, here she is. An enigma I'm struggling to comprehend. It's only when I speak the words out loud that their meaning begins to register.

"You're my grandmother."

She nods, the corners of her mouth drawing downward, a frown creating deepened lines across her forehead.

My instincts tell me to run.

To remove myself from this situation. At least until I can have the time to process it.

But I can't leave without asking her the one question that has plagued me most of my life.

"Where is she?" I murmur. "Where's my mother?"

Even before her face crumples in agony, before her weathered hands begin to shake, before she opens her mouth to speak, I know.

I know something isn't right.

"Gone."

Gone? What does that even mean? The definition of gone is vast. It could mean anything in this context. She could have gone into town, gone on vacation, fled the country to the other side of the world, but there's a heaviness in the way she says the word that lets me know. A finality unsubtle in its meaning.

"Gone where?" I dare to ask, knowing full well that the answer she's about to provide is not the one I want to hear.

Her voice breaks, reaching a pitch I've never heard from her before. "She passed away, Mackenzie. Almost a year ago now."

A fierce pain rips through my chest. "No," I wheeze, shaking my head in denial. I am not ready to hear this. I'll never be ready. "You're lying."

I back toward the door as she reaches for me, tears now streaming steadily from her eyes.

"Please, don't go!" she pleads. "Please don't leave like this. We need to talk."

I pull away from her, saying the one thing I know in this moment to be true. "I can't be here."

The bell above the door chimes as I throw it open, ringing more haunting than inviting in my ears now. As I step out onto the street, I feel as though I'm living someone else's life.

But of course, this is happening to me.

Of course, it is.

I pick up speed, no real idea where I'm heading, just knowing I need far away from this place. When my lungs are burning, my muscles spent, I find myself near a small shopping village nestled in a bay. My feet carry me to the water's edge, and I collapse down onto the sand, the full weight of what I've just been told sinking through my bones like lead.

Truth be told, I don't know how I'm supposed to react. My mother has been gone for most of my life. I didn't know if there would ever be a day that I'd see her again. It's only now that I know that day will never come that I realise I had hope.

A tiny slither of faith that maybe one day she'd spring back into my life. That she'd tell me how sorry she was, and I'd have the chance to forgive her.

How could she be gone?

I don't know how long I sit here, the silence of the beach a total contrast to the overwhelming volume of my thoughts, but it's long enough for the sky to change colour.

When the sun has almost set, I find a bus stop across from the shopping village and board a bus back to Cliff Haven.

My tears hold out until I'm about halfway home and I wonder then if I'll ever be able to stop them. I've never been much of a crier, but they pour out of me soundlessly now like rain through a floodgate.

My thoughts take me to places I don't want to go, leaving a myriad of questions in their wake. How will I explain all of this to Kristen? Does my father already know? Surely, he wouldn't have left me wondering about her existence if he did.

Fat heavy droplets begin to fall on the roof of the bus, cascading down the windows, blurring the world outside. I'm so caught up in my grief, I forget to look at where I am. I squint out at the dark street, realising I've missed my stop.

"Shit," I curse as I stand up, swiping at my eyes. I stumble down the aisle to the bus driver. "I need to get off."

The bus comes to a halt a little further down the road. When the door swings open with an audible hiss, I burst out onto the street.

I scan the area, gathering my surroundings. I'm at the beach. If I take the shortcut through the beach trail, I might be able to cut a few minutes off the twenty-minute journey across town.

I cross the street, startled by a car horn and the screeching of tires. I hold up a hand in apology as the headlights blind me, leaving a trail of silver along the wet road. Then I race toward the trail, my hair clinging to my shoulders in thick strands, the crop top and jeans I'm wearing completely soaked through.

There's been a sharp temperature drop, the icy wind blowing through the fibres of my wet clothing. I know the cold should bother me, but I'm numb.

Tears fill my vision as the ground blurs in front of me, the trees creating black shadows in the darkening night. I make it to the start of the trail when everything starts to spin.

I stumble, tripping over a tree branch. My hands shoot out in time to brace myself from the full weight of the fall, but they hadn't been able to stop me completely.

I push myself up into a sitting position, my jeans now coated in mud, my hands filthy.

"Mackenzie!" A voice cuts through the air. "Mackenzie!"

Panic replaces the air in my chest, my body frozen in place.

"*I'm coming for you, Mackenzie. You can run but you can't hide.*"

"*Ethan! No!*" *My scream echoes through the trees.*

His hands are on me now, smothering and all-consuming.

He's going to kill me this time. I'm sure of it.

I scramble to my knees, but he still claws at me.

My body feels so heavy. I don't know how much fight I have left.

I'm losing the will to get back up as his voice begins to fade into the background.

I close my eyes, surrendering.

"Mackenzie, it's me."

Chapter 22

DYLAN

For the first time in a long while, I wish I didn't have to work tonight.

I'm not entirely sure why. Maybe it's the conversation I'd had earlier with my mother, the feeling that I'm constantly disappointing the two people who brought me into this world.

Or maybe it's because I know Mackenzie isn't rostered on, and the shifts I have with her have become my favourite.

Maybe it's the weather.

But also, maybe it's Mackenzie.

The rain hasn't let up for the past hour and I'm already half-drenched before I make it to the car. I reverse out of the driveway, turning onto the quiet street when a bolt of lightning illuminates the darkness.

I slow down a little further along the road, giving way to a bus, but soon after I press my foot to the accelerator, I'm hitting the brakes again as a figure darts out in front of me.

I lurch forward, my hands braced tightly on the wheel, staring through the blur of thick rain that tumbles down the windshield at the woman in front of me.

She pauses, a deer in the headlights, her long curls dampened straight by the downpour. She raises her left arm to shield her face from the light.

A face that I know all too well.

She darts off across the road, tripping at the entrance to the beach trail. I squint through the rain-soaked window in time to watch her fall to her knees. I don't know what the hell Mackenzie is doing out here. I only know that I need to get to her.

Awareness kicks in as a car horn blares behind me, a reminder that I'm still stopped in the middle of the road. I swiftly pull over to the side and launch myself out of the car, racing in her direction.

"Mackenzie!" I call out as I reach the trail's entrance. "Mackenzie!"

As I draw nearer, her light, denim, mud-splattered jeans come into focus, but it's not until she pushes her hair back from her panic-stricken face, that I realise something is very wrong.

There's a jolt in my chest at the sight of her distraught expression, her cheeks caked with streaks of mud as tears stream from her eyes, her petite rain-soaked body wracking with sobs.

"Mackenzie."

Even if she can hear me, she doesn't respond, scrambling to her feet and bolting further down the track. At this point,

I'm concerned for her safety, so I sprint after her, settling a hand on her shoulder when she comes within reach.

She turns, thrashing at me with wild arms. "Get off me!"

"Mackenzie, it's me," I say as tenderly as I can over the pelting of the rain. I try to be gentle as I attempt to restrain her hands. She's a small woman but she's strong.

"No!" she screams again.

Reaching my arms around her, I pull her back into my chest. I squeeze her wrists tighter, hating that I need to use force to calm her down. Dropping my chin to her shoulder, I speak softly into her ear. "It's me. It's Dylan."

The fight suddenly leaves her, her body sagging against mine. Her breathing is ragged as she slowly turns to face me, the terror in her eyes still there. "Dylan?"

I nod, my chest rising and falling with heavy breaths. "It's me."

"You're not him." She gasps the words out.

It doesn't take a genius to guess who she had mistaken me for. Her ex has put her through more than any person deserves to go through. A few choice words come to mind when I think of him, but she doesn't need to hear those right now. She needs my reassurance. To know that she is safe. Her mind has gone somewhere dark, and I need to bring her back to me. "I'd never hurt you, Kenz."

Her bottom lip trembles as she takes a hesitant step forward, pausing before closing the final gap between us.

She collapses into my chest and I envelope her in my arms, wrapping one hand around her waist, caressing the back of her head with the other. My fingers thread through her damp hair as she chokes out another sob.

"It's okay, Kenz. You're gonna be okay."

The rain pelts down on us harder now as another bolt of lightning cracks through the otherwise black sky, illuminating Mackenzie's distant icy blue stare as she pulls back from me.

"It's not okay," she murmurs just loud enough for me to hear. "Nothing is okay."

My brows pinch as I search for meaning behind her words. I want to know what has happened to her. What has changed since the kiss we shared on the boat?

But it isn't safe here.

"Come on," I say. "Let's get you somewhere dry."

I lead her to my car through the onslaught of rain. This time, when I open the passenger door for her, she doesn't fight me with some silly remark. Instead, she slumps into the seat, pulling her knees up to her chest and tucking her head down in between them.

This is definitely not the Mackenzie that I've come to know and seeing this version of her has me rattled. It's incredibly out of character for her to show emotion like this. To admit vulnerability.

I tug my phone out of my pocket and pull up Jesse's contact as I race around to the driver's door. He answers on the second ring. "Hey, bro."

"Jesse, hey. Is there any way you are free right now and can do me the hugest favour?"

"You need me at the tavern?"

I raise the volume of my voice to compete with the pouring rain. "Yeah. Look, I wouldn't ask if it wasn't crazy important, but I need you to start earlier. Like, now. If you can. I don't think I'm going to make it in there tonight."

"Sure. Everything okay?"

"I'm not sure," I say, as I pull open the door. "But I'm going to find out."

I end the call as I slide into the car. The windows quickly fog up with our body heat, the driving rain still blurring the occasional oncoming headlights.

"Kenz," I say gently. "What's wrong? Did something happen?"

I watch as her chest rises with an unsteady breath, but she doesn't answer my question. Her stare is directed at the dashboard, her arms still wrapped around her knees.

"Kenz, I'm worried. Is it Kristen? Is everyone okay?"

I don't miss the slight crease between her brows before she turns her cold, blue gaze on me. Even with bloodshot eyes and blotchy cheeks, she's still the most beautiful woman I've ever seen.

"It's not like that," she whispers. "Everyone is fine. Do you think you could just drive?"

She squeezes her eyes shut and a tear runs from each corner and even though I have no idea what has caused them, I feel her sorrow like a punch to the gut. I understand that she isn't ready to talk about whatever has her upset and I can respect that.

"Okay. Is Kristen or Henley home?" I reach across her to retrieve her seatbelt and click it into place around her shivering body.

The quick shake of her head that follows is so slight I could have missed it. Then she's resting her chin on her knees again. There's no way I'm taking her back to an empty house in this state. I can't bear the thought of leaving her alone right now.

Within two minutes we're pulling into the tiny driveway out the front of my beach shack. I round the car, opening Mackenzie's door and carefully helping her to her feet. She's trembling profusely now, the cold rain having soaked her skin. "Come on. Let's get you dry."

There's no sign of Chance on the porch as I lead Mackenzie up the weather-beaten steps, but I'll have to deal with him later. He's a smart dog and knowing him, he's found refuge underneath the house somewhere.

I guide her through the front door and straight down the hall to the bathroom. Her own arms are wrapped around her waist, the water from her jeans pooling at our feet. Her tears seem to have run out, but she still hasn't spoken another word and I'm rendered utterly helpless. I need to know what I can do to make things better for her.

I lean down, pressing my lips to her cold, clammy forehead. "I'll get you some towels."

I duck into the hall, retrieving the nicest bath towels I own from the linen closet and place them near the bathroom sink. She hasn't moved, her teeth chattering as she stares down at the porcelain tiles. I go to her, wrapping my arms around her again, rubbing at the goosebumps on her arms. I'm not sure how much it does for her though, given that I'm soaked through as well.

"You're freezing, Kenz. We need to get you warm." I pull the shower curtain aside and reach an arm out to turn on the hot water, adjusting the faucet until the temperature is right.

She begins unbuttoning her jeans and my heart races as they drop to the floor. She seems dazed, completely disconnected. I still have no idea what has gotten her so upset but watching her battle this inner turmoil breaks me.

I can't resist drawing her near to me one last time before I leave the room. My fingers slide up her neck until I'm cupping her face in my hands. "I'm going to get you some dry clothes, okay?"

The subtlest of nods is the only sign that she has heard me. I leave the door ajar as I sprint to my room and rummage through my drawers in search of something suitable. Whatever I choose is going to be way too big for her, but I settle on a pair of grey sweatpants and a black t-shirt with the logo of the local surf shop on it.

When I return to the bathroom, the door is still partially open, and I can see that the shower curtain has been closed over. I reach a hand in between the crack, placing the clothes on the basin for Mackenzie to find.

Once I've returned to my room, I remove my own wet clothes, dressing in a pair of sweatpants and a plain white t-shirt. The pipes in this house are noisy as hell, so I instantly know when Mackenzie shuts off the water.

A few minutes later, she emerges from the bathroom, wandering awkwardly into my room, her legs bare, the hem of the t-shirt I gave her falling mid-thigh.

"I tried the pants," she says, brushing her wet hair back from her face. "But they wouldn't stay up."

A sad smile tugs at my mouth as I watch her pull at the bottom of the shirt before folding her arms across her chest. I move to the dresser and open the top drawer, reaching in for my light blue hoodie. It's oversized on me so I know it will hang a little lower than the t-shirt I gave her to wear, plus it will keep her warm.

She raises her arms above her as I approach, allowing me to loop the soft fabric over her head. She fumbles with the sleeves as I gently tug her hair from the hood and smooth it out behind her. I frown when her face crumples slightly, a sign she's holding back more tears.

"What is it, Kenz?"

"I'm sorry," she sobs.

"Hey. Look at me," I beckon. She raises her glacial gaze to mine. "You have nothing to be sorry about."

"But you're missing your shift."

I shake my head. "Don't worry about that. I'd miss my shift a thousand times over if it meant I got to see how gorgeous you look in my hoodie."

A mangled laugh leaves her as she chokes back another sob.

"Seriously." I turn her cheek, drawing her eyes back to mine. "There's no place I'd rather be than here with you."

I wish I could scoop her up in my arms and hold her until her sadness disappears, but this is Mackenzie. I need to practice some restraint with her, though I know that despite her tough exterior, she's more fragile than she lets on.

She is a domestic violence survivor and I know next to nothing about what that means for her. The way she'd freaked out at the trail tonight only proves that she's wrestling demons I know nothing about. I'm going to have to muster up more patience than I ever have before.

But I can do that. For her, I'd do anything.

"Come on." I slip my hand in hers and lead her to the living room.

"I like your place," she says, dropping down onto the couch, her eyes scanning the small dining table by the window and the closed, white curtains that primarily hide the french doors at the back of the room.

"Thanks," I say, rubbing the back of my neck. "Better than a vacation mansion out on the cape?"

The hint of a smile pulls at the corners of her mouth, but it doesn't meet her eyes. "Definitely."

I take the space beside her on the couch, leaving a little distance between us. It's then I notice the purple-blue bruises on her kneecaps. She must have got them when she fell down at the trail. I don't know how I hadn't noticed them before. Maybe the heat of the shower has brought them out further.

"Shit, Kenz. Your knees." I rub a distraught hand over my face.

She glances down and gives the slightest of shrugs. "It's fine. I've had worse."

My eyes flash with fury in response to her words, my jaw clenching in anger. "Don't tell me that."

I can't hear that these bruises are nothing to her. That she's had worse inflicted upon her at the hands of a man that never deserved to be graced with her existence.

She draws her knees up, hiding them under the long hem of the hoodie and I hate that I've made her feel like she has to cover up. She has nothing to be ashamed of.

"Kenz, I'm not going to push you to tell me what it is that has you so upset tonight. But I want you to know… I need you to know, that I'm here for you. Whenever you want to talk. Or not. I just…" I trail off, swallowing the lump that builds in my throat at the sight of a silent tear tracking its way down her cheek.

This amazing woman here is hurting and I've never felt so powerless. I don't know whether to draw her near or give her space. I wish I knew what she needed but she isn't easy to read.

"My mother died." The words leave her mouth so easily that I'm not sure if I've heard them correctly.

"What?"

"She died. She's gone."

"Oh, Kenz." I shuffle closer to her on the couch, my hands reaching for hers. "How? I thought you had no idea where she was."

"I don't. I didn't." She slides her fingers from my grip, swiping at her eyes, then the words rush out of her. "I met this woman at the pier one day and she told me that she liked my art. She runs a studio in Seabright Cove. I took her up on her offer to go to her art classes there and today she told me…" She pauses, inhaling deeply as though she's internally mustering up the strength to get the words out of her mouth. "She told me that she is my maternal grandmother."

I blow out a long breath, bringing my hands to the bridge of my nose. For her to have learnt that her mother has passed away the same day she discovers she has a grandmother? It's no wonder she's in this state. "That's a lot to process."

"I asked her where my mum was but somehow, I already knew. She told me she'd passed away not all that long ago." Another tear falls down her cheek. "But I don't even know whether to believe her. I mean, how did she even find me at the pier that day?"

I don't know what to say, so I just listen. I place a hand on her knee, careful to avoid the bruise.

"It's stupid," she says, swiping at her face with the sleeves of my hoodie. "I feel like an idiot. I didn't even know her. I don't have any right to be upset when she wasn't even a part of my life."

"Of course, you do," I tell her. "You have every right to be upset, or angry even. All of your feelings are valid."

She nods. "I guess there's always been this small part of me that had hope. This naïve idea that one day she'd walk back into my life. And now that dream is over. I never got to know my mother. I have no idea where I came from. And now I never will."

"I'm sorry, Kenz." I wrap my arm around her shoulder and she nuzzles into my chest.

I pull her closer, leaning back into the couch cushions behind us. We stay like that, listening to the wind howl through the sheets of roofing over the front porch and the tinny echo made by the battering rain. I hold her until her tears stop falling, knowing that there isn't anything that I can say to ease her heartache.

"Thank you," she whispers. "For taking care of me."

"Always."

She tilts her face up to mine and my arms tighten around her. I lean in, the memory of her mouth on mine in the warehouse still fresh in my mind. What I wouldn't do to live that moment all over again. I glide my fingers along her jaw, pressing my thumb to the centre of her full bottom lip.

Then my heart jerks in my chest as something crashes loudly against the back doors.

"What was that?" Mackenzie startles, her eyes brimming with fear. She unfurls herself from me and I pine the loss of her warmth.

A low groan leaves me. "That," I say, getting up and walking to the french doors, "was Chance."

I throw open the curtains to reveal a mud and rain-soaked kelpie-border collie mix.

The smile that lights up her face is real and it's almost enough to make me forget she was ever sad. "Oh my God. He's the most adorable thing."

"Are we looking at the same mutt?" I ask her sarcastically.

She rises from the couch and meets me at the doors, looking down at my brute of a dog who looks pretty damn proud of himself for getting as dirty as possible. "Hi, Chance."

Chance offers a bark in reply, his paw lifting to scratch at the other side of the door. Mackenzie laughs as I aim a warning glance at him. If only he had any idea what he had just interrupted.

"Aren't you going to let him in?"

"Are you kidding?" I ask. "Look at him. He's filthy."

She aims a pout at me. "But it's cold out there."

I could argue with her that this dog has seen much worse, having been a stray that wanders the town for sometimes days at a time, but Chance here seems to have lifted her spirits in a way that I doubt I'd ever be able to. Maybe he's just the distraction she needs.

A deep sigh deflates my chest as my eyes roll back. "Feel like helping me give a dog a bath?"

She nods, the smile on her face growing just that little bit bigger.

I open the door and wrangle Chance before he has the opportunity to cover Mackenzie in muddy paw prints and carry him down the hall. I wrestle him into the bathtub, the sound of Mackenzie's laughter resonating off the bathroom walls like music to my ears.

There is so much healing left for her to do, but for now all of that can wait. She's been through enough today and if this scruffy loveable dog can help her forget her trauma for a couple of hours, I'm happy to let him.

I hold Chance down while she shampoos him and before long the bathroom is covered in dog hair and water.

Another job that can wait for tomorrow as far as I'm concerned.

While Mackenzie dries Chance off with the blow dryer, I go to change out of my muddy clothes. My phone rings from the top of the dresser and I stare down at the screen. It's my father again, but I don't have time to deal with whatever it is he has to say right now. My priorities lie with Mackenzie. I ignore the call, leaving the phone in its place.

When I return to the living room, Mackenzie is laying on the couch. Only this time Chance is curled up against her chest. She giggles as he rolls onto his back allowing her access to give him tummy scratches and I can't help the grin that spreads across my face at the sight.

"What's this?" I say, splaying my hands out as I glare down at Chance's puppy dog eyes. "You trying to steal my favourite girl, huh?" He barks loudly in response, flipping over onto his stomach with his tongue hanging out. "Yeah, whatever. Traitor."

I give him a pat on the head, not missing the pink blush that crawls its way up Mackenzie's cheeks. I hope I haven't crossed a line with that comment, but it's slowly but surely becoming the way I feel. I wander across the room and drop down into the armchair, reaching for the remote on the coffee table.

"You want to watch something?" I ask, then realising that probably sounded presumptuous I add, "Or I could take you home if you wanted. It's completely up to you."

Her eyes drift over me and then back to Chance as she contemplates her decision. "I think I'll stay a little longer."

"Are you enjoying my company? Or my dog's?" A smirk lifts one corner of my mouth.

"Your dog's," she replies immediately.

"Oh! Ouch." I laugh, clasping a hand over my chest in mock heartache.

She grins deviously, but then her eyes soften. "But you've been pretty great too."

"Any time," I say, and I hope she knows I mean it.

I swallow down the emotions her words have conjured. I care about her more than I've ever cared for anyone else. When she's upset, so am I. And that's a completely confounding notion for me. To be at the mercy of someone else's feelings.

"I might order us a pizza." I launch myself up from the chair, suddenly unable to sit still. "What do you like?"

She chews on her bottom lip, her fingers still lost in Chance's fur. "Pepperoni?"

"Cool. My favourite too."

I fetch my phone from the bedroom and search the number for the local pizza place. Once I've placed an order for delivery, I head back into the living room to report to Mackenzie.

"The rain is delaying delivery so should be about forty minutes..." My voice trails off as I catch sight of her.

She's fallen asleep, the hood of my favourite blue hoodie bunched up around the back of her neck, one arm draped over Chance who's still curled up in front of her. His own eyes are closed now too, completely content. I've never seen anything more perfect.

I wander back into my room and pull up Kristen's number in my contacts. She answers on the first ring.

"Dylan? Is everything okay?" I can understand the alarm in her voice, given what we went through with Henley last year. Calling Kristen isn't something I do often.

"Yeah. Everything's fine." This is only a half truth, but it's not my place to tell Kristen what her sister has been through today.

"Okay. Good, but have you seen Mackenzie at all? I didn't think she was working but she isn't answering any of my texts."

"Yeah. She's with me," I tell her. "She's had a bit of a rough day today is all and she's here at my place."

"Is she okay?"

"Yeah. Of course. She's fine. She's safe," I inform her. "But she's fallen asleep, and I don't really want to wake her. I just wanted to let you know so you didn't worry."

"Okay. Thanks for letting me know." Kristen's relief is obvious, but her voice is still laced with sisterly concern. "She seems to be having a hard time opening up to me lately. I'm glad she has you."

"I'm glad I have her too."

In all honesty, I'm glad Mackenzie has both of us, and Henley and Harper too. Something tells me that after today, she's going to need all the support she can get.

"I know you are. You're good for her Dylan. Even if she doesn't know it yet."

"Yeah," I say softly.

But all I can think about is how wrong Kristen's got it.

Mackenzie is the one that's good for me.

Chapter 23

MACKENZIE

I can hear the ocean. The turbulent crashing of waves. But that's not the only thing that overloads my senses as my eyelids flutter open.

My fingers twitch against the ball of fur curled up against my stomach as the morning light streams from the open curtains in Dylan's living room.

Dylan.

Memories of last night forge their way to the forefront of my mind. I hadn't made it home last night.

I roll over, the sleeves of the too big hoodie tangled up around my wrists, emanating the scent of him. I remember the way he'd so tenderly looped it over my head, gently tugged my hair out from the hood. He'd found me on the trail as the rain beat down around us. He'd taken care of me.

Because my mother was dead.

I believed Dylan when he'd said that all my emotions were valid, but the thing is, I still don't know what I'm supposed to feel. Right now, I just feel empty.

And hungry.

My stomach grumbles loudly as I turn onto my side. I never did get that pepperoni pizza.

Chance responds to my subtle movements, lifting his head to lick my nose. "Hey, Chance," I whisper, throwing my arm around his warm, furry body to stroke his belly.

"Morning, sleepyhead." Dylan's voice travels down the hall and I slowly sit up, pushing away the soft, thick blanket that he must have covered me with last night.

I wipe the sleep from my eyes as he emerges from his bedroom, his chest bare, boardshorts hung low on his hips.

It's not a bad view, I must admit.

"Sorry I fell asleep." I push my hair back from my face, grimacing at the thought that I probably have an extreme case of bed hair.

"And I'm sorry my couch isn't more comfortable," he replies, drawing the curtains further open. I blink as bright light filters into the room, an ocean breeze wafting in as he swings opens the french doors. There's no trace of last night's storm except for the waves in the distance crashing a little harder than usual. "I was going to trade places and let you have my bed, but I didn't want to risk – "

"Me freaking out and attacking you?" I interrupt, shuddering as I recall how Dylan found me at the trails.

When he'd grabbed me and held my wrists firm, all I could think about was the day that Ethan abducted me. I was terrified, but to him I must have seemed insane.

"I was going to say I didn't want to wake you up." He moves to the couch and sits down, careful not to crush my legs as he occupies the space beside me. He's so close now that I can feel his warmth, catch the subtle scent of his shampoo.

"Oh." I drop my gaze to the soft, furry canine that's practically wormed his way onto my lap. "I'm sorry, by the way. For lashing out at you. I tend to get a little psycho from time to time."

The laugh that follows comes out strangled, but he doesn't reciprocate it. Instead, he lays those whiskey-coloured eyes on mine. "You have nothing to be sorry about. You acted on your instincts. You were upset."

I nod, giving Chance a scratch behind his ear. "He grabbed me right near that trail."

Dylan stiffens on the couch beside me. "Ethan?"

"Yeah," I answer. A veil of concern falls over his face, a hand coming up to rub the back of his neck. A move I've noticed he does when he's feeling stressed. "What's wrong?"

He shifts uncomfortably, turning his body toward mine. "You called out his name in your sleep last night."

A sick feeling sinks in the pit of my stomach, my vulnerability reaching a whole new level not knowing what else I might have said for Dylan to hear.

As usual, I cover it with another sarcastic joke. "Typical. I haven't seen that asshole in months, and I still can't seem to keep him out of my nightmares."

Again, he doesn't laugh. His brow pinches as he chews on his bottom lip. "Do you wanna talk about it?"

I huff out a short laugh. "You sound like Kristen."

"You haven't talked to her about him?" he asks.

"Not really. I'm not really interested in being psychoanalysed by my sister."

"Fair enough," he says. "Can I ask you something though?"

"If you have to."

He hesitates a second, leading me to believe I might not like his question but the sincerity in his eyes is unmistakeable. "How did you get involved with a guy like Ethan Davis?"

I breath out a sigh as I absorb his question. "No one's ever asked me that before."

"No one? Not even Kristen?"

"No," I say, shaking my head. "I mean, she's asked me how I'm coping. She's questioned a lot about my past, but never once about how I met Ethan. I think most people just assume that I'm this bad girl that goes around looking for trouble, but that's actually the last thing I've ever wanted."

"I'm sure that's not what Kristen thinks." He reaches over to gently pat Chance, who's fallen asleep with his head resting on my thigh.

I shrug. "I don't know."

"So, how did you meet him?"

"I met him at school," I begin, my gaze roaming out the back door to the sand. "He was the new kid in town. He'd just moved into the area with his dad, and they seemed like good people. I was fifteen and he was seventeen. All my girlfriends thought he was so charming and cute. This charismatic older guy. After a few weeks he asked me to hang out after school one day. He took me to the local café and bought me a milkshake." A bitter laugh leaves me. "I'd thought he was so sweet. My friends were jealous as hell of me."

I look across to Dylan. He swallows hard, still watching me

intently, awaiting my next words.

"My home life was difficult with my father's drinking. My mum was gone." Pressure mounts behind my eyes, tears threatening to spill at the mention of my mother. I push them back down. "I guess Ethan gave me the attention that I craved. I didn't know he was a bad guy. His dad was the new chief superintendent."

"A corrupt cop," Dylan guesses.

I nod. "I had no idea. I wasn't looking for trouble. I was looking for comfort. I'd thought Ethan would be my safe haven, the one to rescue me from a life of neglect. Turns out I was looking in all the wrong places. By the time I realised what was happening, I was already caught up in his web."

"Kenz." Dylan reaches up and swipes a tear from my cheek. One I didn't even realise I'd shed. "I'm sorry. You don't have to say anything else."

"I know," I tell him. "But I want to."

And that's the truth. For once in my life, it feels like talking is helping. And Dylan is easy to talk to.

"Okay."

I pause as Chance jumps from the couch and bounds out the back door, his tail wagging as he disappears down the steps and onto the beach. "I tried to break up with him. That's when the violence started. It started with threats at first. He made me do illegal things. Help him with his drug runs. He said if I told anyone I'd be going down with him. Not long after that I became his own personal punching bag."

Dylan's jaw clenches, a vein bulging in his neck that I'd never seen before. His nostrils flare, his eyes wandering over my body as I lift the hoodie up to bare my upper thigh.

"This scar? I got that when he shoved me into a wall mirror. And this one." I pull up my sleeve to reveal a purplish streak on my forearm. "When he held my arm over a stove."

"Stop." The word comes out broken as he curls an arm around my shoulder, pulling me into his chest. My first instinct is to push away from him. I'm not used to letting myself get close to people, but instead I revel in his touch, in the way his fingers comb through my hair. "I'm sorry, Kenz. I hate that you had to go through that. It isn't fair."

My eyes flit upward, taking in his glassy stare. In this light, I can see the golden flecks that streak across his irises.

I bring a palm to his chest, absorbing the thrumming of his heart beneath it. He inhales sharply as my fingers trace along the length of his collarbone before gliding upward to his neck. He swallows, pressing his forehead to mine, his chest rising and falling with every breath.

When he pulls me tighter against him with strong arms, it's all-consuming. Then the world falls away completely as his lips crush softly against mine.

This kiss isn't like the last. It's patient. It's comfort and protection. And about a hundred other things I could never put into words. It's more. It's a promise.

I've never really known what home feels like, but if I had to guess, I'd say this is it. It's him. He feels like everything I've waited for, but that seed of doubt is planted too deep.

Good things like this just don't happen.

Trust is not something I have to give.

My body goes rigid as Ethan's face flashes through my mind, and Dylan being so completely in tune with what I need pulls back almost immediately, scanning my face for a reaction.

I drop my hands down into my lap, the anguish and despair I'm experiencing no doubt written on my face. I can barely look him in the eye.

I'd forgotten. For a moment I'd let myself forget how easy it is for someone to insert themselves into your life, for one kiss to change everything. Dylan makes it easy to forget, but sooner or later, one way or another, those fragmented reminders find me. They always find me.

"Kenz, I'm sorry. I shouldn't have…" He launches himself off the couch, walking to the back door with his fingers thrust into his hair.

Pressure builds in my chest, knowing that once again, I've given him a reason to feel that he needs to be careful with me. Like I'm some fragile thing that might break.

"No, it's me." I shake my head, my wavy hair bouncing around my shoulders. "It was my fault."

His hands fall to his sides as he turns his gaze on me. "Don't say that, Mackenzie," he pleads with me. "It's never your fault. Never."

It's jarring to hear him use my full name for once and it stills me in place. I nod, understanding the undertones in his words. I know what he's really saying. That this situation is completely different.

That he isn't like Ethan.

But Dylan is still dangerous, for an entirely different reason.

I push myself up from the couch and follow him to the french doors, reaching up and pulling his left hand down from his face where he anxiously pinches the bridge of his nose. His hand is warm as I take it in mine, pressing my body up against his, my cheek against his chest. I curl my arms around his waist and breathe him in. The scent of sunscreen invades my senses, coconut with a hint of vanilla.

It might not seem like a grand gesture, but this is me letting him know that I want this too. I want to be close to him. My heart just isn't ready.

He doesn't react for a few seconds but then his arms find their way around me, encasing me in his warmth. "Kenz, you need to tell me what you're thinking," he says as he drops his chin to rest on my head.

"I was thinking that being around you is dangerous for me," I murmur into his golden skin.

His chest rises with a sharp breath beneath my cheek. "Why?"

"Because you make me feel safe."

With a hand on my chin, he tilts my face to his, his eyes swirling with emotion, his expression one of hurt. "What does that mean? What's wrong with safe?"

"You give me a false sense of security. There's no such thing as safe."

His jaw hardens, his eyes still searching mine and I worry I've upset him, but then he threads his fingers through my hair, gently cupping the back of my head. "You're safe when you're with me, Kenzie. Always."

I don't know what surprises me more. The way my words have affected him or the fact that I believe his. Still, whatever this thing is between us, it can't go anywhere. Not yet.

I unfurl my arms from his waist, pushing against his bare skin, my fingers finding the tattooed script on his ribs, lingering there for longer than they should. "I should go."

"Stay," he pleads, reaching for my hand. "I mean, of course

I'll drive you home if that's what you want. But I really wish you would stay."

I look up at him hesitantly. "You do?"

"Yeah." At that moment, Chance comes leaping through the back door, his paws finding my upper thighs. Dylan smirks as he gently pushes him away. "And it looks like I'm not the only one."

A soft laugh bubbles up from my throat as I reach down to scratch the dog's head. "I guess I could hang around."

"Good." The hint of a smile graces his lips. "Because you haven't even had a chance to try my famous chocolate chip pancakes. Come on."

He takes my hand in his and leads me to the kitchen.

Chapter 24

DYLAN

I know what she's trying to do. She thinks that if she keeps herself busy, she can avoid her mind wandering to the things she doesn't want to think about.

I know because I do it too.

And she's failing, like I also often do. I can tell by the way she carries herself, her posture stiff and poised, and by the way her jaw ticks. The most obvious sign though, is the frown that pulls her eyebrows down when she thinks no one is looking.

I'd driven her home this morning after she practically inhaled the stack of chocolate chip pancakes I'd set in front of her. It made me feel a little guilty for not waking her up when the pizza had arrived last night. She must have been starving.

After the serious conversation we'd had this morning about her past with her bastard ex, we'd filled the silence with talk of trivial things, like the crazy weather we've been having and whether it would have been a good morning to go for a surf.

She hadn't mentioned anything else about her past, though what worries me is the fact that we also didn't touch on the life changing news she received yesterday. I had tried once and she had shut me down, using a game of fetch with Chance as an excuse to avoid the subject.

I insisted she didn't need to work this afternoon but in true Mackenzie style, she stubbornly refused to take the day off. I knew it would be pointless arguing with her, but now that she's here, greeting customers with fake smiles and forced cheeriness, I decide it's time to give her another opportunity to make a trip into Seabright Cove. If she won't talk about her mother, maybe she needs to talk to the next best thing.

"You really shouldn't have come to work today, Kenz," I tell her when she rounds the bar with a tray of empty glasses. "I could have had someone cover for you."

She slams the tray down, the glasses rattling with the force. "It's not like sitting at home would have helped my situation. You know that."

"Maybe not. But making a trip into a certain art studio might," I suggest.

She turns a hard stare on me. "I told you already. I'm not going there."

"For what it's worth, I really think you should. You need answers and you're not going to find them here." I still her with a hand on her arm as she tries to walk away from me. "I keep thinking about what you said yesterday. About not knowing where you came from."

"What about it?" she mutters, not meeting my eyes.

"You may not have had a chance to get to know your mum.

And that sucks more than anything. But you can get to know *her*. Your grandmother. You can still find out where you came from."

"Dylan." She says my name like a warning, then she blows out a shaky breath and grits her teeth.

I hate that I've upset her, but I believe she needs to hear what I'm saying. "I'm sorry, but if this woman sought you out, she must want to get to know you."

"Why now? After all this time?" She throws her arms up in the air directing her frustration at me. "I've lived my entire life not even knowing she existed!"

"Maybe there's a reason for that. You have to at least hear her out."

"I don't owe her anything, Dylan."

"I'm not saying that you do. But maybe you owe it to yourself."

She shakes her head, moving to serve a customer at the end of the bar. She supplies him with a schooner of beer and a bowl of salted peanuts and then returns to me. Having to witness the sadness in her eyes is like a form of torture.

"I'm scared," she admits softly. "What if she tells me a whole bunch of stuff I don't want to hear. She knew my mother. Probably better than anyone else in the world."

I rest my hand on her upper arm, giving a sympathetic nod. I can't even begin to imagine what this is like for her. All I can do is show her that I'll be here when she needs me. "I could go with you. If you need support."

She seems to think this over for a few seconds, then letting out a sigh she leans into the bar. "No. It's something I need to do alone. But it's too late to go today anyway. It's almost two.

By the time the bus gets there she probably would have left for the day."

I reach into my pocket and pull out my car keys, dangling them in the air between us. "You know how to drive, right?"

"Yeah," she shrugs.

"I mean, you *can* drive? Like, legally?" I smirk. "As in, you have a licence?"

She rolls her eyes at me again, the hint of a smile on her face. "Knowing my background that's a fair question, I suppose. Yes, Dylan. I have a driver's licence."

The smile falls from her face suddenly and I lower the keys, concerned by her change in demeanour. I hadn't wanted to offend her. It had been a stupid joke.

"Sorry," she says. "It's just that Ethan used to control my every move. He didn't want me to have a licence. It was the first thing I did when I got to Cliff Haven. That, and get an RSA to work in a bar. I had to rope Henley into giving me lessons."

"Look, I'm only going to say this once." My nostrils flare, my jaw clenching in anger. I feel my heart rate rising with every breath. "I don't like to talk shit about people, but your ex is a fucking dick. He deserves to rot in prison for the rest of his life. And not even God will be able to help him if he ever sets foot anywhere near either one of us."

She blinks back at me, obviously surprised by my blatant honesty. "Wow." Her lips curl up in a smile. "You're kinda hot when you get all macho."

My eyebrows shoot toward my forehead. "Kinda?"

"Kinda heaps."

I turn her hand over in mine, dropping the car keys into her palm. "Here. You'll get there a lot faster."

"You sure you trust me with your car?" Her blue eyes glisten as a smirk twists her lips. "I know she's your pride and joy and all."

I scoff at her attempt at humour, then with a shrug I say, "Hey, she's no Ferrari, but I do love her. Just come past the tavern and pick me up later."

I don't miss the glassiness in her gaze as she swallows, squeezing her fist tightly around the keys. "Thank you."

I pull her into my chest, my arms enveloping her. I'm getting used to the way her body stiffens at my touch, but she allows herself to relax into me a little faster this time and I take that as a victory.

I know it isn't personal. That it's not me she's reacting to. She isn't used to being held or allowing herself to confide in others.

Her free hand fists the fabric of my t-shirt as she withdraws from me, blinking away a tear.

"You've got this," I tell her, catching it with my thumb.

She nods and then releasing me from her grip, she turns and heads for the exit.

Chapter 25

MACKENZIE

The scent of coconut and vanilla surrounds me in the driver's seat of Dylan's car. It takes me back to this morning, when I'd wrapped my arms around him in his living room, my cheek pressed against his bare chest. It reminds me of the way he kissed me while we sat on his couch, the way he held me like his life depended on it.

It had been everything, but the memory still sends a wave of unease through me because I had torn away from him first.

Again.

I keep wondering what it will take for me to be able to truly let go of my past.

I stop at a set of traffic lights as I near the studio and fan my face with my hand. The air con still isn't working and a quick glance over at the passenger side door determines the window winder is still broken.

I've spent the entire drive into Seabright Cove wondering if I'm doing the right thing. Just as Dylan said it would be, the journey to the studio by car has been a lot faster than by bus, which hasn't left me with enough time to contemplate all the things I need to say. The questions that need to be asked.

I discover there's a carpark behind the building the studio is located in with plenty of vacancy, so I pull into a corner spot. I smooth down my curls, take a deep breath and exhale.

"Come on, Mackenzie. You can do this," I whisper, psyching myself up. "It's no big deal. Just a little meeting with your long-lost grandmother. How bad can it be?"

With a racing heart and a mind riddled with the fear of all the things I might be about to learn, I slam the car door shut with a clunk. The gravel crunches underneath the soles of my boots as I stride toward the building.

I'm still struggling to come to terms with the fact that I have a grandmother, let alone how she may have come to find me in Cliff Haven.

When I round the corner, it's the bright red 'closed' sign on the door of the studio that grabs my attention first.

"Damn it," I mutter under my breath.

I'm disappointed but I'd be lying if I said I didn't feel a little relieved that maybe this dreaded conversation could be put off for another day.

That relief is dampened as I catch sight of a silhouette in the window. She's here, standing with her back to me, a mop of wavy, greying curls cascading around her. She turns and her swollen eyes and blotchy cheeks take my breath away. We may not know each other at all, but we're still connected and my heart aches to see her in such distress.

I raise a hand in a wave. The smile Grace aims at me in return is laced with sadness before she moves toward the door to let me in. The lock clicks loudly, then the door swings open, the tinny ring of the bell sounding from above.

"You're closed," I say, stating the obvious.

She curls her hair behind her ears, nodding in response. "I didn't feel much like being creative today. I cancelled all my classes."

Guilt twists in my gut knowing that I've been a factor in that decision. "I can go," I offer.

"No. Please stay," she pleads. Her response is quick, her hands coming up cautiously before she moves aside, allowing me to enter the studio. "Come in."

"Okay." I shuffle inside.

"I owe you an apology," she begins. "For how I went about saying what I said. There's just so much I need to tell you and there was no easy way to go about it. I'm sorry that I sprung that on you."

I nod, though I feel somehow that I should be the one apologising to her. I have so many things to say but the words are caught in my throat. Instead, I find myself gravitating to the painting hanging on the wall above. The image of the woman, arms spread wide, palms open, the golden strands of hair floating out around her like a halo.

Grace's gaze follows mine. "She was talented."

"My mother painted this." It's more of a statement than a question. Somehow, I just know.

"I hadn't seen her in a long time, but then she started visiting the studio all of a sudden. She painted that picture while she was here. Little did I know it would be the last time I would see her for many years. If my calculations are correct, she painted this one not long after you were born."

"It's amazing," I say, my eyes not leaving the painting. "So ambiguous. I can't seem to figure out whether she's floating or drowning."

"She was drowning," she chokes. "I didn't realise it at the time."

"I don't know how I'm supposed to feel," I say, my eyes tearing up. "I've spent my life being angry at her. For leaving me with a father that couldn't properly care for me. I didn't know her. I never got to know her, but I still feel this overwhelming sense of loss."

"No one can tell you how to feel, Mackenzie," she replies. "There's so much to process."

Bracing myself for an answer I know will be painful to hear, I dare to ask the dreaded question that's plagued me since learning of my mother's death. "What happened to her?"

She lets out an uneven breath as she curls her lips into a thin line. "Breast cancer. A very aggressive form."

My heart picks up speed, a sick feeling turning in my gut. I feel like I'm going to throw up. I sink down into the nearest chair and Grace joins me, occupying the one across from me, resting her elbows on the table.

Suddenly I'm angry, rage igniting from somewhere within. I'm furious about this whole situation, but I have nowhere left to direct it except at Grace.

"Why did you only come to find me now?" I cry. "Why couldn't you have visited when I was little? Do you know how nice that would have been? To have a grandmother there to care for me? I had no one!"

"Oh, Mackenzie." Her eyes mist over, but the genuineness in them remains. "I wish I could have, but I didn't know about you."

"What?" I had no clue this woman existed. My father had always told me that my grandparents had passed away before I was born, but how is it possible that she didn't know about me either? Realisation dawns on me. "My mother never told you she was pregnant, did she?" I suddenly feel drained. "Was she that ashamed of me?"

"She was never ashamed of you, Mackenzie." Grace reaches to the centre of the table and plucks a tissue from the box resting there. "If anything, she was ashamed of herself."

"What do you mean?"

"She had an affair with a married man and got pregnant with his child. There were a lot of things at play." She sighs as she shakes her head, looking as exhausted by this conversation as I feel. "She was always a bit rebellious growing up, and I admit, I was too strict on her as a teenager. I was too controlling and all it did was make her rebel. I had only wanted what was best for her, but I guess I never made it easy for her to tell me things like that."

"You can't blame yourself for that. She had a choice. She could have told you."

"But I do. I blame myself for her not feeling comfortable to come home and tell me about you," she replies earnestly, looking back up to the painting on the wall. "If I'd have been paying attention, I would have been able to see that this painting was a cry for help."

I track her gaze to the canvas, my own eyes now seeing it in a new light. After hearing her explanation, I can only see the sadness in it. "How did you find out about me then?"

"She came home when she got sick. She stayed with me in the weeks leading up to her passing. When she was nearing the end, she gave me an envelope with strict instructions not to open it until after she was gone. Sometimes I wish I hadn't honoured that wish, but there's no point in dwelling on the 'what ifs'."

She rises from the chair, wandering over to the set of drawers and retrieves a wrinkled sheet of A4 notepad paper. My heart jolts at the sight of the shaky script scrawled across its lines as she hands it to me.

I don't want to read it. I'm not ready to know what it says, but I can't look away.

Dear Mum,

If you're reading this, it means I'm no longer here. I know we've always had our differences. I haven't always been the best daughter. I've made countless mistakes throughout my life that I wish I could take back, my biggest regret being that I never shared with you my greatest achievement.

Her name is Mackenzie. And she is your granddaughter.

I'm sorry I didn't tell you that you were a grandmother sooner, that I kept her hidden for so long. I did it out of selfishness, because by admitting to you that she exists, I also need to admit that I failed as a mother.

I'm writing this letter to you in the hopes that you will find her. It's my dying wish for you to connect with her because you deserve to know her. And she deserves to know you, because any kid would be lucky to have you as their grandmother.

I love you, Mum. You were the best mother I could have asked for.

I'm sorry I never said that enough.
Love always,
Beth
PS: She lives at 23 Woodville Road, Coledale.

The letter drops from my hands, some of the words partly smudged by the lone tear that's trickled down the page.

"She told you to find me. That's why you were watching me by the river," I say, sniffling.

"I went to the address she gave me, but the house was abandoned. I didn't know if I'd ever be able to find you after that. I had no idea where to look. And then one night, I heard them say your name on tv in a news report. When I saw your photo flash up on the screen, I knew. You look just like her."

"I do?" I ask.

She nods, reaching into the envelope and pulling out a tattered photograph. "She left me this too."

I take it with trembling hands. Tears obscure my vision as I look down at the picture. A happy toddler with bright blonde hair and big blue eyes sitting in the lap of a young woman, not much older than I am now. Her long blonde ringlets hang down past her shoulders, the smile she wears signifying happiness, but there is trouble brewing within her eyes.

This is my mother. This is the woman that brought me into this world and then left me to fend for myself. Now that she's gone, I know I should feel sad, and I do, but I'm still so angry about her abandonment. In a way it feels as though she's left me twice now.

"I know this is a lot for you to process," Grace says. "It's a lot for me too. I want to be a part of your life, Mackenzie, but

I understand if you don't want me to be. I'm so glad I got to meet you. I know you've been through so much in your young life, but I also know you're going to be okay. You're strong. Just like she was."

It's utterly surreal, yet bittersweet to hear Grace make comparisons between my mother and I. Knowing my strength is something I have in common with her sends a rush of comfort through me. I'd always wanted to know where I came from, but I have to wonder about all the bad traits I may have inherited too.

Grace is right. This has all been so much to process, but I am grateful that she entered my life.

"I'm glad you found me," I say, placing the photograph gently down on the table in front of me. "So, do I have a grandfather floating around somewhere?"

"Not anymore," she answers with a sad smile. "He left this world when your mother was still a teenager."

"I'm sorry."

"Me too. He would have loved to have met you." She reaches across the table to give my hand a squeeze. "But you do have a great aunt. My sister lives about an hour away from here."

"Wow." I raise my eyebrows in surprise then my eyes find hers. "Well, if she's anything like you I'm sure I'm going to like her."

She laughs. "We're polar opposites, but I think you'll still get on like a house on fire."

The idea of meeting another long-lost family member sends a wave of nausea through me. It's been difficult enough to learn that I'm someone's granddaughter, let alone somebody's great niece. I'm suddenly overwhelmed. I think I've taken in enough information for one day.

"I should probably get going." The chair legs screech across the wooden floor as I stand.

"There is something else," Grace says, once again reaching into the large envelope and turning over another folded note in her hands. "She wrote a letter for you too."

"No," I say, furiously shaking my head. "I don't want that."

I can't think of anything that my mother could have written in that letter that could possibly undo all the hurt of the last twenty years. I'm positive that reading it will only be my undoing.

She holds it out to me. "Please take it. I think you need to read it."

"Did you read it?" I ask her.

She nods. "I did. And you should too. In a way, it has given me so many answers. It's given me a sense of closure. I hope it might do the same for you."

Hesitantly, I reach for the letter, another A4 sheet folded in two. I fold the paper over again, hastily tucking it into the front pocket of my skirt. "I'll think about it."

I'm almost at the front door of the studio when I hear Grace's trembling voice behind me. "Mackenzie?"

I turn, looking back at the woman that I can now call my grandmother. "Yes."

"Don't be a stranger, okay?"

My forehead crumples as I nod, before pushing the door open and stepping out onto the street. I head to Dylan's car, hyperaware of the note in my pocket, wondering how something almost weightless can feel as heavy as lead.

I know that when I get back to the tavern, Dylan will have questions and I already know that I won't be in the right head space to answer them.

I feel as though I'm living in a world of uncertainty right now, but there is one thing I am sure of.

I do want to get to know Grace. This woman may have barged into my life with life-changing consequences, but I know in my heart that she is a good person. One that, like me, knows what it's like to suffer an unbearable loss.

And maybe she needs me just as much as I need her.

Chapter 26

DYLAN

"How were things on the boat this morning?" I ask Jade as I slide her a glass of Coke across the bar.

"Great," she replies with a sassy grin. "You weren't missed at all."

"Haha," I say with dead eyes. "You're hilarious."

"You better have a good excuse for calling in sick." She quirks one eyebrow as she twirls her straw around inside her glass. "You missed out on seeing the biggest octopus I've ever seen in my life. Not to mention the massive grey nurse feeding frenzy."

"You're kidding." I groan. "I missed out on feeding time?"

"Yep," she says with a smug smile on her face.

"Shit. I picked the worst day to call in sick then."

"Speaking of," she says, eyeing me from head to toe and back again. "You don't actually seem all that sick."

"You caught that, huh?" My mind drifts back to this morning. Mackenzie curled up on my couch, Chance tucked into her side. "I had something important to take care of this morning."

"Something?" Jade scoffs, then her eyebrows lift. "More like someone. Like, maybe a certain cynical blonde we've all come to know and love?"

"Maybe," I admit.

"Maybe?" She shakes her head at me, aiming a sceptical smirk in my direction. Clearly, she sees right through me. "It's so obvious you like her. Why do you think I invited her on the boat in the first place?"

"That's why you invited her? You meddler!" I cry in mock shock, swinging a rolled-up dish towel at her.

"Hey, I did you a favour." She pauses to take a slurp from her straw. "You're welcome, by the way."

"Why, thank you, Jade." I hold my hand over my heart, a gesture that earns me a laugh. "It might be the nicest thing you've ever done for me." I'm not even kidding.

"Okay, settle down," she says. "Where is she, anyway? I swear I saw her behind the bar when I walked in."

"She wasn't feeling well," I lie, knowing it isn't my place to disclose Mackenzie's whereabouts.

Jade drops her straw back into her drink and flashes me an accusing glance. "What did you do to her?"

"I did nothing," I retaliate, my hands raised in defence. "She had something important that she needed to do, too."

"Well, this is all very cryptic," Jade muses.

My smile falters. Mackenzie has been gone for almost two hours. Either she's making progress with this new relationship with her grandmother, or she's sitting by a river sketching her angst-ridden thoughts out onto a page. Either way, I'm worried about her.

"Are you okay?" Jade is clearly in tune with the frown on my face, but I don't have time to answer her before the doors of the tavern open, the atmosphere suddenly sucked right out of the room.

"Shit," I mutter under my breath. "Not anymore."

My father saunters to the bar, swiftly adjusting his tie before sliding his hands into his pockets. His posture is stiff, as it always seems to be in my presence lately. "Son, can we have a word?"

I'm about to tell him no. That I have a job to do. Customers waiting. But then I see Claire stroll up behind him. He's clearly brought her along to add to his persuasion. He knows I can't say no to my big sister.

"Sure," I say reluctantly instead, then I wave a hand at Corey. "Corey, would you mind covering for me for a minute?"

"Sure, boss," Corey calls out from the storage room where he's busy unpacking a pallet of beer.

"This way." I motion for my father and Claire to follow me out the back of the tavern to the lawn area that served as the venue for Liv and EJ's wedding earlier this year. I gesture to the long wooden table, and we all take a seat. The beach is quiet, save for the waves thrashing against the white sand in the distance. "What brings the two of you all the way out here? And where's Mum?"

"She had an important meeting about her upcoming handbag line," Claire answers.

"Oh," I say.

My mother isn't new to the fashion industry, but she'd only recently decided to create an accessories line. She may have married the founder of a successful hotel chain, but she is a businesswoman in her own right.

"I'm not here to beat around the bush, Dylan." My father's words come out clipped. "We're here to give you one last chance to accept the job at the Abbott Group."

A heavy sigh leaves me as I run a hand through my hair. I'm sick of this fight, exhausted by the newspapers reporting ridiculous theories about me and my family. "I really appreciate that, Dad. I really do. And I know that my choices are affecting the entire family. I'm sorry about that, but I'm happy here."

My father grunts but he doesn't argue it further.

"Okay," he says. "If you're certain this is what you want, then I'm sure there's some way we can spin this so the media doesn't drag our family name any further through the mud."

"Okay?" I just about choke on the word in shock. "You're okay with this now?"

"You tell me that you're happy here." His gaze moves sideways to the ocean.

"I am," I confirm. "I'm doing everything that I want to do, Dad. And I'm standing on my own two feet doing it."

He doesn't look happy, but he seems mildly less agitated than usual as he gives a short nod. "Then maybe it's about time I accept that. I've decided to allow Claire to take your position."

"What?" Claire blurts, her eyes wide with excitement. Clearly, Dad hadn't briefed her about his plan prior, though this is unsurprising.

"That's great!" I exclaim, knowing that this is everything Claire has ever wanted.

Some little girls want to grow up and become princesses or ballerinas or nurses. Not Claire. When the question had been asked by her kindergarten teacher, a petite five-year-old Claire had responded with three letters: CEO.

"But," my father says, holding up a hand. I should have known there'd be conditions. "I want you to come to the city for a few days over the next couple of weeks to get her up to speed."

Claire lets out a sigh of disappointment. Just when we both thought he'd come around, our father once again shows his misogynistic colours. What's even more frustrating is the fact that everyone sitting at this table right now is aware of her extraordinary capabilities when it comes to business management.

"Up to speed? Dad, that's ridiculous. Claire could do that job with her eyes closed."

"That's the condition of my offer." He stands, letting me know that for him, this conversation is done.

"I have a job to do here, Dad," I argue, knowing my efforts will be futile. I rub my hand over the back of my neck, thinking hard about how I could make this work. If not for me, for Claire. "I can probably take a couple of days off next week."

"Okay. Next week it is." Dad claps his hands together in finality.

"Thanks, Dylan," Claire steps forward, arms outstretched as she wraps them around my shoulders. "I'm sorry you have to do this. But thank you."

"Anything for you, Claire Bear," I whisper.

She releases me, taking a step backward. "Where's Mackenzie? Is she working today? I was hoping to see her."

"She isn't here," I explain. "She's gone to visit her grandmother in Seabright Cove."

As soon as the words leave my mouth, I know I shouldn't have said them. This thing with her grandmother is new. I don't know what I was thinking.

"Seabright Cove?" my father asks, a curious look passing over his face.

"Uh, yeah," I say. "Anyway, I need to be getting back to the bar now."

"I'll see you next week then," Dad says, holding his hand out for me to shake. I take it and he squeezes it firmly.

"You will," I say. "Congratulations, Claire Bear." The informality of the situation feels odd. Claire has just landed the job of her dreams, but the conditions attached to it and my father's lack of faith in her to do the job simply because she is a woman have put a dampener on it. "We'll celebrate properly next week, okay? We can do drinks in the city. My shout."

"I'd like that." She smiles.

I watch my father and my sister climb into the gunmetal Porshe across the street at roughly the same time Mackenzie pulls up in my beat-up RAV4. I take large strides to reach her as she steps out, a forlorn look upon her face.

"Hey," I say. "How did it go?"

She looks down at the ground. "Okay, I guess. We talked."

"That's good, right?" I ask, but her hunched shoulders tell me otherwise. "Are you okay?"

She reaches into her pocket and pulls out a folded piece of

notepad paper, turning it over in her palms. She looks up at me, opening her mouth as though she wants to say something, but then pure exhaustion falls over her features and she closes up, turning to the beach.

"Yeah," she answers.

"Do you want to talk about it?" I already know the answer I'm going to get.

"Not really," she replies, shoving the paper back into her pocket. "I think I'm just gonna go."

"Okay. I'll go tell Corey I'm driving you home." I swivel around but she catches my elbow.

"No, it's okay," she says. "I feel like walking."

"Are you sure?"

"Yeah." She nods. "I'll be fine."

"Okay." I step forward, wrapping my arms around her. Her body slackens against mine just that little bit before she stiffens, offering me nothing else in return. I don't want her to be alone, but I need to trust that she knows what she needs right now. I press a kiss to the top of her head before I reluctantly release her. "Call me if you need me."

I know she won't take me up on that offer. Last night I'd seen glimpses of the things she keeps hidden from the rest of the world, but she's already tucked her heart away. Secured it for safe keeping behind those protective walls.

"I'll be fine." Her eyes barely meet mine before she turns and walks toward the beach.

I watch her as she disappears from view, knowing better than to believe her. Whatever happened today has just added to the already overwhelming mountain of things she needs to process.

And while I want to help her through it, I can respect that she needs her space.

Bombarding her with questions won't get either of us anywhere.

I'll give her tonight.

Tomorrow is a new day.

Chapter 27

MACKENZIE

The blank canvas stares back at me from the moment I open my eyes, the whiteness of it blinding. I've spent the past week wracking my brain for a subject to put on it, but after yesterday's meeting with Grace, or should I say Grandma – no, that feels weird – I don't even know if I'll attend the exhibition.

I roll over, not wanting to look at it, but then my sight falls on the crumpled up note on my bedside table that I'd carried around in my pocket all of yesterday afternoon. I still haven't been able to bring myself to read it, knowing that the words on that paper, whatever they may be, are bound to shift my world on its axis.

My phone rings, too loudly, as I snatch it up from the bedside table. My chest deflates with a heavy sigh. It's Dylan.

I know he means well but I'm not in the mood to talk.

Especially not at 7am. I ignore the call, slamming the phone down and pulling the covers up over my head. As I'd suspected, it rings again. As usual, Dylan is nothing if not persistent.

I swipe the answer key and hold the phone to the side of my face. "What's up."

"Hey," he says, in a voice that's too bubbly and bright for this hour. "You awake?"

"Obviously."

"Good." He isn't bothered by my sarcasm. "I was thinking you might like to take a little road trip with me. Meet some friends of mine."

Is he kidding? In what world does that sound like something I'd be interested in? "Don't you have to be at the boat in like, an hour or something?"

"You're still in bed, aren't you?" I can hear the smile in his voice.

"Didn't feel much like going out for my run today," I admit. "Why?"

"Go look out the window."

I unwillingly drag myself out of bed and peek through a crack in the blinds. It hasn't started raining yet, but there is lightning striking in the distance, the sky ahead a gloomy shade of grey.

"Shit," I say. "Oh, well. Dark and stormy matches my mood, I guess. I'm just gonna stay here for a while and maybe watch some tv."

"Not a chance," he says, his tone teasing. "Get dressed and I'll pick you up in half an hour."

"I can't," I argue.

"Why?"

"I have to work," I lie.

"Kenz, I'm your boss. I know your schedule. You're not due to start your shift until six. I'll have you back in plenty of time."

"I don't know, Dylan," I say. "I'm not exactly going to be good company. I'm not really up for meeting new friends."

I honestly couldn't think of anything worse at this point.

"Trust me," he replies. "These friends are different."

"No. I'm not going."

"Yes, you are."

I sigh again. "Why do you keep trying to help me?"

"Because." He pauses. "We aren't that different. You and I."

"Yeah, right," I scoff. "What the hell could we possibly have in common?"

My question is met with a short silence from the other end of the line and for a second I think I might have actually stumped him. But just when I think he isn't going to reply, he comes through with an answer that has *me* stumped.

"We're both trying to start afresh." His voice is raspier than usual. "And we're both running from things that have consumed us."

Never in my life has a combination of words left me so speechless. And never has anyone made me feel seen the way that Dylan does.

"I'll be there in half an hour," he says bluntly, as though he hasn't just sent my heartrate into overdrive with a mere sentence.

"No, you wo –" My words are cut off as he ends the call. "Aargh!"

I roll over, dropping the phone onto the mattress beside me as I let out a groan. Knowing Dylan, it won't even take him the full half hour to get here.

I brush my teeth and change into a t-shirt and jeans, pausing at the bedside table, where the crumpled note from yesterday lies. Loopy swirls of handwriting are visible but unreadable through the other side of the paper.

I reach down and shove it into my pocket. I don't even know why. Obviously, there is some part of me that wants to know what it says, but the larger part of me tells me to leave whatever its contents may be in the past.

I'm unable to shake the persistent frown from my face as I stumble out into the kitchen. Kristen looks up from her mug of coffee, her forehead scrunched at my expression. She has her iPad laying on the kitchen counter, an article on Spring weddings displayed on the screen. "What's wrong with you today? You get up on the wrong side of the bed?"

I smile sarcastically. "You know that's something only old people say, right?"

She shakes her head at me. "You forgot to do the dishes last night."

"Sorry," I mumble. "I forgot."

I didn't forget. I just didn't have the energy to do anything but crawl into bed last night. I didn't even eat dinner myself.

"Everything okay?"

"Yeah," I lie.

There's no point going into the details right now. Dylan will be here any minute and, just like yesterday when he had asked me the very same question, I can't summon the momentum to discuss it.

I want to tell her. I will tell her. Once I have everything straightened out in my own head, and when she can focus on anything other than her job or her precious bridal magazines.

Okay. Maybe that was a low blow, but once again, I've found myself envious of her. I wish my biggest dilemma was finding the perfect wedding location and not the single piece of paper that feels as though it's weighing my pocket down like an anchor.

Kristen's mouth opens as though she wants to say more, but she's interrupted by a knock at the front door. An unexpected surge of relief floods through me.

"That's Dylan," I announce, grabbing my hoodie from where it's draped over one of the dining chairs. "I'll be back later."

"Okay." Kristen's expression transforms from dubious to optimistic. She likes it when I'm with Dylan. She trusts him. I guess I'm starting to trust him too. "I'm picking up Chinese takeout for dinner tonight."

"Don't worry about me. I'll be working tonight." I call back as I open the door.

Dylan greets me with a coffee in hand. "Morning," he says. "I got coffee."

"You don't drink coffee."

"No. But you do. There's mineral water in the car for me."

"Thanks," I say, wrapping my hands around the cup, ignoring the way my heart beats out of rhythm when his fingers graze mine. The air is humid when I step outside, the atmosphere charged with the static of the impending storm. "Where are we going?"

"Somewhere awesome," he replies, ushering me to the front

seat of the car. "You'll love it."

"I doubt that," I grumble.

He ignores my complaint as he rounds the car to the driver's door. The first thing I notice is that the window winder is fixed in place. "You repaired the winder?" I ask.

"Yeah," he answers. "That thing ain't going nowhere. I used the strongest superglue they had at Bill's Hardware."

I lean forward and attempt to wind it down. Just like the first time, it snaps off in my hand. "Uh oh."

"Are you kidding me?" Dylan says, slamming a hand on the steering wheel. "I'll be having a stern word with Bill about this. And I need to find some better repair videos on YouTube."

Despite my sombre mood, one side of my mouth twists upward in a smile.

"Oh, you like that, do you?" he asks.

I'm unable to contain a small laugh. "You have to admit, it's kind of funny."

"Well, hell." He snickers. "If it's going to make you smile, you can break the other ones too."

I grin, looking down at my lap. "How far do we have to travel to meet these friends of yours this time?"

"Just over an hour. But there's a pit stop about halfway where we can get some food."

"Thank God," I groan. "I'm starving."

Dylan glances over at me as we pull out onto the main road. "You get much sleep last night?"

"Is that your way of saying I look like shit?"

"You're always gorgeous, Kenz," he says, his eyes softening as they catch mine.

"I guess I am pretty tired," I say, ignoring his compliment.

I know he must want to ask me what happened yesterday at the studio with Grace, and I respect him for not pushing it.

"Have a nap. I can wake you when we get to the diner."

It doesn't sound like a bad idea. I had struggled to get to sleep last night, my head a whirlwind of thoughts. I'd finally drifted off around three this morning. "Okay."

I ball my hoodie up, shoving it against the passenger door to use as a pillow. Soon after, the monotonous hum of the engine has me falling into unconsciousness.

There are fingers in my hair, combing strands away from my face. My muscles clench, my first instinct to panic, but as my eyes flutter open, the little bobble-headed dog on the dashboard reminds me that I'm in Dylan's car.

And Dylan is safe.

That's what he tells me at least.

"We're here, Kenz," I hear him say. "Come on. I'm gonna buy you breakfast."

I pull myself upright. Through the rain-soaked windscreen I can make out the flashing neon sign on the roof of a roadside diner with a bright red door.

For a second it takes me back to that day with Henley in Coledale. I shudder at the memory of screeching tyres, of that blood-curdling scream I've heard in all my nightmares since. The scream that came from me. I shake the memory of that nightmare and turn to Dylan.

"Are you okay?" Concern paints his features, his espresso eyes warm and kind.

"Yeah," I say with a shrug. "Just hungry."

He doesn't look away, his gaze scouring mine and I know he can tell I'm wrestling with past demons, but he's patient.

So fucking patient with me.

He brushes my hair over my shoulder. "Talk to me."

A deep breath leaves my lungs. I haven't talked to anyone about this. I couldn't, but something about Dylan makes me feel as though I can. "This diner. It looks like the one Henley stopped at. The day Ethan was hit by the car."

"Shit," he mutters. "I'm sorry. We can go somewhere else."

"No," I protest. "It's silly. This isn't that place. It's just how my mind works sometimes. For a second, I was back there, you know?"

"Yeah," he replies. "I can understand that."

"I want to go in. I do," I say earnestly.

"Are you sure?"

Nodding, I unclick my seatbelt. The door creaks as I thrust it open and step out into the rain. I stare up at the diner, then Dylan is beside me, placing my hoodie around my shoulders and guiding me out of the downpour.

The bad memories I've resurrected vanish as soon as we enter the small café, met with friendly faces and warmth.

"Dylan!" A short brunette middle-aged woman approaches us, holding out two menus. "I haven't seen your face around here for a while. How are you doing?"

"I've been good, Jackie," Dylan replies as he takes the menus from her hands. "How are you?"

"Same old. Nothing really changes around here," she says with a wave of her hand. "Although, last week we had a rockstar pass through with his entourage. They ordered thirty-five cheeseburgers. I can't remember his name. Brenda, what was that rockstar's name?"

"Emmett Jensen!" A tall, curvy blonde emerges from the kitchen wearing a bright pink apron. "He's so dreamy."

I can't help but giggle, having known EJ since I moved to Cliff Haven and experienced first-hand the effect he has on women.

"He sure is," Dylan jokes, shooting me a knowing look.

"Are you on your way to see Daisy and Cyrus again?" Jackie asks Dylan.

"Daisy and Cyrus?" I mouth to Dylan. Those are some seriously unusual names.

"We are." Dylan responds to Brenda and Jackie with a wink that lets me know they're in on some kind of inside joke or secret. "I'm going to introduce them to a new friend of mine. Ladies, this is Mackenzie."

"Hi, Mackenzie." Brenda greets me, her eyes crinkling at the corners as she smiles.

"So nice to meet you," Jackie says.

"Thanks. You too," I reply, self-consciously shoving my hands into my pockets.

"So, this is your first time meeting Daisy and Cyrus, huh? I'm sure you're in for a real treat!"

Dylan lets out a laugh at Jackie's comment.

"Have you met them too?" I ask the two women. Who the hell are these people I'm going to be meeting today?

"No," they both reply in unison.

"But we've heard a lot about them," Brenda adds.

"Let's get you both seated and some food in your bellies. The weather out there is hideous today," Jackie remarks as she leads us to a booth by the window.

When we're both seated comfortably, she shuffles off back to the kitchen and I find Dylan's eyes across the table.

"Daisy and Cyrus, huh?" I muse. "Dylan, are you taking me to meet some old folk in a nursing home?"

Another laugh bursts from him, his white teeth put on full display, those cute little wrinkles that crease the side of his eyes making an appearance. "No," he replies bluntly.

"Well, are they your grandparents or something?" I don't want to admit it, but I'm suddenly nervous about who I'm going to meet today.

"No," he says again. "They are somewhat more pleasant than my grandparents."

"You come here a lot. To this diner." I look around the space, suddenly feeling silly that we almost didn't come here because of those bad memories resurfacing. This diner is cosy, the staff friendly.

"Every time I visit Daisy and Cyrus," he says.

"You're not going to tell me anything about these people before I meet them, are you?"

"Nope," he replies.

I cross my arms, resting them on the table, a wave of curiosity washing over me. "Do these women know who you are?"

"They know I'm Dylan, yes." He leans back against the cushioned backing of the booth.

"Dylan from Cliff Haven?" I ask. "Or Dylan the billionaire?"

"Ex-billionaire," he corrects.

"Whatever."

"They know," he replies.

"Does anyone in Cliff Haven know that you're an ex-billionaire?" I ask, putting the emphasis on the 'ex'.

"No. Only you," he replies, and as if to let me know he's done with the subject he asks, "What do you feel like eating?"

"Everything."

He lets out another chuckle at my response. "Okay then."

Dylan orders the pancake stack with a side of hash browns, and I order everything.

Well, technically, everything. I get the big breakfast with a couple of extra pancakes. We eat in comfortable silence, something I find myself unable to do with most people.

We argue when Dylan insists on getting the check, but he wins. Then we return to the car to continue on to our destination.

Chapter 28

DYLAN

Mackenzie stirs when I nudge her knee as we pull into the parking lot. She'd fallen back to sleep at around about the halfway point from the diner to here and I haven't been able to stop myself from glancing in her direction every chance I can. She looks so peaceful when she sleeps. The stress she's been going through must be exhausting for her.

"Kenz," I say, nudging her knee again. "We're here."

Her eyes flutter open and stormy blue irises stare back at me. She stretches her arms out in front of herself as she straightens and surveys her surroundings.

Her expression turns to one of discontent when she sees the giant sign that adorns the top of the building in front.

"Dylan, what the fuck." She combs her hair back from her face, her hand pausing on her forehead. Her mouth gapes open as realisation dawns on her. "Daisy and Cyrus are not people, are they?"

I can't help but chuckle at her reaction to the bold block letters that spell out the name of a place I frequent often. The Watercrest Marine Research Centre. "Not exactly."

"If you've brought me here to show me a pair of sharks, Dylan, I swear to God," she threatens, but the hint of a smile that creeps across her face hinders any intimidation.

"Not sharks," I tell her. "I learned my lesson the first time. But there are sharks here if you want to see them. Behind glass of course."

"Of course." She offers a dramatic eyeroll as she shoves open the car door.

The rain has stopped for the time being, but the ground is still wet underfoot. The sun pries its way through the clouds overhead as we walk toward the aquarium's main doors.

Jim, one of the head marine biologists rounds the front counter to meet us as we enter. "Dylan, my man! What's up?" He slaps his palm in mine and pulls me in for a hug. "It's so good to see you!"

"Hey, Jim. You too," I say. "This is Mackenzie." I place my hand on the small of Mackenzie's back as she gives an awkward wave in greeting.

"Hi," Jim says. "So, what brings you two up here today? You here to see Daisy and Cyrus?"

"Yeah," I reply. "I know it's been a couple of weeks since I've been here. Busy with work and all, but I wanted to introduce Mackenzie to them, if that's okay?"

"Of course, man," he replies. "We love having you here. And you know those two. They're always up for visitors."

He lets out a laugh, lifting his baseball cap to rake a hand through his unruly hair underneath.

"Thanks, man."

"No worries. It's perfect timing actually," Jim adds.

"Feeding time?" I ask, throwing a glance Mackenzie's way.

She's playing it cool, but I have no doubt she's freaking out on the inside.

"Absolutely," he answers. "You know where everything is."

"Thanks."

I steer Mackenzie down the hallway in the direction of the supply room. In there, I gather a bucket and the feeding supplies we need to take with us to the pool out the back - a mixture of squid, prawns and crab meat.

Mackenzie doesn't speak as I move around the small room, though she does watch me with a keen interest. I look up to find her giving me serious side-eye, to which I laugh. "It's okay, Kenz. You're not the food this time."

"Ha ha." She deadpans.

I can't help but laugh again as I throw my arm around her shoulder and lead her to where Daisy and Cyrus live.

"Why are there no other people here?" she asks. "Isn't this place open to the public?"

"It is, but this is the one day of the week that it isn't."

"How do you know the staff so well. Why do they just let you in here?"

"I've been volunteering here since I left the city," I explain. "I help out with random jobs. Help keep the tanks clean and maintained."

"And with feeding time?" She aims a sceptical glance my way.

"Sometimes."

We reach the end of the hallway, stepping out into the daylight once again. I turn to gage her reaction to the large outdoor pool before us.

"Do I want to know what lurks beneath the surface?" she asks.

I snort out a laugh as I remove my shoes and step into the shallow end of the pool. "These guys are friendly, Kenz."

"You sound sure about that."

"I'm positive," I say. She watches me with uncertainty, her arms crossed guardedly over her chest as I splash the surface of the water with my right hand. "Daisy! Cyrus!"

I hear her gasp as two large, shadowy figures surface in front of us. "Holy shit," she curses. "They're massive."

I stride into the pool, the water lapping around the middle of my thighs.

"Should you really be wading into the depths of the abyss?" Her voice has become slightly higher pitched. "Like, really? Is that safe?"

"Sure. They're gentle giants." I swipe my hand over Daisy, giving her a rub, then turn back to Mackenzie. "Meet Daisy and Cyrus. The centre's largest pair of stingrays."

"Holy shit," she says again, her hands coming to her mouth. "Are they dangerous?"

"Nah, they're okay." I stumble backward a little as Daisy pushes up onto me.

At 300kgs and almost four metres long, she has slightly more power behind her than Cyrus.

"Why do they look like they're trying to smother you then," she asks, her voice full of concern.

"They're just hungry. And they love me. Don't you boy?" I laugh, gliding my hands along Cyrus's smooth sides. "Can you pass me the bucket?"

She hesitantly lifts the handle of the bucket, screwing her nose up at its contents as she peers inside. "Gross."

I laugh at her reaction as I take the bucket, dipping my hand in to retrieve a large prawn. I hold it down into the water for Daisy to find. Mackenzie startles as Daisy flaps her body around in a frenzy, trying to siphon the food from my hand.

"They have to feel around for their food because their eyes are on top of their head," I explain. "They can't see it."

I reach back into the bucket, this time pulling out a piece of squid for Cyrus. He flaps his body up and down, taking the food from my flattened palm.

Mackenzie bends down, peering closer to get a better look. "Is that why they keep flapping all over you like that? Because they're looking for food?"

"Yeah, kind of. They actually have these electrical sensors around their mouth. They're called ampullae of Lorenzini that help them sense their prey."

Mackenzie's head cocks to the side, her eyes narrowing as she raises one eyebrow. "Totally."

"Sorry," I say sheepishly. "I tend to geek out over these guys. I just think they're the coolest things."

"That seems kind of like some weird evolutionary flaw," she muses. "That they can't see what they're eating."

"Well, it seems that way, but their eyes are on top of their head so they can still see their predators when they've buried themselves in the sand on the ocean floor."

She smiles, her eyes softening, and for a moment, it makes

me forget that she was ever sad. "Nerd alert," she teases.

I chuckle, flicking water up at her. "You wanna have a turn at feeding them?"

"I don't think so," she responds with a wave of her hand.

"Come on," I beckon. "Come and meet my friends."

"You know, most humans make friends with other humans."

"Yeah. Well, that sounds overrated."

"Can't argue with you there." Her bottom lip disappears between her teeth as she contemplates my invitation and then a moment later, she throws her hands up in the air and kicks off her shoes. "Okay. What the hell."

She spends a minute rolling her jeans up to her knees, then I take her hand as she lowers herself onto the step.

"Here," I say, holding the bucket out to her. "Just take a piece of squid and then hold it out in your palm. Keep your hand flat so they don't chomp your fingers."

"That's very encouraging," she says sarcastically as she dips her hand into the bucket, her face screwed up in disgust. "Which one is Daisy, and which one is Cyrus?"

"That's Daisy on your side and this is Cyrus over here."

"Okay, Daisy. Here we go." She blows out a nervous breath, plunging her hand under the water as Daisy glides smoothly toward her. She squeals as Daisy takes the food, flapping and splashing us both with water.

"She's playing with you," I say with a laugh.

"Playing with me? Are they smart?"

"Yeah. Very. And they like to play. Especially these guys because they're so used to interacting with us. They even know their names and when they're being called."

"Amazing," Mackenzie says in awe as she reaches into the bucket for a prawn. "Cyrus! Come here, boy!" Cyrus responds by siphoning the prawn straight from her hand. This time, she's game enough to reach out and run a hand along his smooth body the same way I had. "Wow. Slimy."

"Yeah," I agree with a laugh.

I watch as she surveys the water's surface, waiting for either of the stingrays to return to us, her face full of wonder. I'd hoped that I'd be able to get her out of her head for a while and I feel that I've accomplished that. At least for now.

"Hey, Daisy!" she calls out across the pool. "Can she hear me from all the way over there?"

"Yeah, they can hear us from anywhere in the pool," I explain. "But they don't need to hear us to know that we're here. They can feel us in the water. They can feel our heartbeats."

"They can not," she says in disbelief.

"They can." I nod. "They can even tell if a woman is pregnant because they can feel both heartbeats."

"That's incredible." She holds out a piece of fish as Daisy surges forward, letting out a giggle when she touches on her shins.

My breath is taken away when her gaze meets mine. I'm in complete awe of the smile that stretches across her face. It's a real smile. One that I've waited forever to see.

Then suddenly her chest rises with a ragged breath, her features falling in an uncertain frown. Like she's just remembered that she isn't supposed to be happy. That she doesn't believe she's allowed to be.

It's the same look she wore when she returned to the tavern

yesterday after spending the afternoon with Grace. I'd assumed she'd let me in on what's bothering her eventually, that she'd tell me in time. But then I remember that Mackenzie is a vault, and without a little nudge, maybe she'll keep it all locked up tight.

She wipes her hands on her jeans, drying them before she tucks her hand into her pocket. She pulls out a folded piece of notepad paper, identical to the paper I'd seen her shove into the pocket of her skirt yesterday.

She inspects it quickly, then returns it to her jeans and I realise she was checking to make sure she hadn't gotten it wet. I get the feeling that this note, wherever it's come from, holds the answers she needs. Though maybe she isn't ready to hear them.

"Kenz," I say, a hint of cautiousness in my tone. "Are you okay?"

She turns to me, sadness in her eyes, her shoulders sagging as she says, "No."

She wades over to the side and flops down onto the edge of the pool, her legs still dangling in the water below. It means everything that she can be this honest with me.

I move across the step and take a seat beside her, wrapping an arm around her shoulder. As usual, she stiffens at my touch, but only for a second, before she lets out a long breath and drops her head to my shoulder. Warmth shoots through me as she nuzzles into my neck.

We sit like that for a moment, Daisy and Cyrus looping through the depths below before I finally work up the courage to ask. "Does this have anything to do with that piece of paper that's been burning a hole in your pocket since yesterday?"

She nods in response, her eyebrows pinched together in despair. I hate seeing her like this.

"You wanna tell me about it?"

She simply shakes her head, closing herself off to me.

"Okay," I tell her. "I get that, but you should tell someone though. If you can't talk to me, maybe you should try telling Daisy and Cyrus. They're great listeners. Trust me. I know."

I feel the warmth of her breath on my neck before she lifts her head. She slides her hand into her pocket and pulls out the folded paper and I notice her name scrawled across one side of it. "It's a letter. From my mother."

"Oh, Kenz."

No wonder she's been so sullen. This has to be massive for her.

"She wrote it before she died. Grace told me she came back to her when she got sick. She wrote two letters. One for her and one for me."

"My guess is that you haven't read it yet," I say.

"That would be correct."

"Did Grace tell you what her letter said?"

"Yeah. She showed it to me too." She turns the folded note in her hand. "My mother's letter to Grace was what lead her to find me. Up until she read it, Grace had no idea I even existed."

"Your mother didn't tell her about you?"

She shakes her head. "Grace said she must have had her reasons. That she was wild and rebellious. But I don't feel like any of that is a good enough excuse. I know I should be grieving her loss but I'm so angry. Not only because she left me without a mother, but she took away my chance of having a grandmother. Of having a proper family."

"I can understand that." If I was in Mackenzie's position, I'd be furious too, but this situation doesn't seem at all that black and white. "But you need to know what your letter says."

"I haven't been able to bring myself to read it. I mean, she's gone," Mackenzie turns to me, her eyes suddenly burning like blue flames. She shakes the letter in front of me in frustration. "What could she possibly have written in here that could benefit me in any way?"

"I guess that's something you can only know by reading it. And I think that if you don't read it, you're always going to wonder."

She squeezes her eyes shut. "I know. I just don't know if I have the strength. I don't know how much more I can take."

Daisy glides around the circumference of the pool, grazing its edge until she comes to stop at Mackenzie. The way she slides her body over Mackenzie's shins causes her to startle. "What's going on? What is she doing?"

"I think she can sense your sadness. Stingrays have this strange way of knowing when your emotions are heightened." I lean over and run my fingers along Daisy's fin. "Pretty cool, right?"

Mackenzie reaches down, her fingertips skating over mine before coming into contact with Daisy. "It's very cool."

"Like I said, they're great listeners." I offer a small smile when she raises her gaze to mine. "I know you're scared to read it, but if you want my opinion, I think you should at least take a look at it."

She nods. "I know. You're right. If I don't read it, I'll always wonder."

"I can go. Give you some privacy. I need to take the bucket back to the supply room anyway." I don't want to leave her, but she needs this. And something tells me, she'd like space to do it.

I lift one leg out of the water, then the other, and push myself up to stand. Then her hand is in mine. I look down, finding desperation in her stare.

"Stay," she pleads.

I nod, sitting back down beside her, then I wrap my arm around her again. She unfolds the paper gently, taking the kind of care with it you'd only give to something fragile. She swallows, then with a shaky voice she reads aloud.

To Mackenzie, my little ray of sunshine,

If you're reading this, then it means your grandmother has found you. I'm so glad for that.

I know it isn't going to be easy to put into words the way I feel about you and my constant regret for the way I left you. I was a terrible mother to you, in both my presence and my absence, and for that I'm truly sorry. The cancer that eats away at me is my karma. I know that in my soul. It's what I deserve for never being the person you needed me to be."

She drops the letter to her lap, clearing her throat. Her shoulders shake with an unsteady breath. Those words would have been harder for her to read than they are for me to hear. The pain is visible in her eyes as they slice to mine. I can tell she's contemplating whether it's worth her while to keep reading, but I nod, urging her to continue.

"The day you were born was the happiest of my life. It was also the worst. As a toddler you truly were my little ray of sunshine with those light blue eyes that could light up any room, a head full of shiny blonde curls. You were the best thing to ever happen to me. The best thing in this world.

And that is why I had to leave you.

You were pure light, and I was poison. I tried to love you in all the ways I knew how but I always managed to screw it up.

I knew something was wrong with me the day you almost drowned. Your father found you in the bathtub, the water so high it had started to seep into your nose and mouth. I've never set foot in a church in all my life, but I got on my knees that day, sending praises to the heavens that God didn't take you from me.

I prayed that I could be the kind of mother that wasn't so absorbed in her own darkness that she could leave her pride and joy in a running bathtub because she had a sudden craving for caffeine.

I promised to try harder, to be the woman you needed me to be.

But from there things only got worse.

A few days after that, I accidentally slammed your hand in the drawer, twisting your little pinkie. It killed me to see your little eyes fill with tears, staring back at me in accusation. How could I have done this to my baby?

I stopped leaving the house after the time I left you at the grocery store, tucked up in a blanket in your pram. It was though I had stepped out of my life for a moment.

As though I was pretending to be somebody else.

I got three blocks before what I'd done had truly sunken in and raced back up the hill, but by then the police had already been called.

My failure on display for all the town to see.

It got to the point where you could feel my tension. You'd stare up at me in wonder with that mass of blonde curls, your rosy lips curling up in a smile and I would just get up and leave the room because I couldn't smile back. The depression ate away at me and there was nothing I could do to stop it.

I began to resent you. I'd never asked to become a mother, never entailed how much motherhood would change my life, but I always thought it would change me for the better.

Instead, it made me a monster.

It crept in like a shadow in the night, devouring my joy within its blackness.

Do I hate myself for not looking a little harder for the light? Yeah.

But this darkness was all consuming. And it didn't belong next to your light.

So, I left, unable to take the hurt, the guilt. Little did I know I'd come to experience a different kind of guilt. Guilt for leaving you. For not being there for the big moments in your life.

I'm sorry, Mackenzie. So very sorry.

Love always, Mum."

Mackenzie tightens her grip on the letter in her hand, squeezing it hard enough that it crumples in her grip. She leans forward and when I reach over to pull aside the curtain of hair that has fallen over her face, I expect to see tears, anguish.

Something.

But her expression is stoic, her mouth set in a hard, grim line. The slight flare of her nostrils the only sign that she's working hard to process this undeniably distressing information.

I tuck her hair behind her ear, and inch closer to her along the pools edge. I outstretch an arm to comfort her, but she flinches, inching away.

"Don't." She swallows hard, pushing her tears way down, and I watch as that wall that she's built herself rises steadily, brick by brick.

I want nothing more than to hold her through this moment but instead I tuck my arms away, folding them across my chest, fighting the urge to give her the comfort that she desperately needs but won't allow herself to feel.

"Talk to me, Kenz," I whisper.

She shakes her head, instead reaching forward to glide her palm along Daisy who hasn't left her side for more than a few seconds.

"You can't keep your feelings inside forever."

She pulls her feet from the pool and hoists herself up, running from the stingray enclosure. Within seconds I'm on my feet, following her down the corridor that leads out to the underwater viewing area. She stands in the centre of the dim, empty space, gazing out at the hundreds of colourful fish and reef sharks that swim by.

"I'm worried about you," I tell her.

"What do you want from me?" Her voice is low, determined not to break.

"I don't know. A reaction, I guess. Anything."

"You want me to bore you with the details of my sob story life?" she cries, her expression hard and angry. I get the feeling she's about to direct her temper at me, but if it means she's going to let something out, I'll take it. "You wanna know about how while you were driving your Ferrari out to A-list parties and flashing your corporate credit cards around, I was busy making sure that my dad always fell asleep on his side so he wouldn't drown in his own vomit? Or how I spent hours thinking up creative lies and excuses to cover the bruises after my boyfriend beat me? Hoping to God that a teacher wouldn't question me about them and he'd punish me worse?"

A lump builds in my throat, a sick feeling twisting within my gut until I start to worry I'm not going to be able to keep my breakfast down. Her words are breaking me right now, making me feel smaller, her pain crushing me from the inside out.

How can so much trauma be inflicted on one person? How is that fair?

"Or how about this?" she continues, her voice dropping lower, a calmer tone. "How about how scared I am every single day that I'm going to turn out just like one of my parents?"

I step toward her, not sure how much more I can take. But I need to hear this. Her words are important, and she needs to say them.

"You want to hear about how broken I am?" Her tears are falling harder and faster now. "I am. Okay? I'm broken. I'm lost and I don't know what to do."

"Come here," I tell her, almost demanding. Tears threaten to spill from my own eyes.

She steps forward, closing the gap between us and collapses into my arms, her body wracked with heavy sobs. Her world is crumbling down around her and with it her defences are falling too. I've waited so long for her to let me in, but this isn't the way I wanted it to happen.

"You're not broken, Kenz." I tell her. "You're beautiful. And you're the strongest person I've ever met."

"How could she do this to me?"

"I can't imagine what you're going through. I won't pretend to know what you must be feeling. But your mum had post-partum depression. This has never been about you."

Her eyes find mine, a crease deepening between her brows.

"You understand that right?"

"She could have come to me," she argues. "She could have told me all of this before she died."

"Maybe she could have," I say. "But you can't tear yourself down with questions and what ifs. Your mother loved you. And in the midst of her depression, she felt as though she was doing what was best."

"It wasn't what was best. And I don't know how I can ever forgive her."

I give into the urge to hold her, pulling her close, my t-shirt soaking up the rest of her tears. I don't know what to say. It's not my place to find answers for her and I can't take away her suffering.

All I know is that I'm the luckiest man on this earth to be the one holding her through it.

Chapter 29

MACKENZIE

I'm still processing the words in that letter. I have a feeling I'll be processing them for the rest of my life. And I know that Dylan was right when he said that none of this has ever really been about me. My mother had an illness that had been outside of my control. For her, leaving was the only way out.

I was the collateral damage and I guess in a lot of ways, my father was too. My mother's depression set off a chain of unfortunate events. Her leaving, my dad's drinking, my feelings of worthlessness. The what ifs are sure to haunt me forever.

What if somebody had recognised the signs? What if somebody had been brave enough to help her through it, instead of watching it play out from afar? What if she'd come to find me later in life? What if I'd tried harder to find her instead of thinking she didn't want anything to do with me?

God, I'd been angry when I'd finished reading that letter,

but now I'm just sad. Sad for what could have been, and sad for all that was lost.

I haven't taken my eyes off the window, a blur of green trees and grey skies rushing past as we head back toward Cliff Haven.

Along with the rest of the emotions I've conjured up today, there's an immense pressure in my chest caused by the guilt I'm feeling for what I said to Dylan back at the aquarium. He didn't deserve the way I'd lashed out.

I swivel my head in his direction. His sights are steady on the road ahead. He's given me silence the entire journey home. Not because he doesn't want to talk to me, but because he knows it's what I need. He always seems to know what I need.

"I'm sorry for what I said. About the car and credit cards and parties. I didn't mean that."

He turns to me, giving me a lopsided smile. "It's okay. You didn't say anything that wasn't true," he replies with a shrug. "Truth is, I've been given opportunities that most people would kill for."

"But they aren't the opportunities you want."

"Grass is always greener, right?" He laughs. "You probably think I'm crazy."

"To give up your fortune in search of a bigger purpose?" I shift in my seat, repositioning myself to face him. "I think you're brave."

"Brave?" His eyebrows shoot up.

"Yeah. Working for your father would be taking the easy way out, and let's face it, it's what most people in your position would do. But you're different. You don't want easy."

The irony isn't lost on me that he could be hanging out with literally anyone else right now, but he's chosen arguably the most difficult woman on the planet to spend his time with today.

He glances over at me, his whiskey eyes crinkling at the corners as he smiles. "You're the only person that's ever said that to me."

"Well, I mean, you're also a little crazy too," I blurt.

He chuckles as he steers the car down the driveway of the quaint riverside cottage I call home. He pulls up the handbrake noisily and when he turns to me, his easy-going demeanour leaves him, replaced by one of concern.

"I know this is a dumb question," he begins, his eyes on mine. "But are you okay?"

"No." I sigh.

He nods, offering a melancholy smile. "It would be weird if you were."

The car door handle puts up a fight as I try to open it. "I think it's really stuck this time."

"Hang on. I'll get it." He steps out, rounding the car to the passenger side and after some fumbling and jiggling, he gets it open. "Sorry. I think it's getting worse."

"Thanks," I say as he follows me up the front steps, the soft pitter patter of raindrops sounding on the tin roof above us when we reach the porch. "And thank you for today. For everything. For a while there you kinda got me out of my head."

"Any time," he says. "Kristen and Henley aren't home, I take it."

"No. They won't be back until dinner time, but that's when I leave for my shift at the tavern." I turn the key in the front door lock, then push it wide open. When I glance back, Dylan hovers near the porch swing, his hands tucked deep into his pockets. I've been so focused on everything that's been going on lately, I haven't taken the time to check in on him. "Are you okay?"

He brings his gaze up from the ground and my breath catches when I see those golden flecks streaked across his irises. "Yeah," he answers. "I just really don't want to leave you alone right now."

After a few seconds of contemplation, I nod. "I kind of don't want you to leave me alone either."

Relief washes over him, a smile tugging his mouth upward as I gesture for him to come inside. He follows me to my room where I put my phone and keys down on the dresser. I pull out the crumbled letter, now stained with my tears and tuck it into my top drawer. Somehow, I know I won't be able to stand having it staring back at me from wherever I am in the room.

Dylan scans the far wall, where a few of my sketches are pinned to a cork board I got at Kmart on a shopping trip with Kristen and Liv. Kristen had been so excited to help me pick out a few things to spruce up my room. A new quilt cover and throw rug, the porcelain lamp that adorns my bedside and the cork board that Dylan now stands in front of.

"Wow. You weren't kidding when you said you liked to draw. These are amazing."

"Thanks," I say, shyly.

"Have you told Kristen about Grace?"

"No," I shake my head. "I mean, she knows I've been attending her art class, but not about recent revelations. You're the only person I've told."

"You should tell her," he says. "It might help to talk to her."

"I doubt Kristen would want to mix business with family. It goes against company policy."

"That's not exactly what I meant," he says, picking up one of the sketches on my nightstand. "I don't mean for you to talk to her like she's your therapist. She's your sister. She cares about you. She would want to know."

"Yeah, maybe," I say. "She's pretty pre-occupied with organising her wedding at the moment. I kind of don't want to be a downer."

"She'd never see it like that. She'd always make time for you. You know that right?"

I shrug. "Yeah, I guess."

"She was out of her mind the day she thought she was going to lose you. You aren't alone, Kenz. You need to learn to accept help from others every once in a while."

I know that my sister cares for me. I wouldn't be living in this house if she didn't. She's given me more than any other person on the planet, and I'll always be thankful for her. I just hate this constant third wheel feeling I keep getting in her and Henley's presence.

"I'll tell her," I say. "Eventually."

He offers a small nod before moving to the other corner where the easel that Pamela gifted me stands, the blank canvas perched upon the rail. The paints are all laid out in front waiting for inspiration to strike. "What are you going to paint?"

"I don't know yet," I tell him because it's still true. My head is so full now, of thoughts, emotions, and theories. I don't know if I'll ever be able to move past this block on my creativity.

A cheeky smirk lifts one side of his mouth. "Well, I'd offer to model but I'm not sure if nudes are your thing."

Despite the day we've had, I can't help but crack a smile. His lips twitch at the sight as his eyes slice to mine.

"Thank you," I say again. "For being there for me."

He nods again, lingering on the far side of the room. "Always. I care about you, Kenz."

"I'm starting to see that," I say.

Because I am. Trust has never come easy for me. I've been burned way too many times, but Dylan's constant support has shown me that if there is one person in this world, I can count on to get me through those dark days, it's him.

I move across the room in slow strides until I'm standing in front of him. He reaches up slowly, taking my face in his hands, then he leans down to press a gentle kiss to my mouth. It's so soft, so tender, it makes my eyes water.

"I'm sorry," he says quickly when he sees me reach up and swipe at the moisture.

"Don't be," I say. "I'm not that fragile, Dylan."

"Fragile?" His forehead creases in a frown. "I know you aren't, Kenz. When I said you were the strongest person I know, I meant it. I just don't want you to think that I would ever take you for granted."

"You've already proven to me that you aren't like my ex, if that's what you're worried about." I step forward, filling the space between us, planting my hands on his chest. "I know exactly what kind of guy you are."

"You do?"

"I do." I nod as his eyes search mine. "You're the kind of guy that will stick up for a lowly barmaid when his parents call her a gold-digger."

A soft laugh rumbles through his chest, vibrating the hard, toned muscle beneath my fingers.

"The kind that will take me out for a day just to help me get my mind off things."

His hands slide to my hips as mine travel downward, my fingers twisting in his t-shirt. I move forward, forcing him to take a step backward in the direction of my bed.

"You're the guy that took me home and cared for me when you found me in the rain." My hands find the hem of his shirt, creeping beneath the fabric, his skin hot under my palms.

Another step forward for me sends him edging further back.

"Kenz." The way he utters my name, low and breathless causes my heart to beat out of sync.

"You held me when I cried," I say, inching him back further until the backs of his knees are flush with the mattress. A gentle shove has him sitting on the bed in front of me. His arms curl around my thighs.

"You made me pancakes," I whisper.

I'm suddenly acutely aware of how wrong I had it. The way I feel in Dylan's presence is nothing like the way I'd felt with Ethan in the beginning.

Not even close.

I push away the thought of him, ashamed to have let him take up space in my head in this moment that is meant for only us. Dylan and I alone.

How could I have been so completely mistaken?

He looks up at me with those whiskey eyes. The eyes that have seen me the way nobody else ever has.

"I did," he agrees.

"I trust you." I lean down, crushing my lips against his, my fingers gliding up from the back of his neck into his hair.

He kisses me back, slowly but with intention, then I climb into his lap, pressing my body against him. I shiver when his hands trail up my back, finding their way underneath my shirt.

I've never wanted to be this close to someone. Never needed to be this close to someone, but it's time I admitted what I've been denying all along.

Dylan has my heart.

He strokes my hair, nuzzling into my neck, his breath hot on my skin. Then when he falls back onto the mattress, pulling me with him, I melt.

And this time neither one of us pulls away.

Chapter 30

DYLAN

My eyes open slowly, adjusting to the morning light. The sun filters in through a crack in the curtains, illuminating the light pink table lamp on the bedside to my right. Momentarily, in my sleepy haze, I've forgotten where I am and then all the memories of the previous night come flooding back.

Of Mackenzie's silky, sun-kissed skin moving against mine, the way my hands followed each curve as she clung to my broad shoulders. Without question, it had been the best night of my life.

She'd gone home with me to grab a change of clothes and feed Chance and then we'd worked our shifts together at the tavern. We'd barely been able to keep our hands off each other, almost getting busted by Corey in the office a couple of times. I'm pretty sure he could sense something was up between us. Something good.

Afterwards, we'd wound up right back in her room, repeating yesterday afternoon all over again.

I roll over as gently as I can to avoid waking Mackenzie. She's always gorgeous, but in this light, she is exquisite. A long, toned leg thrown over the covers, her hair streaming out behind her like spun gold. I tighten an arm around her waist, drawing her gently against me.

She begins to stir so I nuzzle into her, peppering light kisses down her neck. If I'm being honest, I'm a little anxious that she's going to wake up with regrets but as she murmurs softly, rolling onto her back, her lips meeting mine, my fears disintegrate. She had said she trusted me. More than that, she had shown me, and that had meant everything.

"Good morning," she says, her eyelids fluttering open to reveal those stormy blue-grey irises I love so much.

"Yes, it is," I agree.

She giggles, then Kristen's voice travels down the hallway. "Mackenzie! Are you awake?"

"Shit," I curse, glancing down at my almost naked body. "Will she come in here?"

Mackenzie laughs again. "Oh my. So prudish," she teases.

"I am not," I retaliate, making sure the comforter is covering every inch of my skin. "I'm just trying to be respectful."

"Such a gentleman," she mocks. "Don't you walk around mostly naked for like, half of every day?"

My mouth gapes open. "I'm a diving instructor, Kenz. You're making me sound like a stripper."

"Mackenzie." This time Kristen's voice is accompanied by a knock on the door.

I throw the covers over my head while Mackenzie chuckles at my attempt to hide. "Yeah," she calls back. "I'm awake."

The door creaks as Kristen swings it open. If she notices the giant blob under the comforter she doesn't let on.

"Hey," she says. "Liv and I are going into Little Beach today to check out the shops and get some lunch. We'd really love it if you came with us."

Mackenzie lets out a breath from beside me and I can already guess what her answer is going to be before she responds. "I can't."

I hear Kristen sigh. "Come on, Mackenzie. I really want to hang out with you. Besides I'm worried about how much time you've been spending alone."

"I don't know." Mackenzie hesitates. I take the opportunity to nudge her in the ribs with my elbow, urging her to accept her sister's invitation. "Ouch!" she cries out. "I mean, okay. Yeah. I'll come."

"Okay, great!" The excitement in Kristen's tone is undeniable. "We're leaving at nine. Liv's driving."

I wait until the door clicks shut to throw the covers back and spring into a sitting position. Mackenzie thumps me in the shoulder with a closed fist. "What was that?"

"You should go. It's important for you to spend time with your sister. And Liv's great too."

"Yeah. I know." She sighs, combing her hair back from her face, then she waves a frustrated hand in front of herself. "Fine. I'll go."

Without warning, the door swings wide open and I pull the covers up over my lap. "Oh, and good morning, Dylan!" Kristen throws her head over her shoulder, one hand still on the doorknob, a devious, smug grin spread across her face.

"Uh, hi, Kristen," I stutter, my eyes bugging out like a deer in the headlights. "You knew I was here the whole time, didn't you?"

"Your car is in the driveway," she says bluntly.

I nod stupidly. "Of course it is."

"Get dressed, Mackenzie." With that, she closes the door and leaves us alone.

Mackenzie eyes me sceptically and then her laughter fills the room as she slaps my knee and shoves me in the shoulder. It's the first time I've seen her so carefree. "Did you really forget your car was out front?"

"Yeah. I did," I tell her. "I think I forgot the whole world for a while, honestly."

"Me too."

The smile falls from her face, and I can tell that like me, she's remembering all the things that have taken up occupancy in our worlds. The issues I'm having with my father and the company. Her newfound grandmother, her mother's death and the letter explaining it all.

"Let's not do this," I say, tilting her chin up.

"Do what?"

"Allow our problems to get in the way of this. Us. Here. Right now." I pull her in close, planting a kiss on her forehead.

She responds by crushing her lips against mine, thrusting her hands into my hair. There's no better feeling than knowing that she doesn't feel the need to hesitate with me anymore.

A groan escapes me when I realise what I need to do today.

"What?" she says, pulling back from me, her fingertips dragging down my bare chest.

"I have to get to the boat," I grimace. "And I should have mentioned this earlier, but I'm not going to be around for a couple of days."

"Why?" She drops her hands back into her lap, retreating from me.

"My father agreed to hand Claire my position in the company," I explain. "But he's making a song and dance about having me come to the office and show her the ropes, which is ridiculous, because Claire could do that job and everyone else's with her eyes closed."

"You mean, your dad isn't on your back about working for him anymore? That's great," she says, the glow returning to her cheeks. "That's what you wanted, right? He'll finally leave you alone."

"Yeah. I just wish I didn't have to go into the city. I want to stay here with you."

I tug at her t-shirt, snaking my arms around her waist, then I fall back into the pillows, pulling her down with me. We share another kiss and when she pulls back there's a silent message in her gaze.

Whatever this is between us, she feels it too.

But just as quickly, the spell is broken as Kristen's voice echoes through the door again. "Mackenzie! Are you dressed yet?"

She sighs, but there's a hint of a smile on her lips. "It's like living with a military officer."

I chuckle. "She's not that bad. I have to go anyway, but I'll call you when I get to the city this afternoon."

"Okay."

I pull her in again and kiss her, deeper this time, knowing it will be the last time I get to have her this close for a few days. I don't say out loud what I'm thinking. That I'm going to miss her like hell.

I pull on yesterday's jeans and t-shirt and hurry down the hall. Kristen is folding clothes in the living room at the front of the house.

"See you, Kris." I offer her an awkward wave.

"Bye, Dylan." She gives me a smile and a knowing look.

I close the front door behind me, then skip down the porch steps and climb into the RAV4. The engine splutters as I start the ignition. It's starting to sound unhealthy again, but there isn't much I can do about it right now. I can only hope and pray that it gets me to the city and back without any dramas. I make a mental note to take a look under the hood later.

When I make it to the boat, Jade is busy hosing down the deck on the port side. "Hey," she calls out. "You okay?"

"Yeah," I reply. "Why?"

"You look a little dishevelled there," she answers with a smirk.

I glance down at my wrinkled clothing, raking a hand through my hair that I didn't have time to run a comb through. "I guess I am. In a good way."

Her eyebrows shoot up in surprise. "Good night last night, then?"

"Yeah. The best." I'm unable to hide the smile that overtakes my face as I climb on board, and I don't even care.

"Wouldn't have had something to do with a feisty blonde, would it?" Jade questions.

My sheepish grin is all she needs in answer.

"'Bout time," she scoffs. "You're totally smitten."

"Who's smitten and with what?" Cameron emerges from below deck, his arms loaded with diving supplies.

"Dylan is in love with Mackenzie," Jade teases. "He's gone all gaga."

"'Bout time." Cameron's reply earns a dead stare from me.

"Oh, come on, dude," I say. "You only met her that one time."

"Yep," he agrees. "And I was lucky to not get burnt by all those sparks flying between the two of you."

"Anyway," I say. "I think I might book Mackenzie and her friend, Harper in for a tour at the end of the week if there's space. Harper missed out last time. I'll pay, of course."

"No problem," Cameron replies as he sorts the dive masks from the fins. "Just check the guest register and add them in."

"Thanks." I rub the base of my neck, preparing myself for the next favour I need to ask. "Uh, there's also something else I need to tell you guys." I steady my hands on my hips, staring at the boat deck between us. I hate that I have to ask for time off and with such little notice. "I need to take a few days off from tomorrow. I have some loose ends to tie up in the city."

"Loose ends, huh?" Jade muses. "Wouldn't have anything to do with a certain hotel conglomerate, would it?"

My jaw practically unhinges, my mouth gaping open like a cod as I swivel in her direction. When I turn back to Cameron, I expect to find confusion in his expression, but he doesn't look surprised by Jade's question at all.

"You guys know?

"Oh sweetie," she teases, laying a hand on my shoulder. "You're smooth, but you're not that smooth."

"Have you known this whole time?"

"Not the whole time. We probably figured it out about a month after you started working on the boat. I mean, Abbott is a common name but it's not that common." Cameron begins casually unpacking a slab of bottled water as though blowing this secret out of the water is the least exciting thing he's ever done.

That would have been around the time my parents cut me off. When news of my leaving had hit the papers. "Why didn't you guys say anything?"

Jade offers a small shrug. "I guess we figured that if you needed to keep it a secret, it must be a secret worth keeping. That you had your reasons."

"Wow," I say, letting out a long breath. "Thanks, I guess."

"You might want to prepare yourself for the rest of the town though," she suggests.

"What do you mean?"

"Here," Cameron says. "See for yourself." He tosses today's edition of the Cliff Haven Chronicle at me. The headline screams at me from the front page.

"IT'S A WOMAN'S WORLD. CLAIRE ABBOTT TO REPLACE HER BROTHER AT THE ABBOTT GROUP."

Below that, there's an old photo of me and Claire linked arm in arm at a red-carpet event. I think it was some movie premiere we'd been invited to attend. Claire looks elegant in a red floor length gown, a string of chunky diamonds adorning her neckline. I look bored, like I'd rather be anywhere else.

"Shit," I curse. "I knew it was only a matter of time."

I scan the article quickly. It appears to be written in a flattering light for Claire, all about the empowerment of women taking on the business world. There are a few lines in there about my so-called incompetency, but I can live with that. I couldn't have handled it if it had been Claire they were tearing to shreds. Not that she wouldn't be able to handle it. And I'm sure in the future at some point she will have to. That's just life. Well, *our* lives anyway.

"So, Mr. Abbott," Jade says. "Care to fill us in on the rest of the details? Your sister's hot, by the way."

"Jade!" Cameron exclaims.

"Well, she is." Jade places a hand on her hip defiantly.

Cameron pulls the newspaper out of my hand and glances down again at the photo. He looks up at me, his eyebrows raised, head tilted to the side. "She makes a fair point."

I pinch the bridge of my nose as I shake my head. Then I give them the cliff notes of my life before our guests board the boat for today's tour.

Chapter 31

MACKENZIE

"You okay, Mackenzie." Liv's voice cuts through my thoughts and I realise I've probably been twirling the same three strands of pasta on my fork for at least a few minutes. I don't think I've heard most of what the two of them have been talking about.

"Yep." I try to sound as chipper as I can, but it falls flat, only piquing both Liv and Kristen's concern.

"You sure?" Liv tilts her head to the side. "Because you've been about to eat that same forkful of fettuccine for the last five minutes and if you aren't gonna eat it, I'll take it off your hands. I don't know why, but I'm so hungry today."

"Maybe you're pregnant." Kristen's suggestion is met with Liv's wide eyes.

"I doubt it," Liv replies, though she seems to ponder the possibility before shaking her head. "Nah."

Truthfully, I've been sitting here wondering how to broach the subject of my mother and grandmother. These aren't the kind of things that you just blurt out over a tiny table at a gourmet café overlooking a pristine bay.

Kristen tries to lighten my sombre mood, offering a wink as she says, "She's probably got a certain surfer slash bar manager on her mind."

"Oh? Tell me everything," Liv demands, her eyes lighting up at the prospect of some fresh gossip.

"It's new," I begin, not sure how much information I want to divulge.

Putting your heart on the line is a sure way to get it broken, though something tells me Dylan will handle mine with extreme care.

You're safe with me, Kenz. Always.

"But they are so cute together," Kristen gushes.

I drop my fork into the bowl and aim an eyeroll her way. "You've literally only seen us together one time."

"Yeah. One time in your bedroom while you were both half naked," she chides. I jolt as she pokes a teasing finger at my ribs. "And you looked cute together."

Liv's eyes look like they're going to bug out of her head. "Are you serious? Wait. Are you talking about Dylan? Oh, you two do look cute together. I can totally see it now."

"Right?" Kristen adds, waving her fork in the air.

"Good for you, Mackenzie. Dylan's hot. And such a sweetie," Liv says. "Although, there's something so familiar about the guy. I swear, it's like I know him from somewhere."

My mouth twitches at her comment. Knowing Liv, it's highly possible that she, in fact, does know him from somewhere, but it's not my place to say. "I'm sorry about this morning," I mumble awkwardly.

"Don't be sorry, Mac. I'm relieved," Kristen replies. "Like I said, I've been worried about you spending so much time on your own lately."

"Well, I haven't exactly been spending that much time alone," I admit. This is my chance to redirect the conversation.

"Well, yeah. I know that now. You've had Dylan."

"Yeah, and Harper," I add. Get to the point Mackenzie. "And there's someone else."

"Someone else other than Dylan?" Liv asks, leaning eagerly across the table.

"Yes," I reply. Then when I see where their minds have gone, I quickly add, "No. Not like that. Geez."

They both deflate with relieved sighs and I'm met with puzzled looks.

"Oh, okay. Who?" Kristen asks.

My chest rises with a nervous inhale. Dylan has been hinting at me for weeks now to open up to Kristen, to make the choice to let people in. Here goes nothing.

"My grandmother," I reveal.

"What do you mean?" Kristen's features are now marred with confusion. "Our grandmother passed away a few years ago."

"Not our father's mother," I say. "My grandmother on my mother's side."

"Wow. Okay," she responds uncertainly. "I thought you didn't have any family left on your mum's side."

"Honestly, I didn't know that I did," I explain. "Dad told me my grandparents had passed well before I was born. It turns out she didn't know that I existed either."

"What?" Now it's Liv's turn to look baffled. "How did she not know about you?"

"She said my mother was troubled. That she never told her about the pregnancy."

"That's a lot to process," Kristen says.

She doesn't even know the half of it yet.

"Yeah, it has been. I've been spending some time with her at her art studio in Seabright Cove."

"Wait." Kristen raises a hand in the air. "Seabright Cove? You don't mean the Abstract Palette?"

"Yeah," I reply. "You know it?"

"Of course. It's been there forever. Grace used to come and help out at the primary school when we were younger." She picks up her fork, stirring her salad around before stabbing at a cherry tomato. "That art class I did with my mum? We did that at the Abstract Palette."

"No way."

"Yeah!" Kristen exclaims. "Small world, huh?"

"So…Grace? She's your grandmother?" Liv asks.

"Yeah," I answer, still in shock that Kristen had unknowingly met my grandmother before she'd even met me. "That's what she tells me."

"Mackenzie, this is insane," Kristen says, her eyes widening. "She would be able to answer so many questions you have. She would know where your mother is. Maybe you can finally – " She stops talking when she sees the silent tear that trails down my cheek. "Mac?"

"She's gone," I whisper. "She died. Last year sometime."

"Oh, Mackenzie." Liv is out of her seat now, scooting

closer to me on the bench seat I'm sharing with Kristen.

I've never had girlfriends like this. At least, not since before I met Ethan. He'd made sure I was kept as isolated as possible from everyone and everything.

Sitting here, sandwiched between these two amazing women as they comfort me, I now know what I've been missing out on. It makes me feel silly for taking so long to confide in them. I wish I had of been able to convince myself sooner that they'd only ever offer me love and acceptance and their unwavering support.

I fill Kristen and Liv in on the rest of the details. About how Grace found me, what I'd learned about my mother, and the letter that she left for me that detailed her depression. By the time I'm finished, both Kristen and Liv have tears streaming from their eyes too.

"Oh my god, Mackenzie," Kristen says, curling an arm around my shoulders. "I should have been there for you. I had no idea."

"It's not your fault," I say, swiping at my eyes. "I shut you out. I shut everyone out. My first instinct was to shut Grace out too."

"Look, I know we haven't known each other that long," Liv begins. "But I know a thing or two about how difficult it is to have to reinvent yourself in a new town full of new faces. I know what it's like to hide parts of yourself away. I did that too. For so long, I was scared to let people see the real me, but it was only when I opened up to them that good things started happening for me. Now, I can't imagine ever being any happier than I am right now."

A hopeful smile warms my cheeks. "I feel like I'm only just learning who the real me is."

"You've been through so much, Mac. But you're strong and brave and beautiful." Kristen tightens her arm around my shoulder. "You might not be able to see the real you yet, but I can. And I bet Dylan can too."

"Does he know?" Liv asks. "About everything that happened with Grace?"

I nod. "Yeah. He thinks I should go back and see her. We didn't exactly leave things on the best of terms the last time I visited."

"I think you should too," Liv says.

"Me too," Kristen agrees. "She obviously came looking for you because she cares. I mean, your mother had her reasons for doing what she did, but it isn't Grace's fault that she couldn't be a part of your life. I'm sure if she'd known about you, she would have done everything she could to help you."

"Yeah. I'm starting to see that now."

"Go see her," Kristen says. "I can drive you there if you like."

"Thanks." I aim a bittersweet smile back at my sister. "I might just take you up on that."

I have every intention of returning to the studio to see Grace, but there's someone else I need to see first. Someone that I should have gone to see a long time ago. The idea of it sends a ball of dread sinking into the pit of my stomach, but I've been putting it off for way too long.

I force myself to eat the rest of the pasta I've ordered for lunch and then we visit a few more shops.

Liv buys some new books at the local indie bookstore.

Kristen purchases Henley a gag gift – a pair of socks that say 'I can't keep calm. I'm a drummer.' I scour the art store for a few extra paint colours. I'm still not certain of what I'll paint on my canvas, but a few ideas have started to form in my mind.

As we head back to Cliff Haven, I think about how glad I am that I listened to Dylan and came out with the girls today. I left home today with a head full of uncertainty, a bundle of nerves in my gut but I'm returning with a grateful heart.

When Liv drops us home, Kristen dumps her bag on the hall table and flops down on the couch. She brings her hand up to rest on her stomach. "God, I'm so full from lunch I might go into a food coma. You wanna watch a movie or something?"

She picks up the remote and starts flicking through the channels as I stand in the doorway, weaving my fingers together anxiously. "Actually, I was wondering if I could ask you a massive favour."

"Sure. What's up?" She sits a little higher, straightening herself when she notices my unease.

"I was wondering if I could borrow your car."

"Okay," she says hesitantly. "Where are you going?"

"Milton." It's the only word I need to say out loud. The rest can be communicated through one look.

Her brow shoots upward and I know she understands what I'm telling her. Suddenly, the atmosphere feels charged, a tension falling over us.

"Do you need me to come with you?" she asks.

I shake my head, knowing I need to do this alone. "Maybe next time."

"Okay." She stands and moves toward the hall table, digging

for the keys in her bag. She places them in my palm. "Be careful."

"Thank you," I say, clutching them tightly in my fist. "I'll be back before my shift starts at the tavern tonight."

She nods as I turn toward the front door. I pause when I hear her call my name. "Mackenzie?"

I swivel back around and then her arms are around me, squeezing me tightly in a warm sisterly hug. It's obvious, at least to me, why I've never been a fan of physical affection. The only human contact I've ever had has been forced or abusive, but I relish this moment here in my sister's arms, allowing her to hold me.

"I'm proud of you," she whispers.

When her grip loosens from around me, we share a knowing look, before I turn and walk down the front steps. She watches from the porch as I reverse back down the driveway, offering a small smile and a wave.

Forty-five minutes later I'm pulling into the Rykers rehabilitation facility. I'd be lying if I said I hadn't considered turning around at least ten times on the way here. I consider it once more now, but I've come this far.

Nerves overwhelm me as I approach the front desk. Again, I second guess whether I should even be here. I know I don't need to be. That this is my choice. I don't owe anything to anyone else, but at the very least, I need to do this for myself. I need to see this through.

"Can I help you, Miss?" I'm greeted at reception by an

older woman with a stern disposition.

"Uh, hi," I say timidly, my voice smaller than I intended. "I'm here to visit Greg Riley."

"Do you have an appointment?" She barely makes eye contact with me as she begins flipping through a stack of paperwork on the desk in front of her.

"No, but I really need to see him." I was afraid she might ask me this.

"I'm sorry," she replies bluntly. "Even if he has visitation rights and you are an approved contact, I can't let you in without an appointment."

"Please. It's really important that I see him. I'm his daughter and – "

"I really can't help you today, but you can make an appointment for next week if you like."

"I have to see him now." Desperation has begun to seep in through my veins. I can't go another week without seeing him. I've already left it too long as it is. "There's been a death in the family."

I realise I'm giving the term 'family' more meaning that it deserves in this context.

The lady at the desk goes still. This time she finally looks up at me, her features softening. "I'm so sorry to hear that. Alright, we may be able to make an exception. Let me see if I can help."

She begins tapping away on the keyboard in front of her. "Greg Riley, you said?"

"Yes," I answer eagerly.

"Can you confirm your father's date of birth?"

I rattle off my father's birth date and she gives a brief nod.

Her expression doesn't give anything away as she continues tapping away some more on the keys.

"And your name?"

"Mackenzie Riley."

"Do you have some ID?"

I pull my driver's licence from my purse and slide it over the counter.

It feels like an eternity passes before she replies. "That's fine, Mackenzie. If you'd like to head down the hall and to the left, you'll come to a visiting area. I'll send for Mr. Riley to meet you there. I'm sorry for your loss."

"Thank you," I say. "Thank you so much."

She offers a tight smile. "Don't make a habit out of it. You'll need an appointment next time."

I nod profusely, my eyes beginning to sting with the tears I push back down. "Okay."

Following the woman's instructions, I head down the hall and as I veer left, the waiting room comes into view. It's a bright and inviting space, well-lit by the floor-to-ceiling windows that line both sides of the room. There's an outside sitting area out the back, lush with greenery and colourful flowerpots. It doesn't seem like a bad place, all things considered.

A few other people are seated off to one side, so I choose a couch along the far-left window. Although, sitting is the last thing I feel like doing.

Anxiety fires through my veins as I pace the space in front of the couch, my eyes on the ground, my forefingers massaging my temples. I contemplate one more time whether I should turn and run from this place.

The last time I'd seen my father, he had been passed out on the couch. His head was dipped back along the headrest, an almost empty bottle of whisky on the floor at his feet. An amber liquid trickled from it, leaving a stain on the already soiled carpet.

I'd reached for his wrist, relieved to feel the faint thrumming of a pulse. Then I'd turned for the door, following the yellow glow of Henley's headlights in the driveway with the intent of never looking back.

Now that I'm here, I can't help but wonder what he might say when he sees me? What will he do?

I don't have to wonder long. I force myself to look up when gentle footsteps fall on the plush, grey carpet in front of me.

There are two things I notice about my father's eyes in this moment. One is how much emotion they seem to convey. Happiness, joy but also guilt.

The other is how clear they are. No longer red-rimmed and bloodshot, the whites whiter. If it weren't for the turmoil that swirls in their midst, I'd say he looked more at peace.

"Mackenzie?" His voice cracks as he questions my name.

He blinks, as though he can't really believe I'm standing in front of him. I don't blame him. I can't believe it either.

He takes a step closer, but I retreat, moving backwards with my arms folded across my chest. I wanted to see him again. I needed to. But now that he's here before me, looking the healthiest he ever has, at least to me, I can't stop all of those bad memories rushing in.

"Did you know?" I blurt, swallowing down the heavy lump that forms in my throat.

His eyes cloud over with confusion, his brow wrinkling as

he shakes his head. "Know what?"

"Did you know that she was dying? Did you know that Mum's gone?" My eyes well as I say the words.

The shock that washes over my father's face tells me that he didn't know. That he's learning this information for the first time right now. He pushes both hands through his hair as he falls onto the couch beside us. "I had no idea."

I don't say anything while I watch him process this information. He chokes out a guttural sob. "Oh, Mackenzie. I'm so sorry."

"Why didn't you ever tell me about her?" I demand, my jaw set hard in anger. "You never talked about her."

"I know." He drops his gaze to the floor. "I'm sorry."

"I needed you to talk to me."

"I'm so sorry. I'm so sorry," he pleads. His hands are cupping his mouth now, muffling the sobs that escape. I watch until I can't bear it any longer. I can't stand to see him break in front of me. I fall down on the couch beside him, and he finally lifts his head. "How did it happen?"

"Cancer," I sniffle as tears sting behind my eyes. "I found out from my grandmother. She came looking for me."

The uncertainty portrayed in his expression is sincere, letting me know that he didn't know about Grace either. "Your mother told me her parents had died."

"Her father died," I tell him. "Her mother is well and truly alive."

"I had no idea." He shakes his head in shock. "She told me she'd never had a great relationship with her mother."

"Why didn't you talk about her, Dad? There's so much I don't know about her."

He squeezes his eyes shut as though he's in physical pain.

"Because it killed me to talk about her. It killed me when she left us like that. I had to drink every day just to numb the pain. And it killed me to look at you, because with every passing year, you began to look more and more like her."

I shake my head, unsure how to take this information. "Is that supposed to make it okay?"

"No, Mac. None of it is okay. None of it." He turns to me, determination in his gaze. "I'm going to make it right. I'm going to get out of here and I'm going to be the father that you need."

"You mean the father that Kristen needs." I spit out the words.

His eyes fill with hurt. "What?"

"You're doing this for her, right?" I accuse. "I mean, you only got off your ass and came here after *her* letters arrived in the post."

A crack tears down my chest as a tear rolls from his eye. "I know I've been a terrible father. I know I've hurt you both. I'm doing this for both of my girls And I'm also doing it for myself. I'm going to make things right."

I want to believe him, but past experiences tell me that nothing will ever change. He will never change.

"You said that last time," I bite out.

"I mean it this time."

I'm just now beginning to comprehend what Kristen had said about forgiveness. Sometimes we don't need to forgive someone to release them from their demons. We do it to free ourselves from our own.

I never had the chance to forgive my mother.

I hope that I'll get the chance to forgive him.

"I need to go," I say, getting up to leave.

I've taken two steps before his gravelly cry stalls my feet in place on the carpet.

"Mackenzie," he croaks. "I loved her."

I turn around slowly, unable to hold my tears back anymore.

"I've only ever loved two women. Your mother was one of them." There's an honesty in his gaze that makes it impossible not to believe him. These may be the truest words he's ever spoken to me.

I nod once as my lips twist up in a sad smile. The hole in my already fractured heart grows wider, mourning the loss of everything that could have been.

I take one last look at this man who has been to hell and back, walked through fire and had the embers burn their marks into his skin.

And I hope with everything I am that he can find a way to rise from the ashes.

Chapter 32

DYLAN

My phone chimes from the desk in front of me and I slide it across the mahogany, tapping on the screen. My lips curl in a smile when I see that Mackenzie has sent me a text.

I open it to find a picture of her blank canvas. Only it isn't entirely blank anymore. There are blue flecks of paint in different shades strewn across the top half of the otherwise stark white.

> This counts as starting , right?

My grin widens as I type out my reply.

> Baby steps. Miss you.

Shit. I hold my breath as I reread the words I've just sent. I'd been wanting to let her know how much I missed her since the moment I left her, but I'd worried it might be too much.

And now the three little dots that persistently bob underneath my text are practically screaming at me that I've freaked her out. I've said too much, too soon. She's taking way too long to reply.

I'm dragging a sweaty palm down my face when the phone buzzes in my hand. Her reply is everything.

Miss you more... 🖤

Maybe I hadn't freaked her out after all. Still, I'll exercise some self-control in the future to avoid that post-text anxiety.

"Are we interrupting your social life, Dylan?" My father's voice booms from across the other side of the room. Glancing up, I find him watching me with wary eyes, my sister Claire flanking his left side.

Claire doesn't seem to hold the disdain my father does for my preoccupation. She winks at me playfully. "Texting that girlfriend of yours again?"

"Yeah," I say, realising that my father and Claire still believe Mackenzie to be my real full-time girlfriend, when in reality, I'm not sure now exactly what we are.

"And how is Mackenzie?" my father asks.

"She's good. She's actually currently working on an art piece for an exhibition night at the Abstract Palette. Her work is amazing. She's got serious talent."

"Abstract Palette?" Claire questions, setting down a pile of documents on the desk beside me.

"Yeah," I say, opening the desk drawer and rifling through it for a highlighter. "It's this little boutique art studio in Seabright Cove. Her grandmother runs it."

"Oh yeah, I know the one. It's part of the Elmwood building." Claire doesn't look up from the papers she's now sifting through on the desk beside me.

"Elmwood building? Hmm." For some reason the name piques my father's interest. He plucks his phone from the top pocket of his Prada suit blazer and begins to saunter out the door. "I'll be back in a second. I need to make a call."

"What's his deal?" I mutter, loosening the tie that my father thrust upon me this morning as I walked through the glass sliding doors of the building.

"He's stressing about the new project," Claire says matter-of-factly.

"Which one?"

"The boutique."

"A boutique hotel?" My nose scrunches up in confusion. "Since when does the Abbott Group specialise in anything other than large chain hotels?"

"He thinks it will be good for business," she explains, tossing her auburn hair behind her shoulder. "He wants to create smaller, intimate hotels for regional and remote areas. I mean, it sounds good in theory. Most of the locations he's been considering don't have luxury accommodation but so far, none of them have seemed the right fit."

"Why not?"

"He's not looking to build from the ground up. To maintain authenticity, he wants to utilise something established. Trouble is finding something suitable."

"Claire." Our father has returned to the doorway. "Will you set up that meeting with Donald Osgood?"

Claire stacks the documents she's been rifling through back into a neat pile. "Sure."

The fact that my father has just asked Claire to do a mundane task fit for a lackey lets me know that he wants her out of the room. For what reason, I'm unsure.

"Claire was just telling me about your boutique hotel idea," I say once I hear the echo of her stilettos fading down the hall.

"Yes. Well, then I'm sure she's mentioned that it's still in planning stage." My father's gruff tone signals he doesn't really want to discuss this with me, but I push on.

"Which locations have you been thinking of?"

He picks up one of the files that Claire has left on the desk, not bothering to maintain eye contact as he answers abruptly. "That information is for company employees only."

My eyes narrow at him. "Well, I'm here, aren't I?"

"Yes. And you are no longer an employee here at the Abbott Group so that information is off limits." He takes a seat in the armchair over in the corner. "I trust you saw yesterday's newspaper."

My lips part with an exhausted sigh. Of course, I'd seen it. Yet another article about my exit from the company. Yet another means to drive a wedge between me and my parents. Maybe a subject change is in order. "How was golf last weekend?"

"Fine." His answer is short and to the point.

"I heard the new restaurant over on the course is amazing."

"Dylan, I'm trying to work here." Clearly, he has no interest in small talk, and I've had about more than I can take.

"Fine," I say through gritted teeth. "I was just trying to make conversation with you, Dad. I figured that now that you aren't my boss you could maybe just be my father instead, but whatever."

I begin shutting down the desktop in front of me, tossing the pens into the drawer to my left and slamming it with a little too much force.

It's my actions and not my words that have finally caught his attention. "What are you doing?"

"I'm your son and I'm not going to stay here and have you treat me like some sort of second-rate citizen. I'm going home." I tuck my phone and keys into my pocket and storm toward the office door.

My father is on his feet now, his jaw set in anger. "You promised me three days here, Dylan. Claire still needs help transitioning."

"No, Dad. She doesn't," I retaliate. I don't believe Claire needs my help at all and I can't figure out why my father is putting me through this for any other reason than just to torture me. "Claire has everything under control and all I'm doing here is assistant work, like filing and answering phones. If I didn't know better, I'd think…" I stop talking, shaking my head in amusement, because I think I've finally figured out exactly what this is all about. "Oh my god. That's it, isn't it?"

"What are you talking about?" My father is losing patience now but so am I.

"You want my presence in the building known. You're hoping it will get the media off our backs if they catch me walking into headquarters. That they won't suspect any more family drama."

He stands with his hands on his hips and lets out an exasperated sigh. He isn't going to admit that I'm right, but his silence says more than words ever could.

Finally, after a long pause, he repeats, "You promised me three days."

"I'll come back next week for the final day," I tell him firmly. "But right now, I have somewhere more important to be."

And someone I need to be with.

I take the stairs down from the fifteenth floor, too impatient to wait for the lift. I don't want to spend a single second longer in this building than I need to. I rip the tie from around my neck, tossing it into the trash can outside the automated glass doors. This suit is suffocating. I strip off the jacket and throw it into the back seat as I climb into my car.

It's not until my tyres are crunching down her gravel driveway that I feel as though I can breathe again. I slam the door shut, rounding the corner of the house to the backyard where I can see Mackenzie lost in concentration as she drags her paintbrush across the canvas nestled upon an easel down on the jetty.

She doesn't see me until I'm barely ten metres away. She does a double take when she finally looks up, the suit pants and business shirt no doubt out of place in this setting.

"You're here." She drops the paint brush into a jar of cloudy, coloured water beside her. "I thought you weren't coming back until tomorrow night."

"I needed to see you."

"But what about your dad?" she questions. "I thought you had stuff to tie up in the city."

"Yeah, I do. But this is more important. I'd choose this any day of the week." I don't wait for her to respond before I wrap my arms around her. I hold her, breathe her in, as she brings her arms up around my neck, but when she pulls away from me there's uncertainty in her gaze. "What's wrong?"

"Nothing." She shakes her head and forces a weak smile as she stares at the ground between us.

"Hey," I say, tilting her chin up with my forefinger. "You can tell me."

"It's nothing. I'm fine. It's just…" She hesitates. "I've never been somebody's first choice before."

The way her eyes prick with tears kills me. The fact that this amazing woman hasn't known unconditional affection *kills* me.

I cup her cheek in my right hand, drawing her body closer with my left. "Then you better get used to it."

I lean in until our foreheads touch before she brushes her lips against mine, lingering there long enough to test my patience. I don't give in though, wanting her to be the one to make the next move. My chest rises with every ragged breath, my need for her excruciating.

What feels like an eternity passes before her hands clasp the back of my neck and she crushes her mouth to mine. She kisses me like nobody else ever has, leaving me wanting more long after she pulls away, breathless.

"So, I guess you really did miss me then," I say, my voice unexpectedly hoarse.

A slow blush creeps across her cheeks. "Shut up," she says sheepishly. "You missed me too."

"I did," I agree. "And I have a surprise for you."

"You do?" She pulls back a little, her arms still draped around my neck.

"Yeah. There's space on the boat tomorrow morning for

you and Harper." I lay a quick kiss on her forehead. "Promise not to feed you to a shark this time."

She laughs softly, a suspicious smirk twisting one corner of her mouth. "Oh, I see. So you want to fake-date me in front of your employees now?"

"No." I shake my head, my smile faltering, remembering that we haven't defined our relationship yet. I know what I want, and I think she may know it too, but in case the message isn't clear, I decide to lay it all out for her. I've never been more serious as the next words leave my mouth. "I want to real-date you. In front of everyone. All the time."

Chapter 33

MACKENZIE

"You really like him, don't you?"

Harper asks me the one question I'm too scared to answer out loud and it has me almost squirming on the bench seat at the back of the boat.

We're about halfway to the reef, watching as Dylan answers questions that a couple of middle-aged women are asking him about his experiences in the water.

We both snicker at his use of overexaggerated hand actions. We can't hear a word of what he's saying over the boat's motor, but from the wide-eyed expression on the women's faces, I can only imagine he's talking about sharks.

"I don't know," I answer, which is an outright lie.

I like him way more than I care to admit.

Harper rolls her eyes at me, seeing through the lie, then her eyes soften. "They're not all bad."

I turn away, my eyes scanning the turquoise ocean before I bring them back to hers. "You sure?" I ask. "Because none of the other men in my life have ever shown me otherwise."

"What about Henley?"

"Yeah, I guess." I shrug. "Henley's like a unicorn though. A total mythical creature."

She laughs. "Maybe Dylan is too."

"Where has all of this sudden positivity come from? I thought you'd sworn off men forever after Noah's dad walked out of your lives. All men are assholes remember?"

She shrugs. "They aren't though, are they?"

She nods toward Dylan who is now obediently smiling for a photo with one of the women. Once her friend takes the picture, they swap places and we both fight to stifle our giggles.

"I guess not," I reply.

"I have to believe in happy endings, I guess," Harper says. "I choose to believe there are good men out there and that one of them will find me one day."

"I hope you're right," I tell her, then glancing back at Dylan I add, "What if I can't trust him?"

"Something tells me you already know that you can." She follows my line of sight back to Dylan and the two women. "Those women are totally checking out your boyfriend's abs, by the way. They couldn't be more obvious if they tried."

I watch the women and sure enough their eyes are trailing their way downward to where Dylan's wetsuit is rolled down at the waist and I can't help but laugh.

"You're so lucky!" Harper says as she playfully backhands my knee.

Her words catch me off guard. I don't think anybody has

ever said that to me before, and up until now, I would never have referred to myself as 'lucky'.

My circumstances have never been the envy of anyone else, and maybe they still aren't. But I'm starting to like this little life I'm building, and all of the people in it that make it what it is. For the first time, I can see a glimpse of what my future could look like. And I want Dylan to be a part of it.

"Yeah," I agree. "I guess I am."

"So do you think you'll go and see Grace again?"

"Yeah. Definitely. I'm going to see her tomorrow." I've put off another visit to the studio for too long. I need to see my grandmother. After having time and space to breathe, I've realised how important it is to me that I maintain a connection with her. "The exhibition night is this weekend and I'd planned to help her set up. At least I did before everything else happened."

"I'd love to meet her someday."

The thought of introducing Harper to Grace brings a smile to my face. Taking your friends to meet your grandmother just seems so normal. And I've never had normal. "I'm sure that can be arranged."

A few short moments later, Cameron throws the anchor in place, securing the boat near the reef. We're in a different location this time, anchored off a small island.

Dylan turns from the two women he'd been speaking with and much to their dismay, begins pulling up his wetsuit. He wanders toward Harper and I, calling for the rest of the group to join him.

"Okay, listen up guys," he calls. "If you are snorkelling today, you will be over there with Jade. Scuba divers can follow me. We'll have plenty of time to explore the reef and those that would like to can also head over to Coral Island over there. There's a nice walking track up to a lookout at the top of the hill. Stay safe, guys. We're all here to answer any questions you might have so don't hesitate to ask."

I love being able to watch him here in his natural habitat. This is where he belongs, not stuck behind some stuffy office desk. I can already imagine him taking people out on his own tour boat one day.

He steps forward, warmth shooting through me when he curls an arm around my waist. "I'll catch up with you soon," he whispers into my ear.

He aims a wink at me, before directing the small group of divers to the edge of the boat. His touch had only been fleeting but my heartbeat stays in overdrive long after he pulls away.

"See?" Harper says beside me. "Lucky."

"Stop," I scoff. "Come on. Let's go find Jade."

We join the rest of the snorkellers on the other side of the boat and one by one, we file into the water.

Just like she had the first time I came out on the boat, Jade gives us a guided snorkel tour, pointing out various species of fish and rambling off facts about the ecosystem. Harper seems to be having a great time and I'm so glad my friend is getting some much-needed rest and recovery.

About half an hour later Jade lets us know that we have another thirty minutes of free time to explore, and Harper and I decide to journey across to the island.

We make it to the shallows, wading to the shore before sliding off our snorkel masks. I follow Harper's lead as she drops down onto the sand and we sit, catching our breaths as the sun pours warmth down on us from above.

"You having a good time?" I ask her.

"Yeah," she replies. Her smile falters, the light falling from her eyes. "I am."

"Why do you suddenly look like you're about to burst into tears on me, then?"

She drops her head between her bent up knees and chuckles. "I'm not. I'm okay. I just miss him."

"You've only been away from Noah for like two hours."

"I know!" She laughs. "Isn't that crazy?"

"No," I say, my tone serious as my eyes meet hers. "You're a good mum."

Harper grins at me, then her smile falls and her eyes turn glassy. "I'm sorry about your mum, Mackenzie."

I inhale a sharp breath, swallowing down the overwhelming emotions that still threaten to arise at the mention of my mother. "Thanks."

"I guess we like to think of our mothers as some sort of amazing superheroes, when in reality, they're only human. Just like the rest of us." She picks up a shell from the sand beside her, smoothing out its sides. "The truth is parents like to think they know what's best, but they aren't always as put together as they like to seem. Trust me, I am one."

I laugh softly. "I guess I'm slowly learning to let go of the anger. As hard as it is to understand, in her own twisted way, she thought she was saving me."

Harper lies her head on my shoulder, and I rest mine on hers. "I'm glad I met you, Mackenzie Riley."

"I'm glad I met you too, Harper Conway."

I mean these words with my whole being. I've never had a friendship like the one I have with Harper, and I doubt I ever will again.

"Hey." Harper lifts her head, squinting at the ocean in the distance. "Is that Dylan?"

I follow her gaze to the figure surfacing from the small waves. He no longer has his dive tank on, or his wetsuit for that matter, but it's definitely Dylan.

He removes his snorkel mask as he wades out of the water, his favourite pair of light blue boardies hung low on his hips. The grin he aims at me as he drops down onto the sand beside me is enough to make me melt.

"Hello, ladies." He presses a kiss to the side of my head.

"See anything exciting down there, dive master?" Harper asks.

His muscular shoulders jump in a shrug. "Not today. Just a whole heap of sea turtles."

"Sea turtles!" Harper squeals. Surprisingly, we hadn't seen any on our way over to the island. "Where are they?"

"They were over on that side of the boat," Dylan says, outstretching an arm to point into the distance.

Harper picks up her snorkel mask and rises to her feet. "Well, lovebirds. This is where I leave you. There are sea turtles to be found."

We both laugh as she pulls her mask down and starts wading back into the ocean. "Have fun!" I call out.

"What about you, Kenz?" Dylan says as he gently tugs my chin to him, drawing me into his warm, whiskey stare. "Are you having fun?"

"Yeah." I press a kiss to his cheek, trailing my lips along his jaw before I nuzzle into the crook of his neck. My fingers find the tattooed script that runs across his ribcage. "I am now."

He threads his fingers through my hair, planting a kiss on my forehead. "Do you wanna come up to the lookout?"

"Sure."

He springs up onto his feet then holds his hands out to help me to mine. I follow him along the winding trail that leads to the top of the hill. Once we've reached the lookout, we step up onto the edge of a small, decked platform.

From here we can see the entire coastline, the coves that make up Cliff Haven and Little Bay and some of the other uninhabited neighbouring islands that I'm yet to learn the names of. Below us, the white sand stretches out underneath us, melting into a crystal blue ocean.

Dylan rests an elbow on the protective fencing, his gaze stuck on something out in the distance. "Hey, look. Dolphins."

"Cool." I slide into the space beside him in time to see a pod of dolphins surfacing off the shore, looping playfully through the water. I curl my arms around Dylan's waist, leaning into his warmth, the scent of coconut and vanilla infiltrating my senses. "You never ended up telling me what happened when you went to the city."

"That's because nothing happened," he replies. "My dad was only using me. He was just hoping I'd get snapped by the paparazzi going into the building so the newspapers would have something new to print."

"That sucks. I'm sorry."

"I spent the whole time doing simple, boring tasks for my sister, while my dad ignored me to take calls about his new boutique hotel project."

"Boutique hotel?" I ask. "That's what your ex had been talking about at the party that night."

"She was? Oh, well. It doesn't concern me anymore. Honestly, I don't even want to go back there." He brushes my hair behind my shoulder, and I shiver as his fingers drag along my neck.

"Do you have to?" I selfishly wish I could keep him here all to myself.

"Honestly, I don't think it matters whether I do or not, but I need to go for Claire's sake. I promised her we'd have drinks to celebrate her new role so I kind of owe that to her."

"Fair enough." The love and respect he has for his sister is admirable.

"I'm going to miss you every second that I'm gone though." He cups my cheek in his palm and kisses me again. Despite the warm weather, a trail of goosebumps descends across my skin.

I'm going to miss him too, a feeling that terrifies me more and more each day.

That fear must be written all over my face, because as I retreat away from him, his forehead wrinkles, his eyes scouring my face for answers he won't find. "What's wrong?"

I take a step back, my chest rising with an anxious breath as my eyes drop to the ground. "Nothing."

"Don't do that, Kenz," he warns. "Don't close yourself off to me."

"It's nothing," I say to him. "It isn't you. It's me."

"Ouch."

"No. That's not what…"

"I'm kidding." He grins, his eyes twinkling deviously before they soften. He reaches for my hand, taking it in his. "Come on. What's going on?"

"I'm scared." I admit, unable to meet his gaze. I'm not sure how to tell him that I'm starting to feel things that I've only ever read about in books or seen in movies. That I've begun to have this constant fear that I need to hold onto everything, and to him, because it could all just go away in an instant. "I've never had this much to lose. I don't know what it all means."

He seems to consider this for a moment. Then his reply comes, confident and reassuring. "I think it means that you're happy."

"Yeah." I feel my lips twitch, curling up in a grin until it builds into a smile that I couldn't contain if I tried. I look down to where his hand clutches mine, squeezing it before he takes me in his arms. "I think I finally am."

Chapter 34

DYLAN

"Thanks for today, Dylan." Harper beams as we reach the end of the jetty. "I had fun. It was just what I needed."

"You're welcome, Harps. Anytime." I wrap an arm around her, squeezing her in a friendly hug.

"I'm going to pay you back though." She slides her beach bag off her shoulder and dips into it to find her wallet.

"Seriously not necessary," I wave a hand at her generous gesture. "I get a staff discount anyway."

"Oh," she says. "Okay. Well, if you're sure."

"One hundred percent," I assure her.

"You need a ride home?" Mackenzie pipes up.

"No, that's okay. I can walk." Harper readjusts her bag on her shoulder, her smile inching wider as she readies herself to leave.

"You sure?" Mackenzie asks. "It's not like it's out of the way or anything."

"What do you mean?" she questions, her brows pulling in. "I live on the other side of town from you."

"Yeah. From me," Mackenzie replies. "But not from Dylan's."

Her eyes rake over me, letting me know that she doesn't intend to go home just yet. It puts a smile on my face and fills my chest with warmth. Nothing makes me happier than knowing she's found this level of comfort with me.

"Oh, I see." Harper's voice is lively as she winks at Mackenzie. "It's all good. I think I'd prefer to walk anyway. I can't wait to get back to Noah, but I also want to enjoy the silence for just a little longer."

I chuckle. "No problem. Say hi to him for us."

"Will do. Have fun, love birds." Harper raises two fingers up to the sky in a peace symbol and turns on her heel, walking down the road in the opposite direction, her skin a few shades darker and her soul seemingly nourished.

"So, my place?" I ask as we walk toward the car.

"Your place."

Mackenzie flips the door handle and climbs into the passenger seat. I round the car to the driver's side and do the same.

We're halfway down the boulevard when she starts fiddling with the dial on the dash, searching through the radio stations. We've never really listened to music in the car before, though it's always played at a low volume in the background of our conversations.

Static hums throughout the car until she finds a station that grabs her interest.

"Hey! I love this song." She spins the volume dial all the way up and the sounds of Led Zeppelin's 'Whole Lotta Love' fill the car.

I watch her from the corner of my eye, a lopsided grin spreading across my face. I try to keep my eyes mostly on the road but when I brake for the stop sign at the end of the main street, she has my full attention.

She is a sight to behold, gorgeous and wild. Lost in the music, her hands wind above her head as she sways in her seat. It's not until the end of the chorus hits that she notices me staring.

Her blue eyes are brighter when they finally meet mine.
Lighter.

It's as though a weight has lifted and I catch a glimpse of the other Mackenzie. The unbridle, unbound version of her. Not the one she openly displays, the one she wears like a shield, but the one she keeps hidden behind it.

It isn't the first time I've seen her. Like, really seen her.

I'd seen the fire in her the day she launched the water tap into that jerk's face in the bar. Her spark, the night we kissed on my boat in the warehouse. I'd been privileged enough to witness both her strength and her humility on so many occasions, including the day we spent at the aquarium.

She came into my life this sarcastic cynic, albeit a stunningly beautiful one with grey-blue eyes, both fierce like the eye of the storm and unwavering like the calm that comes before it.

I've always been drawn to Mackenzie. This woman that has waded through the depths of darkness, still learning to find the light in people.

I'd felt a connection to her when we had our first proper conversation around the bonfire at EJ and Liv's wedding. I'd believed then that we were kindred spirits.

I just didn't know how right I'd be.

She drops her arms into her lap, a shy smile creeping across her lips when she feels my stare on her. "What?"

"Nothing," I say, my voice low and thick.

Suddenly, I can't wait to get her home. I pull up the handbrake and tug her close, kissing her as the sounds of Jimmy Page's iconic guitar solo echo throughout the car. She twists herself around in her seat, wrapping her arms around my neck.

This is everything I've ever wanted. Just this.

She whimpers into my mouth as I take the kiss deeper, but when a car horn beeps behind us, disturbing the otherwise silent street, she pulls away unable to contain her amusement.

A loud laugh bursts from me too as we both straighten up in our seats. I release the handbrake and shift the car into drive, continuing on to my place.

Five minutes later we're slipping down the side of the house, rounding the back porch where Chance awaits us. I call out to him, happy to see him, but like the traitor he is, he bounds up to Mackenzie instead.

"Hey, boy!" She holds her arms out to the scruffy canine as he jumps up on her thighs. "Did you miss me, huh? Good boy!"

She giggles as he drops to the decking, rolling over onto his back, tongue hanging out of his mouth. I unlock the door and slide it open, then Chance is on his feet, bounding inside the house.

"Crazy mutt," I mutter affectionately as I step up to the back door. Mackenzie straightens, leaning against the railing, making no attempt to follow me. "You coming in?"

Her bottom lip slips between her teeth, her blonde waves swaying as she shakes her head. "Maybe later."

"Later?"

She shuffles down the steps, my eyes widening as she pulls her shirt over her head and slips out of the denim cut-offs she's wearing to reveal her red bikini.

"What are you doing?" I ask curiously, one eyebrow shooting upward.

She aims a devious grin at me in response, then I follow her as she struts over to the side of the house where my surfboards lean up against the external wall. "I'm gonna school you in the waves first."

"Oh, are you now?" I rasp as I pin her against the wall, my eyes trailing downward over her red bikini, appreciating the way it covers just the right amount of skin.

"Yep," she replies, her voice a whisper.

"You're on." I crush my mouth to hers as her hands lace around my neck and she allows her body to sag against the wall as she kisses me back.

The moment I attempt to wrap my arm around her, she slides out from under me, swiftly grabbing one of the boards and hoisting it up underneath her arm, her laughter carrying on the wind as she runs toward the surf.

My feet remain firmly planted on the sand as I drink her in, the woman I'm slowly but surely falling for, and all the things that make her her. The things she doesn't let anybody else see.

She glances back over her shoulder at me, her wild, blonde hair bouncing around her in long wavy ribbons, a smile that could light up the darkest night.

There she is.

There's the real Mackenzie Riley.

Chapter 35

DYLAN

I stroll into my temporary office on the fifteenth floor of Abbott Corp at exactly five minutes before I'm required to. I already feel claustrophobic in this suit and tie. It's hard to believe I used to wear one every day. It's amazing how easily I've become accustomed to beachwear and bare feet.

I nod at Claire as I pull out the heavy chair and lower my coffee cup to the surface of the mahogany desk. She's on fire this morning, already in full business mode at seven fifty-five, her facial expression signalling that she's most likely dealing with a less than co-operative client. Her voice doesn't waver as she retaliates to his demands in a seamlessly professional manner.

Once again, I find myself feeling as though I've been rendered useless. Much to my father's dismay I'm sure, there were no paparazzi awaiting my entrance to the building this morning.

After what had gone down last week, I had seriously contemplated not bothering to show today. The only reason I've agreed to work, and I use the term 'work' lightly, is because I'd promised Claire drinks this afternoon. No matter what kind of hell my father is intent on putting me through, it will be worth it to see her shine. She's going to do big things for this company. I can see it now.

There's a manilla folder containing a stack of documents on the desk in front of me, so I decide to busy myself with that while I wait for Claire's instruction. I flip it open, sifting casually through the paperwork when my eyes catch on familiar words. I take another sip of my coffee and freeze when I realise what I'm reading.

This is a real estate contract. For the sale of 31 Palmwood Drive, Seabright Cove. Highlighted in parentheses are two words that turn my blood cold.

"The Elmwood."

The coffee cup falls from my grip, sloshing onto the carpet and up one of my trouser legs. I feel physically ill as I rise to my feet. Claire's voice comes into focus as she wraps up her conversation.

"Okay, Charles. Look into that for me and we can reconvene at the end of next week." Her phone slams down on the desk. "Ugh. Seriously that guy can be so difficult to work with." I look up at her as she pinches the bridge of her nose, then flips her hair over her shoulder. It's a moment before she glances in my direction, no doubt seeing the colour drain from my face. "What's up with you?"

"What is this, Claire?"

"What's what?" she replies, walking toward the desk.

There's a deep crease between her perfectly tinted eyebrows as she slides the manilla folder closer.

"Oh. Dad left this here for us to deal with today. He secured a location for the new boutique hotel. I'm actually really excited about this one. I think it will be a great business move." When I don't reply, she looks up at me again, seeing the hurt in my expression. "Seriously, are you okay?"

"The Elmwood building, Claire? Really?"

"What?" She flips open the folder and her face falls as she scans the top page document. "Oh, Dylan. I had no idea. I promise. This is all Dad's doing."

"Grace is going to be devastated. That studio is her whole life." My nostrils flare in defiance as I saunter to the window, looking out at the traffic below, the pedestrians tiny like ants. "We have to get him to back out. Find somewhere else."

"Find somewhere else for what?" My father's voice jolts me. I swivel around to find him standing in the doorway, his hands tucked casually into the pockets of his suit pants.

"Why would you do this, Dad?" I snatch the folder from Claire's grip and shake it in frustration. "Is this your way of punishing me because you don't like my life choices."

"You're being paranoid, Dylan." My father scoffs. "This is simply business. The Elmwood will be a fantastic location. We have big plans for it."

"Yeah. Plans that involve kicking a grandmother out of the studio she's prided herself on for forty years. Not to mention the other business owners in that complex." I should have known something was up when he'd shown even the mildest interest in the Elmwood when I mentioned it. "Why this building? How did you even obtain it so quickly?"

"We weren't the first company to make an offer. Cyncorp has been trying to get them to sell for years. I made an offer that they couldn't refuse," he explains in almost a boastful tone.

"There has to be something else out there," I argue, though I know I'm fighting a losing battle.

My mother was right. When my father wants something, nothing will stand in his way, and he will resort to drastic measures to get it. It's probably why he's taken my exit from the company so hard.

"Come and work for me," he almost demands.

"What? Dad we've been through this already."

"You and Claire could be co-CEOs," he suggests. "If you can find me a better location, I'll tear up the documents."

"Dad!" Claire gasps, clearly as shocked as I am.

I nod. "I see what this is. So, you *are* punishing me."

"I'm not," he responds. "I'm giving you one last chance. An opportunity of a lifetime."

I'm silent as I move back toward the window. I feel completely defeated. If working for my father meant saving Grace's livelihood, it's an option I should at least consider.

"Come on, Dad," I hear Claire say. "I can look into some more options. There are some great locations near Little Beach that we haven't explored." Her tone is hopeful, and it makes my heart hurt to know that she feels she needs to be the buffer between us.

"That won't be necessary, Claire. It's a done deal," my father says, the finality of his words stinging. "All businesses located in the premises have been notified that they can stay until their rent period is up. It's not personal. Just–"

"Yeah. Just business." I cut him off.

"Exactly." His phone begins to ring, and he answers it, pushing off the door frame. We hear his voice grow distant as he wanders down the hall.

"I'm sorry, Dyl." Claire's hand is on my shoulder. "I had no idea."

My heart aches for Grace. And Mackenzie too. She only just met her grandmother, and this could put serious strain on an already fragile relationship.

But it isn't just their relationship I'm worried about. God only knows what Mackenzie will think of me when she finds out my father is to blame for this.

"This is all my fault." I drop down into the armchair by the window, combing a hand through my hair as I loosen the tie around my neck. "I never should have mentioned the studio in the first place. I put the idea in his head."

"Then I'm as much to blame." Claire sighs. "I'm the one who told him it was the Elmwood."

"He's a snake, Claire. I hope you know what you're dealing with here." What I'm saying might sound harsh, especially when I know that this is my sister's dream job, but I need her to be sure this is the kind of career she wants.

She stares back at me for a long moment before she finally speaks. "I want you to know that I don't agree with what he has done. I'm going to do things differently around here. Maybe I can talk him out of this."

I slump down, my head in my hands. "You heard him. He'll rip up the contract on one condition only."

Claire's frown deepens as she takes in my words. "You're

not actually thinking about coming to work here again, are you?"

"What choice do I have?"

"You can't give up everything you've worked for. And I'm not saying this because it means having to share my job title with you." Despite my frustration and sadness, her words make me smile. "I'm saying it because I can see how this place sucks the life right out of you. You were right. You don't belong stuck between four walls in a concrete jungle."

"I know," I agree. "I just need some space to think."

"You won't find space here." Claire's hand squeezes my shoulder, warm and encouraging. "Come on. Let's go to Cliff Haven."

"What?" My eyes snap to hers.

"It's your home." Her gaze softens. "You belong there. So let's go."

I don't need further convincing. Cliff Haven is the only place I want to be right now.

With my girl and my dog.

Blowing out a breath, I stand and follow my sister to the lift. When she pushes the button for the executive parking level, my forehead creases in a frown. "What are you doing? My car is out on the street."

"Yeah. Fuck that," she aims a devious smile in my direction. "We're taking the Ferrari."

I tilt my head to the side in contemplation. "Fair enough."

Chapter 36

MACKENZIE

I've been standing outside the studio for the last five minutes, contemplating how I'm going to do what I should have done days ago. I wish I'd had the courage to approach Grace earlier, but I needed that time to process. Now, as I gaze through the windows to the woman inside, I feel guilty for making her wait this long to resolve things with me.

She hasn't seen me yet. She's too busy shuffling chairs and equipment around, reorganising the space for the exhibition tomorrow night. She doesn't look up until she hears the tiny bell ring above the door as I step into the room.

"Mackenzie." There's an uncertainty in her stare and I hate that we both feel as though we have to tread lightly around each other.

"Hi," I say timidly.

"I was hoping you would come back." There's a hint of a

smile on her lips as she takes a hesitant step closer.

"I'm sorry it took me so long." I shuffle uncomfortably on the spot, the artwork in my hands suddenly heavier.

"What have you got there?" She gestures to the metre wide canvas that sat blank in my room for weeks, now finally finished.

Chewing on my bottom lip, I flip it around in my hands, revealing the project that's taken most of my waking hours to complete.

Her smile widens then she cups her hands over her mouth, nodding in approval. "I see you took Betty's advice."

"Yeah. I guess I did." I huff out a nervous laugh. "It was a bit of an effort getting it here on the bus."

"I bet." Her eyes are glassy as she takes in the brush work, the colours I spent painstaking hours to get just right. "It's wonderful, Mackenzie. Will you put it in the exhibition?"

I nod, placing it up against the nearest wall. "I'd love that."

An uncomfortable silence settles over the room, both of us standing face to face wondering which one of us will be the first to address the situation that hangs in the air between us. I open my mouth to say something, but Grace beats me to it.

"I'm sorry," she blurts. "For not being there for you throughout your life. If I'd have known about you, you would never have spent a single moment feeling alone."

"I know." Her apology has my eyes stinging with tears. "And I don't blame you for any of this. My mother was right."

She tilts her head to the side, a veil of sorrow falling over her features. "She was?"

I nod. "Any kid would be lucky to have you as their grandmother."

Her eyes are misty as she takes another step toward me.

"I wish I knew," she weeps. "I would have held you through all the bad times."

I close the gap between us, throwing my arms around her neck as tears begin to stream freely from my eyes. I can't hold them back now, no matter how hard I try. I feel safe in her embrace as I melt into her warmth, her fingers gently stroking my hair.

"I'm glad you finally found me," I whisper.

"Me too," she replies.

I'm not sure how much time passes as we stand like this, but it's long enough for the awkward air around us to dissolve.

My heart swells with hope. That a day will come where I will know all of the things about Grace that I would have already known had we been acquainted from the time of my birth. I have hope for a future where we'll have a normal relationship, but for now, this is enough. This is more than I could have ever asked for.

Grace finally unravels her arms from around my back, taking my hands in hers. "You got any plans for the rest of the day?"

I shake my head, running my thumb along my eyelid to catch the moisture. "Not really. I came to help you set up for tomorrow night."

"I was hoping you might say that." She smiles, then cups my cheeks in her soft, delicate hands. "But first, coffee. I have some lost time to make up for with my granddaughter."

I beam back at her, my head bobbing between her palms. "Okay. I'd like that."

She swings an arm around my shoulder and leads me to the

café next door. She orders us two cappuccinos and a slice of the cake of the day, and we find a seat by the window.

Then over the most delicious piece of orange and poppyseed cake with cream cheese frosting, she catches me up on the details of her life and I fill her in on some of mine.

I cry when she tells me about my grandfather's death, and she cries when I tell her about my father and Ethan. I give her the full story on how I came to live in Cliff Haven, about how without Henley's help I don't know where I'd be. I tell her about Kristen, the sister I never knew I had.

Then I tell her about Dylan. She tells me I have a keeper.

When she leaves the table to find the restroom, I find myself lost in thought, staring out at the boats in the marina outside.

I've never been a believer in fate. I'd never had any reason to be. But sitting here in a café with my long-lost grandmother, in a life that doesn't nearly resemble the one I had a year ago, I can't help but wonder where I'd be if Henley hadn't come for me. If he'd never met Kristen.

I can't go down the path of wondering about all the what ifs. I can only be thankful for where I am today, but there will always be a heaviness in my heart when I think of my mum.

"Mackenzie?" Grace's voice jolts me from my thoughts and my head snaps in her direction. She's seated across from me once again, having returned from the restroom. "Are you alright?"

"Yes." I nod. "I was just wondering about my mother. About what she would think if she could see us right now."

"I think she'd be so proud of you."

I squeeze my eyes shut, willing myself not to cry again. I've shed enough tears this week to last a lifetime. "I hope so."

We drain the last of our coffees and head back to the studio. Grace slides the key into the lock and the door flies open with a twist of her wrist, but neither of us take a step inside. We're too preoccupied with the rumbling of an engine behind us as it pulls up to the curb.

Grace cranes her neck, searching for the commotion. "What in the world?"

A familiar woman exits the cherry red Ferrari, her fiery auburn hair ablaze in the sunlight. Her stilettos clack on the pavement as she moves hurriedly toward us.

"Claire? Hey," I say, turning back to Grace. "This is Dylan's sister, Claire."

"Hi, Mackenzie," she replies.

It's not until she flips her Prada sunglasses on top of her head that I notice the worry on her face. "Is everything okay?"

"Not exactly," she replies. "It's Dylan."

"What do you mean?" Panic sets in, my lungs deprived of air as I struggle to take my next breath. "What happened?"

Claire, seeing my distress, waves her hands in front of me. "It's not like that. He's okay. He's just having a hard day."

"Okay," I say. This isn't making me feel any better.

She turns to Grace. "You must be Mackenzie's grandmother."

"Yes." Grace nods, a hint of suspicion in her glance.

"Sorry," I say, realising I hadn't given Grace a formal introduction. "Claire, this is Grace."

"It's nice to meet you." Claire offers a smile, but there's a trace of sadness hidden within it. "I understand that the building your studio is located in has been bought out by the

Abbott Property Group."

"Yes." Grace lets out a sigh, a flicker of sadness in her expression.

"What? You didn't mention that before," I say. "What does that mean?"

"It means that all businesses on the premises – " Claire launches into an explanation but is abruptly cut off by Grace.

"It means," my grandmother interrupts. "That I'm going to have to find a new location for the studio."

"But you love this studio."

I remember how Kristen had mentioned that the Abstract Palette had been here since she was a young girl. Grace had been running this studio here for more than half her lifetime. Even before I knew she was my grandmother, I had known it meant everything to her.

"I'm so sorry," Claire says, her tone genuinely sincere. "I only found out just this morning that the contract had been drawn up. Our father has plans to turn this building into a boutique hotel. Dylan blames himself."

"Why would he blame himself?" I ask.

Surely, this has nothing to do with him. He wants nothing to do with his father's company anymore.

"He mentioned that you were here at the studio last week," she explains. "I remembered that this was where the Elmwood building was, and the name attracted our father's interest. He must have done some research after Dylan returned to Cliff Haven and sought out the property for the project. Dylan feels that if he'd never mentioned the town at all, you wouldn't be in this mess."

"Oh my god." I can see why Dylan would take responsibility for this but the idea that he's blaming himself has my heart hurting. And so does the fact that Grace will no longer be able to run the studio here. "Grace, what are we going to do?"

"Oh, developers have been sniffing around here for years wanting to turn this place into a cinema, a bowling alley and now a hotel." She casually waves her hand, seemingly unbothered by this news. "The residents have always fought hard to petition against them, but I guess the times are changing. After tonight's exhibition, I'll be closing down the studio."

"But you love art. It's in your blood. It's in *our* blood." I wait for a frown that doesn't come. Instead, a smile brightens Grace's face. "Why aren't you upset about this?"

"Like I said, this isn't the first-time investors or developers have threatened to take the studio, but this is the first time I feel ready to let it go."

"I still don't understand."

She takes my hand in hers, her demeanour reasonably calm for a person who is about to lose their livelihood. "I'm ready to move on. I've secured a new location. It's a beautiful spot right across from the beach."

"You have?"

"I have." She nods, beaming back at me. "In Cliff Haven."

"In Cliff Haven," I repeat dumbly. "Really?"

"Yes. I'm going to sign the lease tomorrow morning. So, to answer your question, *we* are going to open up a brand-new studio."

"We?"

She nods again. "That is, if you'd like to help me run it."

My eyes go wide as I stand there in complete shock. "I don't know what to say."

"Say what's in your heart," she tells me.

When I'd moved to Cliff Haven, my priority was to get a job. Any job. I've never had time to wonder about what my dream career might look like. Only now that Grace is offering it right up to me do I realise that being an artist is my ultimate ambition, and to be able to share my love for art the way that she does, that would be a dream.

"I'd love to."

She pulls me in, squeezing me in a hug as Claire's voice breaks through the air. I'd forgotten for a moment that she was even standing there. "This is so not how I thought this conversation would go. I'm relieved though."

I let go of Grace, my focus now on the man that has put me first every time. The man that now needs me to assure him everything is okay. "Where is he? Where's Dylan?"

"I dropped him off near the Cliff Haven marina," she replies. "He said he needed time and space to think about what his next move would be. He doesn't even know that I'm here."

"Wait. What next move?" I ask, stepping toward Claire. "What are you not telling me?"

She breathes out a long sigh. "Dad told Dylan he would drop the Elmwood Building if he came back to the company."

"Don't tell me he'd actually consider that." I can't believe he would go to such lengths to save my grandmother's art studio.

Except I can believe it.

Because he's the quintessential nice guy. The very quality that made me cautious of his character is now the thing that I love about him most.

"Honestly? I don't think he knows what he's doing right now. He was gutted when he saw the documents on the desk this morning," she explains. "He was mumbling something about selling a boat and giving up diving."

"He can't do that. I won't let him." I turn to Grace, my voice laced with concern. "I need to go to him."

"Go," Grace instructs firmly.

"But the gallery," I say. "Will you be okay?"

"I've got it covered," she replies. "Go get your boy and tell him the good news."

"Come on." Claire says, nodding in the direction of the Ferrari behind her. "I'll take you to him."

Chapter 37

DYLAN

I can't believe this is happening. I'm furious with my father for once again putting business before people. Before family. That's when I realise it.

Mackenzie is family. No matter what happens, I want her to be in my life. Always.

If she can even stand to look at me ever again.

Me and my stupid, big, fat mouth. I never should have mentioned where she was that day. I never should have spoken about her at all. I should have known better how to protect her.

I've been sitting here on the deck of this half-finished boat trying to think up all the right ways I can tell her that my father's company is putting her grandmother's business out to dry.

God, their relationship is so fragile already. If this ruins things between them, I'll never forgive myself.

My anxiety worsens with every second that ticks by. Because there's another relationship at stake here, and I'm not talking about the one between me and my father. Things between us have been shaky for quite some time and I've wondered for the past few months if it will ever be salvageable.

I'm talking about me and Mackenzie.

I never expected to have to make this choice. Do I risk Grace's livelihood for the sake of my own ambitions or give up what I've been working so hard for so that nothing has to change for her?

Of course, I already know what needs to be done.

And maybe returning to the Abbott group to work for my father doesn't have to mean giving up on my dream. Maybe I'd just be postponing it for a little while. I'd be earning way more money. I could afford to keep the boat here in the warehouse.

Maybe I could try to find a way to have the best of both worlds.

Even as the thought registers in my brain, I know it would be impossible. I simply can't run a company on such a large scale and still operate a dive charter boat simultaneously.

Another half hour passes before I hear the unmistakeable rumble of a Ferrari engine.

Claire's come back.

I lean forward, my head in my hands. I'd hoped I'd have more time to think before she returned. I don't look up when I hear the door to the warehouse slide open, nor when I hear footsteps climbing the ladder to the boat.

"Well, don't you look like a fish out of water." The voice

doesn't belong to my sister. I'd know that voice anywhere.

I take in the converse sneakers as they move in front of me, my gaze travelling upward over long lean legs, denim cut-off shorts and finally a wild mane of blonde curls.

"Mackenzie? I thought you were Claire." My lungs are tight as my heart hammers against my ribs.

Time is up. I owe Mackenzie an explanation and she deserves more than to have to wait for me to figure my shit out.

"Claire brought me here."

"She did?" That explains the Ferrari engine then.

"Dylan, she told me everything."

I scour her face for a clue as to how she might be taking the news, but her expression is one of indifference. It gives nothing away.

I manage a deep inhale before blowing out a long and tired sigh that pretty much sums up exactly how I'm feeling right now. Exhausted. Completely fatigued.

I squeeze my eyes shut, hating that my father has put me in this predicament. "I'm sorry, Kenz. I feel one hundred percent responsible, but I know what I need to do to make it right though. I'm going to fix this."

"You don't have to do anything," she says as she slides down onto the floor beside me, resting her back up against the side of the boat. Her hand finds my knee, gliding along the fabric of my suit pants.

I begin to wonder if she has truly grasped the gravity of the situation. "Of course I do. This is so messed up." I rake a hand through my hair before I turn and meet her gaze. "He said he'll drop everything if I go and work for him. And honestly, if it means that I can help Grace, it doesn't seem like such a bad idea."

"What?" Her eyes narrow as they search mine.

"You said it yourself. Working for my father would be taking the easy way out. It would be a piece of cake. And if it's going to help you and your family, it's the easiest decision I'll ever make."

"But you don't want easy," she whispers.

"I want you to be happy."

Never in a million years would I expect her to laugh right now, but that's exactly what she does.

"You are insane, Dylan. You'd give up all of this?" She waves her hands wildly in front of her, gesturing to the boat. "You'd give up your dream?"

My eyes are glassy as they meet hers and its then I realise she doesn't seem all that upset. "If it means that I can fix this. Yes. I'll do whatever I have to do. I could still live here in Cliff Haven. I could commute. As long as I have you in my life, I can be happy."

"Well, it wouldn't make me happy. I would never want you to do that." Her light blue stare seems to see right through me. "Seriously, I love you for that. But Grace is happy. She's going to move the studio."

"What?"

"Yeah. To Cliff Haven," she says, a grin spreading across her mouth. "She's happy, Dylan. Really."

"She is? You aren't just saying that, are you?"

She shakes her head. "Promise."

My chest deflates with relief. "You couldn't have led with that?"

Her laugh echoes off the walls of the warehouse as I pull her into my arms. She kisses me before drawing back, her fingers tugging at the lapel of my suit jacket. "I guess I'm the only one that needs to deliver bad news today."

"What do you mean?" I search her face for a clue as to what she might be about to tell me, but her expression doesn't resemble that of a person about to deliver bad news. In fact, she looks ecstatic.

"I'm giving you notice," she says. "I won't be able to work at the tavern anymore."

"Kenz, what do you mean? What are you saying?"

"I got a job offer," she explains. "I'm going to work at the studio full time. With Grace."

"You're kidding. That's amazing!"

"Yeah. It is." Her grin widens. "So you can call your dad and thank him because he's done us all a favour."

"That's one way of looking at it, I guess." A relieved laugh bursts from me as I draw her in closer. I act on instinct, pure habit to me at this point, as I crush my lips against hers. She leans further into the kiss, wrapping her arms around my neck. It's several moments before she finally pulls away and I notice her eyes are filled with tears.

"Kenz?"

"You'd really have given up all of this for me? Just so that Grace could keep her studio."

I shrug. "You know I would have."

"How did I get so lucky?" she whispers. "Where did you come from Dylan Abbott?"

"I could ask you the same thing." I stare back at the woman sitting in front of me, who has quickly become everything to me. My heart is full, grateful. "Come on. I want to take you home."

"I want that too," she says, though she makes no attempt to move. Instead, she pauses in place before adding, "But there's something I need to do first."

My brows pinch inward as she climbs into my lap, straddling my thighs. She tugs on the tie around my neck, digging her fingers into the knot until she gets it loose. She slides it from the collar of my shirt and then tosses it over the side of the boat.

I stifle a laugh, a smirk twisting my lips. "Feel better now?"

"It's a start." She slips her hands beneath my jacket, pushing it away from my shoulders. I lean forward, allowing her to slip it off. She clutches it in her hands, rolling it into a ball and throws that over the edge of the boat too.

A laugh rumbles up from my throat. "Not a fan of the suit, huh?"

"I fucking hate it." She begins unbuttoning my shirt as her lips come to mine again.

My fingers wind through her curls and when she pulls away, a devious grin lights up her face.

I look down to where her fingers graze my belt buckle. "You know I don't actually have anything else to wear right now, right?"

Her left eyebrow quirks upward. "Oh, I know."

Chapter 38

MACKENZIE

"Are you ready, Kenz?" Dylan's hand finds my knee in the backseat of Kristen's VW Golf, giving it a light squeeze.

I blow out a breath. "Yeah. I'm fine," I lie.

I may only have one painting on display at the exhibition tonight, but that doesn't mean I'm not nervous about everyone's judgmental stares. Though there's only one person's reaction I'm excited to gage, and he's sitting right next to me.

"I can't wait," Kristen pipes up from the driver's seat.

My sister had been over the moon for me when she learned of my new job opportunity with Grace. She'd practically demanded to meet her right away and when I'd mentioned the exhibition night, she'd jumped at the chance to come with me and pretty much dragged Henley along with her.

I could hardly complain when she'd offered to drive us all into Seabright Cove.

"Will there be food?" Henley asks.

His hopeful tone is only met with laughter from the rest of us.

"Relax, babe," Kristen says. "We'll make sure you're well fed."

We pull into the small carpark behind The Elmwood and make our way out onto the street. My nerves are starting to get the better of me as we approach the front door of the studio. I'm starting to second-guess my artistic talent, whether I've gotten the brush strokes just right. I'd spent hours perfecting the colour palette, but I can't help the little voice that tells me that I could have done it better.

"Welcome!" Grace meets us at the door and ushers us inside the well-lit space. "You must be Mackenzie's sister," she says excitedly.

"It's so nice to meet you," Kristen says, leaning in for a hug. "I'm Kristen and this is Henley."

Henley follows Kristen's lead, reaching down to embrace my grandmother. "Hello, Grace."

"That can only mean…" Grace begins. "You must be the infamous Dylan I've heard so much about."

My cheeks warm as Dylan steps forward, offering Grace a quick hug. I can't help feeling that this is what it must be like to feel embarrassed over a family member meeting your boyfriend.

"I've heard a lot about you too. Pleasure to meet you," Dylan says with a smile.

I'm the last to step into the room. I reach forward and wrap my arms around Grace. "Thanks for having us."

"Thank *you*, Mackenzie," she replies. "Your work is exquisite." She turns to Dylan. "She's extremely talented, this one."

"I'm well aware," Dylan replies, his gaze falling to mine as his palm finds the small of my back. "She's amazing."

I smile back at him as Kristen and Henley disperse into the room, surveying the artwork that lines the walls and the temporary dividers in the centre of the room.

"We made it!" A shrill voice carries from the entry way, and I look up to see Betty.

She waves from the door, wearing a flamboyant purple dress and a matching feather boa around her neck. May follows, not far behind her, a straw hat adorned with artificial flowers atop her head. It's impossible to mask the grin that creeps over my face when I see them.

"Uh, who is that?" Dylan asks.

"Come," I tell him. "It's time for you to meet *my* friends."

Dylan raises an eyebrow but allows me to drag him over to Betty and May.

"Mackenzie!" Betty calls. "I can't wait to see your painting!"

"Thanks, Betty. I can't wait to see yours, but first I'd like you to meet Dylan."

"Ah!" Betty's eyes roam my boyfriend's physique from head to toe. "The sexy diver boy!"

I snicker as Dylan's eyes go wide when he registers Betty's comment.

"Manners, Betty," I joke.

"Don't worry about her," May pipes up from behind her. "She's a horn dog."

Betty's gasp is audible as May steps out in front of her, her hand held out in greeting. "I'm May."

Dylan struggles to hold back a laugh. "Nice to meet you, May. And you too, Betty."

"If you'll excuse us, ladies, I'm going to show Dylan my painting now, but we'll catch up with you soon." I link my arm through Dylan's and guide him to the back of the room.

As we walk away from the two older women, Dylan throws a glance back over his shoulder. I turn to see what has caught his attention, only to find Betty still gawking, her eyebrows jumping up and down.

"What is happening? Who is that?" he asks me with wide eyes.

"That's Betty," I giggle.

"She's staring at me like she wants to eat me."

"Pretty sure she does."

"That's not encouraging." He pulls me in close as we reach the back of the room.

"I'm sorry I subjected you to that." I grin as I wrap my arms around his neck.

"No, you're not." Dylan smirks back at me, his eyes shining under the studio lights.

"Okay. Yeah, I'm not." I agree, then lay a quick kiss on his cheek. "Are you ready to see my painting."

"I've never been more ready."

I unfurl my arms from around him and take his palm in mine, leading him through the maze of art and sculptures until we're standing in front of the painting I poured my soul into.

"There it is." I stand stiffly beside him, awaiting his reaction to my work.

To my relief, a slow smile stretches across his face as he takes it all in.

A beachscape. Cool blue waves crashing against a white sandy shore. A cloudless sky above. And there in the centre, a kelpie-border collie mix chasing a seagull into the water alongside a shirtless man wearing a pair of blue boardshorts.

A man, that if I'm being honest, stole my heart long ago, sitting around a beach bonfire at a mutual friend's wedding.

"Amazing," he says, not taking his eyes off the painting.

"Betty told me to paint something that moves me. Something that makes me feel alive," I tell him. Then with a shrug, I add, "Well, that was after she suggested that my sexy diver boy perhaps belonged in my work."

He turns to me now, his eyes searching mine. "Amazing," he says again. "You're amazing."

"Excuse me," a short older woman wearing a black pantsuit interrupts. "Are you the artist of this painting? I'd love to make an offer."

"Uh…yes," I say, taken by surprise. "I'm the artist."

"How do you feel about – " the woman begins.

"I'm sorry. I'm going to have to stop you right there." Dylan interjects with a palm raised in the air. "I'll pay double whatever you're willing to pay for it, because there is absolutely no way in hell that this painting isn't coming home with me."

The woman smiles. "Sounds like you already have an eager buyer here, but I'd love to commission something in the future," she says to me. "Your work is fantastic. I'll be in touch."

With that, she turns and wanders across the room, continuing to peruse the other paintings on display.

"Did you hear that, Kenz? Looks like you have a future buyer," Dylan says enthusiastically. "You could really turn this into a career."

I think back to what I'd said to Harper on the pier a few months ago. About how putting prices and deadlines on the things you love to do only turns them into chores.

Then I smile, a surge of happiness rippling through me at the possibility that I could make a living out of doing something that brings me so much joy. That I could share my art with others. It seems my pessimistic outlook on life has come a long way.

"Yeah, I guess I could."

"I'm sorry I scared her away, but I have the perfect spot reserved for it." He eyes the painting again, before his gaze returns to mine, a flicker of a grin tugging at his lips. "Also, I just really wanted to be your first customer."

"You don't have to pay for it, Dylan. It was never for sale." I wrap my arms around his neck and lay a kiss on his lips. "It's yours. And so am I."

Epilogue

DYLAN – 6 MONTHS LATER

Mackenzie emerges from the art storeroom at the back of the studio. "I've finished unpacking that order and taken inventory, Grace," she calls out. "Just have to get the supplies sorted for today's first class."

"I'm one step ahead of you," Grace replies. "I've already laid everything out on the tables."

The brand-new Abstract Palette re-opened in its Cliff Haven location about three months ago and Kenz and Grace have been doing an amazing job with it. Henley and his crew had done the fit-out according to their vision and the space looks incredible. It's bright, airy, and spacious, with an epic view of the beach across the road.

And as if working in the studio and running art classes wasn't enough to keep Kenz busy, the commission orders have been flowing in. I'm so proud of her.

As I sit and watch my girl here in her element, I'm in complete and utter awe, my chest warm with gratitude that the universe somehow managed to align my path with hers.

"Oh, awesome," I hear her reply. "But what happened to those new fine line pens. They were right over here this morning when I arrived."

I snicker, a smile lifting the corners of my mouth. "I kind of borrowed them."

"Shit!" Mackenzie shouts, clutching at her chest in shock as she spins around. Her eyes settle on me in the corner of the studio where I sit at one of the back tables. "Where did you come from? Grace, did you know he was here?"

"Yes. I saw him sneak in." Grace beams and the bell above the door chimes as she opens it. "I'm going to the Haven to pick up our coffee order. Would you like anything, Dylan?"

"No, thanks," I reply.

"Okay. I'll be back in time for opening." The door closes gently, and I turn my attention back to Mackenzie.

"How long have you been sitting there?" she asks.

"I snuck in while you were out the back." I stand up and stride over to her, a piece of art paper and the missing pens she was searching for clutched in my hand. "I've been working on something for you."

Her eyes narrow, a twinkle in their icy blue as a dubious grin spreads across her face. "For me? What is it?"

"I drew you a picture."

"You did not," she challenges.

"I did," I tell her. "And I put all of my heart and soul into it so you better like it."

"Okay." She chuckles. "Let's see it."

I'm definitely not an artist and I can't wait to see her reaction. I hand her the scrap of art paper and watch as her grin expands. She begins to laugh as she takes in my stick figure art.

"This is me here," I say, pointing to the badly drawn character. "See? Those are my abs there and that's my boat in the background. Oh, and there's Chance." I gesture to the little dog stick figure in the centre.

"And is this supposed to be me?" She chuckles, pointing at the stick figure on the left that I've clearly tried to make look female.

"Obviously," I scoff. "Because you've got long hair and boobs."

She laughs louder now, bringing a hand to her mouth. "It's brilliant. Can I frame it?"

"Not yet," I say. "I haven't finished."

"You haven't?"

I snatch the drawing from her fingers and grab one of the markers, pulling the lid off between my teeth. "Turn around for a sec."

She shakes her head but does as I've instructed while I add the extra additions to the page. "Okay. Finished."

I click the lid back on the pen as she spins around, reading the text aloud that I've written in the speech bubble alongside 'stick figure' me. "Will you move in with me?"

It's a question I'd been wanting to ask her for a while now and it's really only a formality at this point. She stays over at my place almost every night anyway and I'd cleared a couple of drawers for her to keep her things in my dresser months ago.

Waking up next to her is my absolute favourite thing in the world.

Her bottom lip disappears between her teeth as she plucks the marker from my grip. "Turn around."

I do as she says. I'm pretty sure I know what her answer will be, but my heart beats out of sync all the same. After a painstakingly long moment, she taps me on the shoulder, extending the drawing back to me.

I read the text she's written in a speech bubble next to 'stick figure' Mackenzie. "Only if I get to be in charge of the TV remote every night."

I roll my eyes, pretending to think this over, then I pull her into me, enveloping her in my arms. "Deal. I guess I'm doomed to a future of watching Outer Banks on repeat."

"You know it. Pogues for life." she says, bringing her lips to mine.

"Oh! Get a room, you two!" May's grumpy voice interrupts the otherwise quiet studio.

Mackenzie grins and then lifts the drawing up, one eyebrow quirked. "Should we tell her we're about to?"

We both turn to find Betty and May watching us. May is completely disinterested, but Betty's gaze is intent on me, her eyebrows wiggling high on her forehead. Man, that woman knows how to creep me out.

"I think this is my cue to leave," I say, reluctantly releasing Mackenzie from my grip. "Meet me later at the marina?"

"Wouldn't miss it." She lets go of my hand, a wistful smile on her lips.

Then I lean in and whisper into her ear, just loud enough for her to hear. "Happy birthday, Kenz."

Her smile remains but there's a warning in her glance. Mackenzie doesn't like to talk about her birthday and if it wasn't for the fact that she had to include the date in her employee profile at the tavern, there would be no way I'd even have known when it was.

I get it. Birthdays have never been something to be celebrated for her and the attention is unwanted, but I'm desperate to show her that it doesn't have to be like that.

"Have fun, ladies," I say to the two older women as I exit the shop.

Twenty minutes later, I'm on the dock heading to my boat when I hear someone call my name from behind me. The voice is one I could pick a mile off, but in this setting it's completely unexpected.

I turn to find my father, strolling down the dock, his hands tucked casually into the pockets of his pants. I'm not angry at him anymore, though I am curious as to why he's here, given that we haven't seen each other in months. I'd stopped making any real effort after the day he tried to bribe me to take my old job back.

"Dad. What are you doing here?"

"I came to apologise," he says.

"Okay."

He looks away, taking a deep inhale before he brings his gaze back to mine. "I'm sorry, Dylan. I regret the way things are between us. I should have let you exit the company quietly." His eyes seem to mist over as he thinks about his next words. "I should have believed in you."

"Thanks, Dad. That really means a lot."

My father isn't generous with apologies. He doesn't like to admit when he's wrong, so the fact that he's here truly does mean everything to me.

"How's Mackenzie?" he asks.

"She's doing really well. She's busy with the new studio." I can't help but smile as I speak of her.

"I'm glad." He scratches the back of his neck before he continues. "I don't want you to be a stranger. I want you to visit us frequently. And if it's okay, I'd like to visit you and Mackenzie."

I nod. "I'd like that."

"And one more thing," he says.

"What's that?"

"I've reinstated the original conditions of your trust. The money should be available to you by this afternoon."

"Wow. Dad. Thank you." I almost choke on the words.

I've gotten used to living from paycheck to paycheck, never even considering that I might one day gain my inheritance back.

I had asked myself the questions though.

Would I still live in a run-down beach shack with a stray dog if I was a millionaire? Would I have kept working on a boat that needed loads of work instead of buying one brand new?

Would I still have the same dreams?

And the answer is yes. To all of them. Yes.

I know that without that money I would have been just fine, and I have no intentions of spending it right away. I'd like to make sure that it's used for a greater purpose, but it helps to know that I could use it to help Mackenzie too. That after everything she has been through in this life, financial hardship won't ever be something she has to worry about again.

"I'm proud of you, Dylan," Dad says, placing a solid hand on my shoulder.

I nod, swallowing down the emotions his words have resurrected. "I'm proud of you too, Dad. And I'm sorry if I ever seemed ungrateful for everything you've done for me. I know how blessed I am."

"I know you do, son." He pulls me into a half hug, slapping me on the back with his other palm. "I'll let you get on with your day. I'm sure you have a lot to do."

"Okay," I say. "Thanks, Dad."

He clamps his lips together to form a thin line as he turns on his heel and begins to walk back down the dock.

"Hey, Dad," I call out.

He spins around slowly, his hands still in his pockets. "What are you doing right now? Would you like to come aboard?" I point to the newly refurbished diving boat moored in front of me.

He smiles and his face lights up. "Yeah. Sure, son. I'd like that."

MACKENZIE

Dylan glances back at me from his position at the boat's steering wheel. I don't think anything could wipe the smile from his face. When he stands behind that wheel, it's as though nothing can touch him. This is his happy place.

Now that the boat is finally finished, he has been looking into starting up his own dive charters and I can't wait to see him living his dream.

Chance bounds from one end of the boat to the other, barking furiously, his attention on the pod of dolphins that emerge beside us. This is only his second voyage on Dylan's boat, and he hasn't become accustomed to marine life yet. I tug gently at his collar, pulling him in to give him a scratch behind the ears and it seems to settle him. For a moment, at least.

I move across the deck to Dylan, curling an arm around his neck. He reaches for me, tucking me into his side.

"This isn't so bad, is it?" he asks me.

A reluctant smile forms on my lips. I know that he's referring to the fact that I hadn't wanted to celebrate my birthday today. I hadn't needed to explain to him why all my other birthdays sucked. As usual, he just understood.

But I have to admit that he's right. This isn't so bad. In fact, if this was to be how all my future birthdays would go, I wouldn't have a single thing to complain about.

"Yeah. It's not so bad."

"I love you, Kenz," he says as his chocolate eyes bore into mine, their golden flecks made all the more prominent under the pink-orange sunset.

"I know," I say. Because I do. He doesn't even have to say it. The way he cares for me and puts me first every time speaks louder than any of his words ever could. "I love you, too."

His fingers drag along the small of my back as his grip tightens around me. "You ready to head back in?"

"No," I say. "I could stay out here forever."

He laughs. "I'm sure you could, but we're losing daylight, and I don't want to be out here alone with you when you start getting hangry."

"Fine," I say. "But I'm not cooking."

"Of course, you're not. It's your birthday," he says as he turns the wheel and steers us towards the marina. "I was thinking we could grab something at the tavern."

I ponder his suggestion. Honestly, I can't wait to get back to his place. Our place. Especially knowing I have free rein of the remote control now. Who am I kidding? I always have.

But on the other hand, dinner at the tavern sounds good too. "Okay."

Within minutes, Dylan has navigated us back to the dock. He climbs out first, then holds his hand out to me. Chance waits for neither of us, energetically bounding over the side of the boat and racing up the jetty.

"Chance!" I call out. I chase him as Dylan secures the boat, clipping his leash to his collar once I've reached him. "Good boy."

I lead him to a park bench, where we wait for Dylan, then a few minutes later, all three of us are piling into the old RAV4.

We cruise down the boulevard, where we find a parking spot on the curb outside the Tavern. Chance isn't allowed inside so we opt to sit in the outdoor courtyard around the back.

We take the laneway down the side, but when we round the corner to the lawn area in front of the shore, I stumble back at a sudden disturbance that sets my heart racing in my chest.

"SURPRISE!"

Several people spring forward and it takes me a moment to realise that this display is for me, and that the voices are coming from all those I've come to know since moving to this tiny seaside town.

"Oh my god." My eyes are wide as I clutch at Dylan's forearm, only letting go of him as Pamela and Ben embrace me in a group hug.

"Happy birthday, Mackenzie," they both say in unison.

Next, it's Kristen and Henley's turn, followed by Liv and EJ and then Grace and Harper. Even Corey and the other bar staff are here, smiling at me from the tavern's back doors.

Lastly, my father approaches, encasing me in a hug. "Happy birthday, Mac."

"Thanks, Dad," I say, a tear slipping from my eye as I wrap my arms around his shoulders.

My father left rehab a few months ago, and against all odds, has remained sober. Though our relationship could still be best described as fragile, I'd have to be blind not to see the effort he's been putting in to repair our broken father-daughter bond.

He releases me from his embrace and shakes Dylan's hand, the other resting firmly on his shoulder. "Thank you. For taking care of her."

Dylan merely nods, though there's a hidden message conveyed through his eyes as he squeezes my father's hand in response. Once my father moves aside, he takes a step in my direction, watching as I take in the scene.

I scan the large wooden table set up on the lawn, the various platters scattered from end to end and the simple chocolate cake that sits in the centre. "This was all your doing?"

"Happy birthday, Kenz." He leans into me, his breath warm on my cheek as he pulls me close.

"Thank you," I say. "You always know how to make me feel special. I can't believe you got everyone here just for me."

"You are special," he says, tucking a curl behind my ear. "And I couldn't keep these guys away even if I wanted to. Everyone here loves you, Kenz. Whether they're blood related or not, this is your family."

I smile as he thumbs away another tear that rolls down my face.

Family.

My heart used to ache hearing the word, but now I realise that family isn't just one thing.

Family means unconditionally loving someone in spite of their flaws.

It means having a soft place to land. A light in the dark. A safe haven from the storm.

Family doesn't always mean the one you're born into. It's finding the ones who will stand by you, unflinching, even in your darkest times.

It's cuddles with a stray dog during a thunderstorm. It's chocolate chip pancakes on a rainy day.

It's finally finding a place where you belong.

Family isn't just one thing.

No.

It's everything.

And this is mine.

Playlist

⏮ ▶ ⏭

Girl I Am Now KAIBRIENNE	**Ho Hey** THE LUMINEERS
Little Runaway BENSON BOONE	**Rainbow** KASEY MUSGRAVES
Ceilings LIZZY MCALPINE	**Trustfall** PINK
Name THE GOO GOO DOLLS	**I Don't Want to Be** GAVIN DEGRAW
Front Porch JOY WILLIAMS	**Whole Lotta Love** LED ZEPPELIN
Wild Horses THE ROLLING STONES	**Belong Together** MARK AMBOR
Because of You KELLY CLARKSON	**What Was I Made For** BILLIE EILISH
Speak Too Soon WILD RIVER	**Hold You in My Arms** RAY LAMONTAGNE
The Story BRANDI CARLILE	**Here Is Gone** THE GOO GOO DOLLS

About the Author

Eve Blakely writes contemporary romance novels with an edge. She currently resides in a small town south of Sydney, Australia with her husband and two crazy kids.

She's an avid daydreamer and a self-confessed chocoholic who ditched her city-based career to enjoy a simpler life. When she isn't writing, she's probably trying to get through her never-ending TBR pile, painting or rewatching One Tree Hill for the millionth time.

@eveblakelywrites

@eveblakelywrites

www.eveblakely.com

BOOKS BY EVE BLAKELY

-The Cliff Haven Series-

The Other Version
Versions of Us
The Version You Hide

The Other Version

CLIFF HAVEN BOOK 1

Book #1 in the Cliff Haven Romance series, The Other Version is a heart-breaking yet hopeful story about love and loss, that delves deep into the human psyche.

"She's running from herself. He's determined to save her."

Olivia Petersen had it all. Or so she thought. Until one devastating night, her world fell apart.

Now, Liv Peters is torn between the person she used to be and the person she longs to be, haunted by the past version of herself. From city socialite to loner, she's well aware of the mistakes she's made in her life. Too many things have happened to ever go back.

When Liv finds solace in Cliff Haven, a small seaside town nestled below the cliff she resides upon, she believes she has a chance to reinvent herself. But her plans to live out her meagre existence anonymously are threatened when she meets EJ, a dreamy bartender that wears his guitar around his neck and his heart on his sleeve.

With his flair for music and his love of life, EJ has the ability to make Liv feel alive again. But behind his grey-green ocean eyes, he hides his own pain, and when their worlds collide, their secrets could destroy them both.

If Liv can let go of her demons for good, maybe there's a way out of the darkness. Maybe they can save each other.

Told from dual POVs, Versions of Us is a wholesome story of second chance love and finding hope in the darkest of places.

Versions of Us

CLIFF HAVEN BOOK 2

One phone call can change everything…

Kristen Riley has a tough exterior and an elastic heart, forged from the abandonment of her father at a young age. She's always held her cards close to her chest, never allowing anyone to get too close.

Except for Alex Henley – the boy, who at sixteen was a fun-loving prankster that never took life too seriously, and as a man, hides the deep-seated fear that he will never be enough behind a veil of nonchalance.

Despite their reluctance to dive head-first into a fully committed relationship, they've always known they were endgame and when Kristen notices a quiet change in Henley's character, an understated attentiveness and maturity, she opens up to the possibility of a future with him.

Then without warning, Henley does the one thing she can never forgive him for. He leaves. Six months later, Henley arrives back in Cliff Haven, the seaside town they've always called home, with a mysterious blonde in tow. But the man that returns is a far cry from the one Kristen once knew, his easy-going nature and cheerful disposition supressed by a constant storm cloud hovering above his head.

Kristen is furious, determined to leave Henley in the past, but she can't deny that her heart still belongs to him. She wants answers that he isn't ready to provide.

Why did Henley leave the life they were building behind? Who is the enigmatic blonde woman that doesn't leave his side? And does she know more than she's letting on?

Told from dual POVs, Versions of Us is a wholesome story of second chance love and finding hope in the darkest of places.